Praise for *Witch Trial*:

'Audacious, mind-bending and brilliant. I couldn't read it fast enough!'
Lisa Jewell

'Harriet Tyce's best book yet. Gripping, original and so very clever. I was captivated by this deliciously twisted thriller. And what an ending! Genius. I loved it!'
Claire Douglas

'Daring, different, clever and compulsive – a truly original novel. Delicious.'
Andrea Mara

'Absolutely superb. Grips like a vice throughout and has a perfect, bold ending that no one will see coming. An utter masterpiece of the murder mystery and the legal thriller genre.'
Sophie Hannah

'I loved this. Harriet Tyce is a master storyteller. Supremely plotted, elegantly written and with an ending that will shake you up! An absolute triumph of a book that takes the legal thriller to new heights and will stay with you for a long time. Best thing I've read this year.'
Abir Mukherjee

'A legal thriller unlike any you've ever read, this witchy, mind-melting page-turner is Tyce at her whip-smart best.'
Ellery Lloyd

'Brilliantly clever and utterly addictive, I loved it. Courtroom drama at its finest.'
Clare Leslie Hall

'*Witch Trial* is like the lovechild of Alfred Hitchcock and *The Crucible*. Dark, wry and slippery underfoot, I adored it!'
Sarah Pinborough

'Tyce creates a swirling miasma of meaning and counter-meaning that keeps the reader enthralled and tantalised – and in its audacious final act, revealing layer beneath confounding layer, *Witch Trial* pays fitting tribute to the James Hogg classic that inspired it.'
Chris Brookmyre

'I utterly adored this. Harriet Tyce is truly the queen of plotting and suspense. This is a riveting, rip-roaring ride through a murder trial, which confounds expectations at every turn. I was torn between being desperate to rush straight to the end, and not wanting the story to finish. Simply brilliant.'
The Secret Barrister

'Compulsive reading – I was totally immersed in the story. One of the best courtroom dramas I've read in a long time.'
Araminta Hall

'Give me witchcraft, a mind spiralling into madness and questionable narrators any day – just my cup of tea. A brilliant and twisting new novel from Harriet Tyce. I flew through it.'
L. V. Matthews

'Cancel all plans because this book is going to grab you by the throat and not let go until you turn the final page. It's a startlingly original courtroom drama, and a psychologically astute depiction of a man in freefall. Deliciously chilling and like nothing I've ever read. I ate this up.'
Chris Bridges

'An unputdownable, twisty legal trial from the queen of the courtroom drama. Spellbinding and sinister. A masterclass in plotting and pace.'
Kate Gray

'I read *Witch Trial* then I read it again. Compelling and twisty with perfectly drawn characters. Never have I said "Oh My God" out loud at the end of a book and meant it more.'
Rachel Wolf

'Clever, propulsive, with a wickedly satisfying twist. Excellent. My favourite Tyce book yet.'
C. E. Hulse

'Totally original and impossible to put down, Harriet Tyce has shown once again that she is the absolute master of the legal thriller with a twist. Brilliant!'
G. D. Wright

'At first sight a legal thriller, *Witch Trial* is multi-layered and subtle, delving deeply into the intricacies of the relationships between teenage girls and perceptions of female cunning. We are plunged into a world where nothing is as it seems. Brilliant.'
Heather Critchlow

'Harriet Tyce's masterful courtroom drama is intense, terrifying, and utterly addictive, with a devilish twist in its tail.'
Gilly Macmillan

'I loved this clever book! Stunningly written and may be one of the best endings I've read. Despite being deliciously dark, I found myself chuckling in places. Harriet's best book yet!'
Niki Mackay

'Dark, twisty and unrelentingly brilliant. Tyce in top form.'
Femi Kayode

'Tense, creepy and very, very clever with a genuine jaw-drop of an ending.'
Susi Holliday

'Will spark a million water-cooler debates! Bold and brave, but eminently readable.'
Jo Furniss

More praise for Harriet Tyce:

'One of the best openings I've read in forever. I devoured it.'
Alex Michaelides on *A Lesson in Cruelty*

'Dark, twisted and utterly nerve-jangling – a sharply structured thriller that left me breathless.'
Lucy Clarke on *A Lesson in Cruelty*

'A shocking, provocative, standout thriller. Harriet Tyce at her twisting, wicked, razor-sharp finest.'
Chris Whitaker on *A Lesson in Cruelty*

'An edge-of-your-seat thriller. Harriet Tyce's eye for people – their foibles, missteps and cruelties – is sharp as a blade.'
Abigail Dean on *A Lesson in Cruelty*

'Inventive, chilling and utterly compelling . . . further cements Harriet Tyce's place amongst the great British crime writers.'
M. W. Craven on *A Lesson in Cruelty*

'Perfect plotting, utterly brilliant.'
B. A. Paris on *A Lesson in Cruelty*

'An imaginatively told (and very bingeable) thriller.'
John Marrs on *A Lesson in Cruelty*

'Tyce's denouement pulls things together skilfully and surprisingly.'
Sunday Times on *A Lesson in Cruelty*

'A masterclass in the dark art of plotting. A propulsive read that crafts a scintillating and vivid story out of characters that gnaw and claw from the page. This is a great crime novel, and the chills last long after the final page is turned. Absolutely stunning.'
Janice Hallett on *A Lesson in Cruelty*

'Takes us into the deepest, most toxic recesses of human behaviour. With the author's signature blend of courtroom suspense and relationships in mortal crisis, this is another delicious treat from Tyce.'
Louise Candlish on *It Ends at Midnight*

'A cinematic gut-punch of a book that will linger in your memory long after you've finished it.'
Mark Edwards on *It Ends at Midnight*

'Fantastic, intricately plotted, skilfully woven and beautifully tricky.'
Helen Fields on *It Ends at Midnight*

'Intense, clever, important and deeply chilling . . . proves that Harriet Tyce is a writer at the top of her game.'
Phoebe Morgan on *It Ends at Midnight*

'Harriet Tyce cements her position as Queen of unreliable narrators. A must-read high stakes-thriller.'
Fiona Cummins on *It Ends at Midnight*

'A breathless read – with a shocker of an ending!'
Shari Lapena on *The Lies You Told*

'Every bit as intriguing, well-written and addictive as its predecessor.'
Sara Collins on *The Lies You Told*

'Gripping and intelligent.'
Stylist on *The Lies You Told*

'A classy thriller with complex and compelling characters.'
Clare Mackintosh on *Blood Orange*

'This brilliant debut from Harriet Tyce has it all – a tricky murder case, a complex and conflicted female barrister battling her own demons and a breath-taking ending.'
Rachel Abbott on *Blood Orange*

'Breathes new life into the domestic noir genre and grips until the final page.'
Daily Express on *Blood Orange*

'A heart-pounding . . . and deliciously twisty plot.'
Good Housekeeping on *Blood Orange*

'A dark and disturbing thriller – we were gripped.'
Closer on *Blood Orange*

'Fans of *Apple Tree Yard* and *The Girl on the Train* will love the atmosphere of clenched ambiguity Tyce sustains so well.'
Guardian on *Blood Orange*

'Dark and immensely readable. An impressive debut.'
The Times on *Blood Orange*

By Harriet Tyce and available from Wildfire

BLOOD ORANGE
THE LIES YOU TOLD
IT ENDS AT MIDNIGHT
A LESSON IN CRUELTY

HARRIET TYCE
WITCH TRIAL

Copyright © 2026 Harriet Tyce

The right of Harriet Tyce to be identified as the Author of
the Work has been asserted by her in accordance with the
Copyright, Designs and Patents Act 1988.

First published in 2026 by Wildfire
An imprint of Headline Publishing Group Limited

4

Apart from any use permitted under UK copyright law, this publication may
only be reproduced, stored, or transmitted, in any form, or by any means,
with prior permission in writing of the publishers or, in the case of
reprographic production, in accordance with the terms of licences issued
by the Copyright Licensing Agency.

All characters in this publication are fictitious and any resemblance
to real persons, living or dead, is purely coincidental.

Cataloguing in Publication Data is available from the British Library

Hardback ISBN 978 1 0354 1191 7
Trade Paperback ISBN 978 1 0354 1192 4

Typeset in 12.18/15.37pt Sabon LT Pro by Six Red Marbles UK, Thetford, Norfolk

Printed and bound in Great Britain by Clays Ltd, Elcograf S.p.A.

Headline's policy is to use papers that are natural,
renewable and recyclable products and made from wood
grown in well-managed forests and other controlled sources.
The logging and manufacturing processes are expected to conform
to the environmental regulations of the country of origin.

Headline Publishing Group Limited
An Hachette UK Company
Carmelite House
50 Victoria Embankment
London EC4Y 0DZ

The authorised representative in the EEA is Hachette Ireland,
8 Castlecourt Centre, Dublin 15, D15 XTP3, Ireland (email: info@hbgi.ie)

www.headline.co.uk
www.hachette.co.uk

*To my father Bill, with much love and gratitude
for everything that he has taught me*

Exhibit 1

MONDAY

1

How to describe it, the fug of shit and blood that hit the back of his throat the moment he walked into the dark of the wooden shed, so pungent he nearly gagged. All he wanted to do was turn round and get the hell out of there. Instead, he switched on a torch, moving it slowly across the plywood floor. Feathers everywhere, that's what he registered after the smell, blood smeared everywhere too. Not randomly, though. As he scanned the area, the light beam picking out the marks, he saw that there was a deliberate pattern to it, a five-pronged star.

A pentagram. And at its heart, a dead pigeon, headless, its breast cut open down the middle, its wings spread out wide underneath in its last bloody flight. A scene he will never forget.

2

She puts her hand on her daughter's gravestone, the granite rough under her hand. The day is clear, the sun bright overhead, the loch so still it's a bottomless mirror, the hills reaching down as far as they climb to the blue sky above. She's blind to all that.

Sorry, she says. Sorry.

She'll never stop saying sorry.

3

First, do no harm.

But there's always a moment when it's too late, the point past which the decision could have been made, the one from which no harm was done. So many smaller choices leading up to that moment, each a nail hammered into something we see only afterwards is a coffin.

Matthew Phillips doesn't know that this is one of those moments. As he walks through the door of the High Court, he's not thinking about the forks ahead, the road less travelled that brought him here. It's all behind him – work, wife. Other woman. The moment the jury citation arrived on his doorstep he knew what he wanted to do. And now he's here, every finger crossed that he'll be one of the lucky ones actually drawn to sit on a jury trial.

The longer the trial the better.

He could have told the court straightaway that he had a holiday booked. The citation said explicitly they'd take that into consideration, he'd be able to move his jury duty to a different date.

He didn't. Nor did he tell Rosalind he wouldn't be going away with her on a long-awaited week away, the first holiday without their daughter now that she's safely packed off to university. The holiday he'd explicitly promised wouldn't be cancelled because of work, regardless of what might be happening.

He didn't discuss it with Rosalind at all.

Nor Olivia. Though he's not thinking about her just now.

He could have cited work as another reason to be excused. Matthew can't be spared. Dominic made it very clear. Mrs O'Neill is a triple bypass – *Adam is far too cack-handed to trust with it, however keen he is* – there's a stent to fit and a dinner that night at the New Club at which he's due to stand proxy for Dominic, the senior surgeon's trip to New York with his new girlfriend (brunette, young, the opposite in every way from his soon-to-be ex-wife) taking priority over even such an honour as this invitation. *I can't believe they won't let you off. Haven't you written to them? Since when were doctors eligible, anyway?*

They're eligible. They're also eligible for excusal as of right, if they bother to apply to the court within seven days of receiving the citation. All Matthew needed to do was tell them what he did for a living and he'd be off the hook. A rare benefit of always being up to his elbows in someone else's blood. He didn't say that to Dominic though. He didn't say anything. No point. Dominic never listens, even at the best of times. Too many letters after his name.

Matthew knows perfectly well that in trying to escape, all he's doing is piling up the problems that will be waiting for him when he returns to work. He's not a man who dodges his responsibilities; he takes his job seriously. It's always a matter of life or death. But opening the jury citation, he felt like he'd won a golden ticket. If he's stuck in court, no one can get to him.

And now he's here. He waits outside the entrance for his turn to go through security, a queue to the only kind of holiday Matthew can permit himself to take. A matter of civic duty, with only one responsibility, to determine whether someone is guilty or innocent? Sign him up, please. It'll be a welcome break from all the usual shit. And God knows, he needs a break. He's so tired ... Regardless of the sun, sea and sangria Rosalind was seeking, it was never realistic to expect a man in his position to spend a week lounging about on a beach as though there were nothing more important to be done. She knows it, too, deep down. Or at least she will, once she's calmed down. He'll explain it all to her. Soon.

As soon as he's through the metal detectors, he sees the court official he's been told to expect, a man in a suit and a long black gown. Matthew tells him who he is, shows him the folded piece of paper he pulls from his pocket. Before Matthew can say anything else, he's directed off to a small room, nothing in it but a few rows of chairs occupied by a couple of people already waiting.

The room is steadily filling up. All the potential jurors are keeping themselves to themselves, perched on hard seats, eyes fixed to their phones. Every one a smartphone. Matthew thinks smugly about his basic brick phone, the way he's avoided the addiction from which the rest of the world suffers. An analogue man in a digital world, proud of it too. He's come prepared with a paperback, a reissue of an old classic with an introduction by a Scottish author he likes. It seemed appropriate with its crime themes and Edinburgh setting. But gripping as it is, it fails to capture him. He's too on edge.

He puts it down to reread the instructions that were sent with the letter, though he's read them so often he can quote most of it from memory, he's been so keen to be involved. He's held hearts in his hands; Matthew wants to know how it would feel to hold someone's liberty, too, delving into the depths of someone else's dark desires for once, rather than constantly being confronted by his own.

He glances round the room, checking out the competition. There's around thirty people in the room now. The chairs are nearly all full, the air beginning to thicken with conflicting perfumes, sweat. A faint whiff of old cigarette smoke from a woman by the door. With any luck he won't get stuck next to her, the ashtray pall sickening him to his core. He cut someone open the week before last who was on forty cigarettes a day and he could have sworn the same stench came off the man's greying lungs, seeping through Matthew's surgical mask, crawling into his mouth.

He shifts from side to side in his seat. The caffeine from an espresso he drank earlier is jangling through him, his tongue thick and his foot twitching. One of his eyelids, too. The man sitting opposite him doesn't look comfortable, either. He keeps crossing and uncrossing his legs, constantly in motion, as is his neighbour, a woman in her mid-forties with a fair, brittle bob and a large handbag through which she keeps rummaging. Matthew glances at her only briefly but she catches his eye, her irises a washed-out blue, as pale as her sandy-coloured hair.

'I'm not going to be able to do this,' she says.

'How do you mean?'

'If they call me, I won't be able to do this. I can't. I need to be at home for my daughter. There isn't anyone else.'

'How old is your daughter?'

'Sixteen. But she's a very young sixteen.'

'Right,' he says. The man sitting next to her rolls his eyes as if he's heard her say this a hundred times already this morning.

'It'll be fine,' Matthew says. 'You just explain it to them if they call your name.'

'You really think so?'

'I've told her this,' her neighbour says. He stands up, stretches, wanders away.

'He keeps saying it'll be fine, but I've heard they're strict. They don't care about anything other than their precious trials. What if I can't get out of it? What if I get caught up in something that goes on for weeks? What if it's a child abuse case? I really couldn't cope with that. I mean, as a mother it would kill me to have to look at any terrible photographs . . .' Her voice trails off.

'I'm sure it'll be fine,' Matthew says again, the words automatic. He's looking at her more closely now, a prickle in his scalp. Her voice might sound jumpy but there's something calculating in the way her eyes are set, the tip of her nose pink, almost quivering. Like she's thinking about potential horrors, relishing the thought. Matthew stands up and moves away too.

A woman in a black gown comes into the room. 'I'm the Clerk of Court,' she says. 'Before we go into the court for the ballot to empanel the jury, I'm going to read some names to you. If you have knowledge of any of the people that I name, if you know them personally in any way, I'd ask you to speak to me privately. Attract my attention and I will come over to you.'

A pause, an intake of breath.

'Isobel Smyth. Eliza Lawson.'

Girls' names, not the neds he was expecting. There's a ripple in the room, a gasp of recognition. Something stirs in the back of his mind, a vague sense of familiarity.

'Does it count if it's from the news?' the awful woman says. Matthew glances over at her, repulsed by the excitement he sees shining in her eyes.

'Beyond the news,' the court clerk says. 'If you know them personally, as I said.'

The woman shakes her head. No one else speaks.

Matthew's wracking his brain but he can't place the names he just heard, despite his normally excellent memory. A headline he's read, maybe? Not like he ever has time to spend reading the news, surfing the internet. The others certainly seem to have heard of them, all of them sitting up a little straighter, heads alert instead of slumped down into their phones. Matthew'll find out soon enough, if he's lucky.

Last chance. He could choose to make his excuses, get out of this. It's not like his job isn't important. A literal heart surgeon, as his daughter would say.

But he doesn't want to. He wants the escape of this.

He wants to run away.

'Please follow me.' The clerk is now standing by the door. No one has pulled her aside, all obediently lined up behind her instead. The sandy-haired woman from before stands beside him, the calculating expression still on her face. She licks her lips, the tip of her tongue flicking from one side of her mouth to the other. She wants gore, Matthew can see that now. She wants to pore over photos of pain, of extremity, twisted limbs and bloodied flesh.

Matthew is about to turn away, but not before she meets his gaze, an eyebrow raised as if in recognition. For a moment it's as if she sees his soul, greets it as like meeting like. Shame writhes in his stomach, a tightening and twisting. He might know her voyeuristic desires, her longing to wallow in the horrors inflicted by a crime, feast on the suffering of those hurt by it.

But with that one glance, straight into the core of him, she knows that these are his longings, too.

4

Court to Matthew's mind means dark wooden panelling, an imposing space. He watched *Witness for the Prosecution* on his laptop when the jury letter arrived, keeping the screen hidden from Rosalind. She'd only have made some snide remark about how he'd be lucky to find anyone like Marlene Dietrich popping up on the stand.

Any thoughts of old films or antique courtrooms go out of his mind as soon as he's through the door. It's office-bland, light wood and glass. But not without pomp, slick and modernised as it might be. A coat of arms above a chair on a dais where he assumes the judge will sit, NEMO ME IMPUNE LACESSIT written on the wall in black letters glaring down at him – *no one provokes me with impunity* – as if the thoughts of Matthew's mind have been weighed in the balance and found distinctly wanting, try as he might not to be provocative. He shifts from foot to foot, uneasy. Something dark in him is writhing too close to the surface.

As all the potential jurors file into the courtroom, the air hums, excitement growing. Matthew feels it too, his palms tingling. A loud rap-rap from the side of the courtroom makes his heart jolt, miss a beat. He looks over to see a man in a black gown carrying something like a lantern on a pole over his shoulder enter through a door to the right of the dais. The clerk shouts the word 'Court' as he does. There's a flurry as the advocates all rise to their feet as the judge walks in, a woman in a wig, resplendent in robes, white satin over crimson, red crosses down her front, a white silk scarf round her neck like a tie. The man puts the object into a holder on the wall behind the judge, next to the coat of arms.

'What the hell's that?' the man next to Matthew mutters but Matthew doesn't move. He's transfixed by the pageantry of it, a ceremony of centuries, beyond now or then, a timelessness that picks him up and carries him with the tide of it.

'Call the diet. Her Majesty's Advocate against Eliza Lawson and Isobel Smyth.' The man in the gown is declaiming again.

Matthew is about to look more closely at the girls in the dock but one of the advocates sitting at the curved table in front of the judge's clerk gets to her feet, distracting his attention.

'My name is Miss Brodie. I appear for the first accused, my lady. Eliza Lawson. She pleads not guilty to the charges in the indictment.'

Another advocate pops up as soon as the woman sits down. 'I'm Miss Goodly. I appear for the second accused, Isobel Smyth. She also pleads not guilty to all charges on the indictment.'

So the male advocate on the other end of the table must be the advocate depute, the person prosecuting the case. Matthew tingles with momentary pride that he's remembered the proper name.

Movement from the dock, a hand rising, falling again. Matthew looks over properly for the first time. It's raised to the same level as the judge, containing two smaller figures sitting hunched between burly security guards, stern-faced women in uniform at each end of the dock, dwarfing the slight figures who are both wearing grey hoodies, heads bent down. One fair-haired, one dark. A third security guard separates the girls from each other.

Witch Trial

Behind the dock is the public gallery. It's packed, the rows of chairs all full. Only a few people stand out – a blonde woman sitting in the front beside two men, all with notebooks in their hands. A large group of teenage girls huddled together, younger than Daisy. School uniformed, burgundy V-neck jumpers and white shirts. Matthew is surprised to see them – it's not half-term yet. That's the whole point of Rosalind's diatribes about the holiday, to get there before schools are out. Maybe the girls are studying law.

Back to the dock again. Three security guards, glass walls at each end of the dock separating the accused girls from the rest of the court; a tumbler over spiders to keep them enclosed. They don't look like spiders, though. None of the menace. They look like children, small, pale faces peeking out behind masses of hair, shoulders hunched over. The fair-haired one straightens herself upright. Her skin is clear. The one with dark hair stays stooped though, a greasy fringe flopping down across her face. Matthew can't see too clearly, but it looks like she's got a piercing under her lower lip, a large stud sitting amongst a cluster of angry spots.

The clerk of the court is speaking. She's got a glass bowl in front of her full of slips of paper from which she's going to pull out the names. Matthew drags his gaze from the back of the courtroom to the front.

'Will the ladies and gentlemen whose names she calls out please come forward and take their seats in the jury box.'

At that she gestures over to the space at her left, three tiers of seats, computer screens attached to the desks before them, one between two.

The potential jurors shuffle. The court clerk coughs, clears her throat.

Christopher Patel
Emma Fraser
Alistair Macdonald

Harriet Tyce

Aisha Ahmed
Roderick Davidson
Russell McLean
Michael Reid
Dharam Singh
Jasmine Lewis

Called out in turn, each makes their way up to the jury box and takes their seats. The sandy-haired woman is there. Emma Fraser. She makes no effort to extract herself from the situation, a smile lifting one corner of her mouth. She catches Matthew's eye again and the smile spreads. It's a taunt.

Neil Mackay
Leroy James
Sarah Thompson

Only three spaces left now. It isn't going to be him. He can go back to work, back to Rosalind. Back to normality. Everyone will be happy.

Nicola Wilson
Elliot Graham

The Clerk of Court leans back for a moment, takes in a deep breath. One space left. She runs her hand around the rim of the bowl as if to prolong the agony. It won't be Matthew, he knows it now. He can see Olivia's eyes smiling at him above her mask, across the operating table. A question. *Later?*, one eyebrow raised. It'll be sooner than he thought.

Matthew Phillips

He walks over and takes his place.

5

There was never a doubt that he'd do it. The only uncertainty was whether he would be called. But here he is.

Relief, that's his biggest emotion. The die cast, he can be honest with himself. He's been desperate for this. A get out of jail free card to send someone else down, nothing else for him to do. Better than a holiday. They'll have to leave him alone here.

The woman who gave him the creeps – Emma – is sitting in front of him. He'll have to do his best not to look at her. At least she won't be able to see him, though she keeps turning her head, checking everyone out. They're all looking round though, heads turning left and right, fifteen meerkats on high alert, doing their best to avoid each other's eyes. He glances down his row – the four people sitting along from him all seem normal, at least, no one overly gleeful. Nothing like the sharp look he saw from her.

A number of people in the public gallery are staring straight at the jury, weighing them up – they might not be sitting that close but Matthew can tell they're being evaluated. Not by the teenage girls – they aren't paying any attention. They're restless, flicking their hair, their heads moving from side to side. One of them is chewing gum, her jaw moving constantly.

Matthew is restless too, his curiosity building, desperate to know what the accused girls are supposed to have done. He peers at the advocates sitting in front of the judge. The advocate depute accompanied by a man in a suit, the defence advocates with two younger women next to them also wearing wigs and gowns, men in suits sitting behind them. There are piles of papers and laptops open before them, though Matthew can't make out any details from where he's standing, squint as he might.

He doesn't know much about court proceedings, but his gut tells him that the more lawyers are involved, the more serious the matter.

They're so young, though, the girls sitting in the dock. Younger than Daisy. Vulnerable, up there between the security officers who are each twice the size of the girls. One would be enough to take them both down. He checks himself at the thought. He's no idea what the girls are capable of, pathetic as they may seem.

Matthew knows this is how the system works. Some of the most serious cases in the country are heard in this room. He can imagine a row of beefy men sitting up there charged with multiple robberies, murders. But these children? Daisy always bollocks him when he calls her a kid, but nineteen or not, that's how he sees her, and these girls are clearly younger than her.

'I will now read out the indictment,' the court clerk says. A ripple through the jury. At last he'll find out.

The girls stand.

'Please confirm your name for the court.' He points at the girl on the left, the one with fair hair.

'Eliza Lawson,' she says. Her voice is quiet but clear. There's a firmer set to her jaw than Matthew anticipated from the meek expression on her face. Perhaps not so pathetic, then.

'Date of birth?'

'The eighteenth of June, 2001.'

2001. Matthew was right. She's seventeen. A couple of years younger than Daisy. The hairs on his scalp lift.

'Your address is Ardvulin, Longniddry Road, North Berwick.'

'That's right.'

'Please be seated. Will the second accused please stand and give the court her name?'

Eliza sits down, still confident in her movements, her head held high.

Isobel, the dark-haired girl, is not the same. She gets to her feet slowly, her shoulders still hunched, her arms hanging loose at her sides with her hands hidden by the sleeves of her hoodie. Unlike Eliza, whose face was bare of make-up, she's wearing heavy black eyeliner and there's a ring through her nose as well as the stud under her bottom lip. Looking more closely at her hair, it's clear that it was dyed some time ago, the ends nearly black while the roots are greasy and mouse-coloured. She's not very prepossessing.

'Isobel Smyth.'

'Date of birth?'

'The fourteenth of November, 2001.'

'Your address is 14 Cluny Gardens, in Edinburgh. Is that correct?'

'Yes.'

Cluny Gardens. That's somewhere out Barnton way, Davidsons Mains. Near the supermarket. Not that it matters now – he needs to pay attention. He pulls himself together, looks at the judge. She has a notebook in front of her, a pen in her hand, businesslike. The grey of her wig matches the grey of her hair, the two seamlessly blended together.

The clerk speaks again, her words blurred at first, then razor sharp as Matthew tunes in '. . . that on or about first May 2018, in Inverleith Park, Edinburgh, you did assault Christian Shaw and did threaten her with a knife, thus causing her to believe that she was at risk of imminent attack, and you did so knowing that this action would result in her death or were wickedly reckless as to that risk given your knowledge of her pre-existing heart condition, in consequence of which assault she sustained a heart attack whereof she died; and you did murder her.'

Murder. He blinks. So much for schoolgirl high jinks.

At the mention of the victim's name, there's a loud sob from the public gallery. Matthew looks over; one of the girls in school uniform is covering her face with her hands. He turns his head to see that Isobel is looking up at them too, her dark hair pushed back from her face as she tips her head towards them. Her expression is set, stern, a line between her eyebrows.

A shimmer in the air. The lines around her eyes deepen, darken, her brows knitted together. Her hair seems to move, writhe, twisted in dull hanks that stir around her head, snakelike. Her lips are thin, tightly pressed together. A cold rage beats out from her.

She shakes her head once, twice, glancing over at the jury box, catches his gaze. Holds it. Freezes him to the spot.

One beat, two. The air shimmers again. Matthew blinks, rubs his eyes. He's still looking at Isobel but she's herself again. A girl in her late teens, similar age to his daughter.

Only a child.

The air's shifted. A cold breath on Matthew's face. *Run away, get away before it's too late*, a voice says in his head, so clear it's as if someone's whispered to him. It is too late, though. He's in for the ride. A murder trial – less escapism to be found here than he hoped. Not an escape from the pressures of his day job – different sandpit, that's all. The middle-aged man in the public gallery looks as tense as any relatives waiting outside one of his operating theatres. At least no one can say that he's in charge of anything, though. Or that he's to blame if it all goes wrong. Not like . . .

Witch Trial

The judge coughs, clears her throat.

'Ladies and gentlemen, you have had the indictment read over to you. Shortly you will be asked to take the oath, but before—'

The oath. He'd forgotten about that. He's been flipflopping for days about what he'd do, take the Bible or affirm. He's still undecided, agnostic to the core. What would carry more weight? Does he even believe in God any more? The judge is still speaking and he tunes back in.

'Do any of you know of any reason why you could not impartially serve as a juror?'

Matthew looks over at the girls in the dock. Eliza at least is indistinguishable from many of Daisy's friends, centre parting, head bowed low. That's not a reason not to do it, though.

The clerk takes over, briskly asking all the jurors to raise their right hands. They're all still standing. Before Matthew has fully clocked what's happening, the clerk has rattled through asking if they swear by Almighty God that they will well and truly try the accused and give a true verdict according to the evidence. A mutter of *I do*, the words barely leaving Matthew's lips, before the clerk gestures to them to take their seats.

Is that it? His solemn promise? It doesn't feel very binding. He looks sidelong – the woman next to him is rigid, her lips a tight line. The words of the oath ring in his ears. He'd have liked to have sworn on the Bible, after all. There'd have been a comfort in the grip of the book in his hand. It would have felt more sincere, somehow. Laden with more meaning.

He shakes his head, dismissing the thought. He's too rational to need a prop. Matthew believes in facts, in experts. He seeks the opinion of scientists, making a point of walking under every ladder he sees.

Perhaps something of his childhood lingers. Christened, confirmed, Sunday schooled. His family's God sawest all, although it's been years since he went inside a church, turning his back on it all the moment that he went to university and started to study medicine. Matthew's gods took on human form – it would only be a few years before he could join their ranks, weighing life and death in his own hands, as soon as he was allowed to wield a scalpel. He measured everything in numbers, peer reviews and blind testing his new testaments.

This way of swearing in a jury should appeal to him. But instead he just feels small.

Before he can brood more on it, the judge starts speaking again. She's adjourning the court, giving them the chance to go to their room, take off their coats. Choose their lunch. 'One final matter before you do that. I shall mention this in more detail on your return, but even at this stage, you must not, even out of idle curiosity, carry out any investigation about anyone or anything relating to this case. I say this in recognition that by means of mobile phones it is now very easy to use these devices to gain almost instantaneous access to information on almost any subject, and some people are very adept at doing so.'

Matthew shifts from foot to foot. He feels seen, the God of his childhood suddenly replaced by this woman in a wig with dark, piercing eyes. He wants to protest immediately. He wouldn't dream of looking anything up. He knows how serious it is. But his fingers are itching to type the words *Isobel Smyth Eliza Lawson murder* in his search engine all the same.

6

The judge leaves and the jury go out through a door at the side of the court, along a corridor and into a room dominated by a large table. The familiarity of the scene reassures Matthew. The courtroom might have fallen short of *Witness for the Prosecution*, but this is pure *Twelve Angry Men*, even if there are actually fifteen of them, of whom more than half are women, and no one looks particularly angry. At least not yet.

Unlike the messages that arrive on Matthew's phone as soon as he switches it on, fury throbbing through the ether, repeated pings of irritation. Everyone is angry.

```
Where the hell are you?
You can't be spared.
Why didn't you tell them you were
unavailable?
```

He sends the same message to Rosalind and Dominic, to the registrar at the hospital. To Olivia.

```
On a jury for the next two weeks.
```

After a pause, he types out another message. Sends it.

```
It's beyond my control.
```

His phone starts ringing. It's Rosalind. Matthew doesn't need to answer it to know what she'll have to say. She knows him too well. Knows the system, too. He could hold the line that the court refused to excuse him but she'll never believe it. He turns the phone off again without looking at the screen and pushes it back in his jacket pocket. He never has his phone on at work – they're used to it by now. They'll give up calling soon.

Anyway, he doesn't really care. Perhaps he should, but it's relentless, the ringing of the phone, the shrillness of Rosalind's voice, the way she keeps telling him what to do. It's her fault, what he's done. He'd never have been so irrational if she hadn't been so bossy, dictating to him what his obligations were.

'Coffee?' one of the other jurors asks. Roderick. He's in his forties, wearing jeans and a checked shirt. Matthew will do the same tomorrow, not bother with the suit and tie he's wearing today, by far the smartest of anyone in the room.

Dressed to impress.

'Yes, please. Black,' Matthew says, smiling.

With the interruption, his thoughts do an about-turn. He's a dick. It's not Rosalind's fault. It's his. He's in dereliction of his duties. He's abandoned his family, his work too. It's unforgivable.

'What do you think of all that?' a voice sidling in at his shoulder, sly. He knows without turning it's that woman. Emma.

'We shouldn't discuss it,' he says. 'Only when all of us are talking about it together.'

'They're all around us. Don't be such a stick in the mud. You know you're dying to talk about it.' Her lips are moist, her eyes blinking fast.

'We're not meant to discuss it, not like this. We should just listen at this stage to what they've got to tell us.'

'Ooh, look at you all high and mighty. After the job of foreman, are we? All booted and suited like that.'

She's leaning in close, her breath stale. There's something musty coming from her hair and it catches in the back of his throat.

'Here's your coffee,' Roderick says. The interruption is extremely welcome.

'Thanks,' Matthew says, as Emma turns to him.

'What do you reckon? Do you think they killed her? I know who they are. I heard about them on TV.'

Matthew shakes his head, Roderick also. His nose wrinkles, just a little. Matthew moves closer to him.

'I have no idea,' he says, 'and we shouldn't talk about it.' He starts to move away from her.

'They're the witch girls,' Emma says. 'This is the witch trial.'

7

Witch trial. Something's flickering in Matthew's mind, a glimmer of a memory of a headline he's glimpsed, beckoning round a corner before fleeing out of sight.

'You heard what the judge said,' Roderick says, and turns his back to her, shutting her out from any further conversation. She snorts and walks away in search of easier prey, though none of the other jurors look exactly keen to speak to her.

'Roderick,' he says, holding his hand out.

'Matthew. Matt. Nice to meet you.' They shake hands. Matthew forces himself not to repeat what Emma has just said. *Witch trial.* 'Causing any difficulties for you, being called like this?'

'My boss isn't happy,' Roderick says. 'Not much he can do about it though. I'll have to work around it to an extent. I'm an accountant and it's the end of the tax year. All those returns to wade through.'

'Unfortunate timing.'

'I could have tried to put it off, but to be honest, I was interested in what being on a jury would be like.'

Matthew nods. Someone else gets it. 'I didn't want to put it off either. Though God knows they all told me to.' He gestures out wide with his hands at the word *they*; Roderick looks sympathetic. Perhaps Matthew has found an ally.

26

Witch Trial

The other jurors are chatting to each other, too, everyone standing round the table, only a couple of people choosing to sit down.

'I hope it doesn't go over the two weeks though,' Roderick says. 'That will cause problems.'

'Hopefully not.'

'Can we talk about it now?' Emma says loudly. 'It's only us. I know all about this case.'

Murmurs. They're all looking any direction but at her. The judge's warnings are running through Matthew's head.

'I just don't see how they can be saying such terrible things about those wee girls. The one with fair hair – she doesn't look like a witch.'

Is this what Emma really thinks? Or is she just fishing? Either way, no one replies. She looks around them all, the eager expression in her eyes subsiding as she realises that they're not going to play.

'Let's wait until we've heard all the evidence before we leap to judgement,' Roderick said, his voice not unkind. Matthew bites back a sharper response. It's as well that just then they are called back into court.

They file to their seats. The same rigmarole but this time Matthew knows the name for it; he asked the court official who brought them back into the jury box. The macer leads in the judge before placing the mace in the holder on the wall. A ceremonial function. There was more to it but Matthew loses track of the explanation. All part of the arcana of it, the ritual.

Like witchcraft. Emma's words have stuck in Matthew's head. Witch trial. He looks over at the girls in the dock again, trying to make sense of it. Not a wart or hooked nose to be seen. No one is green. It's only the judge speaking that stops him from snorting with laughter at the thought. She's lecturing them again about who does what, her voice so calm and modulated that it soothes Matthew almost to the point of sleep, his head nodding as she explains it all to them. It's only at the end he zones back in.

'The background of this case has attracted some media attention. If you have seen or read anything like that you must ignore it. The internet also carries material about it. You must not access such material throughout the course of this trial.'

She pauses for breath. In other words, don't fucking google it, dickheads. A big red button marked DO NOT TOUCH. Matthew's got the point. He's bored now, ready to get on with it, hear the real meat of the case. It's a murder – there's going to be blood and guts. What he lives for. Not this prissy laying down of the law. She is the law, motherfuckers, Judge Dredd in a frilly wig.

He folds his hands in his lap, digging his nails in sharp on both sides. Start taking this seriously, for God's sake. He knows exactly what he's doing, taking the piss in order to puncture the dignity of the place a little. Matthew's intimidated by it all, out of water, and he doesn't like it.

'As I say, this case must be decided solely on the evidence you hear in court. If you become aware of any fellow jury member who has conducted independent investigations, please inform the Clerk of Court at once.' She fixes them with a hard stare. Matthew feels every part of him contract, withering inside. 'I may say that after this warning, if I become aware of any juror carrying out such investigations, I shall take a very serious view of it. It may very well result in the trial collapsing with all the attendant cost that would involve. It likewise may constitute a contempt of court. If it did constitute a contempt of court, all sentencing options are open to me.'

Matthew stares up at her, the rest of the jury too. All sentencing options? Meaning?

'Prison.' She adds one word in clarification, seemingly annoyed by the blank stares she's receiving from all fifteen of the jury.

He blinks. She's not messing around here. He glances at Emma, to see if she's taking the point. Her head is bowed, her hands moving in her lap, a repetitive motion like she's working through a rosary, or worry beads, though her fingers are empty.

There's more to the speech. Way more. It goes on for about half an hour. Matthew is doing his best to listen, but it's difficult. The wine he drank last night to let go of the strain of the tricky operation he'd carried out that afternoon, the fact he'd woken at three, excited as a child at the prospect of getting picked for a jury; all of it is catching up with him now. He'd thought he'd be witnessing the cut and thrust of a cross-examination, shouts of *my learned friend* and *I put it to you*, not this droning on about rules and housekeeping, not to *talk* to anyone about it or allow anything to influence his *decision*. To report any *strangers* who approach them outside court and attempt to discuss the case with them.

Come off it, this is hardly a spy story. They're not in fifties Berlin. The caution is over-egged – pettifogging, procedure-heavy. All the things he wants to leave behind in the reality of his day job. This is meant to be swashbuckling fun, the stuff of movies. But it's dull. Dull, dull, dull.

His head nods down once, twice; if he doesn't watch it he's going to fall asleep, start snoring before the case has even begun. When he thought he was foreman material, too – what a joke. That's clearly going to be Roderick, all neatly combed hair, pen in his right hand, as he scribbles down furiously while the judge keeps on and on. Matthew picks up his pen and starts doodling on the paper in front of him to try to keep himself awake, birds taking flight across the page surrounded by a constellation of rough, five-pointed stars.

But this can only hold his attention for a few moments. Soon he puts his pen down, hoping to God it's going to finish soon. Surely there can't be much more to say? The faces in the public gallery look the same as he's feeling, tense and bored. No one in the room is hearing what they really want to know. Who's dead, how did she die, and did these girls in the dock really kill her?

Now the judge is introducing the jury to the main players. Matthew's ears prick up; he turns the page to a clean piece of paper. Something worth noting at last.

'The prosecution is brought by the Crown. That's the name given to the public prosecutor in Scotland. The Crown has to prove the charges and it seeks to do so by presenting evidence. The case for the Crown is presented by the Advocate Depute, Mr Alexander, and he is assisted by Mr McLeod and they are sitting at the table to my right. You have already been introduced to Miss Brodie who represents Eliza Lawson and Miss Goodly who represents Isobel Smyth, who are sitting at the table to my left. In Scotland there are no opening speeches—'

Matthew puts his pen down, stifles a cheer. He's been dreading another lengthy session. Although having said that, they need to get on with telling them what this is all about.

Not yet though. Still more speech. Details of evidence, of legal procedure. What time lunch will be served. The fact that the trial is being recorded. At this moment the judge waves her hand in the general direction of the side of the court where the blonde woman is sitting. Matthew glances over at her. Her hair's twisted up into a bun at the back of her head, an elegant sweep of it away from her face. Her head's downturned, intent on the notebook on her lap, a beige trench coat on the seat next to her, but as he gazes at her she looks up, catches his eye; red lipstick, a blue-green gaze.

Witch Trial

A pulse beats hard at Matthew's neck. He sits tight, swallows. She smiles, turns away.

Another ripple in the air. He's not confronted by a monster, though, no crone here. A melody from a half-remembered Lloyd Cole song plays in his head, about an actress in a black and white film. He understands the pull of the words now.

No Marlene Dietrich, but he's found a film noir star.

8

The judge is getting into the minutiae of the law now, throwing around words like *credibility* and *corroboration* with abandon. Matthew has given up all pretence of listening. He's transfixed by the woman sitting at the side of the court. She doesn't look up again – all he can see is the soft wing of pale blond hair, the curve of the top of her red lip. With an effort, he pulls his eyes away from her, looks at the accused girls instead.

Eliza is looking down, her hair still across her face, but Isobel is alert, the rage still crackling off her as she turns her head slowly to look around the court. Matthew freezes, a rabbit about to be caught in a headlight. He wants to look away, he can't move his head, a moment of paralysis where any minute she's going to see him, fix him with her eyes and then— the girl coughs and it breaks the spell. Matthew looks down, sinking back into his chair. Relief courses through him at the close escape.

One glance more at the woman with the notebook then he forces himself to look back to the judge. She must be winding up by now; the modulations in her voice have an air of finality to them. Though that might just be wishful thinking.

She's explaining reasonable doubt: *the sort of doubt that would make you pause or hesitate before taking an important decision in the practical conduct of your own lives.* Is that all it needs? The sort of doubt that would make you pause? He thought it would be more than that; a crushing sense of apocalypse, more like, a presentiment of certain doom. Matthew's doubted every decision he's made, in his personal life at least. Proposing to Rosalind, that was nothing but doubt, the strongest desire he's ever had to run to the hills and not look back as she sat there, hand extended, waiting for the ring she had no doubt that he'd provide.

You must be certain so that you are sure. Familiar territory again, but only in work. When he's poised with the scalpel, about to cut open a patient's chest, Matthew's always sure. He knows exactly where to cut, making the eight-inch incision with total certainty, pulling the ribs apart and connecting the heart–lung bypass machine, breath held for the moment that the patient is clinically dead until the mechanical pump takes over. He never doubts that. Fixing the accused girls with a stare, Matthew promises himself that he'll only convict them if he can feel that sure, powerful as the cut made by his obsidian blade.

But the doubt faded about Rosalind. He needs to remember that. The moment of panic followed by a lifetime of happiness, his partner in everything that he does. If he puts Olivia to one side, that is, the other Olivias who came before. But temporary doubt doesn't mean doubt enough to acquit someone, not when it's murder . . .

More of the about-turns. He blinks, dizzy for a moment, disorientated by the sense that this is not his world, these are not his rules. He doesn't even know enough to break them. He needs to pay more attention, however hard it feels.

Everyone is standing now, and Matthew realises that the judge is leaving the courtroom again. He jumps up to his feet, catches the eye of the woman with the notebook who smiles at him, striking straight to his core. Who is she? A pause. The question repeats itself, this time more ominously. Who the hell is this woman? Why does she keep looking at him? The notebook in her hand – he's assuming she's here to cover the trial. But what if she's got another agenda? What if Dominic's sent her? The hospital?

Matthew's head is about to explode. He rubs his eyes hard. He's being neurotic now, uncertain of himself in this new environment. He mustn't let his paranoia go out of control. He looks over again at where she was sitting but she's gone now, her seat empty.

He's got to stop being daft, hold on to what he knows for sure. No one is here to spy on him – she's just a pretty girl and there's a mutual attraction. That's all. Rules against speaking to people outside the jury or not, he wouldn't say no if the opportunity presented itself to talk to her.

The jury files back to the room to find that lunch has been laid out on the table for them. Matthew selected the sandwiches earlier, meat variety, and picks at the chicken salad on wholegrain he's been served. He's not hungry, even though he had no breakfast. The emotion of the morning is catching up with him, the knowledge that his phone is burning a hole in his pocket, waiting to start yelling at him the moment that he switches it on.

As he was last into the room he has no choice about where to sit – there's only one space left, next to the dreadful woman. She's That Emma in his head now, the contrast between her badly bleached, straw-like hair and the silken, Hitchcock blond of the woman with the notebook hitting him with such force that he almost recoils from her. She's eating a jacket potato with tuna and sweetcorn in mayonnaise and the smell only reinforces his revulsion. She must sense his movement, though, as she turns to him, smiling with a bit of corn stuck to her front tooth.

Witch Trial

'I saw you,' she says. 'I was watching.'

'You saw me what?' he replies, after a moment. He doesn't want to engage but despite himself he wants to know what she's talking about.

'You were staring at that pretty journalist. Couldn't take your eyes off her.'

'You think she's a journalist?' The question slips out despite himself.

'Notebook? What else would she be?' Her smile has broadened. More knowing. He's going to have to be more careful. Even sitting in front of him this woman's eyes are out on stalks.

The woman sitting on Matthew's other side is clearly listening in because she interrupts. 'I didn't think journalists were allowed to sit in court. What if we get identified?'

Matthew moves his chair back a little so he can take a proper look at her. Someone else with fears, too. She's young, probably the youngest member of the jury by some years. Jasmine Lewis. Not long out of her teens. Her eyes are close together, a greasy fringe of dark hair clumped across her forehead.

'Those wee girls hardly look like mafia dons.' It's Neil Mackay, another man in his fifties. He looks like he's trying to control a smile.

'Someone might hex us,' Jasmine says. Matthew looks at her intently – it's hard to tell from her tone whether she means it, though he thinks he can discern a note of sarcasm under the comment. She points at Emma. 'She said the girls are witches.'

'No one is going to hex us,' Matthew says. 'There's no such thing.'

'You don't know that,' Emma says. She's leaning forward, both elbows down on the table. Matthew breathes through his mouth to avoid the tuna stink. 'Lots of people believe it's true. The co-accuseds, for one thing.'

Roderick holds up his hand. 'I don't want to know what

you've read in the papers about this case already,' he says. 'You heard what the judge said. We're going to hear everything that they want us to know. We shouldn't talk about anything we know from outside.'

'Stop being such an old woman,' Emma says. 'I'm entitled to say my piece. Just because I'm the only one who bothers to read the newspaper round here.' She looks around the table. 'Come on, everyone. Don't you want me to tell you what this is all about?'

Roderick shakes his head. 'Enough. Do you want to get us all kicked out before this has even begun?'

'They're not going to do that,' Emma says. 'How would they know?'

A deep voice from the end of the table. Dharam Singh. 'Because I will tell the court officer myself that you keep trying to talk about what you know about the case and I will ensure that you are kicked off this case if you don't shut up now.'

Matthew leans back to take a look at the man. He's in his sixties, dark turban, gold-rimmed glasses, silver beard. Another foreman contender. Dharam catches his eye and the two men nod to each other. Matthew has no doubt that Dharam will do exactly what he's threatening to do if Emma doesn't shut up. The humphing noise then silence from Emma suggests that she's realised too that he means what he says.

'This isn't a game,' Dharam says, quietly but with such command that the whole jury turns to look at him, their jaws ceasing chewing for a moment, their phones ignored in their hands. 'This isn't a witch trial, either. It's a murder trial, and it's serious. We need to do what the judge says, listen to the evidence, and reach a verdict. That's it. No more of this tittle tattle.'

Emma opens her mouth.

'I said, no more of this. Do you agree?'

She closes it again. Gives one nod, such a slight movement of her head that it might not even have happened. But the whole room sees her back down.

Matthew heads out with the smokers after they finish lunch to skulk round the side of the court building. Not to have a cigarette – he's seen too many blocked arteries for that to hold any appeal – but because he can't bear to stay in the stuffy room another moment, inhaling the stale tuna fury that's emanating from Emma. Also (though he is barely admitting it to himself) he's hoping to get a glimpse of the blonde woman. He's with Neil Mackay (roll-ups), Jasmine Lewis (a bright pink vape that gives off the smell of fake strawberries) and Nicola Wilson (Marlboro Gold). The latter is in her thirties, Matthew estimates, a sensible-looking woman with brown hair and a strong jawline. Could be a teacher. Certainly doesn't look as if she'll take any shit. A third contender for foreman. They're adding up.

She takes a long drag of her cigarette and exhales, an expression of so much concentrated enjoyment on her face that Matthew finds himself momentarily desperate to ask if he can have a drag, though he squashes the thought.

'If it's like this now,' she says, 'what the fuck is it going to be like when we get to discussing the verdict?'

9

Back into court. Matthew's torpor has lifted. There's going to be evidence now, actual witnesses. The case is going to unfold, its mysteries revealed layer by layer. He makes a point of not checking whether the blonde woman has made it back into court, though there's a flicker of movement in the general direction of where she was sitting which gives him an unexpected sense of reassurance.

'Advocate Depute,' the judge says.

'Thank you, my lady,' the advocate says. 'I would like to call my first witness. Callum Montrose, please.'

A man walks into court behind the macer. When he's in the witness box, the judge stands and asks him to raise his right hand.

'Repeat after me, I swear by Almighty God that the evidence I shall give will be the truth, the whole truth and nothing but the truth, so help me God.'

He's young, ginger hair and pale skin, and he looks very nervous. Matthew can barely make out what he's saying.

The judge sits back down and addresses the witness. 'Mr Alexander is going to ask you some questions now, and then Miss Brodie and Miss Goodly may ask you some questions on behalf of the co-accuseds. Please will you do your best to speak up so that we can all hear you in the court.'

Witch Trial

The witness nods, a red flush creeping up into his cheeks. Mr Alexander moves over to a lectern from which both the jury and the witness can see his face.

'Tell the court your name, please.'

'It's Callum Montrose.'

'And you live at an address near Inverleith Park, is that correct?'

'Yes.'

'Were you in Inverleith Park on first May of last year?'

'Yes.'

'What can you tell the court about that day?'

The witness is now so flushed his face is almost as red as his hair. Only a couple of white blotches remain, high on his cheekbones.

'I was out for a run in the morning—'

'I'm sorry, Mr Montrose, but I'm going to have to ask you to speak up,' the judge interrupts.

'Sorry. Sorry.' The witness takes a deep breath. 'I was out for a run in the morning. Early. I always go around six thirty a.m., especially as it gets lighter. Anyway, I was out, running round the park, down the side by the allotments. That's when I saw her.' He stops speaking and there's a long pause. Matthew holds his breath.

'Saw who?'

The witness swallows. Matthew can see the movement in his throat, an involuntary spasm.

'The girl. The dead girl.' A pause. 'I was running down the side by the allotments as I said, parallel to East Fettes Avenue. It was just before the path joins the big path that cuts through the middle. She was huddled down on the ground, underneath a hedge. Even from a distance it didn't look right . . .' His voice trails off.

'What didn't look right about her?'

The man squints his eyes, focusing on something only he can see. 'Something about her position? Maybe a stiffness to her, something like that. It was a funny place to be lying down, too. You wouldn't be sleeping there. Or sunbathing. She was half under the hedge, half on the path, like she'd fallen over.'

'What did you do when you saw her lying there?'

'I didn't want to go over,' Callum says, a slight reluctance creeping into his voice. 'I wanted to turn round and run as fast as I could in the opposite direction. It was the birds, I think. They were freaking me out.'

'What about the birds?'

'There were about ten crows stood around her. Maybe more than that. They weren't moving, just standing there, looking at her. It seriously freaked the shit— sorry, sorry, I didn't mean to swear. It's just . . .'

'Keep going,' the advocate depute says.

'As I started walking towards her, there was this cawing from the trees as well. I looked up, and the branches were full of crows. Dozens of them . . .' Callum's eyes are wide open now, tension lines tight around them. 'I still dream about it sometimes.'

Matthew's leaning forward on to the desk in front of him, his hands clenched into fists. He's barely drawn a breath since the witness started talking. He knows the park – of course he does, he lives five minutes' walk from it. He knows the park, the path beside the allotments the man is describing.

He's remembering something. The stumbling words of the witness have dredged it up from his memory, excavated it from the layers of work stress and life under which it was buried. He'd walked along the main path that day, glancing up to the left past the place where the forensics tent was up, police tape flapping between the trees. He looked it up on the internet at the time, though there weren't many details. A week or so later, he saw on Reporting Scotland that it was a schoolgirl from the boarding school next to the park, but no further details. Once he'd told Daisy to avoid going there on her own after dark, he'd put it out of his head.

'The crows kept cawing. They were kicking up a real fuss. I didn't want to go anywhere near them. Near her. But I couldn't leave her on her own like that. Even from a distance, she looked really young. Small.' He takes another deep breath. 'So I went over to her. As I approached, the crows all flew up. For a moment I actually thought they were going to attack me. It was like that film, you know. *The Birds.*'

Matthew tries to catch his breath but it's stuck in his throat, the air coming through in juddering sighs. The scene is only too clear in his head. The witness's face is pale now, his hands clenched in front of him, as if he needs to be clinging on to something.

'I got to her, lying on her side, her head looking back. Like she'd been running away from someone and she'd dropped like a stone. But that wasn't the worst of it.' He stops.

'What was the worst of it?' the advocate depute prompts.

'Her face. That was the worst. It had an expression on it I'll never forget.' Another pause, another audible swallow. 'It was set in a scream. Like she'd been scared to death.'

The rest of the evidence passes fast. He'd called 999. Other joggers had joined him, a dog walker. They'd stood as the sky lightened, waiting in a form of vigil until the paramedics arrived and then the police. He hadn't touched her – he hadn't needed to. It was obvious that she was dead. Once he'd given his details to the police officer he'd left. Couldn't run home fast enough. He's never been back since.

The first defence advocate takes her place at the lectern. Miss Brodie is almost as tall as the advocate depute, thin and autocratic in bearing with short grey curly hair that blends into the wig. Matthew's distracted by this for a moment, admiring the way it looks intrinsic to her, rather than the rather sloppy appearance of the prosecution junior, a young man with lank brown hair that reaches past his collar, on whose head the wig perches like an after-thought.

'When you first saw the body lying on the ground, did you see anyone else in the vicinity?'

The witness shakes his head. 'No.'

'You said that the area was surrounded by birds. Until you approached, did they appear to be undisturbed by any other life around them?'

'Yes, they were undisturbed. I was the one who disturbed them.'

'Thank you very much. I have no further questions.'

Miss Goodly stands up. 'I have no questions for this witness,' she says, and sits back down again.

The judge thanks the witness and tells him he's free to go. Matthew watches the man's shoulders drop down as he leaves the courtroom, clearly relaxing now that his part in the trial is over.

Matthew doesn't feel relaxed though. His shoulders are up round his ears. He's staring in front of him, but he's not seeing the courtroom, not even the woman with the notebook. He's seeing the white tent, the hushed police officers walking in and out of it.

The host of black crows on the ground beside it, their caws harsh in the morning air.

10

Some days, Angus Macpherson wishes he were still in uniform. This is one of them. Nothing's fitting him quite right, his suit itchy, his shirt collar too tight round the front of his neck. He never usually thinks twice about how he presents – what you see is what you get with Angus. But today, he wishes he were kitted out in the regalia of the state. It would lend him the *don't fuck with me* attitude that he's struggling to find.

It's a relief to be called into court, escape from the stuffy witness room, the tension that's beating off the other witnesses waiting their turn. Once he's in the witness box, the judge stands and asks him to raise his right hand, say the oath. Angus speaks clearly, puts both hands on the desk in front of him and leans forward, one eyebrow raised as he waits for the first question.

'Please will you give the court your full name and position?'

'Detective Angus Macpherson. I'm a scene of crimes officer.'

'Did you receive a call-out on first May last year, 2018, to attend a scene in Inverleith Park?'

'I did, yes.'

'Can you tell the court about it?'

Angus Macpherson can certainly tell the court about it. It's clear as day in his memory. It haunts his dreams. He won't say that to the court, though. He needs to be dispassionate here, unemotional, matter-of-fact in everything that he says. It's not like he hasn't done it before. He's given evidence hundreds of times in his career.

There's a timelessness to it, this part of the job; different accused, different judge every time, but it feels as if he's never left the witness box. It could be any trial he's done, the legs in the freezer, the head in the bag from the bottom of the harbour at Leith. So many dismemberments, drug deaths, beatings: the blood and horror merge into one in his brain sometimes, as if all that exists is one long scream, the dreadful noise he used to hear whenever he did the death knock.

Friends question him as to why he's ended up in the bowels of it, scraping the bottom of whisky barrels for clumps of bloodstained hair and brain matter (the body in the distillery is still one that he's asked to talk about more than any other, the public's fascination with the embalming qualities of an aged single malt seemingly endless). The dead can't speak – he'll find their words for them.

This death, this body. The things that he saw . . . there was something uncanny about the scene that he's never seen before, for all the blood and guts he's witnessed. There was a silent scream there on her face. And that's what has stayed, imprinted on him. The sight of it sometimes wakes him in the night with a jolt, his heart pounding . . . Few jobs have ever given him nightmares like this, the birds that peck at his eyes every night, Christian's face floating dead behind them as a disembodied voice urges them on.

'Detective, please tell the court what you saw when you arrived at Inverleith Park that day.'

The advocate depute's voice pulls Angus out of his reverie. He shouldn't need to be asked twice, and he and Mr Alexander have a sticky relationship at the best of times. They've butted heads before. But even with the delay he's already caused, he takes a moment to ground himself back in the courtroom, looking around him as he does.

Witch Trial

It's that woman judge, one of the new ones – he's heard she gets the job done. Some of the dead girl's relatives are sitting at the back of the court but Angus tries not to make eye contact with them – he's only met them once, anyway, introduced to various cousins and aunts and uncles at the funeral which he attended as officer in the case. Her parents aren't there – they'll be waiting outside to give evidence. It's a relief not to see her mum; it upsets him, seeing the state she gets into. She always ends up in tears. He doesn't want to tear up himself – he'd never hear the end of that, weeping like a child in front of the whole room.

To galvanise himself he glares over at where the accused girls are sitting in the dock, Eliza first, all fair hair and pretty and butter wouldn't melt. Then Isobel. As his eyes slide along to where she's sitting, the air starts to shimmer. His heart speeds up and he loses focus, bright spots dancing in front of him. A cold breath across his face. He rubs his eyes, looks away – this case has got under his skin far too much.

Finally, he looks at the jury. No forcefield there. His heart rate lowers again. A mixed bag – as usual – but they're all staring at him intently, waiting for him to tell them what this is about. He takes in a deep breath. Time to begin.

'If you permit it, my lady, I'm going to refer to my notebook.' It's in his hand already, and he holds it up towards the judge. She nods.

'I was called to attend Inverleith Park early on the morning of first May last year, as a body had been discovered by a passer-by. I proceeded to the path down the side of the allotments, where I found a small group of passers-by surrounding the body of a girl who was lying on the ground. Two paramedics were also in attendance, and I established immediately from them that life was extinct.'

He's gabbling, his nerves on edge. There's a tremor running through him, a sense that his teeth are about to start chattering as if with cold, his grasp on his notebook so tight that the tips of his fingers are starting to turn white. He takes in a deep breath to calm himself, slow down – the judge is writing down everything he's saying and he can see she's struggling to keep up.

'I cleared the area of passers-by and started my examination of the site. It was the body of a girl, mid to late teens was my estimate. She was wearing grey tracksuit bottoms and a navy-blue hoodie, though this was pulled up for the paramedics to administer emergency care. She was lying on her side, and there were no obvious signs of injury.'

'Can you tell us if there was any immediate explanation as to how she might have died?'

'No, I couldn't see anything out of the ordinary about her.' But as he says the words, he knows this isn't the full truth. Another cold breath across his face, the hairs on his scalp prickling. Angus isn't in the stuffy courtroom any more; he's back in Inverleith Park, the late spring air still chill in the early dawn. He's looking down at the dead girl, his heart tight, his hands clenched. Those damn birds standing all around him, silent as the grave; a cortege of crows.

'Are you sure about that?' Mr Alexander asks, as if he can sense that Angus is withholding something.

Angus swallows. 'There was one thing. It was her face. The expression on it. She looked terrified. Her eyes were stretched wide and her mouth open. I'll never forget the look of it.'

Entirely involuntarily, Angus pulls his lips back over his teeth, opens his jaw to full stretch. It's only the surprise on Mr Alexander's face that pulls him back from following it up with the scream that's been building up inside.

Ever since that time.

11

Angus has had enough. He doesn't want to scream any more, he wants to walk down the steps of the witness box, leave the courtroom. He's had enough of thinking about this case, running over and over the details. Dreaming about it night after night. There's no reason why this should have got into his head so much – he's seen far worse. But it's lingered, stubborn as any miasma of death. He wants it gone for good. Of course he wants to see the accused girls convicted; he believes in their guilt absolutely. But for the first time since he started this job, the first time in decades, he just can't face any more questions, the relentless prodding, the repetition of *what why where how* that's drilling into his head.

No escape from Mr Alexander. 'What did you do next?'

It takes a few seconds for Angus to recover himself. Finally, 'I secured the location and put in a call for the forensics team to come in. While there was no sign of visible injury, it was clearly an unexplained death, and I knew that it would require investigating even if it turned out not to be suspicious.'

'Was there anything else about the scene that led you to a belief that it might not be a death from natural causes?'

'Not at that stage, no.' The inadequacy of the words.

'What happened next?'

'We had to wait for the forensic pathologist to arrive ...'

Angus keeps talking, explaining the steps that were taken, the formality of the dance in which they all know the steps, the calls they need to make, the white-suited officers searching the surrounding area with fingertips, just in case. No obvious cause of death but his gut said it was wrong, even more so after everything else he witnessed, the downright creepiness of it all ... He's not saying that to the court, though. Keep all the emotion out of it, the fact that rule-driven and procedure-bound as his job might be, a good proportion still relies on intuition.

The worst of it was that he had to keep the girl lying there like that for hours. The sun was up, its rays gradually warming the morning air, but he touched her hand and it was cold. Emotion again, but he had to fight the urge to take off his jacket and place it over her. More than anything, he wanted to close her eyes, push the lids shut with his hand, secure them with coins. Their wide blue stare seemed to follow him wherever he moved.

Sometimes he even sees them now, an accusation in them. Or a plea.

Passers-by kept flocking round them until he posted two constables in uniform to direct people away, closed off most of the park. Rubberneckers, all of them, sticking their beaks into a tragedy that was none of their business. An officious man in cycling gear got right up into his face and shouted that he had a right to pass through, it was his entitlement as a citizen. Angus had a flash of intense anger but controlled himself. The guy was exactly the type to register a complaint, make an already difficult job that bit more unbearable. *Sorry, sir, yes, sir, terribly inconvenient, sir,* but the man and Angus both knew that he was only a heartbeat away from telling him to fuck off.

There was nothing on the body to identify the girl, not at that stage. Once all the photographs were taken, they managed to erect a white forensics tent over the body so that there could be some privacy for them all. That was a relief. It was mid-morning by now and the joggers had been replaced by women with prams complaining that their route to the playground was blocked. Angus kept his tongue behind his teeth. Hid his snarl.

'Was there a point when you came to identify the body?'

Mr Alexander's question breaks through Angus's reverie. He's back in the courtroom now, blinking in the light.

'Not immediately. Once the forensic pathologist had carried out her initial investigations and the body was being transferred on to a stretcher –' *the relief, to see that poor girl off the cold, hard ground – he can still feel it –* 'she asked me to have a look at the logo on the back of the girl's hoodie. It showed the name of a sports team, and the name of the nearby school. St Jude's, the big boarding school over the road.'

The advocate depute gestures at the macer and the man goes to a long table on which the items are piled and picks up the hoodie, folded so that its back is visible and sealed in a plastic forensics bag. He holds it up to the court and shows it to everyone, turning round slowly in a full circle so that the printed words are plain to read. Then he takes it over to the jury, hands it to the woman who's sitting in the far left corner and they pass it along between themselves.

Angus scrutinises their faces closely as they do so. His initial impression of them hasn't changed too much, pretty normal, though there's a middle-aged woman in the front row he does not like the look of who grabs hold of the bag and clutches it to her heart for a moment in what looks to Angus like pure mawkish sentimentality. He could swear she's mouthing the words *that poor girl*, but he does his best to ignore it. There's always one.

The rest of them look more sensible, a nice mix of ethnicities, young and old. A couple of people who stand out as potential foreman material. Forewomen too, come to that. An older man in a turban with a distinguished grey beard, a younger man sitting in the middle row wearing a suit with an attentive expression on his face, intelligent eyes. A woman on the front row who's leaning back in her seat in whose hooded gaze Angus can read alertness, concentration.

'When you saw the school name, what did you do?'

'I sent two officers over to the school to ask if any of their students were missing.'

'Did they return with a response?'

'They returned with a teacher. A form teacher, she said. She went into the tent and I heard a cry.'

If he's honest, he still hears that cry sometimes, behind his nightmare of birds, always waking him at the same point.

'She came out of the tent. She was very upset, but once she had stopped crying, she introduced herself as Rebecca Waites. She knew who the dead girl was.'

'Did she give you a name?'

'Yes, she said the girl was called Christian Shaw.'

'We'll hear more about Christian from other witnesses,' Mr Alexander says. 'For now, was this the end of your involvement at that time?'

Angus pauses.

'No, there was something else that happened while we were waiting for forensics to finish up. A member of the public approached us and asked if we would go with her to the shed on her allotment, very close to where the body was found.'

'Did you go with her?'

'Yes. The scene was secured and there were two constables in attendance. I followed the woman through a gate at the side of the fence that surrounds the whole area of allotments, and she took me to the top left-hand corner, near to St Jude's School. She showed me the shed – there was a padlock hanging undone from a bolt, and the door was ajar. I went inside first.'

Witch Trial

Chills in his fingers, prickling in his thumbs. Another thing Angus doesn't like to think about.

'What did you find inside?'

He bows his head. Then he tells the court what he saw that day.

What he'll never get out of his head.

12

Matthew is there with him in the shed as Angus Macpherson describes it. By the intent way that the other jurors around him are listening, sitting upright, shoulders straight, he's not the only one finally to be enthralled by the case. This is what they were waiting for. Blood. Guts. Actual entrails.

A series of images flash up on the screens that sit between each couple of jurors. Matthew can't get his head round the incongruity of it, the juxtaposition of the formality of the proceedings with the fact that they're looking at what's effectively the set of a Hammer House of Horror film.

Fully lit as they are, Matthew knows the photos can't possibly convey the atmosphere that the police officer will have sensed, fresh from the scene of discovering the corpse, picking out each detail by the beam of torchlight. But even illuminated, it's still chilling. The dead bird, the pentagram. Scattered around it are various cards with runes and images on them which Matthew imagines might be from a tarot deck, though he can't zoom in and check properly. There's burnt-down candles, a couple of black rocks, some incense. And over everything, small white feathers, some of them also burnt round the edges.

It must have stunk.

The police officer is a big man, red-faced. Burly. He looks like he could face down any number of joyriding teenagers or feral youth. But Matthew is struck by the hesitant way he describes the scene, the way his face pales when he describes first entering the shed. He's shook. And it's having the same effect on Matthew.

The man's evidence is winding up now. He hadn't gone to the school to speak to the headmistress – that job had been delegated to others. He had taken details from the owner of the allotment in question, but the jury would be hearing from her directly themselves later. He had waited with the body until all relevant work had been done in situ; he'd instructed a fingertip search of the surrounding scene; he'd watched as they'd zipped her up into a body bag and taken her away.

Cross-examination doesn't take long. Miss Brodie asks a couple of questions about how sure he is that there was no one else on the scene other than the jogger when he first saw the body. And one final question.

'You said that when you first saw the body, you were struck by an expression of terror on her face?'

'Yes.'

'That's only your interpretation of it, though.'

'Yes.'

'It could as likely have been an expression of pain, or even an involuntary spasm at the moment of death?'

The police officer pauses before he answers.

'I know what it looked like to me.'

'It's a yes or no answer, officer. Let me break it down for you. You don't know what the girl was feeling in her last moments, do you?'

'No.'

'So when you say it was an expression of terror, that's only your opinion, isn't it?'

There's a mulish set to the man's jaw, but he nods.

'Yes, it's my opinion.'

'Not a matter of fact, though?'

'No.'

Miss Goodly gets to her feet, says again that she has no further questions. Sits down. Matthew's starting to wonder why she's even bothered to turn up.

This concludes the evidence of the scene of crime officer. The man walks out. His shoulders look lighter as he leaves the court-room, his back straighter. He does not look back.

The photographs of the dead girl had been handed to the jury earlier in the policeman's evidence, in a brown paper folder. No one has yet opened this, perhaps too nervous to do so. Matthew himself hadn't felt the need to look at that point, given the vivid description that was given by the officer. But at this challenge, all sense of decorum goes out of the window. He picks up the folder – by the sound of rustling paper around him, he's not the only one.

There are three photographs inside. One shows the girl lying on her side as the officer described, the second the same but giving the back view. The third is a close-up of her face. Matthew's seen some bodies in his time. He's dissected them, sewn them back together, cut holes in some of the most diseased limbs you could imagine. But he's never seen an expression like this; forget subjectivity, the rictus of the lips, jaws at full extension – the defence advocate can say what she likes, this is terror. Pure and simple.

The images of the shed are still on the screen in front of Matthew and he scrolls through them again as he waits for the next witness to be called, his heart racing.

Dead pigeon, tarot cards, candles, pentagram; all the nonsense. Matthew might have felt shaken as the police officer described it but the memory of that fades as he takes in all the ridiculous props. He suppresses a snort of derision as he looks at it. It offends his clinical mind that people could actually fall for this nonsense. He remembers how the policeman's face paled as he gave his description and shakes his head – people are far too credulous these days. Thank goodness he's had a scientific training – Matthew would never be taken in by anything as silly as this.

Other than the trappings of occult mischief, the rest of the shed is tidy, almost obsessively so. Hooks and nails on the wall support a wide variety of garden tools, and there's pastel coloured bunting pinned up across the ceiling. On the wall opposite the door is a large framed poster with a motivational message, *This is our Happy Place*. Matthew tries not to roll his eyes.

'Annetta Worth, please,' the advocate depute says, calling for his next witness. A short, dumpy woman is brought to the stand, her dark hair youthfully long with a centre parting, although Matthew reckons she's way north of fifty. Then he thinks about the music festivals he still attends despite being out of his teens – she's not the only one not acting her age.

Once she's sworn in, she gives her name. As Matthew suspected, she's the owner of the allotment. Totally the sort to have motivational posters on her wall.

'We'd been away for a few weeks,' she tells the court. 'I asked the owner of the neighbouring allotment to keep an eye on the place for us, cut back anything that became too obtrusive. Mike, that's his name. But we left it in good shape so he didn't need to do much. Plus he had all his own tools, so he had no reason to go into the shed.'

'What steps did you take to secure the premises before you went away?' Mr Alexander says.

'I locked it as usual. There's a bolt on the door and then a padlock. It's very safe. I left the key as I normally do underneath a rock at the back. No one knows about it, only Mike.

It was just in case he needed it. He says he didn't open it at all though. And of course he didn't. He was nothing to do with this. I just can't believe that it was our shed that was being used to drive that poor girl to her death.'

'I'm going to stop you there,' the advocate depute says. 'Please stick to what you know yourself directly. Did you give permission to anyone other than Mike to unlock your shed or use the premises?'

'I most certainly did not,' Annetta says, crossing her arms firmly underneath her substantial bosom, an aggrieved look on her face. 'It's a very special place for us as a family. I'd never agree to allow anyone to use it, especially not for something as dark as this. I still haven't got all the blood off the floor.' She shivers, a theatrical movement which fails to convey fear, at least to Matthew's eye. Even though she's wearing dusky pink, a fluffy scarf, Matthew gets the sense that underneath the soft exterior is a core of steel. Her mouth is shut like a trap in a tight, straight line.

Few other details of relevance emerge from her evidence in chief. She and her husband had arrived back from Spain the day before and they were planning on going down to the allotment in the morning, when Mike called them to tell them that a body had been found in the area. They'd rushed down, and then they'd found the shed in this unpleasant condition.

Miss Brodie stands up, all elbows and sharp cheekbones.

'Just a couple of questions for you, Mrs Worth. You said you were away for a few weeks, but it was actually six months. That's right, isn't it?'

'Well, I . . . I suppose that's right.' She shifts from foot to foot in the witness box.

'And you've kept the key under that rock for many years, haven't you?'

'I have, yes. It's all very secure there.'

'Hmmm,' Miss Brodie says. 'Yes. Well. It's right to say that any number of people could know about its being there, isn't it?'

'No. Well, yes. I suppose. But I bet they don't. I'm very discreet about it.'

Is she? Is it? Questions are running through Matthew's mind.

'You have two teenage children, isn't that right?'

'I do, yes, though I fail to see what that's got to do with anything.'

'Just answer the questions, please, Mrs Worth. It's correct to say that they are aware of the whereabouts of the key?'

'Yes, I suppose they are,' the witness says sharply. Any softness in her demeanour is fading fast.

'And there would have been nothing to stop them telling their friends about it, would there?'

'Why would they do that?'

'Answer the question, please.'

'Yes. I suppose they could.'

Miss Brodie nods, as if it confirms what she's been thinking all along. 'So, in reality, you've got no idea who knew that the key was kept there. It could have been anyone, couldn't it?'

'Yes,' Mrs Worth says, through lips now so tight they've almost disappeared.

'And given you were away for six months in total, not just a few weeks, anyone could have let themselves in at any point. That's right, isn't it?'

'I suppose so,' Mrs Worth says. Her eyes have narrowed now too and her cheeks are flushed a dull pink that clashes with her top.

'So the shed could have been used at any point in the last six months, couldn't it? Not specifically the night before the body was found?'

'I suppose that's right,' Mrs Worth says.

'No further questions—'

Before Miss Brodie can finish her sentence, Mrs Worth turns to the judge. Her poise has returned. 'It was close to then, though. It must have been. The pigeon blood was still wet. I know this, because I tried to mop it up.'

Unlikeable witness or not, Mrs Worth has won this point.

13

Miss Goodly pulls her usual stunt of asking no further questions so finally they're out of court. The judge has run through the same stuff as before, no internet research, don't talk to anyone about the case, and they're free to go. They collect their stuff from the jury room. Matthew finds himself next to Jasmine and Sarah, the two younger women who are sitting at the end of his row.

'I wish they'd tell us more about Christian,' Jasmine says. 'I can't get her face out of my mind. I shouldn't have looked at those photos.'

Sarah pats her on the shoulder, consoling. 'You're bearing witness. It was the right thing to do, to look at them. That advocate was trying to get inside our heads to say she didn't look shit-scared, but she bloody well did.'

Matthew nearly nods but decides to hold his own counsel. Time enough to discuss the case when it's at its conclusion. Right now it's too early to say. He doesn't disagree, though.

'What I want to know, is what exactly they're saying happened to her? How does this all fit together?' Jasmine says.

'I guess we'll find out,' Matthew says. 'There'll be more tomorrow.'

With that, they leave the building. He takes in a breath of the late afternoon air, relieved to leave the air-conditioned sterility of the courtroom behind, but any sense of escape is short-lived. Matthew needs to switch on his phone, and he knows it's going to be bad. A series of pings confirms his suspicion. He's at the top of the Playfair Steps now, looking down at Princes Street, the Grecian splendour of the gallery buildings, and an urge takes hold of him to throw his phone away, watch it bouncing down the stairs until its face smashes into a thousand tiny pieces. He lifts his hand, brings his arm back, and—

'Watch it,' a passer-by says. He's bashed her on the shoulder as he's prepared to throw. Matthew brings his phone back down in front of him, the urge suppressed. He needs to catch a grip. While he walks down the stairs, he box-breathes – count for four in, hold for four, count for four out – and by the time he's at the bottom he's regained control.

There's a bit of time still before the dinner at the New Club he's due to attend on his boss's behalf. He could go home, shower, scrub up a bit. But he's already in a suit and it's not like there's traces of any surgery under his fingernails. He'll do. He heads right into Princes Street Gardens, finding a bench that's overlooked by the Scott Monument. Taking another deep breath, he picks up his phone and has a look.

Too many messages. More than he can deal with. There will be millions of emails waiting on his computer at home, too. But what is there to say? It's his civic duty, his public responsibility to spend this time away from the hospital, from his family. He was meant to be on holiday next week, anyway – they'd already taken him off the rota at work. Rosalind will just have to suck it up. Instead of reading everything, wading his way through all their reproaches, he deletes every single message without reading it. No good will come from them, and the senders know all they need to know from the messages he sent out earlier himself informing them that he had been selected for the trial.

Witch Trial

When he reaches Olivia's name, he pauses. She's sent only one message – *Hope it's interesting. I'd love to hear about it if you do get a trial.* The first from anyone today not to be full of reproach. A warmth creeps up him. He'd been getting bored with her; it might be nice in some respects that she's in her twenties, but it's not like they've got much in common. Maybe he should reconsider, though. Rosalind's going to be away for a week, after all. Perhaps they could meet up for a drink . . . He doesn't reply, but hers is the only message that he doesn't delete.

He puts his phone in his pocket. The air is mild and it's nice to be outside, sitting on a bench like any normal member of the public. Even if he doesn't have a smartphone. It's for the best. He can see himself now, typing the letters spelling *Christian Shaw* into it, Eliza and Isobel's names too, sinking into the depths of the online discussions he's sure are easily to be found. Fortunately, that temptation is out of his reach with his basic brick. He leans back against the bench, enjoying the breeze, the sight of the leaves fluttering against the blue sky above him.

A woman walks past and as she gets to the level of the bench, she pauses, a faint floral scent shimmering around her. This catches his attention, and he moves his gaze to her. Immediately he's transfixed. It's her. The blonde from court. He'd forgotten his fixation for a while, distracted by the images of the dead girl and the occult happenings in the shed. Thoughts of Olivia, too. But now it returns full force.

She's older than he thought but it suits her, only a few lines round her eyes giving it away. Pale skin, even white teeth, lips caught in a half-smile as if to say *it's you, of course*. He's struck with a sense of instant recognition. He *knows* her, that's the only way he can describe it. He raises his hand, about to greet her, when a phone rings from somewhere, the shrill sound breaking the spell.

He looks away. When he looks back, she's gone, a faint scent of roses the only sign that she was there. He looks down the path in the direction she was walking but he can only see a group of tourists, schoolchildren weaving their way between them. He blinks, blinks again. He can't have imagined it.

Can he?

It's warm, the air fragrant, his thoughts pleasant. Matthew lingers where he's sitting, his doubts passed. She was there. So maybe she'll walk back, maybe this time she'll smile, sit down next to him, they'll talk, their hands will touch, perhaps her head will move closer, closer to his shoulder and then—

A group of teenagers run past him, boys in red blazers, girls in school uniform with their skirts rucked up nearly past their bums. One of the girls is telling one of the boys to fuck off with such enjoyment that it brings Matthew straight back down to earth. The sun's behind the buildings now and he realises that it's getting chilly, his legs stiff from all the sitting of the day. He checks his watch – time to get to the New Club.

As he walks back along Princes Street Gardens it strikes him that perhaps he should have gone home to change after all. His shirt is less than pristine, his suit rumpled. It's not going to impress the visiting dignitaries Dominic has asked him to entertain, surgeons from Singapore and Australia, here on their way to discuss latest breakthroughs at a conference in Aberdeen.

On the other hand, he's got an excuse. He'll be able to regale them with tales of his jury experience. Obviously not discussing the details of the case – the judge's warnings have landed with him heavily enough – but all human interest is there to be found in the courtroom. At least, by the time Matthew has finished describing it all, it will be. The doctors will be delighted to hear about something that isn't medical – no talking shop at this dinner.

By the time he's at the front door to the club he's almost bouncing with excitement at how the evening is going to go. Normally he hates dinners like this, can't stand the aggression that always lurks under the surface, the *I can cut through a sternum with one hand* kind of thing, but he's got a dead pigeon he can lay before them, spatchcocked for their entertainment.

'What did you say the name was?' the doorman says. He's short, broad. Matthew wouldn't fuck with him.

'Matthew Phillips.'

'Hold on a minute, sir.' The inner door closes. Matthew might be off Princes Street, but he's not inside the sanctum. Not yet. He really should sort out membership, then he'd be spared all this. Stupid he hasn't done it before. But there's always been someone else going, people who can sign him in, stand him whiskies, the school dinners that pass for fine dining in this revered establishment. He'll ask Dominic. Hell, he'd be able to put it through as an expense.

'I'm sorry, sir, but you must be mistaken about the date.' The doorman has returned.

'No, it's tonight. I'm sure of it.'

'We've double-checked our records, sir, and there's no booking in your name. I'm afraid I'm going to have to ask you to leave.'

'But—'

Four men in suits come through the inner door and push past Matthew at that point, a haze of alcohol and stale cigar smoke surrounding them. Matthew tries to push forward into the club, but somehow the doorman manages to manoeuvre it so that as they leave the building, he does too, the large wooden door closing with a click that's more final than any resounding slam.

14

Princes Street. Now that Matthew's shorn of the opportunity to rise above street level, sit in those exclusive windows above him, gin in hand as he watches the hoi polloi trek past, the grime of it strikes him hard. The shop full of polyester knickers, endless stores selling tat to tourists, American candy outlets that can only be a cover for organised crime. Shitty venue. Shitty club. Matthew's always hated that kind of pretentious bullshit anyway.

He resists the temptation to spit on the doorway, strides away, his mouth sour. Dominic must be really fucked off with him to have cancelled his spot on the dinner. Perhaps he should call . . . maybe there's been a mistake? Matthew pulls his phone out of his pocket, switches it on. Switches it off again.

He doesn't know what to think. It feels menacing, though. They're out to get him, his bosses so unhappy with his absence that they've stopped him from attending this. But it's illegal for the hospital to sack him for doing jury duty. Besides, he's one of their most experienced surgeons. Angry as they might be, they'll have to lump it.

What if they don't, though? Matthew knows how unforgiving hospitals can be. An image of the blonde comes back into his mind, sitting in court with a notebook. Could she have been sent to check up on him? His mood darkens further. Maybe he's being paranoid, but he'd put nothing past management. Not even that.

He'll worry about that tomorrow. For now, the evening stretches out in front of him. He could go home, hang out with Rosalind. But Rosalind'll be fucked off, and Daisy's off at uni. Olivia crosses his mind, immediately dismissed. He doesn't feel up to her inane babble right now. He could call a friend, but his mind goes blank as he tries to run through the possibilities. Too many of them have given up drinking in the last years, taken up Ironman challenges. His best friend divorced, married a younger woman and is now wrangling a second family, newborn twins in his early fifties – however miserable Matthew might feel right now, at least he hasn't got that shit to deal with. Another reason not to get too involved with the younger woman in his life.

Never mind. He'll drink alone. It's never stopped him in the past. This is actually quite liberating, a whole night stretching in front of him unexpectedly, no one to please, to placate, no need to worry about not drinking so much that his hands might shake in the morning. Not what you need with a scalpel floating round the left coronary artery.

By now he's walked along Princes Street to the turning with Frederick Street. He doesn't want one of the George Street bars – too corporate – so he heads further down the hill into Stockbridge. He'll walk off his bad mood at being barred – fuck 'em, it would be a shit night. It's much better this way. And thank God he's talked himself out of the nonsense of applying for membership. Of course Dominic's a member, he's exactly the kind of wanker who's into *exclusivity* and *selection committees* (the words hiss in his brain), but Matthew doesn't need any of that validation.

Down in St Stephen Street now, place of basement bars and many a drunken night out as a student. He's more relaxed, his top button undone, his tie in his pocket. This is freedom. Hours to drink and nothing to lose. He walks into the basement of the Antiquary.

'Laphroaig, please. Double.'

Might as well start as he means to go on.

Later, much later, when he's seeing double and the doubles aren't slipping down as easy, that's when he knows it's time to go home. Sure, it doesn't matter if he has the shakes in the morning, hardly a matter of life and death if his notes on evidence are less legible than they could be, but he's going to carry the stench of it, a miasma of single malt seeping from his pores. Not that anyone'll appreciate his discernment. They'll just smell booze.

He stops for a pizza on the way home, refusing to worry about what the deep-fried offering will do to his arteries. The alcohol will cut through all that. Ramming the last piece in his mouth, he snorts. Who's he trying to kid? It's not like he does it all the time. Matthew's all over the gut bacteria, the intermittent fasting, running up and down hills. All that shit. He's owed a blowout every now and again. Fuck it, they can say what they like about setting a good example – no one wants a heart surgeon who looks like he's on the brink of a cardiac arrest, after all – but who's to see what he's up to now?

He stuffs the pizza box into a bin at the turn near the Botanics before turning left to his house. The sight of it, the light still shining for him in the hall, brings him up short. Rosalind, that's who's going to see. She'll smell the grease on him, the deep-fat-fried aroma. She'll waft her hand round to get rid of the booze smell, tell him to shower. Maybe even sleep in the spare room.

She did that once, the cow. When they were at uni. He'd had a kebab and she barely opened the door of her room before telling him to fuck off and wash, clean his teeth before he dared to

Witch Trial

come back. Well, she can't do that this time. It's his house too. He's got the key right here in his hand.

He strides up the front path, decision in every step. Straight line. He's totally sober now – he could walk any line put in front of him. She can fuck off if she thinks she's going to have anything to say to him about this, about jury service, about any of it.

He puts the key in the lock, turns. Pushes it.

It opens a couple of inches, no more. Then it sticks.

There must be something caught under the door. Post, maybe. Or the doormat. He pulls it to, pushes it again, harder this time.

It stays stuck. Total resistance however hard he pushes. What the fuck? He peers at the door, pulls it in, out again. Maybe he's got something wrong with how he's opening it. He'll admit he's not totally sober. He's confused himself somehow, that's all. Not totally sober, OK. But not bad.

And again. Again it hits a barrier.

Seriously, what the fuck? He stands back, looks at the door. Peers round the side of it. The chain. She's put the chain on. That's what it is. He's not going mad. Christ, she must be livid with him. He takes another step back and rings the doorbell, trying not to lean too heavily on it. A misunderstanding, that's all this is. He should have listened to the voice messages he's sure she's left him.

No reply. He rings on the bell again. She's there, she must be, the light's on, the shutters are all shut. It's not that late, only just past midnight. She won't be caught in the deepest of sleeps, not yet.

He rings the bell a third time. This is the charm. Footsteps down the stairs, slow, reluctant, but at least someone's there.

'Go away,' the voice says. Rosalind. She's not sounding shrill, not now. Deep and resolute.

'I'm home,' Matthew says. 'I want to go to bed.'

'I messaged you,' Rosalind says. 'I said if you were drinking, not to come home.'

'Open the door. Please. I'm sorry.'

'It's late and you're drunk. I'm not letting you in.'

He's trying not to shout, reining it in, but he knows it's there, ready to burst out.

'Go to the flat.'

'Fuck you,' he says. The control's slipping.

'That's enough, Matthew.' The footsteps retreat. The light's turned off.

Matthew looks up at his own front door, the one he pays for, the one he painted himself one summer's day a few years ago, dark green in accordance with the restrictions of the Edinburgh heritage requirements. The shiny brass letterbox, the doorknob. The door that doesn't fucking open.

The face of the house is shut against him, sullen as Rosalind's must be inside. This is pointless. Fuck her. Fuck them all.

TUESDAY

15

Running through Inverleith Park and there's a demon at his heels, speeding Matthew on like never before. The skyline is red with dawn, the castle silhouetted black against it. His feet are pounding, his heart ready to burst in his chest. Now he's running down the side of the park, no one around, but in front of him there's someone on the ground, someone lying still like they're sleeping, but he knows they can't be sleeping, no one would be sleeping under a hedge like that, halfway on to the path, and he's there now, his heartbeats exploding out of him so hard his ears are ringing, and he's looking down at the dead girl on the ground, and for a moment she's a total stranger to him, her features blurred until his focus sharpens, the veil lifts, and he knows the dark hair, the face, he knows the face only too well—

'Daisy!' he says, and he wakes himself with his own scream. Matthew's wringing with sweat, his mouth dry, his heart pounding hard as a sprinter's. But it's OK, he's in bed. He's not looking down at the corpse of his daughter. He opens his eyes fully, sits up.

Not all that OK. It's his bed, but it's not his house. Not his home, anyway. Memories of the night before seep back to him. He's looking at the bare walls of the first flat he ever bought, that he moved out of years ago. The yellow wallpaper is faded, darker rectangles where student tenants must have hung up posters contrary to the agreements they all signed. Sheets on the bed – that's something – but they're rough, mismatched, a hodgepodge of sets that he and Rosalind owned separately and together before they discovered the joys of high thread counts and the White Company.

He can't believe she'd put the chain up on the door on him like that. Sure, she says she hates it when he drinks, but it's not his fault that she's so oversensitive. It was nothing to do with him going out. She's pissed off that he's not going on holiday with her and she decided to make a show of him. She's lucky he didn't make more of a fuss. He can't be blamed for the way the night turned out.

How was he to know that Dominic would get him barred from the club? He's going to have to dig into what happened there. It must have been a misunderstanding. He's sure he didn't get the date wrong. Though maybe . . . He's been so fixated on the possibility of being on the jury, maybe he's messed it up. At least Matthew didn't make a scene; he's wracking his memory and he's sure he didn't. He clutches at his head, trying to wring out of it any hidden shame of shouting, punches thrown. Nothing.

It's all OK. Unless he sent a message? Made a call? Adrenaline spiking again, he spies his phone on the floor next to his discarded clothes. Slowly he crawls over, switches it on. Two calls to Olivia, both unanswered. Nothing else outgoing since the one he sent first thing about being on the jury. He can live with that – it's not as if Olivia hasn't drunk-dialled him on occasion, too. They know how to ignore each other.

He didn't even disgrace himself at home, despite the provocation. He'd have been well within his rights to force the door down, smash a window to let himself in to his own bloody house. He kept his cool though.

Witch Trial

The sense of panic starts to subside. It could have been worse. It has been worse.

At least he's in the flat. The last tenants moved out a year ago and Matthew and Rosalind decided to keep it empty for a while for him to stay in for the nights that he was on call for theatre. It's good he wasn't left out on the streets, though no thanks to *her*. Unbelievable behaviour, to bar him from the house like that. All he's done is do what he's been told. All Matthew ever does is do what he's told.

Maybe it's time that changed.

His phone starts screaming and he jumps out of bed, ready for action. He grabs it up only to see that it's his alarm, not an emergency call from the hospital. Matthew can step down – his lifesaving skills are not required. He's not a puppet on anyone's strings today.

Which, when he squints at himself in the bathroom mirror, he can see is just as well. What you'd expect after a night on the malt: greasy, creased, bloodshot. Less silver fox, more decrepit old bastard.

A shower, shit and shave later and there's a fractional improvement in his appearance. He scrubs his teeth with a toothbrush, swills his mouth out with mouthwash, trying not to retch when the sharp fluid hits the back of his throat. Mercifully there's a clean shirt hanging up in the wardrobe as well. He'd planned on wearing more casual clothes into court today, but on balance it makes sense to be smarter. Less obvious that he was on a bender last night.

He makes coffee on the stove in the moka pot from his student days, strong and black. It wakes him up even more. Practically human now. Ready to face whatever horrors the trial brings today. He'll deal with Rosalind and Dominic later – they're not important now. Olivia will call him back, she always does. Maybe that's something for tonight? He banks the thought.

What he does need to do is check his emails. The mix-up at the New Club could have been avoided – for all he knows, messages were sent to cancel that he just didn't see. He turns on the old desktop that lives in the corner to check.

No work emails – the word must have got out that he's unavailable. Nothing about last night, either, but he's not going to worry about that. He sets up an out-of-office auto-reply, closes down the email browser. The page defaults to Google, a cursor blinking at him in a way he finds almost hypnotic. It would be so easy to input the names, see what information he can find out.

The judge's warning rings in his ears. It would interfere with the course of the trial. He's been told not to. Surely, though, that kind of instruction can't apply to someone like him, with his level of education? He types the name *Christian Shaw* in the box, looks at it for a moment. Then he deletes it. Not because of the judge's warning, though. He's going to come back to it later. But with time to do it properly, not in a few snatched moments before he's due to leave.

He shuts the computer down, takes stock of his surroundings. Of his relationship. The chain on the door at his house last night said more clearly than any words how Rosalind is feeling. Bleak as the flat may be, he's going to stay here till the trial is over. Best to be on his own anyway so he can concentrate properly. Starting with some proper research into what this trial is all about.

Back in court, waiting for the first witness of the day, who seems unaccountably to have gone missing, or to be refusing to come in. It's good to feel more familiar with the set-up, to walk in past security knowing exactly where to go, what to do. He's walked up the hill at a fair crack and it's a relief to sit down, wipe the sweat from his brow, discreetly smelling his hand to check that it's not smelling too much of booze. Roderick has his notebook out already, pen lined up neatly beside it. Sarah and Jasmine are chatting quietly to each other, their heads close together. That ghastly Emma is staring straight in front of her, her jaw moving incessantly as she chews a piece of gum.

He scans the courtroom, hoping the blonde woman will be there. The scent of roses still plays in his memory from their brief encounter the evening before. Her seat is vacant though, the public gallery more sparsely attended than yesterday.

'Maybe we're going to hear some more about the dead girl,' Aisha says. Matthew's neighbour, sitting to his left. She's talking to herself; a thoughtful woman. Probably the same age as him, though more accepting of it – she's cushioned, comfortable in her own skin. Matthew has a sudden urge to lean against her, rest his head against her cardiganed shoulder and go to sleep.

His head nods down, his eyes heavy. Until a noise splits through his head, a caw of crows. He jumps, sits upright.

Isobel is staring straight at him, eyes defiant, lined in kohl.

He is the first to look away.

16

Rebecca Waites doesn't want to give evidence. She wants to be in her classroom, wiping down the whiteboard, setting up the room for discussion about Shakespeare or Miller, not facing all these strangers, forced to talk about one of the worst days of her life, support a cause she thinks is intrinsically wrong. She can't think about it without crying, let alone explain it to anyone new. She's going to make a complete fool of herself, burst into tears in front of everyone. Word'll get back to the school that she's a total incompetent, a hysterical idiot, and then she'll lose her job, and the accommodation that comes with it.

Even worse, she might lose her temper, tell them all what she really thinks. *De mortuis nil nisi bonum*, sure, but the high-minded Roman who came up with that dictum clearly hadn't encountered a teenager as difficult as Christian.

'You need to come in now,' the macer says. He's been very kind to her, allowed her a few extra moments to pull herself together, but his patience is wearing thin. She's got to sort herself out. She's a grown woman, shouldn't be behaving like such a child.

'OK,' she says, barely audible, and she follows him.

At least the courtroom isn't exclusively filled with men. That's what she feared, when she allowed herself to imagine it. All men in black, like crows, pecking the flesh from Eliza Lawson's bones, witch prickers in their hands. Though she minds less about the idea of Isobel suffering ... Rebecca risks a glance over at Eliza – the co-accused, she'll have to get used to saying. The girl looks well enough, pale but not more than you'd expect, but Rebecca knows what a torment this case will be to her.

She refuses to look at Isobel. She'll never look at her the same way again.

Jurors might not be allowed to read about cases online, but no such rules apply to Rebecca. She's been on internet forums since the day that they were arrested. She hopes Eliza knows how much support there is out there for the girls in witchy subreddits and WitchTok hashtags. Persecuted for their beliefs, no less, though Rebecca's sure that Eliza was never truly sucked in to all this rubbish. Isobel's the one with the problem.

'Do you swear to tell the truth, the whole truth, and nothing but the truth?' Rebecca nods. She needs to concentrate now. Hold herself together. Now she's here, her mind is focused. It's not about keeping up appearances, not making a fool of herself in front of the court. She's fighting a more important battle than that. She might have been summoned as a witness for the prosecution, but that is not why she's here. One more glance at Eliza and this time the girl's eyes meet hers.

I won't let you down. I'll defend you. It's beating in her brain, the words repeating over and over. She wants to scream it out loud but the intensity of her stare will have to do. A small movement of Eliza's head, almost imperceptible, but a knot loosens in Rebecca's chest. The girl's seen. She knows.

'Can you repeat that, please?'

She's missed the first question the prosecutor has asked her. Not a nice-looking man, all spiky and aggressive. He'll do his best to catch her out. She may be a witness for the prosecution but only because they made her do it. She won't say anything to get Eliza into trouble. This is all Isobel's fault. Christian's too, for bringing it on herself like that.

'Can you tell the court what happened on the morning of first May last year, please?'

'Yes. I don't think I'll ever forget.' She takes a deep breath. 'It's the day I had to identify the body of Christian Shaw.' Another deep breath, shudders running through her.

'Please take us through the events of the morning.'

This bastard. He's going to make her say it all, the way the girl was huddled on the ground, her hands stretched out as if to ask for help. The terrible expression on her face. It was almost enough to make Rebecca pity her. Though not quite enough. She knew how unpleasant Christian could be. She hopes she can make the court understand that, too.

'Christian hadn't turned up for register that morning,' Rebecca says. 'She was often late so I didn't worry particularly, but I did need to inform the office of her absence. Someone needed to check the boarding house, dig her out of bed.'

'Why were you taking the register?'

Does she have to spell everything out? 'I'm her form teacher – sorry, *was* her form teacher.'

'Did you know Christian well?'

'I tried. She wasn't very forthcoming. I made an effort to form a bond with her like I do with all my pupils, but she didn't want to engage. It could be difficult.' Her head tilted, her voice sweet. Everyone knows what teenagers are like.

'Please could you look at the photograph in front of you.' A pause before a headshot appears. Rebecca swallows, repulsion running through her. Christian. Large as life and twice as ugly, the photograph overexposed, light glinting off the grease on the girl's forehead, reflecting off the whiteheads that littered her cheeks. Her hair, overdyed, too black, the roots growing through mouse-coloured, piggy eyes a washed-out blue, lined inexpertly with black kohl. God, Rebecca had wanted to take the girl and scrub her down, wash all the crap out of her hair and off her face, get her on to proper acne meds and applying make-up properly. She couldn't bear to look at her. Like Isobel. If anyone's to blame, it's her.

She glances over at the photograph again, trying to suppress a shudder. Her ears are prominent in the picture; probably Christian's worst attribute, though the competition was tough. God, Rebecca hated Christian's ears. Over-full of piercings. Five hoops in one, seven in the other, studs through her tragus and cartilage and God only knows what else. She'd have had a face full of metal too if the school rules had allowed – as it was, the girl had stretched them further than Rebecca herself considered at all acceptable.

'Can you identify the person shown in the photograph?'

Rebecca draws her cardigan close around her.

'Yes. This is Christian Shaw.'

Such a selfish child. Typical that she'd be the one to end up dead, kick off all this trouble for everyone. Even from beyond the grave.

'Returning to that morning, you said that you needed to inform the office of her absence. Did you do that?'

'I did.'

'Were Isobel and Eliza in the same form as Christian?'

'They were, yes. They were in class as they were supposed to be, though. Both seemed totally normal. That friend of theirs, Sasha, she was there too at register. I saw them all at breakfast, too. There was nothing weird about their behaviour. Nothing weird at all.' She shivers, chilled at the memory. 'The only person missing was Christian.'

'What did you do after reporting Christian's absence to the office?'

'I returned to my classroom and got myself ready for classes later that day. Then Mrs Hall came along – the school secretary – with a police officer and he asked me to go to Inverleith Park with him. That's when I saw her. On the ground.'

17

Matthew can't be sure, but he doesn't feel this witness likes the dead girl very much. Something about the twist of her mouth, the way she's turning her head away from the photograph that's up on everyone's screens. A nice-looking girl, if you scrubbed off all the muck. Daisy went through a phase like that a couple of years ago, but fortunately discovered boys and acne face wash at around the same time so started to look a bit more – what's the word, *mainstream*? *Normcore*? He does his best to keep up but inevitably he gets the terms that the youth use wrong.

Anyway, pretty blue eyes and the hint of a smile. He feels sad for the girl, a heaviness that she'll never get to grow out of the eyeliner phase. It doesn't make sense to him that this teacher is sounding so sharp about the girl's tardiness, a faint air of revulsion emanating from the witness box.

Now she's describing how the girl was lying on the ground, her impressions of the girl's expression.

'Yes, I did notice that her face looked emotional. I suppose you could call it scared. But I don't see how you'd know.'

Interesting, she's arguing with the advocate depute. Maybe she's got an agenda. Matthew straightens his back, pays closer attention. The drama is picking up.

'It could have been pain, it could have been surprise. It could have been something that just happened at the moment of death. I wouldn't want to use the word *terror*.'

Matthew flicks open the brown paper file that contains the photos of the body. He tries to angle it so that none of the other jurors see it inadvertently, peering at it furtively. Terror is what it looks like to him.

'Let's move on,' the advocate depute says. 'What did you do next?'

'Once I had seen her, I went back to school and told the headmistress. The police took a statement from me about the identification.'

'Did they ask you any other questions about Christian?'

A pause. The witness shifts from foot to foot. Matthew doesn't think she looks comfortable.

'They asked me what I knew of her, who she was friends with, that kind of thing.'

'What did you tell them?'

A longer pause. 'That I didn't know her very well at all. And that she didn't really have any friends. There had been reports made about her behaviour—'

'We won't go into that now,' the advocate depute interrupts.

'Well, she used to be friends with a group of other girls in the class. Then she stopped being friends with them, by the look of it. She spent a lot of time on her own, as far as I could see. She carried a lot of library books around with her so I assume that she spent time there as well.'

'Did you ever ask her whether everything was all right?'

'She had made it clear she had no interest in opening up to me. I did my best. She knew where my room was. I have amazing relationships with many of my girls, they tell me everything. But not Christian. She didn't want to know.'

The woman crosses her arms in front of her. Defensive.

'Did you give the police the names of her former friends?'

The woman flushes. An ugly dark red that spreads up her neck, staining her cheeks. Even though she's only in her thirties, Matthew reckons, she looks suddenly middle-aged.

'Yes, I told them she used to be friends with Isobel. And with Eliza, too. With the co-accuseds.'

The last word is barely audible.

'Going back a few weeks before Christian's death, was there a time that you overheard Christian having a conversation with someone?'

The flush goes, the witness's lips tighten. She looks like she'd punch the man if she were close enough.

'What does that have to do with anything?'

'Please just answer the question, Miss Waites.'

'I don't see that it's relevant.'

'Miss Waites . . .' a warning in his voice.

'All right, all right. Yes. I overheard Christian arguing with the two girls, Isobel and Eliza, though Eliza barely played a part in it. I barely heard her say anything.'

'When did this happen?'

'It was a few weeks before Christian died. Maybe in the February or March, I can't remember exactly. Before the end of the spring term. Anyway, they were shouting at each other. The door of the classroom was ajar and I was about to walk in, but I didn't want to interrupt.'

Wanted to eavesdrop, more like. Matthew knows what kind of woman she is. He's not taken in by the cardigan, the nice blouse. The fade-away airs.

'Christian's voice went on and on. She was ranting, in my opinion. The other girls were shouting too, but more to get Christian to calm down. Though there was one point . . .' her voice fades out, rallies again. 'One of the other girls yelled it so clearly. *You're going to die.* It was Isobel, I'm sure of it.'

'What happened next?'

'It quietened down – all I could hear was sobbing, I presume from Christian. There was silence for a moment, then Isobel spoke again. It was weird what she said, though I suppose it makes sense now. *You can't be angry with me. I'm just passing the message on. I can't help it if it's true.*'

'Did Christian reply?'

'Yes.'

A long pause.

'What did she say?'

Through gritted teeth. 'This is what I remember. It was Christian speaking. She wasn't shouting. She sounded very sad. She said, *You keep telling me I'm going to die. Of course I'm angry.*'

A ripple through the court. Matthew feels a movement, a breath on his cheek. Only fleeting, but freezing cold. When he turns, there's no one there.

To Matthew's surprise, Isobel's defence advocate stands up first.

'You pride yourself on your relationship with your pupils, don't you?'

'Yes, I do. I become very close to them.'

'But outside of work, you don't have many friends?'

'I . . . well . . .'

'To be more specific, there was a time in October 2017 that you told Isobel that you didn't have many friends outside of work, wasn't there?'

'Yes.' The woman's voice is sullen, the words forced out of her.

'And you said to Eliza that you'd love it if you and she could hang out one weekend, isn't that right?' Miss Goodly says *hang out* with so much disdain, Matthew can almost see inverted commas hanging in the air in front of her.

'But Isobel laughed when you said it, didn't she?'

'Yes.' The teacher's flushed now, her chin wobbling.

'And after that time, you never spoke to Isobel again outside of any school-related matter?'

'I don't think, I mean . . .'

'And in your capacity as Isobel's form teacher, from that point you singled her out for unfavourable treatment, didn't you?'

'I don't think that's fair.'

Miss Goodly picks up a piece of paper, hands it to the macer who takes it across to the witness.

'This is a list of all the detentions that you gave to Isobel from November 2017 until May 2018. Do you agree with this chronology?'

'I suppose so, I don't really remember. I'd have to check . . .'

'It's a register in your handwriting from your school diary, isn't that right?'

'Yes.' The teacher's shoulders slump.

'And what it shows is that Isobel received at least one detention a week from you from that point onwards, yes?'

'Yes.'

'I'd suggest that once your advances of friendship were rejected by Isobel, you went out of your way to penalise her, didn't you?'

'I . . .'

'And when you say it was Isobel shouting at Christian that she was going to die, you're not telling the truth, are you?'

'I know what I heard.' Lips tight, chin jutting forward.

'It was Eliza who said that, not Isobel, wasn't it?'

Head shaking. 'I know what I heard.' But the teacher's voice is faint. Matthew is not convinced.

Eliza's defence advocate stands up. She clears her throat, folds her arms. Aha, jugular time. But Matthew is disappointed. The tone Miss Brodie takes is low. Conciliatory, even.

'You're a very caring, compassionate teacher, aren't you?'

Total softball. The teacher laps it up.
'I do my best.'
'And normally you'd have a close relationship with every girl in your class?'
'Yes.'
'Eliza, she was in your form too?'
'Yes.'
'And Isobel?'
'That's right.' Distinctly less warmth in the teacher's voice.
'Eliza confided in you regularly, didn't she?'
'Eliza certainly talked to me a lot. We were close. I was really worried about her around the time this all happened. She seemed very unhappy though she never said exactly what was troubling her.'
'Returning to the morning that you identified Christian's body – was anyone else missing from registration?'
'No.'
'Please just answer this question with a yes or a no. There was a time Eliza told you that she was very unhappy because of friendship difficulties that she was having?'
'Yes.'
'And this was a month or so before Christian's tragic death?'
'Yes.'

Tragic death. Not murder. Matthew wonders what she's getting at. He's desperate to piece together what the defence is going to be.

'Turning now to Christian, you said that you did not have a close relationship with her, isn't that right?'
'Yes.'
'But there was an occasion that you had a meeting with her mother, isn't that right?'
'Yes.'
'Did she raise any health concerns about her daughter?'

'Nothing specific, no.'

'But she did tell you that she and her husband were going through some difficulties, and asked you to keep a special eye on Christian?'

'Yes.'

'Did you attempt to discuss the matter with Christian?'

'Yes.' The teacher's gone bright red again. 'I did ask her if she wanted to talk to me about it. I said she could talk to me at any time.' A pregnant pause, something bursting to come out of the woman. 'But she told me to fuck off.'

18

They break for coffee. Matthew's relieved to get up, stretch his legs. He gulps down as much black coffee as he can get his hands on in the time allowed, shaking his head when asked if he wants to go out with the smokers. The worst of the hangover has passed but one whiff of a cigarette and he might still barf.

He sits down at one of the tables, phone in hand, but he doesn't switch it on. Russell McLean and Michael Reid are chatting at the other end – they're both in their mid-thirties, both wearing North Face fleeces in different colours of sludge green. Kindred spirits. They certainly seem united in their dislike of the teacher who's just given evidence.

'She didn't like Christian at all, I don't reckon. Did you see the way she flinched when the photo came up?' Michael says.

'Well, yeah, but that doesn't necessarily mean anything. It might just have reminded her of identifying the body. It can't have been fun,' Russell says.

'Nah. It was more than that. She looked disgusted when she saw the girl's face.'

Emma joins in at this point. 'Fair enough too. Far too young to be wearing all that make-up. All those piercings, too. She did not look like a nice little girl.'

Matthew has been trying his best not to engage with this

dreadful woman, but this tips him over the edge. 'I don't think you can say that at all. She had very nice eyes.'

'How could you tell? They were totally obscured. She looked like an angry panda.'

'I like pandas,' Russell says. 'We should remember the girl's dead.'

'Not that we have any real idea how,' Emma says. 'I wish they'd get on with it. I really want the details.'

Matthew bites his lip. He's damned if he'll agree with her. She's right, though. He's desperate to know the specifics. All this stuff about scared expressions, outstretched hands, arguments with friends. Nothing's adding up yet, and he's getting impatient.

To Matthew's relief, the next witness turns out to be the pathologist who carried out the post-mortem. Some science will add clarity. He's a lugubrious man in late middle-age, eyebags on him to rival a basset hound. His delivery is slow and methodical. If Matthew had been given lectures by him at university, he'd have quit the course. He controls the temptation to go over and shake the man, tell him to get on with it.

First up, a picture appears on everyone's screens. Not the body on the slab – it would probably be too much for everyone – but a line drawing on which some marks are shown on hands and knees. No other injuries to be seen. Matthew can picture the corpse, though. The Y-shaped incision, the ribs sheared straight through. When Matthew cuts open someone's chest for heart surgery he must employ as much delicacy as is possible, to aid healing. It's brutal though, whatever his best attempts. But in a post-mortem, they're not going to bother with any delicacy at all, no part left unstudied; unsullied.

They'll have sewn her up after, that's something. But he'll bet that they kept her body wrapped when they finally showed the girl to her parents.

So what killed her? Word by tortuous word, the story emerges. First the technical terms. Sudden and fatal cardiac arrest caused by dilated cardiomyopathy – Matthew knows exactly what that is, though he'll bet none of the other jurors will. Heart muscle damaged, replaced by fat or fibrous tissue, unable to pump blood properly. Boom. Given the right circumstances, sudden death from an abnormal heartbeat can happen. Lopped off with time's scythe just like that.

Matthew had a case like that once. Fifteen-year-old boy, fit as a fiddle, but he collapsed one day on the football pitch. Only quick first-aid action on the part of the referee kept him alive, and the restrictions he was placed under from that point onwards in terms of any strenuous exercise pissed the boy off so much he said he wished he'd died. Matthew knew the boy would come to terms with it eventually, but the anger depressed him, just the same.

Did the girl know she had a dodgy heart? Often kids didn't, only finding out when they dropped down dead. So to speak.

'I was given medical records that laid out a history of a childhood infection leading to myocarditis. This in turn led to the cardiomyopathy that was behind the cardiac arrest. She was on medication – beta blockers – which will have controlled her heartbeat, but of course it's not possible to tell if she was taking these regularly,' the pathologist says. 'I believe there may be evidence coming from her doctor?'

Mr Alexander nods. 'That's correct.'

'He will give the court a more detailed account of the health of the deceased. But as an overview, in these cases, very often the first sign of trouble is sadly also the last. In this case, it is clear that the deceased's cardiomyopathy was more advanced than had been realised.'

Mr Alexander nods again. 'Could you explain the term to the court?'

'It's an inflammation of the heart muscle, which reduces the heart's ability to pump blood properly.'

'So, if someone is suffering from these conditions, what external occurrence could cause sudden death by cardiac arrest as you've stated is the cause of death here?'

'Given the situation was being managed, it would need to have been a considerable shock to her system. Something totally out of the normal way. There's medical evidence to say that she was involved in school sports, that she did cross-country.' The pathologist pauses, takes a breath. 'Over-exertion would have played a part. I note the body was found in a position that could indicate she had been running. But that would not have been enough on its own. Not in my opinion. My professional view is that this cardiac arrest was brought on by extreme stress. The expression on her face indicates this. You'll note the rictus in which her mouth was stuck, almost like a scream.'

'Is there anything else to indicate that this might have been the case?'

The pathologist clears his throat. 'You'll notice the abrasions that are shown as these marks on her knees.' He points to the marks on the large screen beside him. 'These were fresh grazes, bits of gravel in them, still oozing with blood. One explanation is that she was running, fell over and hurt herself but still got up again and kept running. As if she was running away from something. Or someone.' There's a tone of defiance in his voice.

Miss Brodie snorts, shakes her head. It's the first time she's shown irritation, normally motionless as the witnesses give evidence. Not surprising. That sort of speculation seems well out of line for a pathologist. Post-mortem reports are usually dry as a bone.

'Returning to your findings with regard to the girl's heart, what else can you tell us about that?'

Maybe that's why the man feels more involved. The pathologist will have plucked Christian's heart from her chest. It'll have lain heavy in his hand there, all quarter of a kilo of it, half a pound of flesh. Matthew knows how that feels. The omnipotence of it. When someone's alive, that is. The muscle gleaming, quivering red in the bright lights of the theatre. After death, though, a different matter. Drained of blood. White.

A ghost heart.

An image appears on the jurors' screens, a photograph from the post-mortem. It's the heart itself, lying pale, flat and lifeless on a stainless-steel tray. Other photographs follow, cross-sections of the heart. Matthew's transfixed – he never normally gets to see the organ presented in this way, past any working order. The ones he handles are still pink, glistening. The images in front of him show the heart as grey, but as he stares at them, his eyes flicking from one picture to the next, colour starts to grow in them, a bleeding in, not a bleeding out.

The heart that was lying still and misshapen on the tray is red now, monstrously distended, blown up like a balloon of flesh, a pulse beating through it so hard it looks as if it's going to explode. The pathologist is pointing out various features that support his findings, the words *thinned, deformed, asymmetric* falling from his lips, but they aren't sinking in, a meaningless sound.

Blood is rushing through Matthew's own head now, too, the thrum of it matching the thrum of the heart on the screen that's moving now, pulsating, possessed by something Matthew can't explain but which is causing his own head to pound and if it doesn't stop soon something's going to burst, Matthew knows it, the pain behind his left eye growing and growing until suddenly it ends. He leans back in his seat, winded, his hands ice-cold.

The heart lies still again in the photograph in front of him. The pain in Matthew's head has gone. The pathologist is still speaking and slowly Matthew tunes back in. No other physical abnormalities. Nothing untoward in the toxicology report – all standard tests carried out as Matthew would expect. No opioids, no cocaine, all normal. Matthew inhales, exhales, grounding himself back into the courtroom. More hung-over than he realised, clearly.

Miss Brodie. Contempt radiating off her, the ends of her hair crackling with it. They must have had run-ins before, she and the pathologist.

'It's your job to comment on the medical findings, isn't it?'
'Yes.'
'To avoid any subjective interpretation of the evidence that's in front of you?'
'Yes.'
'So, it's entirely out of your remit as pathologist to speculate on whether it's a scream on the girl's face?'
'I am merely describing what I saw.'
'In emotive terms though, professor. Yes?'
'I suppose so.'
'To suggest that the grazes on the girl's knee meant that she was running away from something or someone just before her death is also pure speculation, is it not?'
'I—'
'No further questions.'
She returns to her seat. Matthew shuts his eyes, the image of the heart beating there still.

19

The jury are sent out at this point, told to be back in court at 2 p.m. prompt. It's only half past twelve but it probably makes sense; there wouldn't be much time for another witness to get started before it was time for lunch anyway. Matthew isn't complaining. The weird hallucination has left him a little shaky, at the stage of hangover where the initial agony has shifted, a dull headache left in its place. All he needs now is lard and a can of Coke. Nothing chosen for lunch – he'd felt too nauseous to contemplate the food list the jury were given earlier – so he heads out of the court building.

Lots of choice, most of it tourist traps. There's a nice fish restaurant opposite the High Court but that's a bit too over the top for a working lunch. Sucking the juices from a dozen oysters before going back in to listen to the grim details of a teenager's fatal heart attack feels a bit off somehow. He does have time for a sit-down meal, though, so after standing on the corner of the Royal Mile for a moment, he heads right before taking a left down Advocate's Close and heading into the Devil's Advocate. He's passed it a few times in the past and never gone in – it's the perfect choice for a juror in the middle of a trial.

He's in luck: while it's busy, there's a small table free. He sits down, orders a burger. That'll sort him out. Nearly asks for a pint, too, but stops himself. Not appropriate. Instead, he asks for a pint of Coke, not too much ice. Food mission accomplished, he leans back, shuts his eyes.

The phantom heart has gone, thank goodness. He's calm now, able to think properly about the evidence the pathologist has just given. By the sounds of it, the girl had a weak heart. A pre-existing condition. She clearly knew if she was taking beta blockers, but did anyone else know about it? They've been pushing this silent scream business, the prosecution. Someone mentioned it yesterday, he remembers that. Are they saying she was scared to death? Hard to see how that might lead to a murder charge, though they'll be told, he's sure. With another ten days to go of this there's bound to be a load more evidence.

The teacher, that was another odd one. The way she was simpering over Eliza, the animosity towards Isobel, the twist on her mouth when the photograph of Christian was shown on screen. Matthew has not taken to her.

The waitress puts his drink down in front of him, and a knife and fork wrapped in a napkin. His mouth is starting to water at the thought of the food, and the cold sweetness of the Coke hits him like rain on a parched garden. He sighs out in relief, takes another gulp and burps. When the burger arrives he barely pauses for breath, swallowing mouthfuls washed down by the Coke. His hangover recedes even further, defeated by fat and sugar. He'll go for a run tonight, demolish what's left of its residue.

Sated, he checks the time. Still nearly half an hour before he's due back into court. He could have another Coke, a coffee maybe, but his legs are restless. He pays his bill and wanders up towards the Royal Mile. Instead of going back to the court building, he takes a right up to the top, into the Castle Esplanade. There's a memory stirring of an impassioned piece he'd read in the paper a couple of months ago, calling for there to be a new memorial for the women executed as witches there, saying that what there was in place wasn't fit for purpose.

Witch Trial

He can't remember what the issue was. Nor can he explain the compulsion that's driving him to take a look at the place. Not until he's standing looking at the open space over which the castle looms. Then he clocks it. *Witch trial.* The words muttered by the irritating juror Emma, before they all shut her down. They've only touched on this so far, not really gone into any of the meat of it since the description of the pigeon sacrifice.

Daisy had got really into all of this stuff a couple of years ago. She'd tried to drag Matthew and Rosalind off on a witch tour of Edinburgh, one of those foolish late-night performances put on for gullible tourists. Matthew had laughed at the thought, told her to go with her friends. She'd come back brimming over with outrage and facts about the terrible number of women killed in the eighteenth century – *way worse than England, Dad. Or Salem. They only killed nineteen women there. But there were hundreds of women killed up at the Castle. At least three hundred.*

He should have listened more. She was still young enough to try to engage him then, but he was always so distracted she gave up. At least he'll be able to tell her about this trial. She'll find it more interesting than his tales of the operating theatre. Once you've saved one life you've saved them all, as far as an unimpressed teen is concerned.

Looking at the Esplanade now, he can't explain why he didn't pay more attention. Three hundred women. How would they have died? Hanged? Burned? There's a piper playing 'Flower of Scotland', a large group of teenagers carrying multicoloured backpacks, clouds of fruity vapour coming off the kids at the back, but that's not what Matthew is seeing. He's seeing fire, smoke, terror on a woman's face. A crackling fills his ears, baying from an invisible crowd, the heat building on his cheeks from the flames as they grow higher and higher and he stumbles back and—

'Watch where the fuck you're going.'

He's walked straight into a mum and her three kids, all of them chewing gum, their jaws moving incessantly.

'I'm sorry,' he says, hands up in apology, but she stares at him blank-faced, the children around her as impassive, and the vacant hostility of it chills Matthew. He could be bleeding out in front of them, desperate for help, and he's convinced they would look at him in the same way, nothing but an obstacle in their path.

He pushes through them, apology withered on his tongue, legs unsteady beneath him. He's heading for the wall so he can lean against it for a moment, catch his breath, put his hand on the cold stone and bring himself back. There's still a faint hissing of flames in his ear, a residual heat. But where he finds himself is in front of the memorial, the Witches' Well, an engraved metal drinking fountain with a trough of geraniums in it, a snake's head peering over the red flowers. Matthew looks up at the inscription above: . . . *witches burned at the stake . . . some used their exceptional knowledge for evil purpose . . . evil . . .* The word drums in his head.

To the left there's a sign explaining the history of it but that isn't what Matthew sees. He doesn't read any of the information. What he sees is an old engraving, a ship foundering in the background, groups of women clustered together, held at sword point. And looming on a tower above them, claws out, wings aloft, the Devil, all in black. Matthew's gaze is trapped. He can't look away, though his hands are cold, his gut twisting with the sense that he needs to get out of here, now, immediately, and as he tries to move, to turn, the head on the sign in front of him moves too. The Devil turns to look straight at Matthew, his horns proud above him, and as Matthew backs away in horror, the head rears up from the sign, a form pushing up in three dimensions from the two dimensions in which it's been trapped.

Witch Trial

It's the eyes that render Matthew motionless, amber, flame-ringed, the pupils not round but rectangular. The mouth opens and Matthew steps back, terror finally giving him strength, and the head laughs and laughs, a noise that rips through Matthew, a stench from its breath that nearly fells him, sulphur and rot and shit. He backs away, gagging, before turning and running fast, the hounds of hell at his heels.

20

'Good lunch?' Emma says as Matthew walks back into the jury room, throwing himself into a chair at the end of the table. He's struggling to catch his breath, terror still bubbling underneath.

'You look like you've seen a ghost,' Russell says, more observant than the irritating woman who's sucking her fingers with a loud, slurping noise, an almost empty plate of chips in front of her.

'I'm fine.' Matthew forces the words out with difficulty. 'I went for a walk when I suddenly realised the time. Had to run back.' Despite his best efforts there's a tremor in his voice.

Someone pushes a glass of water over to him and he gulps it down, nodding his thanks. The fear inside him gradually subsides. As does the final remnant of his hangover, driven away by the shock. Though between this and the pulsating heart earlier, last night's booze must still have some kind of a hold on him. He's never had hallucinations like this before. Definitely time to lay off the whisky.

It was so real, though. The stench of the Devil's breath still lingers in his nostrils, the taste of it on his tongue no matter how much water he swallows to try and wash it away. An early night tonight for sure. He's going to look after himself properly from now on.

Everyone has returned now and they're milling around,

Witch Trial

waiting to be called back into court, which happens punctually at 2 o'clock. Matthew takes his seat in the jury box, almost fully composed now. He's glad to be back. The more boring the evidence they hear this afternoon, the happier he'll be. Scientific analysis, maybe, or some data. Numbers will calm him down.

Even more calming is the fact that the blonde is back, sitting in her corner of court again, notebook in hand. The very sight of her is balm to Matthew's frayed nerves. This is the second day she's come into court now; it means that she'll be there for the duration. The creeping doubt he'd had about her return is dispelled – now there's no rush. There will come a point when they stand together and they talk, and from then, her place in his life will be assured. As soon as the thought forms, Matthew shakes his head, laughing under his breath at his absurdity. She's just a journalist, that's all. Nothing to him.

But the tremor in his hands he's felt since the hallucination at the Witches' Well has gone. Whatever the woman might mean to him in future, he's grateful for that.

He glances over at the co-accuseds as he waits for the next witness to come into the courtroom. Eliza is staring straight ahead, twirling the ends of her fair hair round her finger. Her expression is calm, no sign of tension in neck or jaw. Isobel, though . . . As he shifts his gaze towards her, she turns to look at him full on, eyes blazing, her hair moving around her head though the air in the courtroom is still. Matthew swallows.

Before the fear has a chance to conquer him fully again, the macer brings in the next witness. The man is sworn in. As he says the word *God*, Matthew shudders, an involuntary movement. He shakes his head at the irrationality of it, the idea that people would buy into this rubbish of devils and ghosts. Not him. He's stopped being scared, the feeling gone with the tremor he'd felt. Even so, the idea creeps in that maybe he'll dig out Daisy's old school Bible when he gets home, just for old times' sake.

The witness starts speaking and Matthew focuses on what he's saying, listening intently as he explains that he's a family doctor who knew the dead girl Christian as his patient for many years, from the first time that he was introduced to her during a medical emergency when she was still a baby.

'They brought her into the surgery without an appointment,' he says. 'I remember it distinctly. I was about to leave for the day, but I heard them in reception. They were in such distress.'

'Who were in such distress?'

'The baby's parents. They lived over the road and had rushed into the surgery with her as she'd gone floppy and unresponsive. I took one look and said that they needed to get an ambulance.'

'What did you think was wrong with her?'

'At that stage I didn't know, but she seemed to have a very high temperature. Her cheeks were flushed and there was a rash on her chest. I was afraid that she might have meningitis.'

'Did the ambulance arrive?'

'Yes, very soon after it was called. Christian and her mum were taken into hospital, and her dad made his way separately. I didn't see her again for another two weeks.'

'Were you sent any reports from the hospital that treated her?'

'I was, yes.'

Mr Alexander turns to the judge. He's holding a sheaf of photocopied pages in his hand. 'Could a copy be put in front of the witness?' The judge nods, the macer crosses the court and puts the papers down on the witness box.

'Is this a copy of the medical records that relate to that incident?'

'Yes, it is.'

'Could you describe what it says, please, bearing in mind that you are addressing a court of laypeople here.'

Witch Trial

The doctor nods. The screen in front of Matthew has flashed up with a scan of the records to add to the jury bundle. He skims through it, grateful for the chance to employ his professional knowledge to bring himself back from the weird unpleasantness he's just encountered. Notes, indecipherable to any but medical initiates, a litany of attempted diagnoses and treatments before a phrase pops out at him on the final page of the hospital report.

Kawasaki disease.

Another shudder goes through Matthew. He's beginning to see the picture emerge.

The doctor explains it well. An acute illness that is usually seen in young children. A temperature that lasts for days. Red eyes. Sore mouth. A skin rash. A disease that causes the blood vessels to become inflamed and swollen which can lead to complications in the arteries that supply blood to the heart. Even with treatment, some children go on to develop complications. In Christian's case, myocarditis. An inflammation of her heart muscles, which led to some long-term damage.

Her mother had reported symptoms over the years – fatigue, abdominal pain. Chest pains sometimes. Incidents when Christian's heart raced with no cause.

Cardiomyopathy. Her heart didn't pump blood properly. The girl needed to take medication regularly. She had to exercise carefully. She was monitored by the family doctor regularly and on occasion a cardiac specialist as well.

Matthew's slightly surprised that he's never come across Christian before. He knows most of the young heart patients in Edinburgh, or at least that's how it feels. She must have been seen by one of his colleagues. He could always ask around. Then he looks at the judge, her stern demeanour. Perhaps not.

Given he specialises now in surgery and transplants, it's

not surprising he didn't have dealings with the family. But the trajectory of cardiomyopathy is such that if she'd lived, she'd probably have crossed the threshold of his theatre at one time or another, in need of his life-saving skills.

Sadly, it killed her first.

'Would she have been advised to avoid stress?' the advocate depute asks.

'Yes, where possible. That was a priority and I spoke to her about it every time I saw her. She would come in every six months for a general check-up. I got to know her pretty well, watching her grow up like that.' The doctor's voice shakes. 'She was a lovely girl.' Another pause while the man composes himself. 'They're a lovely family.'

He pauses after he says this, as if to give weight to it. Matthew looks over from him to the girls in the dock. Eliza has her head down, a sombre expression on her face. Isobel is looking straight at the doctor, though, one eyebrow raised as if to disagree.

'I saw Christian when she was a baby. From her cradle. I didn't expect I would see her to her grave.' He shakes his head, putting one hand up to push his glasses up on top of his head, rub his eyes.

For the first time since the trial started, Matthew begins to get a sense of what this is all about. Not a game where advocates in wigs score points, some battle of wits between paid swordsmen. It's about death, and sadness. A life cut far too short. The hairs lift on the back of his neck, the gravity of it sending shivers over him.

'Christian started boarding school in Edinburgh at the age of sixteen, as you know, doctor. Did you continue as her GP then?'

'Yes, I did. Normally, I understand that pupils at the school need to register with an Edinburgh GP. There's one attached to the school. Christian did see her for everyday ailments, but I maintained a relationship with Christian and her family throughout. The continuity was too important in this case to let it go.'

Mr Alexander nods. He shuffles through the papers in front of him. 'Was there a time after Christian started school that she said anything to you that caused you particular concern?'

A pause. The doctor blinks, his face a little paler. 'Yes. She came to see me in the Easter holidays last year, just before she died. I carried out the usual tests on her and everything was as it ought to be, more or less. But at the end of the appointment, as she was about to leave, she turned back and said something.' He stops.

'What did she say?'

'I'd told her that she was doing really well. But she'd seemed quite sad throughout the appointment. Not her usual cheerful self. She was normally very philosophical about the care that she needed to take of herself. This time, though, she was more offhand.'

'So what did she say at the end of the appointment that gave you concern?'

'She stopped at the door, turned to me. And she said, "There's no point in all this, though." I asked her what she meant, told her that there was every point. If she took good care of herself there was no reason that she wouldn't live to a ripe old age. Even as old as me. I thought she'd laugh, but she shook her head.'

'Did she say anything else?'

The doctor's head is bent, his hands twisting in front of him. Matthew has rarely seen a solid country family doctor in such a state of distress – it's as disturbing as when he saw his father cry for the first time.

Finally the doctor raises his head, swallows, his Adam's apple moving up and down. 'She said that I had been very kind to her over the years, and she thanked me. Then she said, "You won't see me again. I'll be dead before summer." Before I could ask her what she was talking about, she'd shut the door behind her and gone. I contacted her parents immediately and they agreed to bring her back into the surgery before term started so that we could sort out whatever this nonsense was.' He pauses. Swallows. 'But I never saw her again.'

21

I never saw her again. The words echo in Matthew's ears after the doctor stops talking. It's sent a chill through him, the starkness of the phrase, the contrast between the ruddy normality of the doctor's countenance and the horror of what he's relayed to the court. He's not the only juror to be affected by it, either. He can sense that just by a quick look around the rest of his number. They're shifting in their chairs, holding themselves closer. When he glances down, he can see that Emma is shaking, as if she's in tears, though he dismisses this immediately as some kind of performative emoting. But Matthew can see the tension in Dharam's shoulders and knows that none of that is for show.

Mr Alexander takes his seat back at the table and Miss Brodie stands up in his place, ready to cross-examine for Eliza. Matthew can't think how she can argue with anything that the doctor has said. But at least she's trying. Not like Isobel's advocate, who seems to have given up, as far as Matthew can see.

'You said in your evidence that everything was as it should be, *more or less*. It's right that you'd seen a deterioration in Christian's condition, hadn't you?'

'I wouldn't go as far as that,' the doctor replies. 'But I had seen her in better health. I was concerned that she might not be taking such good care of herself.'

'You asked her if she was smoking, didn't you?'

'Yes.'

'And she replied yes.'

The doctor shakes his head, but agrees. 'I told her she needed to stop. I said it was one of the worst things she could do to herself.'

'And you asked her if she was taking drugs or drinking alcohol?'

His eyes close for a moment. 'I did, yes.'

'And her reply?'

'That it was really none of my business if she wanted to, but that yes, she was drinking. She'd started hiding vodka in her bedroom.'

'Did you explain to her how bad this would be for her heart, given her condition?'

'I did, yes.'

'You said that you contacted her parents immediately after the appointment?'

'Yes.'

'But you didn't think to tell them about your concerns?'

The doctor's shoulders go back, head high. 'She was sixteen years old. There is such a thing as patient confidentiality, you know.'

'Even under circumstances like these?'

'Even under circumstances like these. I told her she needed to be careful. I told her she should talk to her parents if she was unhappy. But she shrugged it off. There was nothing more that I could do.' He speaks with conviction, but Matthew senses doubt in his eyes.

It's too late for that now.

As usual, Isobel's advocate doesn't cross-examine. *No further questions.* It's really starting to look off. All the jurors comment on it as they're sent out to their room after the doctor leaves the court.

'What the hell is she even being paid for?' That's Jasmine speaking. She bangs her water bottle down on the table. 'No one has spoken up for the girl at all. There's Brodie asking question after question on behalf of Eliza, but Isobel is being totally ignored. Her name's Goodly but she's doing her job a bit shit-ly if you ask me.' She snorts at her own joke.

'There will be some plan,' Aisha says. Matthew's assessment was correct – a very sensible woman. 'The advocate will know what she's doing. I'm sure we'll find out.'

'Maybe,' Jasmine says. 'But I don't like it. I'm feeling really sorry for the girl.'

Matthew can't argue with this.

The jurors mill around getting themselves coffee and tea, most of them sitting down at the table while Russell and Dharam stand at the window and look out. Matthew joins them.

'They've set the scene,' Dharam says. 'I wish they'd get on with telling us what the girls have to do with it, though.'

Matthew nods.

'Easier if there'd been a full opening speech. We'd know exactly what the prosecution case was by now.'

'But where would be the fun in that?' Aisha says, moving over to stand next to them. 'This way it's all a surprise.'

'You're enjoying it?' Dharam says.

'It's more interesting than work, I'll say that.'

'What do you do?' Matthew says.

'I work in a funeral parlour,' Aisha says. 'There's not much conversation.'

'At least they don't argue back.' It's Emma. She's pushed into the group even though no one seems keen to include her. 'I have to deal with arguments all the time.'

No one replies until Aisha takes pity on the woman. 'What do you do?'

'I'm a teacher,' Emma says. 'I work with teenagers. I know all about this age group. They're a fucking nightmare. Most of them, at least. I'd believe anything you said about them – they're totally capable of murder.'

Great. Just what the jury needs – an unbiased member of the public who is willing to listen to the evidence with an open mind. They've only just managed to shut down her desire to tell them more about the case than they ought to know; now they need to battle her preconceptions as well.

But before Matthew can work out a suitable response, the jury officer calls them back.

'I'd only just made my coffee,' Emma says, but no one listens to her complaint. They all file past her back into court. Matthew, for one, is relieved to walk away from her. Between her and the demonic experience, he's had quite enough of the day already.

22

'One more witness for today,' Mr Alexander says as soon as they are all sitting back down. 'Please call Muriel Fleming.'

The macer leaves the room and returns leading a middle-aged woman into the witness box. She takes the oath in a crisp voice, very businesslike. She's wearing a black trouser suit with a purple blouse underneath, a chunky silver necklace round her neck. Professional she might look but not corporate, Matthew reckons. The moment she starts to speak she confirms this.

'I'm a psychiatrist attached to the Royal Edinburgh Hospital,' she says. 'I've been qualified for nearly twenty-five years. I specialise in the treatment of children and young people with diagnoses of severe mental illness. I've acted as an expert witness in numerous legal cases over the last fifteen years.'

'Did you have cause to examine the accused, Isobel Smyth?'

'I did, yes. I spoke to her at some length on three separate occasions.'

Matthew looks over at Isobel. She's scowling. But not at the psychiatrist. At her advocate, by the direction of her stare.

'At whose instruction?'

'At the instruction of the Crown,' she says. 'I was asked to determine whether the accused is fit to plead. In layman's terms, whether she is mentally well enough to understand the court proceedings and engage with them.'

'Is this a copy of the reports that you made?' Mr Alexander says, brandishing papers at her. She nods. The papers flash up on the screen in front of Matthew. He restrains himself from reading through them immediately. Better to hear from the psychiatrist herself.

'On examination, did you reach a determination about the accused?'

'I did, yes,' the psychiatrist says. 'Despite her avowed belief in magic and witchcraft, the accused is not suffering from schizophrenia or any other diagnosable mental illness. I could discern no trace of a personality disorder, or any kind of intellectual disability that would derogate from her ability to participate fully in proceedings.'

'You mean that she's fit to plead?' the advocate depute says.

'She's fit to plead.'

Mr Alexander sits back down.

Miss Brodie has no questions to ask. It's Miss Goodly who leaps up to her feet, striding over to the lectern with great purpose.

'I'm going to take you through some parts of your report. Go first to the fourth paragraph down on the second page of the bundle.'

The psychiatrist turns the page of the bundle.

'Please will you read out that paragraph to the court.'

The psychiatrist clears her throat. '"The patient reports that on the first occasion that the coven met, they did a tarot card reading. The cards disclosed a very troubling pattern in which death was foretold for one of the girls. The patient states that she has total conviction that the tarot cards held meaning and were not just a selection of randomly selected images."'

Witch Trial

'Thank you,' Miss Goodly says. 'Now I'd ask you to turn to the first paragraph at the top of the fourth page and read that to the court.'

Another throat clear. '"The patient states that she fell asleep in her dormitory one afternoon only to find herself flying across the rooftops of Edinburgh to the site of the old church in North Berwick, where she landed to find herself in conversation with someone that she calls Old Nick, otherwise known as the Devil."'

Matthew wraps his arms close around him. His hands have grown suddenly cold. Someone must have turned the air conditioning down.

'"He was an imposing figure with a tail and horns on his head. His eyes were particularly remarkable – amber in colour, ringed in flame. Most notably, the pupils were rectangular in shape."'

Tremors running right through him, the horror of what Matthew experienced on the Esplanade completely real again to him.

'"When he spoke, she had to keep her head down, because the smell of his breath was so terrible. He told her that she was his chosen one and that the people around her would soon recognise her power. Then he turned round and bent over, presenting her with his anus, which he invited her to kiss. Under the circumstances, she felt that she had no alternative but to comply, even though the smell was even worse than his breath. But she was happy to pay homage to her new lord."'

It's entirely still in the courtroom. No one is moving. No one even looks as if they're breathing. Matthew is frozen in place.

Miss Goodly puts up her hand to stop the witness from reading further. 'Do you remember Isobel's demeanour when she said this to you?'

'I do, yes.'

'How did she present?'

'She seemed entirely normal and matter-of-fact in the way that she related the dream.'

Miss Goodly shakes her head. 'You are using the word *dream*, but she never referred to it as a dream, did she?'

The psychiatrist leafs through the pages. 'I suppose not, no. Of course it *was* a dream, though.'

'Isobel related this account to you as something that had actually happened to her, didn't she?'

'I think that would be taking it very literally,' the psychiatrist says.

'Well, it's your job to listen to what your patient says and report accordingly, isn't it? Not interpret things as you think they should be.'

'I beg your pardon?' the psychiatrist says. Her lips are tight.

'I'd suggest that you have got this entirely wrong,' Miss Goodly says. 'It's quite clear that what Isobel was describing to you in the run-up to Christian's tragic death demonstrated that she was in the throes of a psychotic breakdown.'

'I don't agree,' the psychiatrist starts to say, but Miss Goodly keeps talking through.

'I will be presenting evidence to the court to support this assertion, but suffice to say that you have given a diagnosis that is entirely wrong, haven't you?'

'I stand by my findings.'

'And that rather than finding that someone who believes she has flown cross-country to pay homage to the Devil is entirely mentally healthy and operating within a normal parameter of acceptable beliefs, you should rather have found that this was evidence of mental illness such that she was not responsible for her actions at the time.'

Mr Alexander rises to his feet, his hand upraised. 'My lady . . .' he says to the judge, who nods.

'Miss Goodly, I need to remind you that this is ground that we have covered already.'

'Yes, yes,' Miss Goodly says, 'I'm not seeking to reopen the question of fitness to plead. I am, however, raising the fact that in the run-up to the time of Christian's death, Isobel was extremely unwell.'

The court falls quiet while the judge digests what Miss Goodly has said. Matthew is trying to keep up with the argument, the fear that gripped him so close fading, but not entirely. It's clearly only the tip of the iceberg of arguments between the lawyers, but he knows that jurors are the last people to be kept informed of any legal disputes. The sub-text is there but not for him to read, especially not when he's feeling as shaken as this.

As the judge starts to speak again, there's a commotion from the dock. Isobel.

'I told you not to do this,' she says. 'I wasn't mad. I'm not mad. There's nothing wrong with me.'

'Silence in court,' the judge says.

'You can tell me to shut up as much as you like. But the Devil is real. The magic is real. You just don't want to see it.'

'If you do not stop interrupting your advocate, I will have to order you to be removed from court. You will have the opportunity to give instructions later,' the judge says. Isobel subsides back into her seat. Her cheeks had gone pink with the intensity of her emotion, but the colour drains away from her almost as Matthew watches. She seems to shrink into herself, huddled inside her hooded top.

Miss Goodly takes a moment before addressing herself to the psychiatrist again. 'There is a difference between religious belief and religious delusion, is there not?'

The psychiatrist nods. 'Yes, that's right.'

'And religious delusion can be a symptom of an impending mental health crisis, such as a psychotic breakdown or schizophrenic episode. That's correct, isn't it?'

'It is correct,' the psychiatrist says. 'But—'

'You cannot rule out the possibility that at the time of

Christian's death, Isobel was suffering from such an episode, can you?'

'I can't rule anything in or out at that time given that Isobel was not then my patient.'

A triumphant expression creeps across Miss Goodly's face. Only a twitch of her mouth, but Matthew can tell she's delighted with the reply she's received. 'So you would agree then that it is a possibility, given the account that Isobel gave to you of what she says she was experiencing in terms of astral projection and devil worship, that this went beyond belief into delusion? Even if when she later described it to you, she presented as being of sound mind?'

'It is a possibility, yes.'

'No further questions.'

They're free to go. Most of the jury members head back into their room to collect anything they'd left earlier, but Matthew only brought his hangover to court with him today, and mercifully this has gone. He's a thirst on him now, a craving for a pint and a chat with someone who knows what he's been going through the last couple of days. He wants a reality check, someone else to talk to about what bullshit it is to believe in the occult. Looking at the other members of the jury, though, there's no one he wants to spend any more time with now.

Instead of hanging round in the room to see if anyone else fancies the pub, he takes off immediately. If he's quick, maybe he'll run into the blonde. He can't explain why, but he's drawn to her. He wants to know what she thinks of the case. Sure, there's a risk she's there to spy on him, but he can charm her out of it. He knows how charismatic he can be. They could go back to the Devil's Advocate for a drink – it was a nice bar; he was impressed with it. She'd like it, he's sure of it. He gets out to the top of the stairs and sees her head bobbing in front, about to leave the court building.

Witch Trial

Taking the steps two at a time, he bounds past an old man who's taking it very carefully, clinging on to the banister. But she stays maddeningly ahead, out of reach. By the time he's at the bottom of the steps, she's out of sight, too.

Baulked of this solution to his evening, Matthew stops walking, pulls his phone out of his pocket. He'll call Olivia. She'll be nice to him; give him the TLC he needs. But his call goes straight through to voicemail – she must be in theatre. He leaves a message, telling her to call back whenever she can, however late it is. As soon as he's finished speaking, though, he regrets his tone. Too keen. Too needy.

Too late to do anything about it.

Today can do one. He's had enough. Between hangover, evidence, the weird hallucination on the Esplanade; he's done in. He starts his walk home, shaking his head. That demonic moment was a warning from his sub-conscious, his conscience asserting itself. It's the only logical explanation for it. Time to stop trying to talk to beautiful women in court, to stop cavorting with Olivia too. He needs to start being decent. He's not like Dominic, he should remember that. If he's nicer to Rosalind, maybe she'll be nicer to him. A virtuous cycle. He's going to shake the Devil off his back, be a better man. He practically skips down the Playfair Steps, a chorus of angels singing in his mind.

WEDNESDAY

23

Sasha Kayode hasn't slept all night. She hasn't dared. She knew what dreams would pursue her – no way were Isobel and Eliza going to let her have a good night's rest before she came into court and destroyed their lives. She's drunk so many energy drinks to keep herself awake that her hands are shaking, her right eyelid twitching a frenetic beat.

She knows what they'll have done last night. They'll have taken a cow's tongue, split it down the middle and put a photograph of her inside. Sprinkled it with death oil (a quick glimpse at her own bottle, nestled on her altar). Then they'll have sewn it up with black thread. Her words rendered worthless.

But Sasha was ready for that. At five o'clock this morning she drank the dandelion tea, said the incantations. Pissed out all their venom. Her tongue is free.

'You nearly ready?'

At least her mum's coming into court with her. She'll sit at the front and smile, unlike everyone else.

'I don't want to go.'

'I know you don't, sweetheart. It'll be over soon, though.'

She rubs the last of the moisturiser into her face, checks that the twists of her hair are secure. Black top, black skirt, solemn as an executioner.

'Is your back feeling all right?'

'It's fine.' This isn't true, but there's no point worrying her mum with it. She doesn't want to take any painkillers, not this morning. She needs to feel it all, everything that they've done to her – they've made her do. It's the only way she'll bring herself to get through this.

Slowly she pushes herself to her feet, picks up her cane. Progress, the doctor said, looking at the silver-headed griffin on top of the fine oak stick, a legacy from her grandfather. Better than crutches. Sasha wishes she could agree.

She paces downstairs, drinks a coffee that her mum has left out in the kitchen for her. The caffeine perks her up, but she knows as soon as this is done she'll collapse. Not yet. Her mum is still upstairs getting ready, so Sasha has a minute to go to the fridge and take out what she needs – a sprig of rosemary, a clove of garlic. She tucks them into her pocket along with the blue glass evil-eye charm she brought back from Greece the year before. With the mirrors she's visualising placed all around her, she'll be protected from anything those girls can throw at her.

'Let's go.'

They sit next to each other in the taxi on the way to the court, holding hands. Sasha looks at their interwoven fingers, brown against white. She remembers her mum's face, the first thing she saw when she came round in hospital, the desperate hope and sadness combined, the cry that sprang out from her mum. *She's alive. She knows me.* Sasha is not the only victim here. She's all her mum has left after her dad died when she was a baby.

'Are you going to be OK?'

Sasha nods. She's got this.

Into the court building. Sasha keeps her head down in case she sees anyone she knows who's stickybeaking at the trial, but she gets through to the witness room undisturbed. She knows what to expect – Victim Support has talked her through it, shown her a video of a High Court so she knows where everyone will be sitting, what it'll be like. The prosecution said she could ask for a screen if she was too scared to look at Isobel and Eliza, but she's not that much of a wet wipe.

Besides, a screen wouldn't stop them if they wanted to get at her. But Sasha's prepared for that. She clasps her protections close to her.

When she first went to St Jude's it was a long few weeks waiting for someone to befriend her. Sure, going to boarding school was her choice – she'd been pushing for it for years, really, her mum only agreeing once she was well into her teens. But everyone was in cliques already, factions formed through the years. Sasha wasn't sure where she could fit in. Not sporty enough, not clever enough either. She looked at the girls in her dormitory, so cool, so together, and quailed at the idea of trying to get them to talk to her. It didn't help that the two coolest – Isobel and Eliza – were best friends, inseparable since they both joined the school years ago.

At last they started to bond. It started with *The Craft*. Sasha was up for watching it that October night long ago when Eliza asked her to join them. She'd have said yes to anything, flattered to be asked. The other new girl, Christian, she was there too, but she didn't say anything. She never really did.

They cleared everyone else out of the common room and watched it in silence. Even the popcorn went uneaten. Sasha knew perfectly well even then that aspects of the film were deeply problematic. The way that Rochelle's character was so underdeveloped, the lack of backstory given to the only Black character. But at least she was there. Sasha could see herself on screen, felt the moment of empowerment as the curse Rochelle cast started to come true. All those fucking blondes . . .

Isobel drove it. Every step of the way. But Eliza and Sasha were right behind her, at least for the first couple of weeks. They did their research, read the books they were able to find in the library, the Tumblr posts written by magick practitioners (Sasha always has the 'K' – this isn't some stage rubbish. They have other uses for rabbits than pulling them out of hats). Blood sisters, the drops their fingers squeezed mixed into one, however reluctant Eliza was becoming.

It might have started with *The Craft*, but it was a couple of weeks later that it began to go dark. Isobel and Christian were keen to bring the coven together that Saturday night, Eliza less so. She'd seemed to be getting bored with it all, ready to move on to a new interest. She was a lot less keen on being friends with Sasha and Christian, had thrown a massive strop when Isobel went off shopping with Christian that afternoon to an occult shop they'd located in the city centre.

But Sasha knew she was all in, the world of it making more sense to her than any reality she'd previously known.

Under protest, Eliza joined them, giving in to the demand that all four of them were needed for the ritual to be fully effective. Again, they cleared the common room. Some of the younger girls objected but Isobel snarled at them and they ran off, shrill giggles fading into the night. Sasha went round and shut all the curtains, sealing out the night.

That's when they turned off the lights, lit some candles they pulled out of the shopping bag from their earlier expedition. With an air of excitement, Isobel took a box out and brandished it at the others in triumph. *Look what Christian bought me*, she said, and set up a wooden Ouija board – Sasha remembers it as clearly as if it were yesterday.

They put their fingers together on the planchette, Eliza's face full of disgust at the proximity she was forced to keep with Christian. With Sasha too, for all she knew. The candle flames

Witch Trial

flickered, Sasha's heartbeat so loud she was sure the others would hear it, laugh at her for her fear. But when she looked round, they were all afraid. Even Eliza, though she tried to sneer. Isobel the least scared though, her voice clear and loud as she invited in the spirits. The planchette was still, a piece of plastic, nothing more, then suddenly off it went, a force stronger than anything Sasha had ever felt. Stuttering, jerking.

EDIEDIECHRISTDIEDIEDIE. The pull on their fingers so strong it was impossible to resist. The candles went out.

'What the fuck was that?' Sasha said.

'I don't know,' Isobel said. White as a sheet.

'Did you do that?' Eliza says.

Christian just sobbed.

Christ. Christian. On whom was that death wished?

24

As she finishes recounting this, Sasha steals a glance round the courtroom. No one is looking impressed. She knows she's done a poor job in telling the story – now, in this over-lit room, it's impossible to conjure up the way she'd felt then. Too many doubters. But she'd believed. And so had the others.

'That's right.'

She's doing her best to avoid looking at the girls in the dock. But every now and then she steals a glance. It's funny, they're not looking the way she thought they would. It's as if their powers have reversed. Eliza's the strong one now, staring intently at Sasha, barely blinking as she takes in every word that Sasha says. But Isobel is diminished. It looks as if her hair has thinned, less lustrous than it used to be. Sasha almost laughs, the sound catching into a sob. Life imitating art indeed, the curse from *The Craft* that landed on the racist palely replicated now. That scene as the blonde cheerleader cried in the shower as her hair came out in handfuls is one that has stayed with Sasha ever since she first watched the film.

'What happened next?' The advocate depute is asking her a question. Sasha needs to pay attention. She swallows, gets back to it.

What she's struggling to convey is how real it felt. She went from being an outcast, homesick, missing her mum, to fitting into the coolest group in school. OK, they weren't the coolest in the most traditional sense. They didn't play hockey, excel in any sporting achievements. But they were smart, they were funny, and they knew things that no one else knew. They knew why Charlotte Nussey kept missing goal whenever she tried to hit the ball, why her maths had suddenly escaped her and every attempt she made to hiss racist invectives at Sasha failed. They knew why Carol-Ann Napier couldn't bully the smaller girls any more, but had instead grown terrified of the dark, insisting on sleeping with her light on, moaning whenever she dozed off because of the ferocity of her nightmares.

Those were deserved victims, though. They were mean to other girls, strutted round with superiority as if they thought no one was better than them. Sasha didn't mind that – their hexes wouldn't recoil on them, the Rule of Three would be respected. No harm done. It was when Isobel decided that she wanted to get Noah to dump Freya so Eliza could go out with him that the problems arose.

Sasha told her that she couldn't hex someone just to get what she wanted. It wasn't the right way to go about it. But Isobel didn't care. She was doing it for Eliza, so it was fine.

'The easiest way is to take Freya off the scene,' Isobel said.

'How are you going to do that?' Sasha asked her, not really wanting the answer.

'I'm going to curse Freya so she becomes ill. I know exactly what we need to do – all of us will have to be a part of it though so the magic is stronger.'

'Won't that rebound on Eliza? Given this is for her benefit?'

'I think the risk is worth taking.'

Eliza had looked really pissed off at that. But she had such a thing for Noah, she couldn't resist.

As she recounts it all now, Sasha can hear the scepticism in the advocate depute's voice. She knows he doesn't believe in the truth of what she's saying. Not that he thinks she's lying, but he thinks the magic stuff is bullshit. She gets it, she really does. All she can do is speak her truth, though. Even if they all think she's crazy, at least they'll see the kind of power that Isobel wanted to wield, even if they don't believe that she did.

This was the first time they'd gone to the shed. Isobel found it one day when she was foraging for herbs in the park, the gap in the railings, the unattended structure, the key hidden under a rock. She had a sixth sense for getting what they needed, this space perfect for more complicated rituals. There were only so many times they could kick the younger kids out of the common room before it blew up in their faces, and the prefect in charge of the dormitory was way too fond of telling them to shut up. She didn't care if they went out after lights out; she just didn't want to be disturbed while she chatted on her secret phone to her even more secret boyfriend.

They'd wait until lights out, then they'd sneak out of the school grounds. It was easy to squeeze through the small gap in the fence round the school perimeter, the smaller gap in the fence that ran down the side of the allotments. It really wasn't very big. But neither were the girls.

'How do you know it's disused?' said Christian, panicking as usual. Isobel had the answer to that.

'I've walked past multiple times to be sure; no one ever does anything there. Also, look at the place. Everyone else looks after their allotments – this one is overgrown and tired.'

A moment's hesitation, then they were in.

It was dark in the shed, cold. Its décor was cheerful, but this only made its air of abandonment more sinister. Spiders lurked in the corners, the webs catching at Sasha's face as they crept in. Isobel wouldn't let them put any lights on so candles had to

Witch Trial

suffice, the shadows on the ceiling seeming to lean in around the girls, threatening to suffocate them.

Isobel was carrying a black tote bag from the occult shop in Candlemaker Row, the place they'd bought the Ouija board. She emptied the contents out on the floor. Sasha stared at them, transfixed. Something cold lodged itself at the bottom of her stomach.

'What frightened you?' Mr Alexander says, pulling Sasha back into the courtroom.

'She'd brought all the components for the curse. The candle, the death oil—'

'Sorry to interrupt, but what is death oil?'

'It's an oil which has been treated to have magical powers. Dead insects, soil from a graveyard. We said incantations over it. It gives force to any spell you cast.'

'Thank you,' Mr Alexander says. Sasha is impressed that he's treating what she's saying seriously. She knows it's a lot. 'Please continue.'

There was all the normal stuff that they'd used to hex people. But this time Isobel had brought something else with her. A poppet of Freya. Sasha looked at the cloth doll with growing horror. Christian and Isobel had made it together, giving it Freya's features. Isobel had stolen a shirt of hers which she'd made into the top part of the doll, and she'd sprayed it with some of her perfume.

Worst of all, she'd filled it with Freya's hair. With a grin, Isobel pulled open the seams and showed Sasha, chilling her to the bone to see wispy auburn curls of Freya's hair peeking out from the gap in the top of the doll. She'd taken it from Freya's hairbrush that morning, she told Sasha with glee. Then Isobel had picked up a plastic bag, opened it. A stench of fish had filled the shed.

'What the fuck is that?' Sasha said.

'Rotten sardines. That'll put Noah off for sure.' Isobel stuffed the fish into the poppet before sewing the hole up roughly with a needle and thread. Then she pulled out a packet of pins, gave a handful to each of the girls who had been watching on silently as Isobel made her preparations.

'Now we stick them in,' she said. 'It'll make Freya so ill she'll have to leave school. Then Noah will dump her and the way will be clear for you, Eliza.' It was terrifying how matter-of-fact Isobel sounded.

'We can't do this,' Sasha said. 'It's going to go badly wrong, I'm sure of it.'

'Don't be such a coward,' Christian said. One of the few interventions she ever made, but backing Isobel up. At that stage, Christian always did exactly what Isobel said. It's like they were one person. No room between them for anyone else.

'Something terrible is going to happen, I swear it. We can't do this,' Sasha said again.

'You can go if you don't like it.'

After a moment's hesitation, Sasha left, sneaking back in through the dark, getting into bed without anyone seeing her. It was one of the hardest decisions she'd ever made, to walk away from her friends like that. She had no choice, though. What they were doing was too dangerous. When she got into bed she thought she'd be awake for hours, staring wordlessly at the ceiling, but she was asleep before the others came back to the dorm, the stress of it all too much to bear.

'Did anything happen to Freya, as far as you know?' Mr Alexander says.

'She did become ill, though I don't know what was wrong with her. She had to go home for a couple of weeks.'

'Do you know what happened to Noah?'

'He didn't dump her. He was far too devoted. Eliza wanted Isobel to cast a love spell on him but she refused. She said that could only end badly. Eliza would have to seduce him herself. I watched at the half-term disco and all I can say is that she tried, but it went nowhere. Eliza was really upset. She ended up passed out in the toilets, so drunk that she had to have her stomach pumped.'

'Did anything happen to you after you walked away from the shed?' Mr Alexander says.

Sasha doesn't answer him for a moment. Words have temporarily failed her. How can she describe the nightmares she had to this man in his wig and gown, his friendly yet sceptical smile as he humours her, letting her spout her nonsense in return for her telling them what Isobel and Eliza are really like. But she has to say something.

It was like hell. They never told her exactly what they did in the shed after she walked away. But Sasha's guess is that they hexed her for breaking the sisterhood. She may have slept that night when she got back early, but that was the last time that she slept for days.

It would start with a crawling sensation. As soon as she closed her eyes, it began. Something moving under her skin, multiplying, woodlice when you lift a stone but they were crawling out of her ears, up her nose, round the edge of her pants while she flailed her hands at them, desperately trying to brush them off. That was the first night.

The second night it was grasshoppers. She knew why; she'd told Isobel once how scary she found them, the way they jumped. Hundreds of them, thousands, crawling all over her, tangled up in her hair.

The third, midges. An incessant scratching, every part of her bitten. But when the morning light came, not a trace of the intolerable itching, other than the long scratches she'd inflicted on herself in a vain attempt to make it all stop.

The fourth night, she was so tired, she'd fallen asleep despite herself. However bright the bedside light in her eyes, the music she kept blaring through her headphones, she was unable to keep awake any longer. Up and up she flew in her dream, soaring above the streets and houses of Edinburgh, Arthur's Seat a tiny lion crouching beneath her, till suddenly she lost the wind beneath her wings, falling falling falling until she woke with a scream to see Isobel perched at the end of her bed, a manic grin on her face.

That was nearly the last straw. But it was what happened to her mum that flipped it.

'What happened to your mum?' Mr Alexander says.

'She found a lump in her breast. They had to do loads of tests to see if it was cancer. I knew they'd done it to her. That's when I knew I had no choice. I had to join back in.' She takes a deep breath. 'And that's when it all went terribly wrong.'

25

Matthew is getting more and more pissed off with this. The advocate depute is treating the bullshit that's spilling out of the girl's mouth as if it's gospel truth when it's clearly a load of nonsense. He shouldn't give any more attention to this guff about spells or curses. The idea that a group of schoolgirls could induce breast cancer in a grown woman is laughable.

He's going to have to put up with it, though. There must be a point to all this shit. But he hopes she's torn apart in cross-examination.

'I told you before about the Ouija board. How it had said DIE, and we weren't sure if it was trying to say Christ or if it meant Christian. Well, shortly after I rejoined, the next thing happened. We were doing tarot cards. Isobel said the situation was too big for us to ignore, that we had to keep asking questions now that we had direct communication with the other side.'

Matthew tries not to roll his eyes. Fails.

'We'd read up all about it, but Eliza was the best at it. She'd memorised the card meanings so she did the quickest readings. She was our reader.'

'Where were you at this time?'

'We were back in the shed. They'd persuaded me that they weren't going to do anything like the poppet again, that they'd learnt their lesson about cursing people for the wrong reasons.'

As if there's ever a right reason. Matthew holds in a snort of derision. Mind you, he wouldn't mind some of these powers himself. He can think of a few people he'd like to hex.

'So Eliza was doing the readings. I went first, drew three cards. The first two were all right, nothing special. But I was really shaken when I turned over the Hanged Man, especially when Eliza said it showed I'd been a traitor in the past, betraying friendships. She paused there for a moment, then she said the other cards showed that everything was all right now.' Sasha stops, swallows, as if the words have hurt her throat on the way out. 'Then it was Isobel – I don't remember anything much about hers. But after that, it was Christian's turn.' Sasha's voice changes as she says this. It's quieter, more strained.

'What happened with her cards?' the advocate depute says, coaxing her along.

'The first one she drew was the Knight of Swords. That means something sudden and shocking is going to happen. Then she drew the Death card. After that she drew the Four of Swords. That means mourning.'

'Together did all of that convey a meaning to Christian?'

'Yes,' the girl says, her voice still hushed. 'Yet again, it was telling her that she was going to die.'

Matthew had been about to laugh, but the sound dies in his throat. Hokum it might be, but this witness's belief is rock solid. Beyond any sneering of his.

Besides, Christian *is* dead. Hokum or not, the fact of it is true.

'How did Christian react to this?'

'She was shaken. You could tell. She went very white, kept her head down. But she didn't start crying. I think I would have, but she kept it in. She shrugged, said, "It is what it is."'

'What did you think about that?'

'She was a lot calmer than I would have been.'

The words drop into the quiet of the courtroom. Everyone is

hanging on her evidence, listening almost without movement, as if they don't want to break the spell.

A pause. Mr Alexander is clearly thinking of how to phrase his next question. At last he works it out. 'I understand that you think that these experiences were real.'

'Yes.'

'But do you accept there is any possibility that they could have been set up by one of the other participants? By one or other of the accused, or both of them?'

'You mean, was it faked by Isobel or Eliza? I really don't think so. But I suppose it's possible. One of them could have pushed the planchette round. The cards could have been set up. But I saw Eliza shuffle them properly. I saw it with my own eyes.'

They've stopped for a coffee break. Matthew is relieved for the chance to stretch his legs. He's not in his suit today – chinos and a sweater, pale blue shirt. It's a relief not to be hung-over. When he woke he loved the clarity of his vision, the lack of any ache and pain.

The smart-casual wardrobe came courtesy of Marks & Spencer. He stopped in on his way home, down the hill towards the flat in Comely Bank, filling a bag with what was necessary for presenting himself respectably at court for the next week or so, a pile of microwave meals in a second bag. Health purists wouldn't approve, but a week of highly processed ingredients won't hurt. Besides, they're not just normal microwave meals. They're M & S . . .

He knows what he's doing. He's descending into the banality of advertising slogans because he's so cross about the way the advocate depute is letting this girl talk about magic as if it's real. It's an insult to his intelligence – to everyone's intelligence. Alexander should be getting a grip.

'What do you think of all this?' he says to Jasmine. They're standing outside round the corner from the door into the court building while Jasmine puffs on her vape.

'It's a bit weird,' she says. Blueberry-scented smoke weaves round her head. 'I can't believe he isn't being firmer with her that it's all bullshit.'

'Is it though?' That's Neil. He's wearing his green fleece again, looks very sensible. At odds with what he's saying. 'I got my tarot cards done once. It was freakishly accurate.'

'No, it wasn't,' Jasmine says. 'You were played.'

He looks surprisingly cross to be challenged, puffing his chest up. 'She saw stuff that I hadn't told anyone else.'

'They're brilliant at cold reading,' Jasmine says. 'It's all a scam. I bet they fixed those cards for Christian to find.'

'There's more to it than that, I know it,' Neil says. He walks away to finish his cigarette, his shoulders hunched against them.

'Do you believe in it? You can't do. No man in chinos thinks that ghosts are real.' She laughs, smoke billowing out from her again.

Matthew shakes his head. 'Of course not.' But Neil's certainty has cracked his scepticism, just a little. And under the fake blueberry scent that surrounds him, there's the faintest tang of shit and rotten meat.

The Devil's breath.

26

Sasha doesn't want to go back into court. It isn't easier now she's started – it's even harder than she'd thought it would be. The advocate depute is being nice but he clearly thinks she's barking mad. The rest of the court, too. It's full of sceptics – she can tell from the vibes even with her eyes shut. She's pushing against the tide of them, every step heavier than the last.

'Tell the court what happened next,' Mr Alexander says.

Deep breath. Now it gets really dark. She looks round the courtroom but there's no escape. Other than her mum, smiling at her in what's meant to be a reassuring way. Sasha can read the panic behind the smile, though, the fear rendering it a grimace. Her mum knows what happens next. She knows what Sasha doesn't want to say.

'We went to Christian's house that October half-term. Well, I say house. I mean her country estate.'

The advocate depute nods, encouraging her to go on.

'It's like a stately home. Not like a normal house at all. Loads and loads of land. They do grouse shooting there. It's up in the north of Scotland, right up in the Highlands.'

'How long were you staying there?'

'The whole week. My mum was away, Isobel and Eliza both wanted us to hang out as well.'

* * *

Sasha remembers what it was like to arrive. Christian hadn't warned them that this was what it would be like, that they would have to drive for half an hour to get to her house even after they'd turned into her gate. Even Isobel was quiet in the car, her normal arrogance subdued by the scale of it all. The road got rougher, narrower, the trees surrounding it denser and denser, pine trees in serried ranks. They'd just finished doing *Macbeth* and Sasha couldn't help shivering thinking of the threat of the woods of Great Dunsinane. These trees could do some damage if they decided to gang up on you.

It was even worse when they got to the house. Gothic, looming turrets, the front door huge, wooden and heavy. The hall was full of dead animals, stags' heads, a stuffed eagle hanging from the rafters. Glass cases of dead game birds lined the walls, their bright plumage deceptively cheerful. Still dead.

A man in a black suit had opened the door silently to them, ignoring Christian when she said hello. Sasha had felt that he'd sneered at the sight of her, though she might have been imagining it. Everything about the environment was setting her teeth on edge.

'Why are there so many dead animals?' Eliza said. She didn't look unhappy about it, though. There was a glee to her. Her nerves were clearly subsiding.

'They came with the house,' Christian said. 'It used to belong to these people back in Edwardian times. They liked to go to Africa and shoot things. Wait till you see their museum.'

'Does your family shoot things?' Eliza asked. Sasha knew it was said with hope, not disapproval.

'They try. I succeed. Had some luck earlier – that's dinner next week sorted,' a man said from behind them. He'd walked into the hall while they were looking at a display of stuffed pheasants. Sasha turned to face him – dark, handsome, wearing an Aran jumper and a kilt. 'Hello, Christian.'

Christian had blushed. She mumbled something incoherently. Isobel and Eliza stood on either side of her, eyes beady as hawks.

'Take your friends to the museum – it's not locked. Your parents will be back soon so it'll fill the time nicely until you see them. And I'll take you all out shooting in the morning if you like.'

'Not birds!' Christian said, the words finally coming out clear.

'Clay pigeons, you half-wit. I'm not wasting pheasants on this lot.'

They followed Christian out of the main house and down a path to a smaller building to the side of the lawn that stretched out in front.

'Is he your gamekeeper, Christian?' Isobel said.

'Are you fucking him, Christian?' Eliza said.

'Does he take little flowers and weave them into your pubes while calling you my lady, Christian?' Isobel said. Both girls collapsed into fits of laughter.

Sasha said nothing. They went into the museum and all laughter stopped.

'What the fuck?' Isobel.

It was a temple of death. Hundreds of stuffed animals. From tiny hummingbirds to a baby elephant standing proud in the middle of the room, surrounded by antelopes, there wasn't an inch of space left uncovered.

'Think of all the spells we could cast with these,' Eliza said.

'I don't know,' Isobel said. 'They might be a bit too dead, if you know what I mean.' She turned to Christian. 'Is there any way of getting anything a bit more recently dead? I mean, like something that's been shot? I've been looking out for dead cats on the roads round school but that would be way better.'

'Why do you want a dead cat?' Sasha said.

'It would be useful,' Isobel said. 'This whole place will be perfect for it.'

'After everyone was asleep, we sneaked down to the game larder. That's what they called the room where they put anything that they'd hunted. It needed to be hung, or something,' Sasha says. 'Anyway, Isobel wanted to see. She was practically slavering at the thought of getting her hands on something dead. Eliza was almost as bad. It was really creepy.'

'Did they say what they wanted to do with it?' the advocate depute says.

'No. Isobel and Eliza were the ones planning it all. They kept looking at each other and giggling, going off into corners and whispering. They were barely sharing anything with Christian, absolutely not with me.'

'What happened when you went down to the game room?'

'We crept in. I think we were expecting to see pheasants or something like that. Eliza wouldn't let us put the lights on. She just had the torch from her phone. It was quite scary. There were these hooks hanging from the ceiling and there were two things hanging from them. I thought they were rabbits to begin with, but as we got closer, Isobel started freaking out,' Sasha says. Her hands are cold. She remembers the light dancing on the ceiling, the shadows that the corpses cast, big as men.

'Did she say why that was?'

'She realised that the dead things were hares. The gamekeeper had shot them earlier through the head. Isobel burst into tears. She kept saying that hares were sacred, they were magic. They shouldn't be harmed. This meant that something terrible was going to happen.'

Isobel Gowdie. Isobel Gowdie. That's what Isobel had kept saying. This could be Isobel Gowdie. *I shall go into a hare.* Sasha didn't want to look stupid so she said nothing at the time but she looked it up later. One of the old Scottish witches; she'd turn herself into a hare. Her namesake. No wonder Isobel was so upset.

'What happened next?' the advocate depute says. Sasha snaps back into now.

'Isobel took one of the hares down from the hook, wrapped it in a tea towel and we went to the chapel.'

'The chapel?'

'The house was so big it had its own chapel. We went to look at it after we'd looked at the taxidermy museum.'

'What did you do there?' Mr Alexander says.

Sasha sighs. It's getting harder and harder to speak, like something has hold of her tongue, stopping it from working. She glances over at Eliza but the girl's face is blank, her hair over her eyes. Sasha shivers, turns away. 'They said we needed to desecrate it, to punish the house for the killing of the hares. This would be the only way of righting the wrong that had been done to such a symbolic creature. I wasn't sure what they meant, but they basically danced round making a mess, knocking the cushions off the chairs and scattering the flowers from a vase on the altar all over the floor. Then Isobel climbed up on to the altar and took the crucifix that was hanging on the wall above it and turned it upside down.'

'Did you take part in this?'

'No. I thought they were being silly. It was creepy, but it was ridiculous. Like they were just kids playing.'

'Was there a point when it felt more serious again?'

'Yes.'

'Tell us what happened.'

The mood had switched just like that. Isobel stripped the cloth off the altar and put it on the floor at the front of the chapel. She was carrying her black tote bag as usual, and she put it down on the ground beside the cloth, pulling out a black candle which she put on the altar and lit. The air shifted – Sasha started to feel cold seeping into her, like she'd never be warm again.

'Did she take anything else out of her bag?' the advocate depute asks.

'She took out her ritual knife. That's what she called it, though it looked like a normal kitchen knife to me. Not that she ever let me have a close look at it. She wouldn't let anyone touch it. Kept it wrapped in a black silk cloth. Anyway, she laid the hare out on the floor. Told us all to stand around it in a circle and hold hands. We had to shut our eyes and she said an incantation.'

'What did she say?'

'I don't remember exactly.' Sasha is lying. She knows exactly what Isobel said. But she can't bring herself to say the exact words. 'She called on the demons, asked them if they would present themselves. That she was going to give this dead hare to them as an offering, to make its death worthwhile, and that she would gratefully accept any message that they sent.'

'What happened next?' Mr Alexander asks.

Sasha closes her eyes for a moment. Swallows. 'She took her knife, and she cut into the hare.'

It was horrific. The smell that came out almost immediately had made her want to retch, something so strong and feral that Sasha had recoiled from it, covering her face with her hands. *Stay still*, Isobel had barked, intent on her work, as she tugged the knife down the hare's belly. Blood was spurting out, so much blood – more Shakespeare, *who would have thought the old man to have had so much blood in him?* Isobel put down the knife, bowing her head in respect, pulled the sides of the incision apart. Reached inside.

'Then she put her hand up. She was holding something. There was so much blood it was hard to see, especially as we only had the light from a phone. But she put her hand fully into the light and I could see what it was.' Sasha pauses.

'And?'

She knows the advocate depute is getting impatient. But she's choking on it, the words refusing to come out. Finally, 'It was a foetus. A baby hare. A leveret. All pink and slimy and covered in blood.'

'What did Isobel do with it?'

'She stood up, walked over to Christian and she held it right up to her face.'

'Did she say anything?' the advocate depute asks.

Sasha nods. 'Yes.' She doesn't even need to shut her eyes to see the scene play out in front of her.

'Using her words, can you tell us exactly what Isobel said?' There's an urgency to the advocate depute's voice.

Sasha nods again. 'This is what she said. I remember it exactly. Her voice was weird, all deep and powerful. She said: "The baby is dead. The hare's baby is dead. Do you know what this means, Christian? Do you? It means that you'll be next. You are going to die."'

27

Lunch. Matthew had ordered roast chicken but when the plate is put in front of him it's a leg, the bone protruding from the drumstick, the flesh dark pink as he cuts into it. Something catches in his throat and he pushes the plate away from him. No one else at the table seems to have much appetite either.

'She really believes it, doesn't she?' Aisha says. She's looking bemused. 'Kids these days . . .'

'I don't like it,' Neil says. 'I always find this stuff too creepy. Never watch films about witchcraft or anything like that.'

Russell shakes his head. 'Don't get sucked into it. They're young, they wind each other up. Social contagion, isn't it, where they all start fainting or whatever? We're all old enough to know better.'

Matthew nods. He's uncomfortable, though. The witness's sincerity is having an effect, however much he's trying to resist it. His experience at the Witches' Well keeps playing on a loop in the back of his mind. He wishes the blonde woman had been in court this morning – he'd have seen at a glance whether she was buying into it or not. Not that he should be putting so much credence in the facial expressions of a stranger, but something about her shouts ally, however fanciful that might seem.

'I'm going for a walk,' he says. 'Get some air.'

No one says that they want to join him, but as he leaves the court building, he finds that Emma has attached herself to him.

'Mind if I join you?'

Matthew looks her up and down. There's nothing in him that wants to further a connection with her. But on the other hand, he should try and be friendly. He might be missing something about her.

'I thought I might go to Greyfriars Kirk and say a little prayer,' she says. 'This is all a bit sacrilegious for me.'

He looks at her, waiting for her to crack a smile. She doesn't though.

'It's kids playing around,' he says.

Emma shakes her head. 'Someone died, Matthew. They desecrated a consecrated space. You think it's nonsense, but there's real evil at work here.'

'Well, don't let me keep you,' Matthew says, moving briskly away, any friendly intentions withered in the face of her last words. He turns left down the Royal Mile, not wanting to go anywhere near Greyfriars Kirk while Emma is in it. He's planning on getting as far as Holyrood Palace, maybe heading up round Salisbury Crags if he has time, but as it starts to rain and the cold wind bites through his jumper, he turns into a close instead, hoping for some shelter.

A group of tourists are already in there, loud in their multicoloured cagoules. Matthew fights his way through them, hoping there might be a café on the other side. He turns to find himself facing a large black sign, a bubbling cauldron with *MAGIC* emblazoned on it straight at his eye level. He's found a museum. The Museum of Witchcraft, Fortune-Telling and Magic. He blinks at the coincidence, but instead of dismissing it as more fodder for the tourists as he might normally, he goes in.

It's quiet, warm, a dog leaping up to greet him from the other side of the reception desk. He pays his entry fee and wanders through, looking at the displays of amulets and voodoo charms. There's a Ouija board on the wall and he goes over to look at it, remembering Sasha's story about it. DIE DIE DIE, that's what it had said. DIE DIE DIE CHRIST. He picks out the letters on the board, looking at the planchette with curiosity. His hand is itching to reach out and touch it, see if he can divine some actual power from it, but there's a notice saying DON'T TOUCH on the wall and he doesn't want to upset anyone, especially not someone who works here.

Over on the other side is a display case full of images of the Devil. He approaches with some caution, mindful of the experience he had looking at the Witches' Well, but reassures himself with the thought that he's not hung-over this time. He's well rested and his blood sugar is normal, even though he didn't eat lunch. Casting his eye over the pentagrams, the brass lamp in the shape of the Devil's head that used to belong to a warlock, he's relieved that none of them comes to life before him.

'Would you like to have your tarot cards read?' a man says from behind him. Thinking the question is addressed to someone else, Matthew doesn't respond, but when the man says it again, he turns.

'We have a resident tarot reader,' the man says.

Matthew hesitates. It doesn't seem wise, given his earlier experience. On the other hand, he can't help but be curious. That juror Neil had seemed so convinced by it.

'Sure,' he said. 'I don't have much time, but I'll give it a go.'

The man leads him behind a black curtain into an alcove at the back of the museum. A woman is sitting in there at a small table, a pack of tarot cards in front of her. Matthew is surprised to see that she's wearing a fleece and jeans, technical trainers on her feet.

'Did you think I'd be in shawls and hooped earrings?' the woman says. She must have seen his surprise. 'I'm not some fairground attraction, you know.'

Witch Trial

'Of course not,' Matthew says. 'Sorry. I just thought . . .'

'I'm teasing you,' she says. 'I do wear ceremonial dress on occasion. Though not today. Anyway, what is the question to which you are seeking an answer, querent?'

Straight to the point. Matthew blinks. He hasn't got that far. But all the same, words leap unbidden to his tongue.

'Will I be happy again?'

The woman starts shuffling the cards. Matthew leans back on his chair, trying to catch his breath. He doesn't know where this has come from. He is happy, perfectly happy, thank you very much. OK, his relationship with Rosalind might be going through a bit of a bad patch, Daisy might not have spoken to him for the last few days, but all this is perfectly normal. Families go through ups and downs, everyone knows that.

'I heard you say that you're short of time,' she says. 'So I'll make this fast. But I want to do a seven-card horseshoe spread. I don't feel that a three-card spread is going to be quite enough for you, sensing your energy.'

Matthew opens his mouth to argue, closes it again. He's the one who came up with the happy question, after all. He watches her shuffle the pack, dextrous as any card shark, trying to maintain the level of scepticism he knows he should keep in mind. But the space is warm, her face comforting – the temptation to sink into the embrace of it and accept whatever fate is handed to him is almost overwhelming.

'Hold your question in your mind and draw your cards. Place them down on the table where I point,' she says, holding the pack spread out in front of her like a fan.

Matthew does as he is told, drawing seven cards and putting them face down one after the other in the shape of a horseshoe. He doesn't linger over the choices that he makes, but he's struck by the pull that he feels towards the cards that he draws out of the pack. There must be more of his hangover lingering from the day before than he realised, his defences still lower than he would like.

'Let's begin,' she says. She turns over the first card, her expression sombre. 'This card represents the past, events that are impacting your current situation. It's the Five of Pentacles. This points to a time of financial strife, indicating that you've suffered a significant financial loss or failure.'

Matthew swallows. He doesn't accept it's true, but it's unpleasant nonetheless. His palms are itching, sweat prickling under his arms.

'I'm not saying this is definitely the case, but often what has caused these financial problems is to do with your emotions – greed can lead to loss, or anxiety to error.'

'I'm not greedy ...' he says, though the words die on his tongue. What's Olivia, if not greed?

She ignores him, turns over the next card. 'This card represents the present, the current events which are circling you. It's the Hermit card, but it's reversed. What this means is enforced isolation. Your refusal to listen to others may result in withdrawal from others in anger or resentment.'

The pile of microwave meals, sleeping alone in his bachelor bed.

'This card shows someone who over-analyses with a tendency to intellectualise rather than allowing feelings to surface.'

She wants feelings? Matthew can give her feelings all right. Any minute now he'll sweep the cards on to the floor, that's what he feels about this. A load of old shit. She's clutching at straws.

The woman pauses, takes a breath before turning over the next card.

A lifetime passes in a second. Dead meat in the air, rot. Flames dancing round amber eyes. Matthew knows the image she's now revealed. Only too well.

Witch Trial

'You think you know what this represents,' she says. 'But don't assume the worst. This card shows the hidden influences on you. The unseen. Obviously you recognise the image – the Devil. It doesn't mean that you're going to hell, though, or that you've done something evil. What it does mean is that there's some kind of negativity in your life. Perhaps you're snared in an addiction.'

The stench of whisky, the fists banging on the locked front door.

'I'm not addicted, there's no way I'm addicted. Not an alcoholic. Very high functioning,' he says, garbling his words.

'Of course you are,' the tarot reader says. Her voice is neutral but it feels like she's hiding a laugh. Like she knows something about him, has heard a rumour. He stares at her, his eyes narrowed. She smiles.

'Or maybe you're being self-destructive in another way. It's all open to interpretation. You're the only one who can fully know the truth of this. But this card should serve as a warning for you to assess your own life and make changes.'

He bows his head. There's nothing wrong with his life. Nothing at all. It's all totally under control. Matthew doesn't need to argue with her about it, though. He's got nothing to prove. Not to this freak with her shitty card set and her playground warnings.

Heedless of the turmoil in his head, the tarot reader continues, relentless. 'And this, the fourth card. This represents you, the querent. The questioner. It's the Eight of Swords.' She holds it out to him and he looks at the image, horror building inside him. A figure stands blindfolded, surrounded by a cage of swords. 'I'm not going to lie to you, this is not a positive image.'

Matthew wants to laugh. Everything inside him is resisting this bullshit. But it's a sob that comes out.

'Bluntly, you're in a terrible situation. The blindfold indicates a high level of denial. You're refusing even to acknowledge that you're in deep shit, let alone deal with it. I'm sorry to be so harsh, but I can only tell you what the cards tell me. It's up to you to find the meaning as it personally relates.'

He'd speak, but he can't.

'Now the fifth card, showing the influence of others. It's the Star, but it's reversed. A creative or emotional block is arising as a partnership loses its way. You need direction, but you also need to beware those who cultivate you for their own purposes. You may need to step out of an illusion and search for your star elsewhere.'

Rosalind? Dominic? Should he be more careful? Trust them less? Relations aren't great right now, but that's while he's doing the trial. Normally it's all fine. He sits on his hands, trying to get his breathing under control. His anger, too. This shouldn't be having such an effect on him – he needs to catch a grip.

'The sixth. What should you do? Aha, something slightly more positive for you. The Seven of Wands. Perseverance. The message is that your goals are worth pursuing. You may not have an easy path to follow, but with perseverance you can get to where you need to be. Keep believing. There is a great chance that you will succeed.'

The tightness in Matthew's chest subsides. A little. A crack of light in the dark of this spread. He watches with trepidation as she turns over the final card. Her face darkens, her eyebrows contracting.

'This card represents the final outcome, factoring in all of the previous six cards into its answer. Your question at the beginning was will you be happy again. Looking at this, I have to say that I can't give you a very positive answer, at least not in the short term.' She holds it out to him to show him the image, a figure sitting up in bed, head in hands, swords hung horizontally on the wall beside him.

More bloody swords.

'This is the Nine of Swords. Despair, confusion, even insanity are imminent. Grief, loss, tragedy, break-ups, job loss or even death.'

It's a litany of woe.

'But like the Devil, it can be seen as a warning sign, a wake-up call. The nine with its dark image suggests that your mind is out of control, that you're creating your own nightmare. You think you know what you're doing, but you're wrong. The universe is telling you to wake up.'

Matthew sits silent, stunned. It's like the woman hates him, as if she's set him deliberately to fail a test he didn't even ask to sit.

'Are you done?' the man asks from behind the curtain, and the woman looks up.

'Just about,' she calls. She looks back at Matthew. Her expression is not unkind, though Matthew can sense that she's putting some distance between them.

'I understand that must have been hard to hear,' she says. 'It's not a combination of cards I would choose to draw for myself. But you must see it as an opportunity. You need to go away and think about all of this, work out the changes that you should make in your life. Nothing is set in stone.'

28

'Are you all right?'

Matthew looks up, confused. He's stumbled out of the museum and made his way back up to the High Court, not even checking the time. He could be late, for all he knows. All he cares, either.

'You look a bit out of it.'

Now Matthew focuses on who is speaking to him. It's the blonde woman, standing behind him in the queue for security. He opens his mouth to reply. Closes it. Opens it again.

'Yes, sorry. In a bit of a daze.'

'Has something happened?' The woman's voice is warm. She sounds genuinely concerned.

'I'm fine. I just had a bit of a shock about something, that's all. Nothing serious.' As he says it, he wants to believe it. The further he's got from the museum the more sense has imposed itself on him, the reminder that this is not true. A random selection of cards is all. However bleak their premise.

'I'm glad you're OK,' she says. They move forward in the queue. A quick empty of his pockets and Matthew is through, looking behind him. He wants to keep talking to her. He can smell that floral scent of hers again and it's lessening the dread by the second, an incense to banish dark spirits.

She's through fast enough and they walk together up the stairs.

'It's quite the case, isn't it?' she says. 'Don't think I've ever heard anything like this in a courtroom before.'

'Do you come to court often?' Matthew says before stopping, scarlet. Such a hammy line . . . Fortunately she just laughs, rolls her eyes at him.

'Not for a long time,' she says. 'But this one looked interesting. I thought I could use it for something. It's all good research.'

At that moment the jury officer comes through the door next to the courtroom. When he sees Matthew he gestures at him, his movements brisk.

'We thought we'd lost you,' the man says. 'It's time.'

Matthew turns to say goodbye, but the blonde has vanished, probably gone into court herself. He follows the jury officer meekly, less shaky than he was when he got back to the main door. The encounter may have been brief, but it's restored him, a little. It's good to know she'll be there in court this afternoon, too.

Sasha's back in the witness box. She's looking tired, her face drawn. It's clear that telling this strange story is taking it out of her. Her head turns this way and that, as if she's looking for an escape. The relief Matthew felt has gone, a feeling of dread heavy on him, in his gut.

She continues her account. The girls were kicked off the estate the day after their escapade in the chapel. All hell had broken loose on the discovery of the desecrated space, the blood and guts all over the floor. Christian had tried to hold it together, telling her dad it was harmless, that things had just got a bit out of control. He wasn't buying it though, furious at the destruction of his property. Besides, Christian couldn't fully hide the effect that the situation had had on her. There was a point in the early morning that Sasha overheard her speaking to Isobel, begging her to say everything was all right, that the discovery of the hare foetus could have another meaning than that Christian was going to die.

Isobel had refused.

The school had got involved on their return in disgrace, putting them in two weeks of detention and moving the dormitories round so that the girls weren't in the same room any more. That had been the end of the night-time escapades, at least for a while. But it hadn't stopped the supernatural activity. Every now and again, Sasha saw Isobel or Eliza go up to Christian and tell her that they'd had another dream, or that they had done a tarot reading, and that it was still looking as if she was going to die sometime soon. They always said how sorry they were, but Sasha didn't think they seemed particularly sad to be passing on the bad news.

The Christmas holidays had provided a welcome escape. Sasha didn't talk to any of them, even though Isobel messaged her a couple of times. She just wanted a break from it. It was all a bit too real, still. But she was getting bored, so when she got back in January, she wasn't unhappy that it all kicked off again. The dormitories had been rearranged over the holidays and the four girls were back together again (albeit under strict instructions to behave themselves). The Ouija board had thus come back out, and the tarot cards, though the messages from the spirit world were pretty harmless for the first part of the year.

'Did the messages become more harmful at any point?' Mr Alexander asks. Matthew sits up. He's been drifting off a bit through the last part of the evidence, nothing dramatic to catch his attention.

'Yes,' Sasha says. 'It was the Ouija board again. It went off one night saying *DIEDIEDIE* again. Then it went a bit further. I really thought we weren't going to get anywhere that night. But suddenly the words appeared.' A deep breath. Her chin up. 'It said *HELPHERDIE*. It was in the middle of a muddle of letters. Isobel took this really seriously. She said we had to obey the spirits if they were telling us to help Christian. She did a lot of tarot readings on her own, carried out some divinations. I don't know exactly what as she was very private about it. She only talked to Eliza. But I thought she was trying to find out what would be best to do. Finally she said we needed to do a funeral.'

Mr Alexander makes a noise of surprise. 'A funeral? But no one was dead?'

'Yes, that's right. The idea was that it would help Christian come to terms with what was going to happen to her, Isobel said. We needed to help her cross over to the other side.'

'Did you get the impression that Isobel genuinely wanted to help Christian?'

A long pause. Sasha's face is lost in thought. 'At the time, I thought she did. She wasn't being nasty. She wasn't being nice, either. She was just acting on the instructions that were given by the spirits, she said. She believed it all implicitly, I'm sure of it. And Eliza believed everything Isobel said.'

'Given everything that's happened, do you still think she was trying to help?'

A long, blank stare at the prosecutor. Sasha glances at the accused girls, turning her head quickly towards them, back again. There's a light shimmering across her, ripples in the air around her, seeping into her face.

Matthew blinks. It's still there, Sasha's face is rippling now, too, the edges of her features blurred, melting into each other. The dread that suffused him at the tarot reading is back, a cold presence that demands his attention.

'I don't know,' Sasha says. 'I just don't know. But I do know that it was very unkind.'

29

Sasha's back is hurting. She's given evidence all morning standing up, refusing the offer of a chair when she arrived, but now she's regretting it. Even though the injuries of last year are so much better now, it still takes its toll if she stands for too long. On top of which, her knees are beginning to shake. It's not a psychic attack – she's got the protection she needs with her, after all – but the brutality of the story that she's telling is starting to wear her out.

She knows what the prosecutor is doing. He's building the case against Isobel and Eliza. Victim Support told her exactly what was going to happen. But she wishes he would look at her with slightly less irritation when she answers his questions. She can't help that the weapons that the girls used were supernatural. They were weapons all the same.

Other than her mum, no one else in the courtroom looks friendly. One of the jurors is even holding a wooden cross in her hands, as if she's brought it in specially for protection. Though Sasha can't really talk, with the bouquet of rosemary and garlic that she's carried with her today. On the upside, at least the woman can't be a sceptic. That's one person taking what Sasha says seriously.

'Tell us about this funeral,' Mr Alexander says. His mouth twists as he says the word. Sasha can see the same expression repeated around the room. Disbelieving, unimpressed. Other than the woman with the cross, who looks angry. Then Sasha catches sight of one of the jurors sitting behind her, a man who looks like he must be in his fifties. He's very pale, looks the way Sasha's mum looked the day that they had to go in and speak to the headmistress after Christian died. Sasha was really worried about her, she looked so ill. This man doesn't look much better.

'The funeral?' Mr Alexander says, a note of impatience leaking into his voice. Sasha turns round, gives him her full attention.

'It was Isobel's idea. But Eliza planned it . . .' she begins.

It took place on 20th March. This coincided with the spring equinox, Eliza told them. Or as the pagans had it, Ostara.

'Why?' Sasha was clueless.

'It's the day when light and dark are equally balanced. As spring takes hold it means there's going to be lots of energy in the soil when we do the burial. It'll be even more powerful.'

'What needs to be powerful?' Christian asked. No one replied.

That was part of the plan. Christian was a dead girl walking, and dead girls don't speak. Isobel and Eliza told Sasha first thing in the morning that she was to pretend that Christian didn't exist.

'We can't stop her from tagging along,' Isobel had said. 'But we need to make sure it's clear that she's dead to us. Otherwise it won't have as much power.'

'Isn't that nasty?' Sasha had said, but Eliza laughed at her.

'It's neither nasty nor nice. It's how it has to be.'

'We'll wait until lights out. But I've got everything we need,' Isobel said. 'I found it on the road yesterday, sneaked it into the fridge wrapped up in a plastic bag.'

'Found what?' Christian said. But it was only when Sasha asked the same question that they replied.

'You'll find out soon enough.'

'And did you find out?' Mr Alexander asks.

'Yes,' Sasha says. A shooting pain comes up her right leg – sciatica. She's had issues with it ever since the injuries, a permanent reminder of everything that happened. She turns to the judge. 'I'm sorry, but is it all right if I sit down? I'm in quite a lot of pain.' The judge nods. Isobel smirks, or at least it looks that way to Sasha. She's not going to react though.

Once she's sitting down, Sasha gets her breath back. This part is going to be hard enough to tell the court without being in agony as well.

'What did you find out?'

'It . . . well, I'll get to that. We spent the rest of the day ignoring Christian, even though she was getting distressed. She really hated being ignored – it upset her more than anything anyone could say to her. She kept trying to get me to talk to her, and I wanted to, but Eliza said it would break the magic. She said we had to behave as if Christian was already dead. I went along with it, even though it was hard. When it got to bedtime, we were all in the dormitory again, and once everyone else seemed to be asleep, around half past eleven, that's when we sneaked out to go back to the allotment.'

'They hadn't stopped the way?'

'No one knew about it,' Sasha says. 'Not then, at least. They only found out about it after Christian died.' She swallows. If only they had . . . 'Anyway, we slipped out. I could see that Isobel's bag was full. It looked heavy and it was bulging. When we got to the shed we were relieved that it was still looking deserted, so we let ourselves in and then Isobel spread everything out.'

Witch Trial

Isobel and Eliza are both staring at Sasha intently now. So is every member of the jury. The woman with the cross is leaning as far forward as she can in her seat. She might be holding a Christian symbol, but Sasha doesn't like her expression. She's almost licking her lips waiting for the next instalment.

'What was in her bag?'

Sasha starts to list the objects. A Kim's Game she'll never forget. The shoebox, the black ribbon. The black string. A big printout of a photograph of Christian (the girl had cried out at that, though no one reacted. Dead girls don't cry . . .). A birthday card that Christian had sent to Sasha (Isobel didn't ask before she took it but Sasha was too on edge to argue).

'There was something else, though. Deep in the bottom of her bag. It was wrapped in a black cloth. When she took it out and unwrapped it, the smell hit us all. Rot. Decay.' Sasha can taste it in her mouth still.

'What was it?'

Sasha shakes her head. She really doesn't want to say. But she doesn't have any choice.

'Go on.'

'It was a dead cat. Isobel said she'd found it on the road the day before when she was out for a walk. It must have been hit by a car. She'd picked it up and put it in her bag.'

Mr Alexander nods. 'What happened next?'

'Isobel cast a circle . . .'

She keeps talking, reducing the experience to the barest of words. But it's impossible to recreate the horror of the scene, the bleak expression on Christian's face as it gradually dawned on her what was happening. The smell from the dead cat was spreading through everything, the candles were guttering, giving off foul black smoke, almost as if they'd been dipped in something toxic, too, or made from rancid animal fat.

Christian was crying and Sasha's eyes were watering so much

from the smoke it was as if she were crying, too. But Isobel and Eliza had risen above it all, their faces pale ovals in the semi-darkness of the room. Isobel had called upon Hecate, her voice deep and guttural, asking the witch mother to guide Christian to the other side.

'Do you know what she meant by that?'

Sasha nods. 'Yes. Christian was dying, that's what the spirits had told Isobel. She had to convey that message to Christian, so that her spirit could be free. The point of the ceremony was to show Christian's spirit that it was time to let go of life, stop fighting her fate.'

'What happened next?'

Another deep swallow. Sasha's mouth is dry. 'We took the dead cat and we wrapped it in Christian's photograph. She was crying but we ignored her. I helped. It wasn't just Isobel and Eliza. All three of us did it. When we'd finished, we put it into the box, and we put the birthday card alongside the dead cat.'

Isobel had started chanting, her voice still deep. *This vessel is the body of our dear departed friend Christian. Ashes to ashes, dust to dust.*

'We tied it up with the black ribbon, the black string. Then we went out into the allotment and we dug a hole. There were some tools in the shed – a spade, a trowel. I had to use my hands, though, as there weren't enough. It had to be deep, we needed to make sure that no fox would dig it up. But finally it was deep enough.'

'What did you do with the box?'

'We put it in the hole, and we covered it with earth. Then we stamped it down.'

'How was Christian reacting at this stage?'

'She'd stopped crying. It's like she'd turned into stone. She'd stopped trying to talk to us, anything. She just stood and watched, her face paler than I've ever seen it. Once we'd finished burying the box, she said only one thing. "But I'm not dead." Her voice was so quiet I could barely make out the words.'

Mr Alexander goes through the documents in front of him. Then he holds up a photograph.

'Is this a photograph of the box and its contents?'

At the sight of the birthday card, the pitiful remains of the cat still wrapped in its cloth, something breaks inside Sasha, the self-control that's kept her talking for what feels like the whole day. She puts her head down, and she cries. For the cat, for herself.

For Christian. She can still hear her now. *Please talk to me. Stop ignoring me. I'm not dead.*

Sasha could have turned to her then. She could have put her arms round her, brought her in from the cold.

Instead, she turned away.

30

'Let's move on to the events that preceded Christian's death,' Mr Alexander says. 'After this funeral scenario, did you and the other girls start to acknowledge Christian's presence again?'

Sasha nods. 'I was the first, the others eventually followed. But Isobel and Eliza weren't happy with me. Isobel seemed particularly stressed about it – she said that there was dark magic at play and that I must stand back, let it play out. Otherwise, I might get hurt. Eliza kept saying it wasn't their fault; the situation was beyond their control. They kept trying to remind me that dead girls don't speak. I thought it was a bit shit, though. Sorry . . . I mean, a bit rubbish. Christian wasn't dead yet, and it didn't seem very kind.'

The advocate depute nods. 'Right. I'm going to take you now up to the end of April last year,' he says. 'Tell us what happened at the beginning of term.'

Sasha remembers it only too well. The Easter holiday had been the most welcome break she'd ever had. Her mum had taken a week off work, and they'd hung out together at home in the Borders, baking and watching bad TV together. The biopsy on the lump had come back normal and the cancer scare was over – that made it all worthwhile, all the time Sasha had spent with the girls doing those things that she hated doing. She'd made that sacrifice to protect her mum, and maybe her mum sensed it because she made a real effort to spend the holiday with Sasha, too – it wasn't her mum's fault that she had to travel so much for her job – Sasha appreciated everything that it brought. It had been Sasha's idea to go to boarding school in the first place, obsessed as she was with boarding school stories like the Chalet School series and Malory Towers and the Kingscote books by Antonia Forest which had belonged to her mum.

She'd spent that holiday tucked up in bed reading those books when she wasn't spending time with her mum. She wanted to go back to an easier time, more innocent, when she still believed that it would be the experience of her life, not an experience that she would do anything to avoid. There were so many times that she could have said to her mum that she'd changed her mind, she'd rather go to the school down the road. But then her mum told her about the promotion she'd been given, the conferences in New York and Dubai that she was leading – it was obvious that she was thriving in the time that she now had to herself with Sasha away from home. Sasha would have to deal with it.

Going back to school was hard. She'd kissed her mum goodbye, jumped out of the car and walked into the grounds without looking back. Her biggest hope was that Christian might have decided to leave. Without her, Sasha had a fantasy that they would all be happy again. Isobel would stop all this witch stuff, Eliza would stop going on about death, and they could be normal teenagers again.

The first person she saw was Eliza, accompanied as ever by Isobel.

'They told me that they'd been talking a lot over the holidays, making plans. Their instructions from the spirits were clear – they knew what they needed to do.'

'What did you understand this to mean?'

'That they'd kept doing tarot readings. Ouija boards too. I

knew they'd done a lot of reading, as well, so they knew about other rituals, though they didn't tell me about them.'

'Did one or other of them seem to be more enthusiastic about this?' the advocate depute asks.

'Eliza was excited. I could sense the energy coming off her. Isobel was quieter about it, more resolute. A messenger, though. Passing on instructions to do something. They didn't tell me what. They were still whispering in corners. They'd shut up whenever they saw me come near.'

'How were you all behaving towards Christian?'

'I was being normal. We had a lot of the same classes and we spent free periods together.'

'And the others? How did they behave towards her when you were in sight?'

'They were better. Not quite as friendly, but not so weird. I can't be sure, but I think that she was trying to stick with me as much as she could – it seemed like she didn't want to be left on her own with them.'

'Was there a point when it became less friendly?'

Sasha nods. She glances over at the dock. Both girls are staring at her. She puts her fingers to the protective talisman in her pocket, bringing her hand to her nose to catch a whiff of rosemary, a reminder of a life beyond. 'Yes. It came to a head at the end of April. Eliza came and found Christian and me in the library. She told us that we were going to have a ceremony for Beltane.'

'Beltane?'

'A witchy word for May Day. The first day of May. Another important date. They'd had messages, she said, and now it was time. I thought she was looking at Christian in a funny way, calculating, but that was all she said.'

She stops, takes a drink of water.

'They wouldn't tell us what they had planned,' she continues.

'They told me to get out of the dormitory at one point and even though I tried to argue, they weren't having it. I had to go away for an hour. So I went for a walk round the grounds. I ran into Ms Waites but she wasn't very friendly. No one else was around, there was no one to talk to. In the end I went back to the library and read for a bit longer. Then it was time, I was allowed back in.'

'Did they tell you then what they had planned?'

'All they said was that we would be getting up at four. Then the lights were off.'

It was dark when Isobel shook Sasha awake, dark as they crept out of school and over the road to the allotments, only a glimmer of dawn in the sky. No part of Sasha wanted to be there – she felt sick to her stomach, cold dread permeating through everything. She jumped at every shadow, certain that this would be when they would be caught, expelled. Or worse. Christian walked slowly beside her, the girl's footsteps even more reluctant than Sasha's, or at least that's how it sounded.

When they arrived at the allotment Isobel led the way into the shed, lighting five candles in jars that were already placed at the points of a pentagram that was drawn on the floor with chalk. She must have been here earlier in the night to set it all up.

'That wasn't the issue though,' Sasha says. 'There was something in the corner of the shed. Isobel's black bag. But there was something wrong with it. Something horrible.'

She can still see it now, the way that the bag writhed and twisted. It had taken on a life of its own.

Or it held something that was alive.

Isobel and Eliza were both wearing black gowns. Sasha hadn't seen these before, and as the girls drew the hoods up over their heads, casting their faces into shadow, she felt even more disturbed. There was a ghostly quality to the set-up, other-worldly. She felt very close to the edge right now, as if she were about to cross over into a place unknown.

Somehow, she can't put that into words. Again, she's trapped by the limitations of language, the difficulty in trying to communicate exactly how horrific it was, to see the bag move and the inexorable quality to Isobel and Eliza's actions, as if they were carrying out a ceremony ordained by an ancient power.

'Eliza picked up the bag and handed it to Isobel. She reached inside. Isobel was being very careful, cautious, and when she brought her hand out I saw why. It had a pigeon in it, a big one, but with an injured wing. It was trying to struggle, but it had clearly lost a lot of strength as she was able to hold it with only one hand.'

'Did you say anything when you saw this?' Mr Alexander says.

'"What the fuck?" That's what I said. I thought I was going to be sick. At least the cat had been dead. But this . . . this was a step further again.'

'What did Isobel do next?'

'She put the pigeon down in the centre of the pentagram, holding it in place. Then she started to chant. Eliza joined in. I don't know what they were saying, exactly – they were calling on various demons by name, bringing in the elements. They must have learnt it while they were together during the Easter holidays. I certainly didn't understand it.'

It should have sounded ridiculous.

It didn't.

'She looked straight at Christian. "The cards have spoken," she said, "the spirits too. You have tarried too long." Then she began to chant. "This bird is the physical representation of our sister Christian. We are going to ease her over to the other side."' Sasha stops. She's fallen into a chant as well, the words sing-song in the court. Everyone is looking at her, she knows it, and her cheeks flush red.

'What did she do next?'

'She took up her knife – it had been in the bag as well. Then she turned the pigeon on to its back and stabbed it through the breast, over and over again.'

'Was she saying anything as she did this?'

The court is completely silent. Sasha can hear the beats of her own heart, pounding in her chest.

'She was screaming. "DIE CHRISTIAN DIE. DIE CHRISTIAN DIE."' A pause. Once more. '"DIE CHRISTIAN DIE."'

'What did Christian do?' The advocate depute is speaking very quietly, every word very clearly spoken, shards of glass.

'She started to sob.'

'What happened next?'

The words are stuck in Sasha's throat. She can't swallow, she can't speak. How to describe it, the horror she felt. Her reaction, so childish – to curl up on the floor, her head in her hands, her eyes tight shut.

Movements around her, a clang of metal on metal, a scream from Christian. Sasha on the ground for a moment, head clutched in hands, but compelled by a force greater than fear, she sat up slowly, opened her eyes, transfixed as she watched Eliza and Isobel advance on Christian, take hold of her, the girl's scream a terrible sound but even worse the screech that came from the two witches. *NOW IT'S YOUR TURN*, the words that still echo in Sasha's head.

'Now it's your turn? You're certain it's what they said?'

Sasha nods.

'And you're certain it was both of them screaming together?'

Sasha nods again.

'I'm certain of it.'

'What happened after that?'

She shut her eyes again, huddled back down. Christian was struggling against the hold of Eliza and Isobel – Sasha could hear the heaviness of the girls' breathing, the grunts and muffled curses. Finally a yell – Christian – followed by shouts from Eliza and Isobel, wordless sounds full of rage. Footsteps, a shout, another clang of metal. The slam of the door. Sasha was paralysed momentarily, pinned to the spot as if by Isobel's knife. Then her strength came back and she got up off the floor to find herself alone, the knife beside her on the floor.

Terrified, Sasha made her way back to the dorm. She didn't look over her shoulder, eyes down as she ran as fast as she could. Isobel and Eliza might turn on her at any moment, that was her selfish fear. She hoped beyond hope that she'd get back to find Christian safe in her bed, all wrapped up. All the beds were empty though. She heard Isobel and Eliza come back in a few minutes later, but she pretended to be asleep and the girls ignored her, whispering furiously between themselves, so quietly she couldn't make out the words.

Christian did not make it back.

Sasha looks out at the courtroom now. 'I never saw her alive again.'

Mr Alexander clears his throat. 'Obviously you can't know exactly what happened while you had your eyes shut, but from what you could hear, what do you think that Eliza and Isobel were doing?'

Sasha stops, thinks back. 'It's hard to separate out all the different noises. Obviously I was scared, as well as tired, disorientated. I think that they went at Christian with the knife, pinned her down, that there was a struggle during which the knife was dropped, and that Christian managed to get out of the shed and run away, them hot at her heels, before it all got too much for her heart.'

'Thank you,' Mr Alexander says. 'Just one more question

from me for this evening. Do you have any idea who was actually holding the knife?'

She contemplates the question, searching through the memory of the incident to see if there's any detail she might have missed, no matter how many times she's gone through it already. There's nothing, though. No new moment of eureka. 'I don't know. Isobel was holding it before. She was the one who stabbed the pigeon. But it was on the floor nearer to where Eliza was standing in the struggle with Christian. It could have been held by either of them.'

As Sasha speaks, she looks directly at Isobel and Eliza. Now that the story is out there, they've lost some of their power. Though as she catches Isobel's gaze, feels it tear through all her defences, reaching for any weak spots it can find, she knows that the grip they hold on her is still strong.

Not strong enough to stop her from telling the truth about them, though.

31

Matthew can't get out of court fast enough. Only the third day and he's done, his head ready to explode with it. The fear on Sasha's face as she talked about the last incident in the shed was infectious – he's shaky, unsettled, a feeling of unease that persists even when he gets outside. It's the most important piece of evidence they've been given so far – an actual act that could be seen as causing the death. Knife-wielding, shouted threats. At last Matthew starts to understand why they're all there. He wants it to be spelt out more clearly, though, the prosecution case to be laid out in bullet points in front of him.

He remembers how pleased he was to discover there wouldn't be an opening speech, only the reading of the indictment before the evidence started – he could punch himself for his naivety. They're all still groping in the dark to find out exactly what it is that the prosecution say these girls have done, how they murdered Christian, but at least there's a bit more information available now.

The rest of the jury were all buzzing with it. For the first time someone raised the idea of going for a drink, although ever-sensible Roderick kicked that into touch. Not appropriate at the moment, he'd said. Matthew thought he was being a bit prissy but didn't argue. There's only one person he wants to discuss the case with at the moment.

He wants to talk to the blonde. He wants a name for her,

for her to explain exactly why she's there, taking such copious notes, intent on the evidence as it unfolds in front of them. She'll have insights that will help, a sounding board for his concerns. He hovers across the road from the court entrance, hoping to spot her on her way out, but she's obviously got out before him. She's never there when he wants her. Does she even exist?

At those words, he blinks. The question hadn't even occurred to him before. But maybe he's so desperate for a friend in this alien place that he's conjured her out of thin air. She seems to come and go as the wind.

Feeling strangely bereft, he wanders down the Mound and makes his way home.

He should clean up – mundane household jobs usually calm his nerves. He makes a start, but he's too restless to finish anything off. He's got to let the evidence they've heard today sink in, process itself through him. It's frustrating to be so docile, such a passive recipient of information, but that's the nature of the job. Matthew needs to trust the process. The wheels of justice are turning. His time for action will come. He folds up some clean shirts and switches on the television.

At least life without his mobile phone is peaceful. He hasn't switched it back on since his drunken night out. There's nothing anyone has to say to him that's of any interest. Dominic might be begging for his help, Rosalind for his company, Daisy for . . . well, money, at least, if nothing else. Olivia, too. Though he might get in touch with her over the weekend. But not before. It's like being young again, free, when he was accountable to no one, at the end of no one's chain. All he needs is a wristwatch and an alarm clock.

Besides, he doesn't risk turning his phone on for more sinister reasons. He knows how much interest there is in the trial – every billboard for the *Edinburgh Evening News* is already emblazoned with the news about the *PIGEON SACRIFICED IN WITCH TRIAL*. It's even made the *Daily Mail*, though he has been strongminded and resisted the temptation to read what's being said about the case, true to his juror's oath. It wouldn't surprise him if someone has managed to intercept his messages and his calls, so they can see what the jurors might be thinking. He wouldn't put anything past journalists with a story this big.

He'd almost said that to the other jurors at the end of the day, while they were collecting their coats and bags from the jury room. Jasmine was updating her Instagram as usual and Matthew was about to tell her to be careful when he bit his lip. Not for him to interfere. He can only take care of his own security. He's not responsible for anyone else's.

At least he's not at home. No one has tracked him down here – they won't be able to bug the flat or anything. Unless of course someone has followed him home . . . At this point he checks himself. He's got to stop getting carried away. Hard not to when dealing with a situation like this, but that's all the more reason for him to keep his cool. He's trained to withstand extreme pressure, moments when hearts stop beating in the operating theatre – it's about time he started applying that training to this trial, too.

And there's another reason to keep offline. Less extreme, but still important. Despite the temptation to conduct his own research into the case, Matthew understands how strict the rules are for jurors. Even though he knows he's sensible, that it wouldn't do him any harm, it's best not. Not while they're still finding out the evidence, at least. He wants to be a blank slate for the prosecution case, let Mr Alexander tell the story to him in his own way without trying to edit the process.

How then to square this with his desire to talk to the blonde woman? Matthew knows there's an inconsistency there. It's different, though. She's sat through the case; she knows the rules. And let's be honest, what he really wants from her is not a detailed discussion of the fine details of the evidence. It's something very different. Unloved by Rosalind, bored by Olivia, there's a vacancy in Matthew's life that's the perfect fit for the blonde.

He flicks through the TV channels. There's a Hitchcock film on Channel 4 – *Vertigo*. Not one he's seen before, though that could be said of many films, to be fair. The life of a medic doesn't leave much room for culture. He's going to take as much as he can get over the next few days, leaning back on the sofa to enjoy Kim Novak at her finest.

He wakes with a jolt many hours later, having fallen asleep sometime after Scottie sees the woman fall to her death from the bell tower. He hadn't quite finished his lasagne, pushing it to one side on the cushion next to him, and he's managed to slump over it, sticking his elbow right in it. He pulls off his jumper, swearing at the mess on the sleeve, before crawling into bed without undressing further or cleaning his teeth.

Sleep comes easy but he's restless, tossing and turning through the night, falling through clouds and waking with a jolt just before he hits iron spikes below. He doesn't wake enough to get up, though, trapped in the gap between dreams and reality.

Before dawn, he lies in bed, eyes suddenly wide open. The blonde woman is in the room, walking around, her back turned. He sits up to greet her, relief flooding him that at last he's found her, tracked her down. He calls out – 'You, hey you, you there with the blond hair!' – and she turns, smiles. Comes close.

That's when he sees her eyes. Amber, flame-ringed. Pupils in the shape of rectangles.

The Devil's eyes.

He screams. She comes closer and closer, the scent of roses around her, until her eyes are right at his and he can smell her breath now too and it's the same as before, rotting flesh. Shit. Matthew rolls over, hiding his head in the pillow. If he can't see her, she can't see him. He's invisible now, he's safe – at last his breath returns to normal.

He's woken an hour later by the alarm, sweat dripping off him, his neck stiff from the angle at which he's slept. The blonde woman is not in the room.

But he could swear that she was, a trace of shit and roses still lingering in the air.

THURSDAY

32

He's shaved, showered, but still looks a mess. Matthew glowers at himself in the bathroom mirror. There's something off about his appearance, his face not fully his own. Even though he's done everything he needs to scrub up, there's still a dissolute air to the reflection, the look of a man who's been living life on the lash. It's not fair. He hasn't drunk any alcohol since the first night of the trial, and he's slept long enough surely that these bags under his eyes should have diminished. He smiles at himself, but the man in the mirror does not smile back.

This case is getting to him. That's the truth of it. If only it had been a straightforward murder, some gangland shooting over a drugs deal gone wrong. Not this weird shit that's taking him places he doesn't want to go. Still, this girl's evidence should be finished soon. At least they'll get back to sensible witnesses soon, not ones who believe that this nonsense is real.

A brisk walk up to court, a double espresso from a café on George IV Bridge and he's himself again, cobwebs blown away. No more shadows lurking in the corners of his mind. He greets the other jurors as they file into the jury room, most of them wearing the same expression of resignation that he feels. They need to get through this, however exhausting.

Sasha is back in the witness box. How much more evidence can she have? Poor Christian is dead now. There'll be cross-examination, though. Not that Isobel's advocate will take up much of their time.

'You told us last night that Christian ran out, and that you returned to school. Can you take us through that again, please?' Mr Alexander says. He's straight back to it.

'I ran out almost immediately – it had gone too far this time. I couldn't cope with it – I was really scared. I went straight back into school and went back to bed, though I couldn't sleep.'

'Did Isobel and Eliza return to the dormitory as well?'

'Yes, about half an hour later. I didn't speak to them, though. We didn't speak about any of it again until after the school had told us.'

'The school told you what?'

'We all went to lessons as usual. I saw that Christian didn't make it to registration, but I thought she might be hiding in the library or something. I knew I should find her and check that she was OK, but I was still trying to get myself together as well. After registration I had double English – still no Christian – and at lunchtime they called us all into the hall.' She pauses for a moment – she's clearly finding it difficult. 'They brought in all of our year. The headmistress was there and she told us that Christian had been found dead, and that while they didn't know if there were any suspicious circumstances, the police were looking into it. Anyone who knew anything could come and talk to her, day or night.'

'What was the reaction to that announcement?'

'What you'd think.' A note of scorn creeps into Sasha's voice. 'Gasps, cries of shock. Lots of hysterics. Three girls from the netball team had panic attacks – there was lots of hyperventilating. Audrey from Year Eleven started screaming and wailing, saying that she was scared. None of them were friends with Christian when she was alive – Audrey always looked down her nose at her. It was such bullshit. They were all being attention seekers.'

Witch Trial

'How did you feel?'

Sasha shakes her head once, twice. Opens her mouth, closes it again.

'I felt like I wanted to die.'

After this Sasha's voice becomes very quiet. The judge has to ask her to speak up at least twice while she rattles through the next tranche of evidence. Matthew can sense her pain.

Neither the police nor school had suspected anything of the girls – not to begin with, at least. Sasha thought that they should go and talk to someone, tell them what they had been doing, but neither Isobel nor Eliza would allow it.

' "They won't understand," that's what Isobel kept saying. "They'll think we did something to cause it, when all we were doing was telling her what we'd been told." ' Sasha pauses, swallows. 'They were pretending that they hadn't lunged at her with the knife, and I went along with that when I talked to them. I felt so guilty – I knew I needed to tell someone what we'd been doing. I was so scared. If they were prepared to do that to Christian, what would they do to me? To my mum?'

She promised them that she wouldn't tell anyone what they'd been doing. For a week or so, this had been good enough, or so she thought. But it turned out that Isobel and Eliza had different plans.

'We had an inset day,' she says. 'A day off school while the teachers did some course. I couldn't go and see Mum as she was in the US that week, so I agreed to have a day out with the girls. They said they had a surprise planned, a special outing. I wasn't excited, though. I was terrified.'

'Where did they take you?' the advocate depute says.

'We went to North Berwick, on the train.'

'Was there any particular significance to North Berwick?'

Sasha nods. 'Yes. It was an important place in the history of

Scottish witchcraft. It's where some of the witches confessed to meeting the Devil.'

The advocate depute nods as if Sasha has said something rational. Matthew is seething. Why can't the man tell her to stop talking shit? But a faint drumbeat of dread thrums underneath his outrage, a pair of amber eyes staring at him unblinking.

'I didn't think about it until we got to the harbour. There's a ruin there of the old church, that's where they said it all happened, where they held the Witches' Sabbath, kissed the Devil's behind. Isobel held me by the wrist – she was hurting me, I told her to get off but she just gripped harder. Then she said she'd made a deal with the Devil. She'd promised him that nothing would be said as long as I kept my mouth shut. But if I didn't, he'd get me. He'd get my mum.'

'Did you believe her?'

'I believe that she meant to hurt me if I didn't keep quiet. By any means possible.'

Stick applied, the girls had given her some carrot by way of lobster and chips from the shack beside the harbour. They'd eaten their food overlooking the sea, the boats bobbing up and down as the tide came in. Bass Rock was in the distance, faint specks of birds to be seen swirling around it. But the peace didn't last. When they got back to school, they were told that Christian was found to have died of a heart attack, and that it was thought that something had terrified her in the moments preceding her death.

'I felt so guilty when I heard,' Sasha says. 'I knew what it was. They'd been building up to this for months, telling her she was going to die. Then they threatened her. Christian was terrified. That's why she ran away – between the running and the fear, it's obvious why she had the heart attack. It would never have happened otherwise. I'm sure of it – it was so obvious to me. I said to the girls we needed to come forward. It wasn't fair on Christian's parents. But that's when everything got even worse. Way worse.'

33

By the following day messages had started to arrive on Sasha's phone, she told the court.

'What kind of messages?'

'Endless messages,' Sasha says. She's speaking almost in a whisper now, so tired she can barely form the words. 'Photos of Christian, photos of a poppet that was made to look like me, a nail straight through its mouth. Threats. If I told, I would die. My mum would die. Even if I didn't tell, I was cursed. I was going to die. It went on and on, and on, for days. I couldn't sleep, I couldn't eat. I was feeling more and more ill the more it went on.'

'How many messages did you receive?'

'I didn't count them at the time,' Sasha says. 'It felt like my phone was going off every two seconds. I looked afterwards and it was three hundred and seventy-three messages that came through over four days.'

'Is this a list of the messages you received?' the advocate depute interrupts, holding up a piece of paper. It appears on the screen, showing dates and times written in blue biro.

'Yes, I wrote that down after it all happened. I was worried something might happen to my phone.'

'Did you know who the messages were from?' He's turned back to Sasha.

'Isobel. Eliza. A few unknown numbers. I think it was probably them.'

'Forgive me for asking, but why didn't you just switch off your phone?'

Sasha looks at him blankly – her mum had said the same to her after it all came out. No way to make middle-aged people understand how you couldn't just disappear like that. They'd never get it. 'My mum was still away. I needed her to be able to get hold of me. I couldn't turn my phone off like that. Besides, it wasn't just on my phone. They were writing notes to me, sending me emails. The threats kept on coming.' She stifles a sob. Out of the corner of her eye, she sees Isobel suppress a sneer and her heart jumps. Even now . . . it's like she's back in the dorm, waking up to find notes full of hatred stuffed under her pillow, or falling out of her school bag like charred confetti.

There was no one to talk to. Her mum was out of the country again; it was out of the question that she'd tell anyone at school. Wherever she went she felt Isobel's eyes on her, Eliza's too, their dark gazes following her round the school, haunting her every moment. The pressure was relentless. Unceasing.

Once she got as far as the chaplain's office, thinking that a clergyman might be best placed to help, but just as she was about to knock on the door the girls appeared as if by magic, one on either side of her, smirks on their faces like the one Isobel's trying to hide now. *Looking for God, are we? Let us pray? Do you want him to tell you to kneel? Altogether now, kumbaya . . .*

Then there were the dreams. The insects were back, the incessant feeling of bugs crawling under her skin, up her nose and into her ears. The flying, falling into an infinite abyss. Sleep was a torment, waking worse. She couldn't even eat, everything tasting of dirt as soon as she put it in her mouth. There wasn't a corner of her life left untouched, untarnished.

'I couldn't understand it,' she continues after a moment, her voice still low. 'They'd be asleep, and my phone would keep buzzing. All day. All night. I didn't know how they could be doing it. I was so scared. All the time. Then finally it came to a head.'

'What happened?'

'I went back upstairs to our dormitory at lunchtime one day, two weeks after Christian died. I couldn't take any more. That's when I found the map.'

'This?' the advocate depute says, holding something up to Sasha. She looks at it, nods. 'What did it say?'

'The map was of Arthur's Seat,' she says. 'There's a place near the top where they found a load of mini coffins that they think were something to do with magic. It's always been associated with witchcraft. They circled the place on the map.'

She points at the screen, where the image has come up. A large-scale Ordnance Survey map with a circle written on it in black ink. Next to it is scrawled in big capital letters, *JUMP HERE*, a skull and crossbones scribbled alongside.

How to explain it, the sense of compulsion which drove her from the warmth of school up the slopes of Arthur's Seat that Saturday morning last year? She was so tired, the beeping from her phone so incessant, Christian's face more and more visible to her, even as her eyes were open. The guilt was overwhelming. She should have done more, she should have stopped it, stopped them, called them out for the bullies they were instead of being such a coward.

She was still being a coward, even after Christian's death, letting them dictate what she should do rather than telling the truth. Tell the truth and shame the Devil, that's another thing her mother used to say to her. Well, her mother wasn't here now. No one was here to help Sasha, no one at all. That Miss Waites had even asked if she was all right, but Sasha wasn't going to talk to her. It was too late now.

'I knew how to read the map,' she says. 'I did an expedition for Duke of Edinburgh. I knew exactly where they meant for me to go. So I went.' She glances over at Isobel and Eliza but their heads are down, curtains of hair drawn against their faces. 'I climbed up the hill, I got to the bit near the top.'

Wind in her hair, voices in her head, *do it do it jump jump.*

'I just wanted it to stop. I wanted them to leave me alone. I don't know if I wanted to die, but I thought that if I did what they wanted, they might leave me alone.'

Standing on the edge looking down at the steep hill below her. Not quite a cliff but enough of a drop. They'd chosen well.

'So I jumped,' she says. 'And the next thing I knew, it was two weeks later, and I was in intensive care, with forty bones broken. Someone found me and called for help. I was lucky to survive.'

Mr Alexander nods at her, his face encouraging. She can tell he's pleased with her, overall. She's been a good witness. She tries to hold on to that thought.

'Before you left for Arthur's Seat that morning, did you write a letter?'

'I did, yes.' Sasha nods as he shows it to her, sealed in a plastic bag.

He turns to Sasha. 'A copy will be given to you. Please will you read it out to the court.'

Dear Mum,

I'm sorry. I can't go on like this. They keep on at me day and night, saying I'm next. They did it to Christian – they bullied her to death, far as I see it, telling her all the time that she was about to die. Now they're doing it to me. I just want them to stop.

I love you.
Sasha

Witch Trial

Sasha is blinking back tears as she gets to the end of the letter. It's sealed in a plastic bag but she can see where it's crumpled at the edges. She can picture it now, crushed in her mum's hands.

'I know this is a hard question to answer, but did you have a fully formed intention to die that day?' Mr Alexander asks. She knows he's trying to phrase it sensitively, but the question feels probing. She jumped off a cliff – what more does he want from her? She opens her mouth to speak but finds herself hesitating.

He speaks again. 'What I mean to say is that the letter does not make any explicit reference to death. Simply to the fact that you wanted them to stop.'

Sasha's defensiveness drops, a little. Maybe she can reframe this narrative. 'You're right, you know. I don't think I did want to die, not exactly. But I was finding the pressure unbearable. Isobel and Eliza just wouldn't leave me alone. They were on at me all the time, telling me that I would be next. By the time I made the decision to go up Arthur's Seat, it was more that I was completely exhausted.'

'Thank you,' he says. 'I know this is a difficult subject.' The advocate depute leafs through some papers, a change in atmosphere now he's past the worst. 'You said that you regained consciousness two weeks later, to find yourself in intensive care, is that right?'

'Yes. They induced a coma because they were worried about whether I might have a bleed on my brain, but I didn't need a head operation in the end. Only to my back. Once I was conscious I started to make a good recovery, though I had to stay in traction for a few more weeks because of the injury I did to my back. I broke two of the vertebrae. My pelvis too.'

There's a little ripple of movement from the jury. Sasha glances over. At least three of the older women have very sympathetic expressions on their faces, their eyebrows furrowed. The two girls in the second row have their heads on one side, tipped in concern, and the older man next to them is scowling with concentration. At least, she hopes it's concentration.

'The police came to see me while I was in hospital. My mum had given them the letter and they wanted to know what I meant. That's when I told them that we'd been bullying Christian.'

'Did the police ask you whether you had any prior knowledge of Christian's heart condition?'

'They did, yes,' Sasha says. 'But I didn't know anything about it. She never said anything to me.'

34

Cross-examination. At last. This nonsense is finally being put to the test. Matthew thought he'd be excited to see it, but now Sasha is being put through her paces it's more uncomfortable than he anticipated. Miss Brodie is doing an excellent job at demolishing everything that she's said.

'This idea that you're some kind of victim is complete rubbish, isn't it?'

'No. I . . .'

'You were in this up to your neck, weren't you?'

Sasha is reduced almost to tears by the questioning. It's all so brisk, Matthew can barely keep track, but the gist of what he can gather is that everything that Sasha has accused Eliza of doing is in fact Sasha's own fault. She faked the Ouija board, back at the start of the bullying campaign, pushing the planchette to the letters DIECHRIST together with Isobel. She helped Isobel make the poppet that looked like the classmate Freya. She helped Isobel set up the tarot cards so that they would spell out Christian's doom. Anytime that Sasha said that she was being excluded, she was lying. She and Isobel were tight throughout, working to cause havoc with the other girls.

'You said that when you visited Christian's country estate, it was Eliza and Isobel who were keen to visit the taxidermy museum?'

'Yes,' Sasha says.

'It was you, though.'

'No, it wasn't.'

Miss Brodie goes through her file. Pulls out a photograph.

'This is a photograph of you, isn't it? From your Instagram account?'

Matthew looks first at Sasha, her face flushed dark red. Then he looks at the photograph now shown on the screen. It's indisputably Sasha. She's a little younger, happier, smiling proudly next to a black cat that's curled up on a velvet cushion. But there's something off about the cat, an awkwardness to its pose, its head at an unnatural angle.

'Please can you read out the caption that you wrote underneath this photograph.'

'This isn't fair,' Sasha says. 'You've got no right to go through my Instagram profile like that.'

'It's in the public domain,' Miss Brodie says. 'Anyone can see it. Please will you read the caption out to the court.'

' "Farewell to my familiar," ' Sasha says, her voice tight. ' "And thank you to Frozen in Time for their brilliant taxidermy course. They helped me preserve my beloved Carbonel so that he can be with me forever." '

'Carbonel is your cat, is that right?'

'Yes.'

'Thank you.' A delicate pause while Miss Brodie waits for the Instagram post to take full effect. Matthew feels slightly stunned, unsure how to react. He tries to imagine telling Daisy that she was going to learn how to stuff their old tabby cat Archy for posterity when he died a couple of years before – even in his imagination Daisy's response is an appalled *fuck off*.

'At the beginning of Year Nine, before Christian joined the school, you had a conversation with Eliza in which you told her all about your love of roadkill, didn't you?'

'I . . . no . . . well, yes, but . . .'

'You told her that when you were a child you were obsessed with keeping a record of everything that you saw that had been killed by cars on the road, didn't you?'

Head hung low. 'Yes.'

'You particularly liked it when you saw a dead cat, that's what you said to her?'

'I . . .'

'My lady,' Mr Alexander interrupts. He has risen to his feet very hastily, so much so that he has knocked his wig slightly askew. 'I would remind the court that cross-examination needs to be relevant to the case at hand. Not just dredging through childhood reminiscences, however eccentric.'

Miss Brodie makes a harrumphing noise. 'Given the nature of the evidence that this witness has made against my client, I would argue that it is entirely relevant to show that she has a propensity towards activity with dead animals. The case I am seeking to put, as I have made very clear, is that far from being a victim of Isobel and Eliza, she was involved in the nefarious activities up to her eyeballs.'

The judge pauses for a moment, nods. 'Very well, Miss Brodie. Carry on. But keep to the point.'

'Thank you, my lady.' Matthew can almost discern the triumph in her voice as she gets one over on the advocate depute. She then turns back to Sasha. 'Let us return to the chapel. You say that it was Eliza and Isobel who made a mess of the place, yes?'

'Yes.'

'That's not true, though, is it? You were the main instigator of this, weren't you?'

'No.'

'And it was you who climbed on to the altar and turned the crucifix upside down, wasn't it?'

'No, it wasn't. It was them, all them. I'm not lying.'

'The jury will be the judge of that. Now, you say that you knew nothing about Christian's pre-existing heart condition?'

'I didn't, no.'

'But that isn't true, either. You were with Isobel when Christian's mother told both of you that you needed to be careful with her, that she was unable to withstand stress of any kind, weren't you?'

'That's just not true! If she told them, I wasn't there! They never told me!' Sasha has pushed herself upright in the witness box. Her face is still red, her voice raised. She bursts into tears. Matthew can see a woman in the public gallery who has the same profile as Sasha – she's also mirroring the girl's distress. Not so Miss Brodie, who stands poised, ready for the attack.

'So from that moment, you knew that if Christian was put under too much emotional pressure, it could have a very detrimental effect on her health?'

'No, I didn't. I didn't know. I tried to stop them.'

'I would suggest to you that you are lying. You and Isobel were in a conspiracy together to bully Christian in the most unkind way possible, knowing that it was dangerous to her health. You actively wanted to cause her harm, didn't you?'

'That's not true.'

'Let's turn now to a conversation that you had with Eliza after that ill-fated visit – you told her how jealous you were of Christian because of her close relationship with her father, didn't you?'

Sasha sobs. 'I . . . yes. I did say that. But I didn't mean . . .'

'I put it to you that the jealousy you felt then festered, and grew, so that when you came back from the Christmas holidays, you made a decision that you were going to start the whole bullying campaign up again.'

'It wasn't me!'

'And it was your suggestion that the so-called coven became active again?'

'No, it was Eliza. Or Isobel. I can't remember.'

'You can't remember.' Miss Brodie says the words slowly. Each one a hammer blow. 'Convenient. As it was convenient that in your version of events, you had your eyes shut so that you couldn't see who it was wielded the knife that you say was used to threaten Christian. You've just made that up.'

Sasha stares at the woman, shakes her head. 'I'm not lying. That's what happened.'

Matthew nearly shakes his head. The advocate has done a comprehensive number on Sasha, the girl left ashen and shaken in the witness stand. He feels sorry for her, but he's putting that to one side. What's important here is justice. Not protecting people from the consequences of their actions.

Defence advocates are clever at twisting things, though. He needs to remember that, too. Looking round the rest of the jury, he's not sure whether they're going to be able to see through manipulations as well as he can. Not that he means to brag, but his experience in the world of medicine has given him a unique insight into psychopathy in action. He knows that he can take no one's honesty at face value. Not even a weeping girl who reminds him of his daughter.

The advocate has been consulting a document in front of her. She asks the macer to hand her one of the items on the exhibits table, which she inspects before having it delivered over to Sasha.

'This is your book, isn't it?'

Sasha looks at the book. She's shaking her head. 'No.'

'Open it, please, and read out what's written on the first page inside.'

'"Sasha's book HANDS OFF".' She sounds strained, as if

the shame that's staining her cheeks with red is strangling her voice, too.

'This is your book, isn't it?' Miss Brodie is not going to let her off the hook.

A long sigh. 'Yes.'

'Will you please tell the ladies and gentlemen of the jury the title of the book?'

A longer sigh. 'It's called *Of Blood and Bones: Working with Shadow Magick and the Dark Moon.*'

'Can you tell the jury a little more about what this is about?'

Sasha tries to speak, but all that comes out is a groan. She seems to be in a lot of distress. Miss Brodie steps in.

'I will read an extract from the description of this book that I took from the Amazon website: "Within these pages, you will also discover methods for hexing, scrying, sex magick, and working with dark deities in addition to the magickal use of graveyard dirt and performing spells to assist the crossing of a dying loved one."' A pause while the description lands with the jury. 'It might be said that this is also an accurate description of your activities in relation to Christian, isn't it?'

'Yes.' A mutter from Sasha. No more.

'It's not unreasonable to suppose that if this is your book, you will have read it?'

'I've read it, yes.'

'And that *you* are the person who generated all the ideas for the ways to torment Christian that you've tried so hard to blame on my client, aren't you? You were the one who planned the progression of events that were visited upon your poor victim.'

'It wasn't me,' Sasha says.

Miss Brodie clears her throat, straightens her sleeves.

She's only just begun.

35

The rest of the cross-examination is a car crash in slow motion. Matthew can't bear to look; he can't turn away. Lion against gazelle, hunter against hunted – Sasha's as stuffed as her cat Carbonel. She was the one obsessed with the mini coffins that were found on Arthur's Seat. She'd even persuaded Eliza and Isobel to go to the Museum of Scotland to look at them. She'd marked the map herself, she'd gone up there herself because she was overwhelmed by guilt because of what she'd done to Christian, herself. She'd written the letter to her mother in order to try and frame Isobel and Eliza. She'd jumped not because anyone had told her to, but through her own volition.

When the jury leave the courtroom for a coffee break, they're all buzzing with it. The advocate has flipped the narrative on its head – look at the twist here. Clearly it's all Sasha's fault. Matthew watches them all fussing around, deciding not to remind them that only yesterday they were fully convinced of Isobel and Eliza's guilt. She's put together a good defence on Eliza's behalf, that's for sure, but it's Miss Brodie's job to put forward Eliza's case. However truthful that might be. Or not.

Miss Goodly is on her feet when they return to court. Isobel's defence advocate has spoken so little that Matthew can't actually remember what her voice sounds like, surprised again by the sound of it. She asks only a few questions.

'Isobel took all the magical rituals very seriously, didn't she?'

Sasha thinks for a moment. Nods. 'She seemed to, yes.'

'And there's no question that you and she were in a conspiracy to fake any of the messages, were you?'

'No. We weren't. I never spoke to her about them. I just saw them happen.'

'At no point did she say that it was her intention to harm Christian, or bully her, did she?'

'No. She didn't say it. Not in so many words.'

'Any accusation you make against Isobel plotting against Christian is based on supposition and assumption, isn't it? Not actual knowledge?'

'She never discussed it with me, no. She spent a lot more time with Eliza,' Sasha says. She's looking confused, as if the narrative has taken an unexpected turn.

'As far as you are aware, Isobel believed she had magical powers, didn't she?'

'Yes. Well, it's definitely what she said.'

'And while she may have misused magical powers on occasion when it came to hexing some people, as far as *Christian* was concerned, she was simply carrying out what she considered to be her duty insofar as she was passing on messages from the spirit world and doing what the Devil told her to do?'

Sasha looks thoroughly taken aback. Not as taken aback as Matthew feels, though.

'I mean, I guess so. Yes.'

'Let me take you back to the first time that you discussed magic with Isobel.'

Sasha nods.

Witch Trial

'She told you that she was a witch, didn't she?' Miss Goodly says.

A pause. Sasha turns something over and over in her pocket before smelling her fingers. A chill passes through Matthew.

'She did.'

'And what's more, you believed her. Didn't you?'

Sasha nods her head, once. Twice. 'I did believe her. I still do. I don't know about Eliza, but Isobel is a witch. I know it.'

The lights in the courtroom flicker, dim. Go off. In the midst of the commotion that follows Matthew can hear only one voice. A strange chant, a rhythm unfamiliar to him. The sound melodious, but utterly chilling.

'I shall go into a hare,
With sorrow and sych and meickle care;
And I shall go in the Devil's name,
Ay while I come home again.'

'Watch out, Sasha, I'm coming!'

A scream. A thump from the direction of the witness box. The lights flicker back on to reveal that Sasha has fainted, slumped over the witness box.

And where Isobel was standing, only an empty space.

It takes so long for everyone in the courtroom to calm down that the judge orders everyone out. 'That's quite enough. I want you back in fifteen minutes, and I will expect there to be quiet in my courtroom.'

'This trial is beginning to mess with my head,' Dharam says when they're back in the jury room.

'Yeah, I actually thought for a moment she'd managed to transform herself,' Jasmine says.

Russell laughs. 'I was looking out for a hare, seeing if she'd jumped all the way to the door. Didn't occur to me she'd just decided to go.' There isn't much humour in his voice though, the laugh more like a bark.

'Thank God we've got tomorrow off,' Neil says. 'I think the judge has had enough too, whatever she's saying about pressing engagements and unprecedented circumstances.'

Matthew can only agree. He's totally shaken by the way that the day has ended. Of course, it turned out that Isobel had just taken herself downstairs to the cells from the dock when the lights went out. But the fact that she's reduced fifteen adults to the state that they were prepared to entertain the slightest possibility that the girl had transformed herself magically into an animal . . . as Neil says, thank God they don't have to come in tomorrow.

There's only one answer for this week. Obliteration.

Matthew knows exactly how to find it.

FRIDAY

36

Next morning and his head is throbbing. He bypassed the pub, shaking his head when Russell and Neil asked him to join them, buying a bottle of malt on the way home, solitude the only way to take his poison in a mood like this. He sat in the flat while darkness fell, watching the lights from passing cars flicker across the ceiling. The whisky was smooth, needed – it slipped down so easy he lost track of how much he poured, absorbed as he was in his thoughts.

Matthew can't remember going to bed, but he's lying under his duvet, naked other than his socks, his clothes scattered in a pile next to him. He's forgotten to pull the curtains shut, but it's grey outside, the sky thick with haar. He looks over at the alarm clock – not yet 9 o'clock. He's not slept too late, can't have passed out too late either.

He scans his body mentally, assessing the scale of the hangover. Legs stiff from lack of proper exercise, back a touch sore from the tricky angle at which he's slept. Liver? He passes over that quickly, kidneys too, passing up through his lungs (the lovely, clear, unpolluted lungs of the non-smoker – one thing he can feel smug about at least) and finally head. The worst casualty of the lot.

Still, it's Friday, a day off – three days off, for goodness' sake. He can put this infernal case out of his mind for a while. He can finish the rest of the laundry, do more endless life admin, throw out the little pile of empty plastic food trays piled up in the sink.

It's a chance for him to catch up with Rosalind, too. She's not going away until tomorrow. He could go round to the house, ring on the bell (*like a fucking supplicant*), ask if he can come in and talk (*to his own WIFE in his own fucking HOUSE*).

Arguably he might still be a little angry. Not conducive to a calm discussion. He'll wait until they're back, until the case is finished. Same with Dominic, too. It's not like he's doing anything wrong.

Olivia? Well, he could. She won't understand what he's going through, though. Besides, she'll be at work. He'll think about speaking to her tomorrow.

Maybe.

He has a pee, drinks some water. He'll go back to bed now, catch up on the years' worth of sleep debt he's accumulated. But the idea of getting back into the fetid sheets makes him feel worse, not better. Stifled. He needs to get out and feel the wind in his hair.

A day trip. That's it. He hasn't done one of those in forever. He casts his mind over the options, weighing up castles and stately homes, a walk up in the Pentlands. Then it comes to him – North Berwick. That girl mentioned a lobster shack, and if there's one thing Matthew has a weakness for, it's eating seafood by the sea. That's his sole motivation – no question that he's doing his own research into the case. Besides, of all the locations mentioned so far, this is surely the least significant. It's not like he's decided to climb Arthur's Seat and see where the girl decided to throw herself off.

A brisk walk up to Waverley Station and soon he's on a train, passing through the stations of East Lothian on the half-hour journey to North Berwick. He'd looked up the site of the old church before leaving the flat, switching his laptop on and checking Google without going anywhere near his emails or message apps, so he knows roughly where he'll need to go – it's over by the harbour, handily close to the lobster shack as well. When the train pulls in, he takes a moment to orient himself before striking out for the sea.

It's still grey and misty, the haar rolling in from the water. He follows the signs to the Scottish Seabird Centre and then, a little further along on the green over the road from the seawall, he sees what he's looking for: a small, white building with some stone ruins. What's left of the church where the witches met with the Devil. According to Isobel Gowdie's testimony, at least, albeit one obtained under torture, but Matthew doesn't want to think about that.

I shall go into a hare. Isobel's chant from the day before goes through his mind. He knows rationally speaking that it's ludicrous that the whole jury believed for a moment that she might have transformed herself, but this case is doing something to all of them. Spend enough time with a believer ... Sasha's belief has shone through her evidence.

Her fear, too.

No one's around. It must be heaving with tourists in the summer months – he remembers trips here as a kid with his parents, ice creams and sandcastles, the Bass Rock in the distance. It's lost that wholesome feel, though, the murk and the mist changing the normally friendly place to one that's full of shadows, a sense that the buildings are telling him to keep out. He steps over the low wall of the ruin into the heart of it, thinking himself back hundreds of years, women circling past him as they dance to the Devil's tune.

Looking over to the sea, the haar is building, intensifying, but there's a white disc suspended low in the sky – the sun's still there, burning yellow against gaudy blue, but it's so obscured it might as well be orbiting a different planet. The mist around it is shifting, thickening in some parts, the sun almost breaking through in others, a constant movement that looks almost as if a shape is emerging...

Matthew blinks. A shape *is* emerging. Head, shoulders, the features becoming increasingly clear. A big nose, eyes sunk deep above high cheekbones, a pointed chin. Matthew's cowering back, terrified to see it emerge, but there's no hiding from it, no escape, as the face shakes clear from the haar, only a few strands of it now clinging to the horns that emerge on either side of the immense head. It opens its mouth and now Matthew is on his knees, bowed against the prospect that once again he'll have to smell the vile stench, the overwhelming effect of the Devil's breath—

'Are you all right?' A woman's voice.

Matthew takes a moment to regain focus. The clouds have lost their shape now. No more horns. His legs are still shaking though, not strong enough yet to get him back on his feet.

'Hello? You OK?'

He looks up with an effort, seeing a figure emerge through the haar. But this time it's solid, corporeal.

Unless he's imagining it. Imagining her. Wish fulfilment; the one person he would have wanted to see. He's conjured her out of thin air.

The blonde.

'Oh God, it's you,' she says. 'That's so weird.'

With that he pulls himself together. It is her, the woman from court. But given they've both heard the same evidence together, it's hardly surprising that they've decided to make the same pilgrimage.

'I wanted to come and have a look,' she says. 'I've been reading about the Scottish witch trials. Apparently seventy people from around here were executed.'

'That's a lot,' he says, cursing himself immediately for the inadequacy of his response. 'It's not something I know much about. Witches, that is.'

'This trial is a steep learning curve.'

He should walk away now. He shouldn't talk to her. The warnings the judge gave were very clear not to discuss the case with anyone outside of the jury. But they're discussing witch trials, plural. Not the trial with which he's specifically involved.

'It must be so interesting to be on the jury for a case like this,' she says. Now he's sure he should walk away. 'But of course you can't discuss it.'

'I'm sorry, I can't.' He's finally managed to get some words out, but the effort exhausts him. He sinks to his knees again. 'I'm sorry.'

'Don't be silly,' she says. 'I'm not here to spy on you. But you do look like you could do with a hot drink.'

He can almost feel the warmth of a coffee cup smooth beneath his hands, the scent of it nearly reaching him. Instead, cold earth, the scent of something sweet, floral. Underlaid with the faintest rot. He starts away from her.

'I can't do this,' he says. 'I mustn't talk to you. It's wrong.'

'I promise I won't tell anyone,' she says, 'but I don't think I should leave you on your own. You look terrible. Come on, let's go and get a cup of tea. Get yourself back to normal. I really don't want to leave you like this.'

Angel on one shoulder, telling him to run. Devil on the other . . . hot drink, warm room, a friendly smile. It's a secret. No one will know.

He pushes himself to his feet and holds out his hand.

37

They walk together to the Seabird Centre. Matthew is still tongue-tied, still shaken, barely daring to look up at the sky in case the Devil's head re-forms. The haar is still heavy. Not the weather for fish and chips on the beach, even if the lobster shack were open.

'I checked,' the woman says. 'That was the main draw here, if I'm honest.'

Common ground. Non-contentious. 'Me too. But it's not open?'

'Not for another few weeks,' she says. 'Out of season still. We'll just have to come back.'

We. Not I. He allows himself to envisage a future with her in it for a second. The thought does not displease him. This is even more ridiculous than the affair with Olivia, though. He can't go down this route. The thing with Olivia is immoral. This would be bordering on illegal. His hangover isn't up to it.

The interior of the Seabird Centre couldn't be more at odds with the menace of the cloud-formed shape that loomed above him only minutes ago. It's bright, cheerful, with displays full of soft toys in the shape of puffins and seals. The air smells of coffee and toast, chocolate and carrot cakes sliced up next to the till in irresistible arrays. He pays for his coffee, the blonde woman's too, and they sit at a table overlooking the water. It's so overcast he can barely make out the Bass Rock, despite its normal prominence.

'What's your name?' he says. Then he stops himself, surprised. He wasn't planning on being so direct. The mystery has been part of the appeal, after all. But he can't keep calling her the blonde.

'Isn't that against the rules?' she says, one eyebrow raised.

Rules are made to be broken. Rules are made to be broken. He controls himself. Says nothing.

'You may call me Gill,' she says. 'Gill Martin.'

'Is that your real name?'

'Does it matter?'

'I suppose not.'

The morning is full of surprises. None of it has turned out as planned, though to say that would imply that there was a plan to begin with. He's probably still drunk, reminders of the whisky from the night before still lingering underneath the coffee on his breath. The clouds swirl together over the sea and he flinches, fearing a return of the demonic head, but they subside. He's nervous as a cat.

'Why are you watching the trial?' he says, remembering only too late that they talked about that days ago.

'It's interesting,' she says. 'I think I'm going to write about it. It's such a fascinating case. I know a bit about law but I haven't seen something like this before. I'm finding it very curious the way the prosecution is running it.'

'How do you mean?'

'I mean it's obvious the poor girl was being bullied. But less obvious that they knew it might kill her. Maybe they've got some more evidence that'll establish that. The internet is all over this one. They think the girls are being persecuted because of their beliefs.' She shakes her head slowly, as if to marvel at the strangeness of the world.

Back off. Run away. Stop talking.
'You know I can't discuss this,' he says.
'You're not. I'm discussing it. But I can stop if you like.' She smiles. It's a nice smile, reassuring. The vestiges of fear still clutching at him slip further away. 'It's funny how much you get drawn into it. I had no real idea what it was all about beyond the headlines – now I'm totally engrossed. And despite the way they're being portrayed, it's hard not to relate a bit to the girls in the dock. Isobel, especially . . .' Her voice trails off.

'How so?' He knows he shouldn't ask the question – the words leave his lips regardless.

Gill pauses. She looks away from him, out of the window, her face lost in thought for a moment. 'She reminds me a bit of me at that age. I had terrible acne, too. Greasy hair. People weren't always very kind to me – I was very angry. I didn't end up dabbling in witchcraft, but maybe, if the right people had come along . . . I can see how this has all ended up happening.'

He looks at her, all shiny hair and clear skin. Hard to imagine her as a spotty, unloved teen. 'You feel sorry for Isobel?' Matthew says. She's the first person he's heard saying anything like that.

'Perhaps a little. More for Christian. I just hate the way that the Elizas of this world get away with things. Life is so much easier for them. Anyway, I would love to know what the jury are thinking. It must be incredible to have so much power over people's fates like that.'

The room's cold, suddenly. Dark. As if the lights have snapped off as they did in court. They're still on, though; it's just that Matthew can't see, a cloud before his eyes, a roaring in his ears, the smell of rot strong in his nostrils. Gill is transforming before his eyes, the skull emerging beneath the skin, her teeth now fangs, her hands a pair of grasping claws. Her eyes . . . he can't even look at her eyes. He pushes his coffee mug away from him and he runs.

Witch Trial

To begin with, he doesn't look where he's going, wanting only to escape from the roaring sound, the predator that Gill has become. He stumbles fast as far away from her as he can get, his back to the sea. When he finally stops to take stock of his surroundings, he's got himself to the foot of North Berwick Law, a hillock he hasn't climbed since he was a child, dragged complaining up each step by his long-suffering father, now long dead.

That phantom is beside him now, urging him to climb, climb, *the top isn't far off now. Look, from here you can see the sea.* Matthew can't see the sea, though, the head of the hill cut off from its body by mist, still that damned mist that hasn't cleared yet, won't go away even though by now the sun should be high in the sky.

Now he's at the top, standing underneath the great jawbone of the whale, hands outstretched to touch either side of it, breath catching heavy in his chest. The connection to something once living, skin on bone, brings him to himself. What kind of man has he become? A coward, running from shadows, scared by ghosts. But look at him now, king of the world! Or at least, he should be. He turns around to view his kingdom, rolling swathes of grey below him, above, that pale disc in the sky the only hint that light may come.

He sits down, head in hands, pulling his strength together. Light will come. This darkness is only for now. He's spent enough time cowed, a coward, doing what everyone tells him to do, like a good boy.

That's it, you stand up to them. His father's voice again, an echo from when he was bullied at school. *You know exactly how to stand up to them.*

He's let himself be tossed by fortune's tide quite long enough. The jury needs him to step up. The court needs him to step up. Not for him the fetters of caution – they all know he can be trusted with information that less intelligent members of the jury can't handle. Matthew has the skill to separate the wheat from the chaff. *The internet is all over this,* Gill said.

It's time that Matthew was too.

He's going to take control.

Yet even as the words form in his head, he's defeated again by the futility of it. He's not in control at all. As his head clears, along with the clouds around him, his reality hits him again in the face. He's a speck of a man, minuscule on this giant planet. Nothing he can do will make the slightest difference. Any agency he had has disappeared, as he follows the judge's lead like a little lemming. A sheep. A cardiologist who can't even work out what the issue is with the medical evidence. It's pathetic.

Not just the trial. In his own life, too. He's not even allowed in his own home, barred from it like a dog even though he pays for the whole thing. The sad little flat comes before his eyes, the inadequacy of his existence. He's so cowed he won't even look this case up, despite all the information that's so readily available.

Well, that's one thing he can change. When everything else is falling apart, control what you can. He can at least start by doing some research. Damn it, this is a case about a girl with a heart condition. He *is* a fucking heart surgeon. At the least he can make some calls, see what he can find out about her.

SATURDAY

38

Saturday's a write-off. He spends most of it sleeping off Friday, the shock he sustained at the top of North Berwick Law, the crushing sense of inferiority that took hold of him, refused to let go. He barely made it down the hill before dark, staggering along to the station, back to Edinburgh on the train. For all he knew, Gill was on the train too, but he paid no heed. As soon as he got back to his flat, he drank what was left of the whisky from Thursday night before collapsing into bed still fully dressed.

It's dark by the time he feels like getting up, the sun already set. He's lost the day and now he won't sleep at night, either. It's all upside down. Fitting for the state of his head, really. Another microwave meal, pushing the pasta round his plate joylessly. Only a few days and this case will be over. Then he can get on with his life.

What's left of it.

Enough of this self-pity. He jumps into the shower, turning the heat up to boiling hot before down to freezing cold, standing under the water for as long as he can bear before rubbing himself dry with a rough towel. He's alive, that's for sure, every part of him glowing from such abrasive treatment. It's broken his torpor, given him a sense of purpose.

He sits down in front of the computer. Now it's time, judge's warning or not. Gill had said Reddit (*Gill*, he rolls the name round in his mind, *Gill*. At last he knows who she is . . .) so he goes on to the site, putting the words *Witch Trial* into the search engine. The first few entries relate to historical matters, mostly Salem. Then he hits gold.

If he can put it that highly. He skims through, disappointment growing inside him at the paucity of material available. There are strong feelings about the case, both for and against the girls. Mostly in favour of Isobel – the consensus is clearly that she believes in the power of what's happened and that spirits have worked through her. No one feels that she should be prosecuted for possession of magickal powers (he can't understand why everyone misspells it so consistently, but he can't be bothered to find out, either). *You can't be prosecuted for scaring someone to death* is a line that's repeated more than once.

Most people think that Eliza's innocent, based on her photo, but they have more respect for Isobel. Gill's words of sympathy for Isobel flash into his mind. She's sorry for the girl but that's not the prevailing view. A true witch, that's how she's being hailed. People wouldn't want to get on the wrong side of her. But Matthew gets the distinct impression that they're saying this with awe rather than horror.

A little further down he finds a thread by someone with the user name *HexyBitch* who is clearly sitting in on the trial. Matthew's chest tightens – he knows it's public property, open to view for anyone who wants to come and watch the process of justice, but this is *his* trial, *his* evidence to consider, not there for the edification of some random person who posts anonymously on the internet.

He skims through it. Anodyne enough – the author is clearly aware of the rules that govern court reporting. Matthew learns nothing from it that he doesn't already know. This is all a bit of a waste of time, really. He's slept off the exhaustion that was making him believe that any of this rubbish might be true, and he can't be bothered giving more of his precious time to idiots who think that any amount of ritual will conjure up what they want.

Annoyed, he deletes the search, leaves Reddit and starts a new search for the name *Christian Shaw*. Any number of news reports about the trial, though no new material that gives him additional insight. Only an article that gives the medical background to cardiomyopathy, most of which has clearly been scraped from the Mayo Clinic website.

Damn it, Matthew wants to do something. He's fed up with just sitting there, waiting to be told what the prosecution wants him to hear. He's never taken such an acquiescent role in his life, always preferring to do first, apologise later. Go fast and break things, his version of the tech bro motto. It's led to advances in the way that he treats patients, cutting through a level of bureaucracy with his forthright approach. There's no way he should wait to be told – Matthew needs to get himself into the driving seat.

He pushes himself up from his computer, paces to one side of the room, back again. He thought it would help, looking things up, but it's only made it worse. He's truly powerless. Everything is slipping away from him, wife, job, position in everything he holds dear. He goes to the side to pour a drink but even that eludes him, the whisky finished now, the dregs drunk dry.

Damn it, damn it. What is there to do? He can't stay in; he doesn't want to go out. Back and forth, back and forth he paces, poring over and over everything that he knows about the case. Then he comes to a halt in front of the computer, the diagram of the cardiomyopathic heart in front of him. A pain starts up behind his left eyeball, nagging at him. There's something he's missing, he knows it. That's what's behind this feeling of restlessness, this sense that there's something out there, just out of his reach, but if he gets hold of it he'll have the key.

He's going to call Dominic. That's what he's going to do. He may not have treated Christian himself, but Dominic might have done. Scotland's not that big, after all, the cardiac specialists in Edinburgh treating a large swathe of the country's population. If Dominic hasn't heard of her, he'll know someone who has.

Calling Dominic means turning on his phone. Still, desperate times. He plugs it into its charger, waits for a few moments until it's got enough juice to fire up. Ignoring the barrage of pings that greets him as it updates with all the messages awaiting him, he dials Dominic's number. It's Saturday night, he'll probably be out on the town somewhere, carousing with his new woman, but Matthew can leave a message. At least he'll feel that he's done something to progress this case.

To his surprise, Dominic replies immediately.

'What do you want?'

Matthew blinks. Not the reception he expected. He's always got on fine with Dominic, not being either young or female.

'Yes, hello to you too, Dominic,' he says. He's not going to let the apparent hostility faze him. He's got a job to do, after all.

'Hello, hello, yes, Matthew,' Dominic says. 'Sorry to be abrupt. I was expecting someone else to call, that's all.'

'No problem, I know I'm off at the moment. I have a question for you, though.'

'You know I can't discuss anything with you . . .'

'It's about the trial,' Matthew says, pushing through. He's more nervous than he realised, now that he actually has Dominic on the line. He'd really been hoping to leave a message. 'I wanted to ask if you've ever had dealings with a Christian Shaw.'

'Trial, what trial?' Dominic says.

'The trial I'm on,' Matthew says with some disbelief. Dominic knows exactly what he's talking about.

'Yes, yes, of course. Sorry, million miles away,' Dominic says, though with little conviction. Maybe he hasn't been paying attention.

'Christian Shaw. Teenage girl with dilated cardiomyopathy. Have you had dealings with her?'

'Right. Shaw. Yes. No. Maybe. Let me think.' A long pause, clicks and thumps at the other end of the phone as if he's digging through a drawer or something. Matthew is used to Dominic being distracted but this is next level.

'Shaw,' he says again. But something's changed. Dominic's voice is normal again. Alert. Switched on. 'Pretty mother?'

'I don't know,' Matthew says. 'Haven't encountered her yet.'

'I think I did see her. Years ago. I'm not completely sure – there was an initial meeting. But one thing I can tell you, the mother felt distinctly off to me.'

'In what way?'

'In a Munchausen's way.' There's a long pause. 'Look, don't quote me. I may be misremembering. I'll go through my files when I'm next in my office. But I do remember getting a very strange vibe from her. She wanted there to be something wrong with her daughter, that much I do know. She was really pushing for a bad diagnosis.'

'Did you give her one?'

'I can't recall the details exactly, not off the top of my head. But I didn't think that any further intervention was required, probably because of the observations I carried out. The mother was having none of it, though. She marched straight out, dragging her daughter with her. They never came back to my clinic.'

Matthew says nothing for a moment. He's trying to absorb the information. So much of the prosecution case rests on Christian's heart condition – what if it turns out that this never existed in the first place?

'Look, Matthew, I need to—'

'Did you report it? Follow up?'

An awkward laugh. 'I didn't, I don't think. It was only a feeling I got. A vibe. She was pushing for a diagnosis, that was all. She wasn't making her daughter ill or anything.'

'Was the girl on any medication? Might that have been unnecessary?'

'Look, Matthew. You're taking this a bit seriously if you ask me. I just got a vibe, as I said. No more than that. Anyway, should you be asking questions like this if you're on the jury?'

Damn it, Dominic is suddenly on the ball. Time to go. Matthew thanks him, cuts off immediately. His mind is whirring. Without having seen Christian's mother yet, it's hard to know what difference this might make, if any. But it's given him something to think about, that's for sure.

Instead of immediately powering his phone off, he scrolls through the messages. Nothing of interest other than a text from Daisy saying she's having fun. And three messages from Olivia. The last one reads: `Hello. Free tonight if you are.`

Tonight? He checks the date stamp. It was sent today. Only a couple of hours ago. He thinks about it for a moment. Then he makes the call.

SUNDAY

A gentleman never tells.

MONDAY

39

They've been in town less than a day and the dressing room already looks as if it's been struck by a tornado. Every item of smart clothing Marianne possesses is on the floor. That skirt was wrong, this pair of trousers, everything falling off her she's lost so much weight. Not that it fucking matters what she looks like – she really couldn't give a shit. But it's not for her. It's for Christian.

There's no style guide for what a bereaved mother should wear on the stand at the trial of the killers of her murdered daughter. Marianne knows the playbook well enough from the criticism made of the parents of Madeleine McCann; she's desperately tried to work out what to look like, the right amount of pathos to put into her face, avoiding levity so as not to provoke the internet trolls waiting in the background to jump on any sign of inappropriate behaviour.

Not that she wants to laugh. Or that there's any ambiguity in what happened. All those fucking years she kept Christian alive, from the breastfeeding to the organic purees, the endless hospital stays, the horror when she had her first febrile convulsion as a baby. The battles she fought to have her baby looked after the way Marianne thought she needed, never caring who she fucked off in the process. Why did she ever let Peter persuade her to change her ways?

'We should never have let her board,' she says. Not for the first time. *You have to let go of self-recrimination*, that's what the bereavement counsellor said. Like fuck she's going to let it go. The guilt she feels will kill her, if she can't kill someone else first.

Peter sighs. 'We've been through this,' he says. 'You know what the consultant said. She wanted the independence.'

'She should have been at home. With me. I wouldn't have let this happen to her. I told you.' Tears spring up in her eyes, the lids already swollen and red from another night without sleep. She rubs at them, irritated, mascara smearing itself across her cheeks.

She's spent the last half-hour trying to do her make-up. What even is the point . . .

Peter's standing behind her, his face hovering over her head in the mirror, concerned, irritated. She wants to punch it, punch him, smash every fucking thing in the room into smithereens and sit in the wreckage and howl.

'Why aren't you wearing the suit you wore to the funeral?'

Black. Chanel. Like some fucking mob wife. She hated that suit, only wore it because Peter asked her to, said it would look better if they made an effort. An effort? It took all the effort she had not to throw herself down on the coffin, cover herself with the dirt.

'Left it up north. I think it's a bit much,' she says. Doesn't feel like her voice, like she's speaking. Clear. Not rough with sobs. The screams that are all she can hear in her head. 'Don't you think this is all right?' It's the first skirt she tried on, before working her way through the rest of the wardrobe. Black, mid-length. White shirt, the collar open over the neck of a black jumper. The locket her grandmother gave her with a photo of Christian in it, a lock of her hair. She never takes it off.

He puts his hand on her shoulder. 'You're right. Am I too smart? I could put on a tweed jacket.'

Witch Trial

He's in pinstripes, faint chalk mark lines on the charcoal wool. White shirt. Navy tie.

'It's perfect.'

Such a meaningless word. Perfect for what? For work, for a meeting with a bank manager. Not for standing in front of your daughter's killers and facing them down. She and Peter should be dressed in rags, daubed in mud, axes in hand as they run into those laughing faces and smash them in, screaming marauders as the grieving parents take their revenge.

'I still can't believe they haven't let us sit in the court already,' Peter says. They're putting their coats on now, checking round the hall to make sure they've got everything. Keys, handbag, tissues. Bloody vengeance. 'It's been going on for a full week and we don't know how it's going.'

'You know what they said. As soon as we've given evidence, we can sit in. We've got to trust them to do their jobs.'

'I'm the only person I can trust to finish those little bitches off,' Peter says. He grips her hand so hard she nearly cries out. 'I want to bury them.'

She pulls him in close, hugs him for a moment. No one understands what she's going through, no one has any idea, what it was like to see her baby dead like that, her beautiful face stuck in so much pain. Only Peter comes close. All thoughts of separation gone, at least for now. They'll only get through this together.

They leave the house. Even now, Marianne is about to call out. *Bye, your dad and I won't be long.* There's no one to hear, though, Christian's room dark, empty of life. She tried to go in last night when they arrived in Edinburgh from up north, couldn't bring herself to do it. The room's been untouched since Christian died.

It's a clear morning, the sky blue, the air crisp. It would be lovely on the hills. If she were at home she could go for a run, sprint around the loch until her muscles ached and her brain was empty of everything other than the burn. But she's not. She's walking to the High Court, ready to give evidence. As she has been for months.

Not long to go now.

They're waved through security, taken to the witness room. A middle-aged woman in a pink cardigan fusses around them with mugs of tea and plates of biscuits. Marianne tries to smile but her face has frozen, her mouth outside of her control. *My name is Marianne Shaw, mother of a murdered child, and I will have my . . .*

'It's time.'

40

The woman in the stand looks as if she hasn't slept for a week. Her skin is so pale it's translucent, a blue vein pulsing on her temple. Her lips are chapped, her nose rubbed red raw. Matthew can tell she's tried to dress for court, but the jumper is too big, the collar too stiff, a child dressed in her mother's clothes.

Her voice is quiet as she gives her name, affirms. No Bible for her. When she explains that she's Christian's mother, Matthew understands. God wasn't there when her daughter died. He's on edge watching her, his nerves tight as wires. His weekend's activities have soothed him, to an extent, but he certainly didn't get enough sleep. Besides, he's on high alert now. He knows what this woman is.

The blonde woman – Gill, he knows her name now; Gill – she doesn't look too comfortable either as they watch the woman being impaled on the advocate depute's questions. Not that he's making a point of searching out Gill's attention, after the way that he ran off in North Berwick. And not that the questions are that searching. Matthew has a feeling that the woman has mostly been brought in to show the human face of Christian's loss. About time, too. The dead girl has reduced to an abstraction, an idea slowly fading from view, a word repeated over and over again that loses its meaning.

Christian's no abstract to Marianne Shaw. The loss of the

girl pulsates off her. Maybe too much so? He's not sure. Hard to calibrate how someone should react to the loss of their child. In such terrible circumstances, too.

She takes the court through Christian's childhood, the disease that so nearly killed her when she was little, the steps that they had to take to keep her alive after the infection led to myocarditis. The lasting damage to her heart. The constant fear under which Marianne lived that each birthday would be Christian's last. The fact that by sixteen, her condition had finally started to seem stable.

Matthew takes careful notes. He's trying to keep an open mind about Marianne's credibility, but Dominic's suspicions linger. He goes back to the photographs of Christian's heart from the autopsy, tries to remind himself of what the pathologist said. There's something nagging at him about it, though he can't put his finger on it. Not right now. He switches his attention back to the witness.

'I didn't want her to go to boarding school. I felt very strongly about it. But she insisted. Her father wanted it, too. She just wanted a normal life. I stood firm till she turned sixteen. Then I gave in. The doctors agreed it would be all right, so long as she was careful. Took her medication. Sixth form – it's a time to be more grown up. Independent. She knew how to look after herself, at least I thought so. We were pleased when she said that she wanted to bring some friends home that October half-term.' A sob, a hand held to her heart. 'We thought she was settling in. But the friends she brought were these girls. Isobel and Eliza. That Sasha, too. We thought they'd look after her, the way friends do.' She pulls her shoulders back, rallies herself. 'We couldn't have been more wrong.'

'Did you tell them specifically that Christian had a heart condition?' Mr Alexander says.

Marianne shakes her head. Her eyes are brimming with tears – Matthew can see that even from this distance. If she's acting, she's doing it well. 'Not in so many words. I did speak to them the morning that they left, after the drama in the chapel.'

'What did you say?'

'That they needed to be more careful with her. This kind of behaviour might be all right for them, but Christian wasn't like that. She wasn't tough. She was very sensitive. It might make her ill.'

'Do you remember specifically to whom you said this?'

A stricken look, a shake of the head. 'I've been wracking my brains trying to remember which of them was there. But I don't know. They might both have been there, it might only have been one of them. I was in shock about the whole thing. Sasha wasn't there – I think she'd left already, her mum arranged a taxi to pick her up first thing. But whether it was one or the other or both . . . I don't know. I'm sorry.'

'How did Christian seem when she got back to school? During the following months?'

'She was very withdrawn. I tried and tried to get her to talk to me, but she wouldn't. Peter – her father – he said I needed to leave her alone. Individuation, he called it. She was working out who she was on her own, now that she'd left home. He said it was perfectly normal.'

'What did you think of it?'

'I thought she was unhappy. But she said she was fine. She wouldn't talk to me. I said to her that she didn't need to go back. That we'd get her back into her old school, she could live back at home with me. With her dogs. But she was clear that she wanted to keep going to that school. I should have insisted . . .'

Isobel's advocate doesn't cross-examine. There's no need. The woman is suffering as it is, and her evidence can't be clarified much further. It's obviously important that she told one or the other of the girls to lay off, but it's clear she can't remember exactly which, and it won't do Isobel any good if she changes her mind and says that on second thoughts, it wasn't the blonde one that she spoke to.

The thought creeps into Matthew's mind that given their striking difference in appearance, she should perhaps have a better idea. Then he rejects it. He'd struggle to tell any of Daisy's friends apart. They all dress the same, wear their hair in the same way. He muddles names and backstories all the time. He hasn't suffered any major trauma like this, either.

Something feels off, nonetheless. He wants to believe her, but there's something that doesn't feel right.

The atmosphere changes when Christian's father comes to the stand. He means business, from the starched collar of his white shirt to the shiny tips of his black Oxfords. His face might look as if it's more at home in a checked shirt and hunting jacket, all red cheeks and weather-beaten nose, but his hair is carefully slicked down and he gives his name in a clipped tone that shows far more control than his wife.

'You would have been happy for your daughter to go to boarding school some years earlier, is that right?'

'Yes. It's a family tradition. I went from the age of eight, myself, and it was the making of me – I learned resilience, how to rely on myself. Self-discipline. All those attributes.'

'Your wife wasn't keen?'

A grim laugh. 'If I'm honest, I thought she mollycoddled Christian. I thought our daughter was fitter than Marianne would accept. It caused some terrible rows between us. But the doctors agreed with Marianne – they didn't think that she was up to going away from home. Not until sixth form, and that was only when Christian put her foot down herself about it.'

'How did you feel about that?'

Peter shakes his head. 'I was delighted,' he says. 'So proud of her. But now? I'll never forgive myself. If I hadn't insisted ...

I should have worked it out from the moment that those girls stayed at our house, that our daughter wasn't safe at that school. But I trusted them to look after her.'

'You trusted who? The girls?' Mr Alexander says.

'No,' Peter Shaw says, briskly moving on without expanding further. 'I trusted the school. After I reported to them what had happened in our house, the violation against our hospitality, I would have assumed that they would have taken stringent measures against those girls. But no. We are taking further action as far as that is concerned.'

Matthew understands this. The other jurors might think it's a dry response, that it reduces Peter to a one-dimensional figure, interested only in pounds and pence. But Matthew would do exactly the same. The only language these schools speak is one of money, the impact on the bottom line. Like hospital management boards. Or insurance companies. Organisations that never admit any liability, show any weakness. Litigation is the only weapon that effects change. Especially when someone dies.

It's probably why Isobel and Eliza weren't expelled after that disastrous half-term visit to the Highlands. The school didn't want to lose their fees.

'Could you tell the court about what you deemed the violation to your hospitality?'

'Certainly.' He proceeds to outline the state in which the chapel was found the day after the girls arrived, the stench of blood and guts, the desecration to the altar. Most of what he says the court has already been told by Sasha.

'This was all terrible,' Peter Shaw says. 'That chapel has been in my family for generations. Nothing like this has ever happened there. The place was wrecked.'

Matthew looks over at the girls in the dock. He's struggling to picture it, the grimness of the scene. Surely not that pretty blonde girl, with the pink cheeks. The incongruity is striking.

'Did you speak to either or both of the girls the following morning after the state of the chapel was discovered?'

'I did, yes,' the witness says. 'I spoke to that one. Isobel.' He points straight at her, saying her name with such force that she looks up, a shocked expression on her face, the first sign of emotion that Matthew has seen from her since the trial began. 'I told her in specific terms that Christian might seem like any other girl, that she was strong. But that if they kept on like this, they'd kill her. Her heart wouldn't take it.'

The man's head lowers. He swallows, his Adam's apple moving up and down. For a moment he's quiet, looking at the floor, or something far beyond. Then he brings his focus back to the jury. 'I thought that it might help. I thought it might waken some compassion in these girls. But now I understand it's as if I loaded a gun and put it straight into her hand.'

'You're lying,' Isobel shouts across the courtroom. 'You're lying. You never said anything!'

'Silence!' the judge says. Her words cut like steel.

A commotion in the dock as the girl seems to be trying to climb out of it, perhaps to get to the witness. The security guards have soon dealt with her, though, restraining her by the arms as they drag her down to the cells.

'Court will adjourn for a brief period. Back in fifteen minutes, please.' The judge stands and walks out of court.

Back in the jury room, there's a lot of strong feeling. Marianne's demeanour has convinced everyone, it seems. They're united in their dislike of Isobel, too. Matthew's not saying anything, though he understands their emotion. But the research he carried out online at the weekend is on his mind. Strange how the internet favours Isobel so. They haven't been sitting in court through this, though. Not like the jury. They don't like her one bit.

'She's looked aggressive the whole way through,' Jasmine

says. 'I've been waiting for her to blow, if I'm honest. She certainly isn't helping herself.'

More murmurs of assent. The room is quiet for a moment, as if thinking about Isobel's various iniquities.

'Her own advocate doesn't seem to be defending her,' Russell says. 'That's what I can't get my head round. Why aren't they putting forward a defence?'

'Maybe there's nothing for them to say,' Neil says. 'Maybe she did it, and everybody knows it.'

Everybody knows. The phrase cuts through Matthew's thoughts. Everybody knows. Everybody thinks the same. Since when was he everybody? The conversation he had with Dominic comes into his mind. He remembers the suspicion he's feeling towards Marianne, takes a step back mentally. Maybe he needs to stop following the herd.

41

Back in court, Matthew shifts in his seat. He's struggling to find a comfortable position today, his body protesting at the length of time that he's been sitting in the same spot.

The girls are back in the dock. Eliza's face still unmoved, beautifully calm. Isobel is calm as well but she looks sullen, her brows knitted as if in concentration. A gargoyle to Eliza's cherub, satyr to her fawn.

Christian's father returns to the witness box. He doesn't look at the dock. Doesn't look at the jury, either, his gaze fixed on a point somewhere at the back of court. Matthew looks over to see that the previous witness, Christian's mother, is now sitting in the front row of the public gallery. Gill is sitting a couple of rows behind her – Matthew catches her eye but doesn't smile.

'To reiterate,' Mr Alexander begins, 'you say that you spoke to Isobel and told her of your concerns for your daughter?'

'Yes, that's right.'

Matthew looks at the dock. Isobel is bright red, her mouth compressed into a tight line. But she keeps herself under control.

'Where were you when you had this conversation?'

'I went into the kitchen. Isobel was sitting there on her own. So I took the opportunity to say something, much as I wish I hadn't.'

Witch Trial

'Let's rewind a bit – what can you say about Christian's general demeanour before she started boarding that year at school?'

'She was a normal, happy child. I had no real concerns for her. Sure, she had the heart condition, but it was under control. She could have gone to boarding school a lot sooner, if her mum had let her.'

If her mum had let her. The phrase jumps out at Matthew. Why was Marianne trying to control the situation?

'She liked our dogs, she liked riding, she liked going out for long walks with her mum and me.' A sob from the public gallery. Marianne is losing control. 'I had *no* concerns for her at all, other than that she should continue to look after her health. Take care of herself.'

'Was there a point when you started to feel more concern for her? Aside from this half-term?'

Peter nods emphatically. 'Yes. The tone of her messages home changed almost overnight. She had always been such a happy, open child. But she became more closed. Monosyllabic, almost. We put it down to typical teenager behaviour, a necessary adjustment as she got used to being away from home. It would have evened out in the end – I was sure of it. I know now that was wrong. I should have asked more questions.'

Matthew's thoughts turn to Daisy, the times that she'd walked upstairs without saying hello when she was the same age as the girls, shutting her bedroom door. He'd never questioned her either. He'd always assumed she'd grow out of it too.

'I blame Isobel entirely. I could never have guessed she'd go this far, though,' Peter says. He hasn't been asked a question and the advocate depute holds up his hand.

'Please wait until I've asked another question, Mr Shaw.'

The witness snorts, an irritated sound. But he does stop.

'Did you speak to anyone at the school about your concerns?'

'Not until after the half-term fiasco,' he says. 'I didn't raise it with anyone until then.'

'What was the school's response?'

'They told me that they would speak to the girls' parents, and that they would break up the dormitory. I understood from Christian that this is what happened. She was very angry with me about the fact that I told the school – she said I'd ruined everything, made her life impossible. I didn't take it seriously, though. I was sure she'd get over it.'

'How was she at Christmas?'

'Quiet. A bit subdued. But essentially herself. At least I thought so. In retrospect . . .'

'In retrospect?'

'I think she was a lot more unhappy than she was letting on. But she wanted to make her own decisions. She hadn't been allowed much independence growing up – it was hard, with her mother's concerns for her health. *Our* concerns. But in retrospect I think that she was hiding a lot of unhappiness from us. And come the new term in January, she didn't tell me that the girls were put back into the same dormitory as her.' He pauses. 'She stopped telling me anything at all.'

Words that could break your heart. Matthew's chest is tight with sympathy. While the circumstances of Christian's death are not the most standard, it's not too much of a stretch for him to imagine himself up there, a bereaved father, alone.

There isn't much more for Christian's father to say. Peter reiterates his point wherever possible that it's Isobel he holds primarily responsible for Christian's metamorphosis from mummy's girl to full-blown goth. The prosecution makes a point of showing a photograph of her from the year before, fresh-faced and smiling beside a group of different school friends – it's clear that something has changed her from that child to the facially pierced, sullen young woman that had flashed up on the jury's screen at the start of the trial.

Looking at Isobel, her badly dyed black hair, her lip stud, the hoops running up each ear, Matthew knows the answer is probably staring him straight in the face.

Cross-examination takes a moment to get going. While Miss Brodie shuffles through her papers, Matthew picks at the skin on his left thumb. There's been a weird burning sensation in it all day, the area at first just red, but now he can see that small, round blisters are starting to form. Not just on his thumb, either, across the palm of his hand. But mostly his thumb. Decades-old *Macbeth* creeps into his mind, *By the pricking of my thumbs, something wicked this way comes.*

Wicked. Such a harsh word to use for a schoolgirl. However badly dyed their hair.

Miss Brodie doesn't baulk at the sentiment, though. 'You're clear that Christian was the target of systematic bullying, aren't you?'

'Yes, I am,' Peter says.

'And that this campaign was waged despite the fact that you asked Isobel to lay off?'

'Yes.'

'You're equally clear that you told Isobel about Christian's heart condition?'

'Yes. I was trying to appeal to her better nature.' A bitter laugh.

'You did not at any point communicate this information to Eliza?'

An emphatic shake of the head. 'No. I did not.'

'No further questions, my lady.' Miss Brodie returns to her seat. A brief exchange, but her point has been rammed home.

To Matthew's surprise, Miss Goodly takes her place at the lectern. Then he remembers Isobel's outburst. *You're lying.* Even this advocate would have to put that point across. She doesn't look comfortable, though.

'Mr Shaw, I am sorry to put such a point to you, but I have my instructions. Isn't it the case that you are lying about the fact that you told Isobel about Christian's heart condition?'

'It most certainly is not,' Mr Shaw says. 'I am outraged at the very suggestion.'

'And that the person you told was in fact Eliza?'

He shakes his head, his face red. 'I am telling the court exactly what happened here. I told *your client* in specific terms that she should leave my daughter the fuck alone.'

The court collectively takes a sharp intake of breath. Not at the language per se – Matthew knows that no one is that naive. But the sound of the swear word coming from this man's mouth has the force of a gunshot.

And in its aftermath, a quiet sobbing from Christian's mother the only sound.

The rest of the jury look over at her in sympathy. Not Matthew, though. It's falling on deaf ears to him. He glares over at her, unimpressed by the performativity. She's too perfect a bereaved mother, playing the part far too well.

There's more to it than this. And whatever it is, he's going to find it out.

42

Fleabag was the worst thing that ever happened to the church. Gerald Thomas puts his fingers up to his dog collar and caresses it gently as he waits in the witness room to be called to give evidence. He's sick of being called a hot vicar, sick of the raised eyebrows, the smothered laughs when he tells people that he's a school chaplain. *Watch out for the naughty schoolgirls*, that's what some of his more outspoken friends said when he took the job at St Jude's. *They'll eat you for breakfast.*

He's grown into the job, though. Five years and not a hint of a rumour that he's anything other than strictly professional. Primarily because he isn't. He's done his best, anyway. He can't help his cheekbones, chiselled jaw, does his best to soften them with pies and pints with some of the more amenable teachers – the geography department generally the best bet for a night out in Stockbridge – but he can't help how he looks.

The jury will hold it against him, though, he's sure of it. When he gets up there to tell the court what he knows about Christian's sufferings, they won't see that, they'll see Andrew Scott telling Phoebe Waller-Bridge to kneel. Or if they're from a generation above, they'll see Richard Chamberlain smouldering in *The Thorn Birds*.

Gerald hopes they can rise above themselves, leave their basic instincts behind. He prayed for it last night, prayed for guidance about how best to judge it, telling the story straight without showing favour to any of the girls he once knew so well.

That was the upside of the cheekbones, at least – he got good attendance at his Bible Studies classes. He never kidded himself that any of the pupils who came were drawn initially by his inspirational take on scripture, but by the time they'd finished a session, more were tempted to come back by the lively discussions that happened than they might have predicted.

'Christian first came to Bible Studies class in November of that term,' he says to the court. 'I hadn't noticed her particularly before, though there was a couple of them who dressed in that alternative way. I saw them in the back of the chapel. They'd pretend to be reluctant, but if it was a well-known hymn they always joined in the singing by the end. Especially at Christmas.' Gerald laughs. Chokes it back. He knows it's not funny, but now he's up here, he's found his voice less under his control than he would like, a tremor setting in through his hands.

'Anyway, she came to the first class I held after half-term. I'd chosen Hallowe'en as the topic. I mean, given it had just passed, it seemed appropriate. I wasn't wanting to be overly serious about the subject, but at the same time, I felt that there was something worth saying. All this talk of magic and witchcraft, but it can be dark, dark stuff. The way it's been commercialised by this whole Trick or Treating . . .'

The advocate depute coughs, loudly. Gerald catches on to himself. He's rambling. So nervous that he's lost all grip on what he is there to say. This is important, though. He needs to set the scene.

'I was pleasantly surprised by how many pupils attended the session. Christian was there, with some of her friends, though I never found out their names. One of them looked like Christian, I mean with the hair and the make-up.'

Witch Trial

He can see them now, sitting as far back as they could, heads huddled together. They burst into giggles throughout his talk, refused to ask any questions.

'Do you recognise any of those girls in the courtroom today?'

'Yes.' He points towards the dock. Isobel has her head averted from him, but Eliza is gazing at him, the same adoration on her face that there always was. He wants to smile at her, to reassure her that it will be all right, but he knows that he can't. Knows that he doesn't even know if it's true.

'I ran through a quick history of the celebration, how the Celts had celebrated the time of year known as Samhain, in a similar fashion to the Mexican celebration of the Day of the Dead. I was light-hearted. But I also made the point that the Bible is quite clear. We must abstain from all appearance of evil. One Thessalonians 5:22.'

'Thank you, Reverend Thomas. Now if we can return to Christian?'

He's got to stop talking. Or rather, he's got to stop waffling. One more piece of scripture though. It is relevant after all.

'My point was that all this might seem like a joke, but it wasn't. Anyway, my talk went down well enough. I finished off with a cracking verse from Deuteronomy. Do you mind?'

Mr Alexander shakes his head, as if he's resigned to his fate now, the vicar on the loose. Gerald straightens his sleeves, stands up tall.

'It's 18:10–12. "There shall not be found among you *anyone* who makes his son or his daughter pass through the fire, *or one* who practises witchcraft, *or* a soothsayer, or one who interprets omens, or a sorcerer, or one who conjures spells, or a medium, or a spiritist, or one who calls up the dead. For all who do these things *are* an abomination to the Lord, and because of these abominations the Lord your God drives them out from before you."'

Gerald's confidence grows as the words pour from him, his

voice ringing. As it did when he said them for the first time in that school room all those months ago. The girls at the back had twitched when he said the word *witchcraft*, he'd noted it particularly, their laughter starting to fade. At the end of the talk they'd filed out, no questions asked, the mood decidedly more sombre than at the start of the hour.

Only Christian had stayed behind.

'She helped pile up the chairs, put them back at the side of the room. After we'd finished I thanked her, said there wasn't anything else to do, but she didn't leave. She just stood there.'

He can see her now, shifting from foot to foot. She was white as a sheet, clearly deeply agitated. He remembers noticing how badly bitten her fingernails were, how chapped her lips. She could have been a pretty girl – she *was* a pretty girl – but he didn't think that she looked well.

'She said that she had something to ask me. I was struck by how scared she seemed. It didn't really make sense to me. But what she said explained it. She asked me if I believed that the Devil was real.'

Someone else might have laughed at that question, but not Gerald.

'What did you say?'

'I said that I believed that evil existed, and that people were capable of many evil deeds, but that if it came down to cloven hooves and a tail, I didn't believe that the Devil was real.'

'Did she ask anything else?'

'Yes. She asked me if I believed that it was possible to speak to the dead, or to predict the future. I answered very firmly to those questions. I said absolutely not, but that it could be very dangerous to try. She asked if I meant dangerous because it might disturb evil spirits, but I said absolutely not to that, as well.'

'Did you explain why you thought it was dangerous?'

'Yes. I said that some subjects, some activities were best left well alone because of the dark direction in which they could take your thoughts. Even though rationally speaking, of course, communication with the dead or with evil spirits isn't possible, it's still unwise.'

The girl started to look calmer, he remembers that. The more he said it wasn't real, that it was impossible, the more colour returned to her cheeks.

'She was about to leave – she'd nearly got to the door. Then she came back. Like she'd saved the question she really wanted to ask until nearly the end. She stood right in front of me, sheer terror on her face. Then she asked me this.' He pauses. Even now, he can't actually believe how it's all turned out. That it's real.

'What did she ask you?' the advocate depute says. The courtroom is completely silent.

'She said that the Devil had told her that she'd be dead within six months. She wanted to know if that was true.' Gerald looks down at his hands, now twisted in front of him. 'I told her no. Of course not.'

That conversation happened at the beginning of November. The Devil might not be real. It might have been a day or two longer than the prediction said. But one thing was true. Christian died on the first of May the following year.

Six months later.

43

The rash is spreading across Matthew's hand, little blisters popping up now all over the palm, creeping up to the finger joints. He doesn't want to keep scratching it but the itch is so intense he can't stop himself. The biggest blister is emerging right in the centre of his left hand, not yet fully formed, hot and irritated. He glares at it, turning his hand over and over to catch the light, give him a better sense of what's happening. Some kind of eczema, he remembers it from medical school. Trivial, as health complaints go. But he doesn't like it. Not one bit.

The vicar is facing cross-examination now. He didn't have much more to say after his revelation about Christian's foreknowledge of her own death. He offered to pray with her and she said no; he never saw her in Bible Studies class again. He was ashamed to say that he hadn't followed up on the conversation. He wishes that he had. The girl was clearly deeply unhappy; he failed in his duties towards her.

Matthew can't imagine why someone looking like that would go into the church – makes no sense to him. Shoulders like that, the man would be an asset on any rugby pitch. Muscular Christianity. He wouldn't be out of place as an eighteenth-century missionary, fighting his way through a jungle with a machete on his way to inflict religion on anyone unfortunate enough to get in his way.

Witch Trial

Wasted on a school. Maybe this was meant to be a stepping stone to something better. Not any more. After this experience, the vicar has lost faith in his ability to provide spiritual guidance. *It was my duty to do more, and I failed in my duty.* His final answer in examination-in-chief still echoes in Matthew's ears. Duty. An outmoded concept these days.

Miss Brodie makes what Matthew is now coming to recognise as her usual point – Reverend Thomas never discussed Christian with Eliza, rarely saw Eliza with Christian, never heard Eliza's name mentioned to him as a source of any trouble.

'The contrary, I'd say,' the vicar says. 'She always seemed very sweet and concerned for Christian, at least in terms of how she acted when I was around. Also, Christian never looked unhappy when I saw her with Eliza. If anything, she looked happier with her than she did with anyone else.'

'Including Isobel?'

'I never saw her alone with Isobel,' he says. 'So I can't speak to that. But when I saw her walking round the school with Eliza, she always seemed very relaxed.'

'Did you have any dealings with Eliza separately?'

He nods. 'Yes, I did.' A warmth has come into his voice. 'She volunteered with some of the younger girls. We ran a mentoring scheme via the chapel for new pupils who had started in Year Nine. She was always very kind to them.'

Matthew looks at the girl. She's got a small smile on her face but it's not smug at the praise. More tinged with sadness. An easier time, long past.

Miss Goodly doesn't bother to cross-examine. Matthew supposes that she doesn't have anything to say. Not that he wants to be prejudiced about appearances, but Isobel doesn't exactly look like the kind of girl anyone would want mentoring someone young or impressionable.

* * *

Lunch break. All the female jurors are fluttering about the hot priest. Other than Emma, who mutters darkly that she prefers her clerics less decorative. At last, something on which she and Matthew can agree. Not that he says anything. His hand is pissing him off, hot and itchy. It's spreading up on to his wrist now, too, a small blister making its appearance on his right hand. He needs to go and buy some cream but the break won't be long enough, not now, not by the time he's eaten. He'll pass by Boots on the way home later.

As usual, everyone is slagging off Isobel.

'You don't think it's a bit convenient, that they're all pinning the blame on her?' Matthew turns in surprise – it's Nicola. He's never heard her speak inside the jury room, only seen her outside smoking. Marlboro, he remembers.

'Convenient?' That's Aisha.

'All this being laid out against her. Maybe that's just what they want us to think.'

'They?'

'Oh, you know,' she waves a hand, 'the prosecution, the family. Pin it on the problem girl.'

Matthew's interested that someone else is possibly thinking along the same lines. He tests it. 'Or maybe it's adding up because that's actually the evidence? There hasn't been anything to suggest otherwise, you know.'

'What Sasha said? That they were both in it?'

'She's just trying to play down her role in the whole thing,' Jasmine says. She's glaring at Nicola as if the woman has insulted her family.

Barring a miracle, Isobel's guilt really is emerging, clear for all to see. But there's a doubt in his head, an ugly growth, like fungal spores multiplying in the dark. He doesn't think she's innocent, either. But it's all starting to feel a little too contrived. Images of the dead heart keep flashing into his mind; there's something not right there, too. But the edges of it are dark; he can't go behind it. It nags at him, just the same.

After he's eaten, Matthew goes out for a quick walk round the block. His legs are feeling twitchy, in need of a stretch, even though they've been stiff ever since he launched himself up North Berwick Law. His fitness is slipping away from him every day that this trial goes on. He scratches at his hands again, feels an itch on his face too, his heart sinking at the thought that he's going to come out in a rash there as well. He's falling apart.

As he left the court building, he saw Gill's head over the road, but he quickly went in the opposite direction, heading down the Royal Mile to the Palace of Holyroodhouse at the bottom before turning round and heading back up again. On the way back up he spots a pharmacy and goes in, showing the pharmacist behind the desk what his hand looks like. Before she can stop it, she makes a face, a moue of disgust twitching her lip up.

'It's eczema,' she says. 'Pompholyx is the most likely diagnosis. Have you been very stressed lately?'

He nods, pays for the cream that she recommends.

'If it gets worse, you need to see a doctor,' she says. He keeps walking.

'Everything all right?' A voice brings him up short as he leaves the pharmacy. It's Gill.

His immediate response is to turn and run. Not because he doesn't want to talk to her – there's nothing he wants more. But he can't . . . She's got such a real expression of concern on her face, though, that Matthew can't bring himself to be so unkind. On the other hand, they're so close to court . . . While he knows there's nothing untoward about the conversations they've had, he also understands that someone else involved in the trial might take a different view.

'I'm fine,' he says, keeps on walking. She trots to keep up with him but he refuses to turn and look at her.

'Matthew,' she says. At that he stops.

'I can't talk to you,' he says. 'Don't you understand that? I can't talk to you, I can't answer any of your questions. You need to leave me alone.'

He strides off without looking to see if she's taken the point or if she's still pursuing him. The distraught state of Christian's mother has brought it home to him how serious all this is, how much is at stake. Whatever happens, he can't be seen to be consorting with anyone outside of the jury. Much as he's intrigued by her, he just can't.

Emma is entering the court building at the same time as him and she raises an eyebrow as she hears him puff his way up the stairs.

'Went for a run, did we?'

'I walked further than I intended,' he says through gritted teeth. He'd rather ignore her but there's no point alienating her. Not yet.

'A little walk with your blonde friend?' She's standing next to him now, her breath hot on his ear. He freezes.

'I don't know what you're talking about,' he says after a moment.

'I've seen you, you know. Exchanging glances in court. Little chats outside. You shouldn't be doing that, you know.'

'I'm not doing anything,' he says.

'I should really tell the jury officer,' she says. 'You know what they told us about jury interference. Pretty woman, too, isn't she? I bet you'd like her to interfere with you.' She lets out a laugh, a low, horrible sound that chills Matthew's blood.

'You don't know what you're talking about,' he says as he walks away. But the sound of her laughter still echoes in his ears.

44

Between Emma's scrutiny and the discomfort Matthew's increasingly in with his skin, he finds it hard to concentrate during the afternoon's evidence. It's as well that it's a police officer on the stand, telling the court what items she found during a search of the girls' dormitory. The exhibits table is soon covered in items that look like they've come straight out of the witchcraft museum down the Royal Mile.

Everything was taken from a black metal box that was found underneath Isobel's bed. The poppet that was discussed earlier is there. It's sealed in a plastic bag as it's handed round the jury but Matthew still thinks that a stink of dead fish lingers around it, making its way even through this air-tight wrapping.

There are bunches of dried herbs, clumps of hair and a rabbit's foot all sealed up in separate exhibit bags. There are five different sets of tarot cards. Matthew blinks as he turns them over in his hands – who would have thought there to have been so many variations? A wooden board that he recognises as a Ouija board. He runs his fingers across the D, the I. The E. A tremor goes through him, as if an electric current is transmitting itself through the contamination-proof sealant.

A collection of books, all containing variants of *Magick* and *Witchcraft* on their covers. A history book – *Witchcraft, A History in Thirteen Trials*. Matthew turns that over in his hands too, reading the back cover with interest. He might get himself a copy of it, mug up a bit more on the subject.

'Members of the jury may find some of the following items rather disturbing,' the judge warns them at one point. Matthew sits up with interest. What could be worse than what they've already seen?

Bottles of urine, that's what, the contents dark and cloudy now. A collection of used tampons, squishy in their clear wrappings as if they haven't yet fully dried out, even though it's been months since they were found.

Matthew has a sudden, horrible image of Isobel lurking in bathrooms, waiting for her prey to finish discarding their sanitary protection before picking it out of the bin and stashing it away. For what, though?

For casting spells. Hexes. Curses. Matthew's research over the weekend has taught him that much. A whole arsenal of intended harm. He's not going to share the thought with anyone else on the jury, though. He knows he needs to be more careful now, make sure that he doesn't attract any more adverse attention.

Finally, a knife with a black handle, the blade plain but wickedly shiny, light reflecting from it even through the clear evidence bag. Matthew sits up straight. The ritual blade, the one used to kill the pigeon.

The one wielded by either Eliza or Isobel to threaten Christian, leading to the fatal heart attack.

'This was found at the bottom of the box. Fingerprint analysis came back negative.'

'What does that mean?'

'It means that it had been wiped clean. There's no way of knowing who handled it.'

Miss Brodie stands up to cross-examine. Matthew can't

think what she can have to say on the subject but he doesn't have to wait long to find out.

'Just to clarify, this box was found underneath Isobel's bed in the dormitory?'

'That's right, yes,' the police officer says.

'And it was tucked right to the back, next to the wall, with a number of other items stashed in front of it?'

'Yes.'

'You've said that the knife had no fingerprints on it. Overall, though, when you took fingerprints from the other items, the ones which you found belonged primarily to Isobel?'

The police officer clears her throat. 'Not primarily, no. There were slightly more of Isobel's fingerprints on the box, but there were also fingerprints found which belonged to each of the other girls involved in this case. The two co-accuseds, the witness Sasha. Even a couple from the victim herself, Christian.'

Dead girl's fingers. Matthew shudders, a cold chill on the back of his neck.

Miss Brodie sits down. She hasn't won the point she wanted, Matthew can tell by the disgruntled expression on her face. To his surprise, Miss Goodly stands up and moves over to cross-examine as well.

'This box wasn't locked, was it?'

'No, it wasn't.'

'And even though it was hidden under the bed, there was nothing to stop anyone from finding it if they spent longer than ten seconds pulling out the items that were in front of it?'

'Well, no. They'd need to know that they were looking for it, but yes.'

'The point is that although this might have been underneath Isobel's bed, it's clear that it was accessible to everyone involved, yes?'

'Yes.'

'And beyond the location in which it was found, there is nothing to suggest that any of these items were specifically owned by Isobel, or obtained by her?'

'I don't quite understand . . .'

'I mean that the tampons could have been retrieved by any of them. The bottles of urine could have been filled by any of them. That's right, isn't it?'

'I suppose so,' the police officer says hesitantly.

'You might have tested the DNA of the tampons, but you didn't test the DNA of the urine, did you?' Her tone suggests triumph, a piss-stained gotcha.

'Well, no. It's hard to get DNA from urine. We took a view . . .'

'You took a view? You took a view that you were going to blame Isobel for everything, so you didn't bother to do any further investigations, did you?'

'That's not the case.'

'Thank you, officer.' The advocate swoops back to her seat, her expression still triumphant.

But if that's the best she's got, Matthew fears she's got a long way to go in convincing anyone on the jury that Isobel isn't up to her neck in this.

45

It's well after 3 o'clock. Matthew is tired; by the way that they're slumped, the rest of the jury are tired, too. There's been everything today, high emotion, grotesque exhibits, a nasty trail of slime left on Matthew's mind as he thinks about everything that they've been shown this afternoon. He's trying not to look at the table of exhibits, trying not to look at Gill in case Emma catches him. While the last thing he wants to see is the squalid little pile of witchy artefacts, now that he knows he can't, the only direction in which he wants to stare is Gill.

Are you OK? She sounded so concerned when she asked him how he was earlier. He can't even remember now why he had such a strong reaction to her in North Berwick. He was being overly conscientious, that was all. He does what he's told, mostly. Some of the guidelines are there to save lives, after all. But this isn't like that. It's not a game of life and death in the way that heart surgery is. As with his research into the online discussions about the case, Matthew knows that his judgement is strong, his objectivity one of his most-prized attributes.

He wants to talk to her. He needs to talk to her. She understands what this case is like. She won't try and influence what he thinks, not like the other jury members. All of them are closing their minds now, the evidence cut and dried for them. Matthew's worried that he's doing the same, too. It would be so easy to make a decision, switch off. The prosecution has made it very easy for them, a brilliant sheepdog rounding up his obedient herd.

'My lady, I could start with the police interview now,' Mr Alexander says, 'or we could pick up on it tomorrow morning and go through it in its entirety. I'm not keen that we should start and then stop, if your ladyship agrees?'

He wants to finish for the afternoon. Matthew doesn't blame him. He's had enough, too. His head is aching, the blisters sore now and popped from his incessant scratching. He didn't have time to apply the cream that he bought and now all he wants to do is go back to the flat, strip off and have a soothing bath before rubbing on a layer of ointment and falling into bed.

Or he'll try to speak to Gill. She's inside it but outside, the perfect sounding board. Well, perhaps not perfect. But the only one he's got.

The judge agrees that they should finish for the day, the defence advocates both nodding their assent, and they head out of the courtroom. If Matthew hides in the gents for long enough, everyone should have left, and if Gill has any sense of what he's feeling, any sense at all, she'll be waiting for him outside, round the corner, somewhere only they will know.

He hasn't even caught her eye, too paranoid to look over in case of Emma, but he has a strong feeling that she does know what he's thinking; the same electrical current that jumped out at him from the Ouija board is tingling through him now as if they're connected by it. He just knows, if he leaves it long enough, it will all be all right. He'll find her.

Emma watches him like a hawk all the time that they're in the jury room gathering their belongings. No one is keen to do a post-mortem – home is calling, the unexpected hour given to them at the end of the day a bonus that no one wants to waste. Matthew says his goodbyes, and muttering under his breath about *bathrooms, something he ate,* makes his way into the gents, locking himself into a cubicle.

Normally he'd kill time by reading a book, but he's stopped bringing it to court. That distraction is lost to him. He sits on the closed loo, counting the tiles on the wall, tracing the patterns made by the cracks in the enamel, the stains. As he stares, a shape starts to emerge, a face, two eyes, ears, a mouth, a nose. It's friendly to start with, but the longer that he looks at it, the more that it starts to take on a sinister appearance, the smile on the mouth turning into a jeer. It's laughing at him, Matthew can almost hear it. He knows exactly what it thinks of him, what contempt it holds for him. *You're just another sheep, going along with the herd. Doing what you're told like a good little boy. Of course you're going to find Isobel guilty – you're stupid like the rest of them. Baa, baa, baa.*

He shakes his head, trying to stop the noises that are now filling his ears. He's surrounded by baaing noises, louder and louder. The white tiles around the face have black faces now, eyes staring out at him, muzzles wide as they *baa baa baa BAA BAA BAA BAA BAA.*

'Stop it,' he says. 'Just stop.' He jumps to his feet, puts his hand to the cubicle lock to let himself out but the lock is jammed fast, it's stuck, the sheep heads getting closer and closer with their infernal *BAAAA BAAA BAAAA.*

'Everything all right in here?' a man says.

The lock moves smoothly back in Matthew's hand, the door opens. He glances at the wall of sheep and it's nothing but tiles, gleaming white under the fluorescent lights.

'I'm fine,' he says as he leaves the cubicle. 'The lock jammed, that's all.'

'I'll have a look at that,' the man says. He's wearing a janitor's uniform, a bucket and mop in his hand. Matthew thanks him, washes his hands automatically. The urge to wait for Gill has been replaced by an urge to get the hell out of here and to stay as far away as possible. He's had enough of this case and everything to do with it.

The cold air hits him as he walks out of the court building. It's a jolt, the immediate transition from claustrophobic courtroom to this open space full of tourists and wailing bagpipes. 'Flower of Scotland' segues into 'Amazing Grace' and the tightness in Matthew's chest increases as the long-remembered words fill his head to the music. *I once was lost but now am found. Was blind but now I see.*

Does he see? Has he been looking at it all the wrong way? Isobel's guilt seems so overwhelming. He's no sheep, though. Matthew's always prided himself on his ability to avoid thinking with the herd. He's lost friends for it in the past.

A woman with a large umbrella followed by a procession of teenagers bashes into him. He needs to get out of here, away from the court building, away from the fake tartan and fridge magnets that litter the street where once mobs bayed for the blood of witches as they were hanged, burned. He looks up and down the Royal Mile and it's as if the centuries have lifted, the history of it now evident to him, its dark beating heart.

He doesn't know enough, though. The ghosts of the past might be more apparent, but they're speaking in a different tongue. A memory comes back to him of the evidence that they were shown earlier, the book that he'd looked at with such interest. The history of witchcraft trials. With sudden decision, all thoughts of Gill out of his mind, he heads up towards the bookshop near the end of Chambers Street, determined to read and find out everything that he doesn't know.

Mission accomplished in the bookshop, he heads into the Museum of Scotland. As he'd paid for the book, the woman behind the till had told him to go and have a look there. 'If you're interested in that kind of thing, they've got a whole display of it up on the fourth floor.'

Up to the fourth floor. He's looking at something described as a talisman of protection, a calf's heart studded full of nails. Protection or not, his own heart beats uncomfortably fast at the sight of the grotesque item. He feels a touch to his arm. He freezes. The devil's head, the face in the tiles – is this another attempt to trick him? Make him think he's seeing, feeling things that don't exist? Another tug, firmer this time, and a delicate smell of flowers that eases his fears. He turns to face Gill, the woman real in front of him, so solid that he could actually put his arms round her and weep.

46

No discussion needed, no words exchanged. Something has shifted in the air between them and neither seems to want to name it in case it breaks whatever it is. She takes his hand and leads him over to a display cabinet where there are eight miniature coffins, the Arthur's Seat coffins, found on the site where Sasha later tried to take her life.

Matthew turns his face away. He's had enough of the case. He's had enough of witches. He wants the here, the now. Nothing nebulous. Something tangible.

Gill.

They get out of the museum on to Chambers Street, straight into a taxi. Matthew gives his address without pausing to think. They sit close on the back seat, not touching, but near enough that he can feel warmth radiating off her, easing the numbness at his core that he's felt since the tiles in the bathroom transformed themselves into sheep and started baaing at him.

'I need to sleep,' he says, suddenly realising that this is what he wants beyond anything else, to climb into bed, a warm body beside him that he can curl himself into until all the outside world has gone away.

'You can sleep,' she says. 'You look like you need it.'

'I feel like I haven't slept since this case began.'

He pays for the cab and takes Gill into his flat. Despite his clearing up last week, it's a tip now, but he doesn't care. He knows instinctively that she won't, either, that she'll see beyond the washing-up, the piles of empty microwave trays. Or if she does see it, she understands that this isn't laziness, the grubby habits of a slovenly man. It's the detritus of loneliness, too many nights spent cold and alone; the time he spent with Olivia feels long now past.

He leads her into his bedroom, takes off his jumper, his socks. He sits on the bed and she sits next to him, unlacing her boots.

'Can you hold me?' he says. 'I just want to be held.' In her face he can see nothing but understanding. He lies down, curled up with his arm under his head, and to his joy he can feel her curl herself around him, pulling the duvet up close. A warmth suffuses him, a sense of peace, and he closes his eyes and sleep comes.

Later, when he wakes, she's not there. He puts his hand out to the empty space on the bed where she lay, panic rising. It subsides quickly, though. There's clattering from the kitchen, the sound of plates being stacked. A scent of frying onions in the air. He gets up, goes for a quick pee before joining her in the kitchen.

She's cleared up. The washing-up is neatly stacked on the drying rack and the microwave dishes have gone.

'I went through the fridge and found some bits,' she says. 'I'm just making a pasta sauce. You can't live off this processed rubbish, you know.'

She's looking after him. Matthew feels almost too grateful for words, though he manages a stumbled thanks.

'I've been worried about you,' she says. 'I've been watching you on the jury. You really seem to be taking it all so much to heart.'

'My daughter's not far off the same age,' he says. 'I think it was Christian's mum this morning . . .' He can't finish the sentence. She nods.

'I know what you mean. Look, I know you can't talk about it, but do you think this is a good jury? I mean, do you think they're keeping an open mind, that they're weighing up the evidence properly?'

'Yes, I think they are. It's all looking a bit of a foregone conclusion, but I guess we'll see what the defence is.'

'I guess we will. Anyway, eat up.'

She puts a plate of food in front of him. It's simple stuff – pasta, tomato sauce – but the fact that it's homemade gives it real flavour against the pap that he's eaten for the last week and he wolfs it down, pausing only to help himself to more when his plate is clean.

'Thank you,' he says again, with more vigour than before. The food and the sleep have both given him his strength back. He feels clearer in thought again, the fog lifted. He clears the plates from the table and puts the kettle on. It's his kitchen – he should take back control.

'Tea?'

She nods. Once it's done he sits back down at the table, pushing her mug across to her. Instead of picking it up, she reaches down and rummages inside her bag, pulling out a box.

'What's this?' he says.

'I bought it from that little museum off the Royal Mile,' she says. 'I wondered what you might think . . .'

He takes the box, looks at it, registering what he's looking at. A game box, the same size as Cluedo or Monopoly. But not as cheerful in its packaging, a spooky grey cover on which the word *OUIJA* jumps out.

Ouija. He pushes it away from him.

'What the fuck?'

'I was curious. I couldn't help it,' she says. 'We've heard so much about this kind of thing. I wondered what it would be like to try it.' She raises one eyebrow, looks at him invitingly.

Matthew recoils, shocked to his bones. He could handle it more easily if she'd stripped off all her clothes and offered herself to him on a plate. That would be straightforward, at least, a simple yes or no. A familiar invitation. Enough women have offered themselves to Matthew in his time. He's not always said no, either.

But what she's offering now is different. Darker. Dirtier. The kind of secret that sends shivers through you, the compulsion that repels yet attracts. *Just one more.* If you do it with your eyes shut, maybe it doesn't count. Though if you do it, it can never be undone. *If I can't see you, you can't see me. We'll do it in the dark.*

'I'll turn the lights off,' he says. 'There's a candle in here somewhere. That'll be better.'

He's crossing the Rubicon now.

47

Fingers on the planchette. Matthew's holding his breath. The tension is palpable. He knows it's a joke, that this is only a game played by impressionable teenagers, but he can feel his heart thumping. Gill looks caught in some private world, her eyes focused down on the board as if there's nothing else in the room. The air's colder, the darkness around the candle more intense. There's something throbbing there, something twitching under his fingertip, though he can't describe it, couldn't ever articulate how exactly it feels as if the cheap piece of varnished wood were alive.

'Is there anyone there?' Gill says, her voice solemn. No reply. Nothing, though the thrumming is growing in intensity, an awakening about to occur. 'If there's anyone there, please give us a sign.'

And what? Matthew feels panic rising in him too, now. They haven't thought this through, haven't discussed the questions that they should ask any potential spirit.

'Is there anyone there?' Gill says again, and this time the planchette twitches, sending a spark through Matthew's finger like an electric shock. He jumps, pulling his hand away from the planchette, the eczema suddenly itching beyond anything bearable, as if the skin is on fire. He scratches and scratches at it to try and get it to stop, to make it go, but it builds and builds, running up his arm now and into his other hand.

Witch Trial

'Matthew, stop,' Gill says. She's moved over beside him and is trying to restrain his hands. 'You're making yourself bleed.'

'I can't,' he says. 'It's too much. It's far too much.' He keeps scratching, Gill keeps pulling at his arms to make him stop, a roaring in his ears and a darkness building in front of his eyes.

Then it stops. All is quiet. So quiet the silence is heavy. Weighing down on him. The itch has gone, the urge to scratch disappears. Gill leans back, letting go of his arms. He looks over at the board and freezes. The planchette is moving, silently, relentlessly, spinning endlessly in a figure of eight. He opens his mouth to cry out but no sound emerges; he can't formulate a word, even a scream.

'What is it?' she says, following his gaze over to the board. 'What's wrong? Why do you look so scared?'

'The planchette . . . it's moving. Look, can't you see?'

Gill shakes her head. 'I can't see anything.'

'You're lying,' he says. 'Look at it. It's going mental. Like a fly trapped in a glass.' As he says the words he realises this is exactly what it's like, the wooden plaque buzzing round and round in an ever-repeating pattern, the buzzing building up in his head so loud it's like it'll explode, and now the itch has moved there too, burning inside his brain, his eyes; however much he claws at them he can't make it stop.

'Stop!' Gill screams, her voice so desperate that it cuts through the buzzing like a knife. The planchette flies off the board straight at her and Matthew launches himself at her in a rugby tackle before it can hit her in the head. Matthew lands on the floor, Gill underneath him.

The buzzing stops. The room is silent again. Matthew clocks where he is, lying straight on top of Gill. She isn't moving and for one terrible moment he thinks that in trying to save her from the planchette missile, he's knocked her out instead, bashing her head on something on the way down. He pushes himself up and as he does so, she moves away from him, scooting into the wall with her arms wrapped round her knees.

'What the fuck are you doing?' she says. 'Why did you do that?'

'I thought . . .'

'You thought what?'

'I thought that the planchette was about to attack you. It looked as if it was firing straight at you.'

She straightens up a little, looks at the board. 'The planchette is where we left it.'

Matthew stands up, walks the few steps over to it. She's right. The planchette *is* exactly where they left it. He puts his finger to it, deeply cautious. But it's dead now, all life gone from it. Just a flimsy piece of plywood. He puts it back in the box, folds the board in two and places it on top.

'I'm going to go,' Gill says. 'I think you need some rest. Maybe you'll be calmer tomorrow.'

'I'm sorry,' he says. 'I didn't mean any . . .'

'I know you didn't mean any harm. But that hurt. You scared me.'

Worse than the itching, worse than the fear, Matthew is struck by a deep wave of shame. He's fucked it up completely, every dealing he's had with this woman.

Not that he should even be talking to her. Any relationship he might have with her is fruit from a poisoned tree. It's a greater betrayal than any affair he's ever had.

'I'm sorry,' he says again.

She touches him lightly on the hand, her touch searing into him. Then she leaves. Matthew sinks to the floor, the Ouija board game still in his hands. He stays there for a long time.

His legs are numb by the time that the sun rises the next day. He's stayed motionless in the same spot, clutching the box, watching the corner of the room where he caused Gill to fall.

Where he tackled her to the floor, if he's going to be honest about what he did. All right, he didn't hit her, but he's used force against her, even if it was for what he thought was her own good. Was she limping as she left? It was hard to tell. But it had taken her a couple of beats to get up, an indication that he'd knocked the wind out of her.

This case. This case is fucking with his head so much. The responsibility of it, the stories they've been told. He can't handle it for much longer, he knows that much.

At least it won't go on for much longer. It can't. They must be near the end of the prosecution case now. He's got the picture of what they say happened, the creepy occurrences, the way that Christian was hounded down. Hard to believe it was anything other than a vindictive campaign. If Isobel had any decency, she'd have admitted what she'd done months ago.

The futility of it all strikes him hard. How can they ever possibly know for sure what was happening before the girl died? Only Christian knows the truth of what happened, who said what to her when. And Christian is dead.

TUESDAY

48

Police interviews take up the bulk of the day. The prosecution plays videos taken of each of the girls being interviewed by police officers, Eliza co-operative, eager to answer questions. Isobel less so. She looks disengaged and bored on the screen, her dark hair lank and greasy; disengaged and bored in court as well.

Matthew struggles throughout to focus on what's said. He stares hard at the screen from the start, not wanting to look anywhere else in the courtroom in case Gill is here and is glaring at him. Shame at his loss of control is eating away at him inside.

The police questions build a narrative, but it's one that he's worked out already from the evidence that the prosecution have presented. Any hope he had that he might start to divine a more detailed defence from Isobel are dashed as she says 'No comment' in a monotonous tone to each of the questions that's put to her.

Initially, the police seem immune to Eliza's charm. Every time she tries to suggest that she's been the innocent victim of Isobel as well as Christian they shoot it down, pointing out the times that Sasha witnessed her being nasty to the girl.

'You were the driving force in this, weren't you?'

'I was not.'

Where she is clear and unassailable is on the point that she was not told of Christian's heart condition by Christian's father or mother, or by anyone else. She had no idea that there was anything wrong with the girl at all. She accepts that sometimes what she said to Christian might have been less than kind, but she had no intention of causing her any significant harm.

One statement stands out. 'I'll never forgive myself for what's happened. If I'd had any idea that Christian suffered from this heart condition, I'd have stopped Isobel from doing everything that she did. I don't know why I didn't stop it as it was – I could tell that Christian was finding it distressing. But you know how it is . . . you get caught up in things. You want your friends to approve of you.'

As the interview builds to its finale, Eliza stays firm.

She did not pick up the knife.

She did not shout threats or run at Christian.

It was all Isobel. Isobel was the person who threatened Christian right at the end. Isobel was the one who put Christian in fear of her life.

Isobel is the one guilty of her murder.

Eliza seems so plausible. The police officers have clearly done their best to resist her wholesome appearance, but they've obviously taken to her as well. Matthew picks up on a big difference in tone between how they speak to her and to Isobel.

Isobel may have replied 'No comment' to every question that's asked of her, but the next witness, who appears near the end of the afternoon when all the videos of the police interviews have been played, has a great deal to say. She's tall, brunette, elegant, wearing a cashmere jumper and a tweed skirt, a string of pearls peeking out from under the white cotton frill of her blouse collar. There's a ripple of shock in the court as she gives her name, shaking her hair back off her face almost with a gesture of defiance.

Witch Trial

'Fiona Smyth,' she says. 'Isobel's mother.'

Isobel's mother is a witness for the prosecution? The jury are glancing around at each other trying to make sense of this. Eliza is biting her lip, an expression of distress on her face. Isobel hides behind her hair. It's impossible to tell what emotion she's feeling, although by the hunch of her shoulders, Matthew reckons she's upset. How could she not be?

'Thank you for agreeing to give evidence, Mrs Smyth. I appreciate that this is difficult for you.'

The woman sighs. Then she raises her chin. 'It's my duty,' she says. 'I love my daughter, but a child is dead. What kind of mother would I be if I ignored another mother's pain?'

A sob from the public gallery where Christian's mother is sitting. She's clutching a tissue, her nose red. Sitting very close to her is Christian's father, staring intently at Fiona Smyth. It looks as if he's trying to smile at her, although the strain he must be under is making it look more like a grimace.

'Please can you tell the court about your family situation, Mrs Smyth?' Mr Alexander says.

She nods. 'It's very difficult. I am what's known as a single mum. My marriage to Isobel's father broke down about seven years ago, partly I think down to Isobel's behaviour, and I've struggled to bring her up on my own ever since.'

'You said partly down to Isobel's behaviour – what did you mean by that?'

'She was constantly in trouble at school. I had to keep going into meetings about how she was behaving towards other girls in her class. There were many allegations of bullying. She'd been such a sweet little girl, but the older she got, the worse she became. Mind you, I'm sure that she was copying what she saw her father doing at home.'

'Can you expand on that?'

A loud sigh. She pauses to dab at her eyes with a small white handkerchief she's clutching in her right hand. 'This is very hard to talk about,' she says again. 'As well as being a single mum, I'm also the victim of domestic abuse. He was deeply unkind to me throughout our marriage.'

'I appreciate that it's difficult, but could you tell the court about that in a little more detail?'

'May I sit down?' Fiona says, turning to the judge. 'I'm feeling a little faint.' The judge nods.

Matthew's hands are clenched on his lap. There's nothing this woman is saying that's intrinsically wrong, in fact, more the opposite, but everything in him is rebelling at the prospect of listening to her speak. Every time she opens her mouth it's like a snake hissing. It makes no sense to him at all. She looks perfectly nice. Dresses like Rosalind.

He couldn't dislike her more.

'My ex-husband is a bully,' she says once she's sitting down in the witness box. 'He delights in undermining me and making me look like a fool. There is nothing he likes more than pushing me to my absolute limit, only happy when he's made me cry.'

'And you think that this had an effect on Isobel?'

'Yes, definitely. It's what every meeting at the school said. That she kept teasing and teasing people until they couldn't take any more.'

Isobel is so hunched over that Matthew can barely see her head over the top of the dock. For the first time since the case started, he feels intensely sorry for her. It must feel terrible to have her mother there, giving evidence against her in this way.

The litany of Isobel's sins continues, honey dripping from this woman's smiling mouth. An exclusion here, a suspension there, the school from which she was told to remove Isobel because of a complete breakdown of a friendship group.

'Did there come a time when you were introduced to Isobel's

most recent friendship group, Eliza, Sasha and Christian?' Mr Alexander says.

'I was, yes. They came round to my house for tea one exeat weekend.'

'An exeat weekend?'

'Although St Jude's is a boarding school, the children are allowed to come home at the weekend if they so choose. Isobel didn't choose to come home very often, but on this occasion, she brought her friends round too.'

'Can you tell the court where you were living at the time?'

'Where I'm still living. In Barnton,' she says.

Matthew knows it well, a genteel area in the north of Edinburgh on the way out up north. Not a difficult commute to school – Isobel had no need to be boarding as far as living close to school was concerned. The thought has clearly occurred to Mr Alexander as well.

'So Isobel boarded by desire, not because she lived too far away to be able to get into school?'

'Yes, that's right. It was more convenient for all concerned,' Fiona says. 'Especially after the divorce. It's so difficult when you're on your own . . .' her voice fades out.

'Tell us about the visit that Isobel made with her friends.'

'There was something off about it from the start . . .'

Matthew does his best to listen to what she's telling the court, a complicated story about who got to sit where when she drove them out to Cramond for tea by the sea, tempers lost and feelings hurt.

'I felt that Christian was very vulnerable,' she continues, 'that was what I thought. She clearly hero-worshipped Isobel.' A look here at the jury as if to say no, she didn't understand it either. 'And I became very uncomfortable with how unkind the girls were to her.'

'Unkind in what way?'

'They kept teasing her. They seemed to have a nickname for her – Dead Girl Walking. I remember it because it seemed such a strange name to call a friend. I didn't understand at all, although I do now, of course.'

'Do you remember who you heard saying that to Christian?'

A long silence. 'I think Sasha. Maybe Eliza.' Another silence, longer this time. She starts to cry. 'Definitely Isobel.'

49

They break for tea while the witness composes herself. Someone's bought a pack of bourbon biscuits and they're shared round the jurors. Matthew can't help himself; instead of eating it like a grown-up, he prises the top off the biscuit with his teeth, chuffed to get it off in one piece, scraping the filling off with delight. He looks up to find Neil laughing at him.

'That's how I used to eat them,' Neil says.

Matthew laughs. It loosens something in his chest that's been tight since Isobel's mother took the stand. Even though what she's said so far has been fairly reasonable, not sticking the boot in too much, he still feels quite stressed that someone should be giving evidence against her own daughter.

'I couldn't do it,' Jasmine says. It's as if she's been reading his thoughts. 'Stand up and give evidence against my own child like this. She's not even saying anything that bad, really. Just a bit of name calling.'

Emma shakes her head. 'I disagree. What it shows me is how dangerous Isobel is. If even her own mother thinks she's trouble, it means she needs to be stopped.'

From the nods around the table, it looks as if Emma's is the view that the majority share. Matthew can't explain his unease. Maybe he's wrong. Maybe he's projecting his irritation with Rosalind and how badly they're getting on right now on to this blameless woman who is doing her duty, after all. It makes a change to see a parent putting someone else's child above their own.

'What's wrong with your hand?' Aisha says.

He glances down at it. The rash has suddenly flared up again, bright red and swollen. As he opens his mouth to reply, he's hit by the unbearable itching again, the burning sensation that he can only calm with incessant scratching. He doesn't want to scratch, though. He doesn't want to lose control in front of this room full of people, all of whom will be keeping an eye out for weakness, any sign of strange behaviour.

'I've got a touch of eczema,' he says through gritted teeth, willing his hands to behave themselves and not start clawing uncontrollably at himself. 'I'll just go . . .'

With every appearance of calm he saunters out of the jury room, only to walk to the gents as fast as he can. As soon as he's inside the cubicle he pulls up his sleeves, horrified to see that the rash has spread up both of his forearms to his upper arms and beyond. The places where he scratched the night before are red and raw. He pulls out the cream that he remembered to bring with him and daubs it all over himself.

It's the strangest rash he's ever had, weirdly unpredictable. It goes from forgotten to unbearable in the blink of an eye, triggered by he knows not what. Chocolate? The bourbon biscuit? Surely not that. It doesn't make sense.

He can't wait for this case to be over. Funny how only a week ago, he was desperate to be on jury duty. Now he'd do anything to escape. All the grief of it, the misery, is leaking into him, his skin no longer an impermeable barrier, broken as it is by scratch marks and suppurating blisters.

The burning has subsided now, the cream doing its job. He needs to get back into court and find out what else this woman has to say. Looking in the mirror, he wills himself into action, staring himself down.

The face in the mirror starts to laugh. But Matthew isn't laughing.

He turns tail and he runs. Whatever might happen in court can't be as bad as what he's facing inside his head. Or in the mirror grimacing out at him.

He's wrong about that. It's worse. Fiona Smyth has come back into court fully composed and full of a story about how Isobel treated her pet hamster when she was younger, how she'd left it without food for days to see how it would survive.

'I think she wanted to see how far she could push it,' she says. 'A bit like she did with me, as well. She'd needle me and needle me to see how much it would take for me to break.'

'Did you speak to Isobel about her treatment of Christian at your house?' Mr Alexander says, returning the evidence to the more recent past.

A little colour returns to Fiona's cheeks. She'd grown very pale talking about the hamster. Now she looks more enlivened. 'I did, yes. I made a point of it.'

'Why did you think it was necessary?'

Pale again. Paler still. 'It was seeing Isobel's face when they were teasing Christian at tea. She was watching her when they were calling her Dead Girl Walking, this expression on her face. I'll never forget it . . .' The woman shivers, wrapping her arms around herself. 'She was enjoying herself. The more that Christian was upset, the happier Isobel seemed. But that wasn't the worst of it.'

'What was the worst of it?' Mr Alexander prompts as the witness falls silent, seemingly lost in thought.

'She had the same expression on her face as she did before, when she was gloating over her hamster. Little Ossie was so close to death you could see all his ribs – I got to him in the nick of time. But Isobel didn't care that he was suffering. She just sat there and smiled. This horrific smile. I can't begin to describe it.'

'That's not true,' Isobel cries out. The whole court starts. Matthew feels his heart jack-hammer at the unexpected exclamation. 'You know it's not true.'

Her voice isn't angry though, it's sad. Desperately sad, hopeless, someone stuck at the bottom of a well who has given up all hope of being heard.

'Silence,' the judge says, but she's already quiet, her head sunk back between her hands.

Matthew glances over at Fiona, expecting to see shock on her face, an expression of distress. But to his surprise, she's smiling, a small, secret smile like she's won a victory in a battle that only she knows she's fighting. Then her face falls sombre again and it's as if he imagined it.

But for a second, he could imagine her staring down at a starving hamster and smiling, too.

'What did you say to Isobel about Christian?' Mr Alexander says.

Fiona closes her eyes for a moment, opens them. 'I said that she needed to stop it. That it was one thing torturing a small mammal. But it was quite another torturing a human being like this. It was clear that the girl wasn't able to take it. She looked more and more ill the more that they kept on at her. I told Isobel that if she didn't watch out, she'd have Christian's death on her conscience.'

'What did Isobel say?'

'Nothing. She just smiled that smile.'

Eliza's advocate doesn't cross-examine. Another nail in Isobel's coffin. Why hasn't the girl just pleaded guilty? He can't make sense of it. Some desperate hope driving her that she'd get away with it? Something might turn up? He has a feeling she's going to be disappointed.

Miss Goodly stands up to cross-examine on Isobel's behalf.

But before she can get a word out, Isobel starts gesticulating at her, hissing something. Matthew can just about make out 'Come here, please come here.' Miss Goodly raises an eyebrow at the judge as if to ask permission and at the judge's nod, she crosses the floor to the dock where she has a muttered conversation with Isobel. Matthew tries to listen but it's nearly impossible to hear anything, right until the end, when an anguished cry breaks the air.

'There's just no point.' It's Isobel, fully in tears now. 'If I died she'd just have me burnt and throw away the ashes. She doesn't love me. She never has.'

Her sobs ring round the court. Matthew looks over at Fiona Smyth, sitting in the witness stand as her daughter has this outburst of emotion.

The woman's face is completely unmoved.

50

They're sent home after this. Miss Goodly has thrown her hands up in the air and sat back in her seat, saying only that no cross-examination will be necessary. Then Mr Alexander said that this concluded the case for the prosecution. Even though it's not yet quite time for court to finish, that's the end of matters for the day as far the jury are concerned.

Matthew doesn't hang around the jury room. Everyone is pretty much in agreement that Isobel must be a terrible person for her own mum to be saying this about her. No one else seems to share his misgivings about the woman in the frilled collar who is just too good to be true.

He's finding it all very depressing. Too much exposure to misery, too much sadness. The mothers. Marianne, her grief palpable; Isobel's mother, unable to muster the slightest sympathy for her daughter, even though the girl is her own flesh and blood. When this case is over, Matthew's going to make much more of an effort with his own daughter. Daisy deserves more from him. At least she's moving on with her life, hopefully living it up on campus rather than sitting at home wondering when he's going to get back from work. In future, though, he's going to do a better job.

Halfway down the Playfair Steps, he suddenly catches sight of a couple walking slowly ahead of him, past the National

Gallery. A slight woman in a coat that's too large for her; a man who would be more comfortable in tweeds. It's Christian's parents.

Matthew glances around him. There's no one else from court in his vicinity. Nothing to stop him following them. His suspicions of Marianne are nebulous, but present. Even if she has exaggerated Christian's symptoms over the years, does that make any difference?

On balance, he thinks it does.

They cross Princes Street, keep walking down Hanover Street, across George Street and Queen Street. At Heriot Row they take a left. By now Matthew is only a few dozen feet behind them, his head bent. They won't recognise him, he's sure of it, Edinburgh so full of middle-aged white men as it is. But no need to draw attention to himself. He stops on the corner of Heriot Row by the railings surrounding the Queen Street Gardens, pulling out his phone so that he can appear to be consulting it while he peers after his prey.

They aren't going into a house. They're letting themselves through a gate into the private gardens. It shuts behind them with a resounding clang.

So that's it then. Nothing more to be done. Matthew jams his phone back in his pocket, ready to give up, when he remembers Sasha's evidence. The girls would sneak into the allotments through a gap in the railings. The least he could do is search the perimeter to see if he can find a space through which he can fit. He shouldn't give up so easily.

Two thirds of the way along he's rewarded by a missing railing. He looks at the gap for a moment, working out his chances of getting through it. Would it be better to climb over? The spikes are off-putting. He doesn't want to end up impaled on them like those unfortunate people after the New Year's party that went so disastrously wrong. If he breathes in, he can do it.

It's a tight squeeze, but he's through. No one sees him, either. He's lucky that it's starting to get dark so he can keep himself hidden, but after a few minutes, he starts to worry that he won't find Christian's parents, however much he keeps out of sight. It's quiet, the only sound the rustling of leaves beyond the rumble of cars over the setts, down the hill.

Finally, a sound of sobs. Matthew is in the middle of the gardens and he stops, trying to orient the direction of the sound. More sobs, now a splashing sound.

'Marianne, for fuck's sake. Get out of there. You'll catch your death.'

Through the gloaming, Matthew can make out the pond with the island in the middle of it, the main feature of the garden. But there isn't just an island in it. There's the figure of a woman standing in the water up to her thighs, fully dressed. He shivers at the sight – it's cold tonight. Her husband's right.

'It's what I deserve,' she says. 'You know it's all my fault.'

'It's not your fault,' Peter says. Christian's father is standing on the edge, his hand held out to his wife.

'I made it happen, Peter. I brought it on Christian.'

'We've been through this. Many times. It was those girls. Both of them. I don't care which one of them had the knife in the end. They both threatened her as far as I'm concerned. They're both to blame for it. Now please, stop being silly. Get out of there.'

'No. It was me. If I hadn't told all those lies about her health, it wouldn't have come true. I cursed her, Peter. I took a perfectly healthy girl and said she was an invalid. Of course she became one.'

Matthew's frozen in place. Dominic was right.

'Marianne. You didn't tell lies. You were a concerned mum, that was all. I shouldn't have kept pushing for boarding school.'

Between sobs, 'You don't understand. You'll never understand. I know you think I'm stupid, standing in here. But it's the only place in Edinburgh I feel close to her. I remember playing with her – she was such a happy little girl.' She starts crying in earnest.

Eventually, Peter coaxes her out. Matthew gets the sense that this is a scene that's happened more than once. The couple trail back towards the gate through which they entered but this time Matthew doesn't follow them.

He's heard enough. Peter might not understand what Marianne is confessing, but Matthew does. Dominic was right. Now Matthew needs to work out what this means.

WEDNESDAY

51

Matthew's exhausted, but he sleeps badly. Weeping women kept drifting into his dreams, starving rodents, Isobel crying out to him, her hands outstretched, though when he got close he saw that her skin was covered in suppurating sores. He's about to reach her, to pull her out of the lake in which she's standing, when he's knocked off his feet by a series of giant inflated hearts, as round as the image he saw from the post-mortem. He turns to see hordes of them rolling down a hill at him, each larger than the next, giant pulsating globes of horror that cover him, weigh him down under the water till he drowns.

Now he's sitting in the jury room again, waiting. They've been here since before ten but no one has asked them to come into court yet. The jury officer said something vague about legal arguments, but Matthew is at a loss. So are the others. Emma is making tiresome noises about supporting animal charities, as if anyone cares what she does. Before Matthew can say anything, the jury officer enters the room and tells them that it's time. Probably for the best.

They file into court and take their seats. To his surprise, he sees that the advocate who was representing Isobel is gone. So is the solicitor. Miss Brodie and her junior are still in place, but the space where Isobel's team were sitting is empty. He glances over at the dock. The girl looks even worse than she did before, pale as death with red-rimmed eyes and scratches on her neck. Maybe she's getting some kind of skin condition too – if the trial is having this effect on Matthew, who's only an observer, albeit one with certain privileges, how much harder must it be for her?

Eliza on the other hand is looking calm, resolute, her skin clear and her hair clean. The contrast between them is painfully striking. *There's no art to find the mind's construction in the face – Macbeth* again. Funny how well he remembers the play. Shakespeare or not, Isobel looks guilty as sin, there's no getting away from it.

As he has the thought, an itch starts on his face. He puts his hand up to find a patch of blistered skin by the corner of his mouth. His heart sinks.

The judge clears her throat. 'Ladies and gentlemen of the jury, you may notice that Miss Goodly and her junior are no longer in court. This is because the accused Isobel Smyth has made the decision to represent herself. She has been fully advised as to the merits of this approach and is aware of the potential drawbacks.'

A gasp from the jury. Matthew's heart skips a beat.

Miss Brodie stands. 'I'd like to call Eliza to give evidence, please.'

Eliza flicks her hair back and walks over to the witness box.

The thrust of her evidence is clear, and as predicted by Matthew. She was a poor, lost soul when Isobel came to the school. Friendless and bullied, the girl had gravitated towards the charisma of the new girl, her self-confidence and the challenge that she presented to established ways of thinking. Glamour and excitement had blinded Eliza to the reality of what they were doing. She admitted that she'd been nasty to Christian on occasion, but Isobel had made her do it.

Matthew doesn't believe a word of it. He's trying to keep an open mind, but every word she says sets his teeth on edge. She's lying, he's sure of it. But he's the only one to see it, too, the little sparks that come from her eyes whenever she says Isobel's name. If anyone is possessed by a demon, it's her.

Head to one side, her voice is low and sincere as she assures the court that no one had ever told her that Christian had a heart condition, or any other kind of health problem. She hadn't spoken individually to Christian's mother or father; she'd been mortified by the way that their visit to Christian's family home had worked out.

'I told them not to do it,' she says. 'I told them that we shouldn't behave like that in the chapel, that we should respect their property, but they wouldn't listen to me.'

'Why did you go with them, then?'

'To keep an eye on it, see if I could stop it from going out of control.'

'Do you think that you would have been better going and speaking to a grown-up?'

She pauses, stifles a sob. 'Of course I see that now. But at the time, I didn't know what to do. I tried to do the right thing, but I wanted to protect my friends as well. I thought that it would all stop.'

She licks her lips. Matthew starts. He could swear that what he sees is a little forked tongue darting out, flicking from corner to corner of her mouth.

'Were you told by Christian's mother that Christian had a heart condition?'

'I wasn't. No.'

'Were you told by Christian's father that Christian had a heart condition?'

'Absolutely not.'

She holds to this line throughout the rest of the examination-in-chief. There's more detail about the imbalance of her friendship with Isobel, how Isobel ran rings around her.

'I now know that it was a form of coercive control,' she says. 'She would withhold affection if I didn't do what she wanted. It was really hard to stand up to her.'

'Did she tell you explicitly that you had to be unkind to Christian?' Miss Brodie says.

'Not in so many words. But it was obvious what she wanted me to do. It always was.'

'Did she tell you why she wished to do Christian harm?'

For the first time Eliza looks uneasy. She's shifting her weight from foot to foot, her calm expression a little tense.

'Not as such,' she says after a pause. 'But there was one comment she made.'

'What was that?' Miss Brodie prompts when Eliza pauses again.

'I think she was jealous of Christian's family. She said she wished she had parents like that. A family that was still together.'

A hiss from the dock. Isobel is shaking her head. The judge looks at her sternly but says nothing.

'Can you remember the exact words she used?'

'Not exactly, no. It was something like that, though. After we stayed at Christian's house.'

'How did you feel about Christian?'

Her eyes flicker from side to side. It looks shifty to Matthew. 'I liked her. Not as much as I liked Isobel – or rather, not as much as I thought I liked Isobel. But she was a nice girl. She didn't deserve this.'

Then it comes to the pivotal moment, the altercation in the shed.

'Isobel didn't tell me anything of what she had planned, just that the Devil had told her what to do, it was all clear to her now. I didn't even know that she was going to kill the pigeon. Do you think I would have agreed to something like that?' She stretches out her hands, plaintive. 'I was so shocked when I saw

Isobel do that I didn't even think to argue when she nodded at me. Sasha collapsed on the floor in a little ball and before I knew it, Isobel was running at Christian, waving her knife at her, shouting "now it's your turn" at the top of her voice.'

'Did you think she was going to stab Christian?'

'Yes. I did.'

'What did Christian do?'

'She started screaming as well. Pure terror. Then she turned round and she ran for her life.'

Mr Alexander cross-examines first. 'You're not telling the court how it was, are you?'

'I am.' The girl does indignation well, her voice rising but not overly so.

'You're telling the court how you wish it had been, isn't that the case?'

'Absolutely not.'

'And you and Isobel were working hand in hand to see how far you could push Christian?'

'No.'

'To see whether you could induce a heart attack in her – that was your and Isobel's plan, wasn't it?'

'No.'

'Isobel might have been driving this but you went along with it, isn't that right?'

'No. I didn't. That's not right.'

'And you both planned to make Christian fear for her life in the final altercation, didn't you?'

'No.'

'You knew Isobel had the knife, you knew what she was planning, didn't you?'

'No.'

'And despite your desperate attempts to put the blame on

to your co-accused, whether you or she was holding the knife when you both charged at Christian, you were in this together, every step of the way.'

The jurors around Matthew are shifting around in their seats. It doesn't look like they're appreciating the tone that the advocate depute is taking with Eliza. But if Mr Alexander senses this, it doesn't affect his approach. He takes every assertion that Eliza has made and suggests calmly that she's making it up in order to shift all the blame on to Isobel.

'That just isn't true.'

'No further questions, my lady.'

Isobel is next. It's a surprise to see her walk out of the dock and go to the lectern. She's shorter than he realised, a slight figure still in her baggy tracksuit. Daisy is taller by at least half a head. Even with her emo, goth-like appearance, she doesn't look scary. But then Matthew isn't a teenage girl.

Eliza on the other hand is looking uncomfortable, some of the cockiness gone from her stance. But she puts her shoulders back and squares her jaw in preparation.

'Remember when we did the first Ouija board,' Isobel says. Her speaking voice is deeper than Matthew realised from the few occasions he's heard her call out from the dock. It's not unpleasant. 'You were terrified too, weren't you?'

'Yes,' Eliza says. She's talking very quietly.

'You believed it was real, when the spirit took over the planchette and spelt out that Christian was going to die?'

A deep breath. 'I did believe it was true, yes.'

'You know that we didn't plant the tarot cards either – the reading that Christian got that was so bad, you know that was true, too?'

Another deep breath. 'Yes.'

Witch Trial

'Every time we called upon the spirits, they answered, didn't they?'

'Yes.'

'When we asked the Devil to come, he spoke to us. Didn't he?'

'Yes. No. I don't know. Isobel, you were making it up, you were making it all up. I know that now.'

'You know that's not true, don't you?'

'I don't know anything any more.' Eliza starts to cry. Miss Brodie starts forward as if to intervene but the judge holds up her hand.

'Isobel,' the judge says, 'you must remember that your questions must be relevant to your defence.'

Isobel looks up at the bench, though it doesn't look to Matthew as if she's focusing on the judge at all.

'Yes,' she says. 'Of course.' It's clear that she hasn't really heard what was said.

'A couple more things. It wasn't me who was jealous of Christian's family. It was you. You were jealous of their house. You always thought you had the biggest house of any of us until you saw hers and you realised that she was richer.'

Eliza laughs. It's not a nice sound. 'No, Isobel. You know that's not true.'

'And you know that Christian's parents never spoke to us about Christian's health. No one ever said anything. They're lying because they wish they had, but the truth is that as soon as they found out what had happened in the chapel, they threw us out. Made us wait outside in the rain until the taxi came to take us away.'

'Oh Isobel,' Eliza says. She's regained some calm now. 'I don't know anything of the sort. I know they didn't speak to me. But they could very well have spoken to you. It's what you said afterwards.'

'That's a lie.'

Matthew tenses up. It looks like Isobel is losing control of herself. She's bright red, her hands clenched tight in front of her. After a moment she pulls herself together.

'You knew exactly what was going to happen in the shed. We'd discussed the pigeon sacrifice. I told you the Devil told me to do it.'

'You know that's not true, Isobel.'

Isobel swallows. 'And you know it wasn't me who went at Christian with the knife. I hadn't been told to do that. It was your decision. You did it on your own. You're lying when you say it was me.'

Eliza shakes her head. Her expression is calm. 'It's not a lie, Isobel. You know it. I wasn't going to say anything, but if you're going to tell these lies about me . . . You told me explicitly that you knew something about Christian, and that you were going to make her wish that she had never been born.'

'You lying bitch,' Isobel says, and hurls herself towards the witness box. She's nearly at Eliza's throat, hands outstretched in claws to attack her, before security get to her, a short, lumbering man who takes hold of her arm and pulls her away, ending the cross-examination abruptly.

52

They break for lunch. Matthew reckons everyone will feel better for getting their blood sugar back up. He certainly will. He's feeling distinctly wobbly, the rash bringing his mood down, exacerbating the tiredness he's already feeling from such a bad night's sleep. He doesn't want to hang around with the other jurors, though. The moment they were out of the court door he could tell what way it was going, the sympathy that they all have for Eliza, the condemnation for Isobel.

He doesn't like it, the way that everyone seems to have made up their minds already. He's not sure what could change their minds, either. To be fair, Isobel isn't helping herself at all, the moody outbursts and outbreaks of anger only serving to compound the impression that's been given of the girl. She doesn't look entirely stable. A psychiatrist said at the very start that she was fit to plead, but other than the cross-examination of the psychiatrist, her mental health has hardly been brought into it. Matthew can't understand it.

He leaves the court building and heads left. He's going to go back to the Devil's Advocate. The mood he's in can only be sated by a cheeseburger, chips, the full works. It's not just that, though. He can't explain it, but he's got a strong sense that Gill is waiting for him there.

Sure enough, as he walks in through the door, he sees her. She's sitting at a table for two in the narrow corridor to the left of the bar, facing outwards as if waiting for him. He raises a hand in greeting before joining her.

'I thought I'd see you here,' she says. It's as if the strangeness of their last meeting has never happened. Any animosity he might have felt has disappeared in the face of the alienation he feels from the rest of the jury.

'How's it going?' she says.

It's on a knife edge. He knows what his legal responsibility is. He shouldn't speak to her about this. He shouldn't even be in the same room as her, let alone sitting opposite her preparing to divulge the secret workings of the court to her. But at the same time . . .

'I don't know whether I should tell you this or not,' she says before he can say anything else. He looks at her in surprise – he's not the only one going through a moral dilemma.

'What?'

'The delay this morning, before the jury were called in. There was a legal argument. Well, rather, Isobel and her advocate were having an argument.'

'What about?'

She takes a deep breath, as if she's decided upon something momentous. 'It was about a psychiatric report. Isobel's advocate said that she had finally been sent a psychiatric report that called into question Isobel's sanity at the time this was happening. She wanted to put in a defence statement to say that Isobel had diminished responsibility at the time of the offence because she was suffering from a psychotic breakdown.'

'I mean, I have wondered, given some of her outbursts,' Matthew says.

'But neither the advocate depute nor Eliza's advocate were happy about this. Nor the judge. They all said that it was being done far too late in the day. At which point Isobel started yelling. The judge let her speak. She said that she didn't agree, that she hadn't been mad at the time and that she wasn't mad now. She didn't want her advocate to run this as a defence and if the woman insisted on it she'd represent herself.'

'So that's what ended up happening?'

'That's what happened. After considering it, the judge said that given there was no dispute that she was fit to plead now, it meant that she was fit to give instructions and that if she didn't want to argue that she was suffering from diminished responsibility at the time of the alleged murder, that was a matter for her.'

A long pause. Matthew tries to digest what he's been told.

'I'm really worried,' Gill says. 'I don't think the girl is well. But no one is looking out for her. It's like she's all on her own.'

Matthew looks at her. A long, steady gaze while he assesses what she's said, weighs it up against his own misgivings. Sure, Isobel might be fit to plead now, but given her whole-hearted belief in the supernatural cause of everything that happened, can it really be said that she wasn't suffering from some delusions at the time of Christian's death?

'At the least, diminished responsibility should be put as an option to the jury. That's what I think,' Gill says. 'That's why I'm talking to you.'

'What do you expect me to do about it?'

A waiter comes over to the table at that point with a glass of wine. It's clearly intended for Gill but Matthew picks it up, drains it. It seems the only answer right now.

'I don't know if you know this, but a jury can find whatever verdict it wants. You know that the decision never needs to be justified. It can't ever be discussed.'

'I had heard that, yes,' he says with caution.

'So you can save her. If you want to.'

Without another word, he gets up and walks out. His head is spinning. Not just from the wine.

He walks around the Old Town for the rest of the lunch break in the hope that the fresh air will bring him some clarity. He should report Gill, he knows it – this is jury interference on a grand scale. But at the same time, he can see that her concern is coming from the right place. It chimes with his fears, that Isobel is being set up in some way, too conveniently the fall guy for this whole set-up. Coupled with his uncertainties about Marianne, his doubts about whether there was truly anything wrong with Christian in the first place . . . he's not sure what to think.

It's only when he gets back to the door of the High Court that he remembers he hasn't eaten. The wine is vinegar in his stomach, no solace to him any more now that the temporary buzz has faded. He burps as he stands in the queue for security, acid reflux adding to his skin condition misery. He learnt about pathetic fallacy at school, when they were studying *Macbeth*, the weather tying in with the narrative mood. Matthew is the weather of the court right now, the misery of the proceedings playing out on his skin and in his toxic guts.

He just wants it to end. He doesn't want to walk this line any longer between doing the right thing and behaving in a way that's legally correct. He knows what his old college tutor would tell him to do – obey the rules, regardless of the consequences. Regardless of the rightness of the rules, either. His not to wonder why, his but to cast a verdict according to the evidence or . . . well, not die. But worry forever whether he did the right thing.

Gill shouldn't have told him. But he's glad she did.

The evidence trails along in the afternoon. It's a team of character references for Eliza, a beauty parade of the great and good, evidently friends of her family who've agreed to do them a favour. Two advocates – Queen's Counsels, no less – and an MSP, her family vicar, her Guide leader and the headteacher of her prep school, a prestigious establishment in the north of Edinburgh.

Eliza was the last person they would have expected to see in court like this. She was a model of perfection, someone held up as an example to the younger children both in school and in her Sunday School as well. She headed up Guides with aplomb, earning so many badges she ran out of room on the sleeves of her tunic to display them all.

At the end of all this, the glorious finale, up stands a woman in tweed, her face pale and drawn, wringing her hands in the witness box. Eliza's mother. They've saved the best till last.

Matthew needs to stop being so cynical. He's doing his best. But his teeth are on edge. Perhaps driven by hunger, his temper is frayed almost to breaking point. The more perfect that he's told Eliza is, the less he believes it. But perhaps this woman will change his mind.

'She's not always been the perfect daughter,' the woman starts. He sits up, takes note. Finally someone is talking about the girl as if she's a real human being. 'But I can't blame her for it. It's that girl who destroyed her.' She points a shaking hand straight at Isobel.

Matthew slumps back in his seat. So much for a more objective take.

The evidence carries them no further forward. All she does is go over old ground. Eliza was wonderful until Isobel joined the school. Thereafter her behaviour became more problematic. She's sure it's because Isobel was a toxic influence, and she regrets the day that she ever let Eliza board and therefore be out of the reach of her own influence.

'Girls need their mothers,' she says. 'It's a fact. I blame myself for letting them talk me into it.'

'Who?' Miss Brodie says. She's struggled to get a word in edgeways through the tide of saccharine bile that's poured from the woman's lips.

'Eliza. And her father.' The woman points to the man who's been sitting in court throughout, stolid in his grey jacket. He stays expressionless.

At least Matthew now knows who he is.

'He said I smothered her, but if she'd stayed at home, she wouldn't be facing a murder charge now.' The woman breaks into hysterical weeping, a hanky over her face, though Matthew can't shake the feeling that she's peeking out of one side of it, careful to check that her emotional outburst is having the desired effect on the court.

53

'That poor woman,' Neil says as they go into the jury room for a quick break.

'It's terrible,' Russell says.

'I'd never let my child go to boarding school,' Emma says. 'As a mother, I think it's our responsibility to keep our children close. Not farm them out to other people to look after.'

Matthew sits down. He doesn't contribute to the chorus of sympathy, or judgement about parenting decisions. It's as if they've watched two different people up in the witness box, so different is his perception from the rest of the room. They're overflowing with empathy for Eliza and her family. She's fooled them entirely.

He catches himself short. He's being irrational. What Eliza and her mother said makes perfect sense, and the fact that his gut is telling him it's not true can't be substantiated objectively. If everyone else in the room is thinking differently, then he must be wrong.

'It's all very sad,' Aisha says. Matthew nods. This is an analysis he can agree with. 'I'm trying to stay open-minded, but it's hard. Isobel isn't making a great case for herself.'

He nods again. She's not wrong in that assessment.

'But maybe she'll be more impressive when she comes to give evidence herself.'

'Maybe she will,' he says. He doesn't add, *I hope*. But he's thinking it.

Isobel cuts a forlorn figure in the witness box. She'd kept her head down, hair in front of her face throughout Eliza's mother's evidence, not bothering to cross-examine, and now she stands in a way that speaks of exhaustion, bone weariness. She's silent for a while, as if gathering her thoughts, until finally the judge prompts her to begin.

'Sorry, yes.' She pushes her hair back from her face now and looks over at the jury. Matthew can see a nose ring through her septum, three small hoops in her left ear, seven in the other, working their way from the lobe up to the top of the cartilage. As ever she's wearing a grey hoodie, but the sleeves are pulled up, and even from the distance she is from Matthew across the court, he can make out rough tattoos, the ink crawling up over the back of her hands and up her arms. Underneath them, very faint, white parallel lines running up her arm. Self-harm scars.

He glances along the rows of jurors. No one that young, no one with tattoos. No one remotely alternative. It's no wonder they haven't warmed to her. But maybe she'll pull something out of the bag now. Maybe.

'I don't have very much to say,' she begins. 'But I want you to know that it's not true that I hurt Christian on purpose. I didn't have any reason to. She was my friend.' A long pause, the word left hanging in the air. A lump forms in Matthew's throat. Friend. Said with such sadness. 'But I couldn't help what the Devil told me to do.'

Matthew looks over at the judge. Surely she's going to intervene? But she stays silent, her face impassive, even as Isobel lists all the ways that she was told by various spirits and demons of Christian's impending death.

'I understand that it looked like bullying,' she says. 'But it was what needed to be done. I was passing on important information, that was all. I couldn't help the way that the tarot cards fell. I couldn't help the Ouija board messages. I wasn't faking them – the planchette was moving of its own accord.'

A hiss from Jasmine. Disbelief? Matthew remembers the way that the planchette flew at Gill. He glances at her, sitting in her usual spot at the front of the public gallery. She does not catch his eye.

'I know that the cat and the pigeon look bad,' she says. 'I know exactly what it looks like, how much you'll judge me for it. But it was what I was told to do.'

She was having visitations in dreams. Awake, too. The Devil's head would appear to her in the strangest of places – peering out of the froth at the top of a cappuccino, faces appearing from patterns in the wall. Matthew tenses up at this. So much of what she says is what he's experienced, a chill runs through him, the jeering sound from the Devil in the bathroom ringing again in his ears.

'Some of it is established ritual,' she says, earnest now. 'There are books. You've seen the one that belonged to Sasha. I found that very helpful. It was a bit reductive, though. I think more sophisticated practices give better results. I've tried to follow some of the rituals laid out by the Golden Dawn, but it's difficult setting up a proper altar in a school dormitory.'

A muffled noise from behind him. Matthew glances round. Russell is trying to stifle laughter, his face going redder and redder in the process.

Isobel looks over at him. 'I know you think it sounds mad. That I'm mad. I'm not, though. Magic is real. It exists. I've spoken to spirits, I've spoken to the dead. About the dead. I've spoken to Christian recently – she knows I wasn't bullying her. That I didn't want her dead. I just knew she was going to die. That's all that happened.'

She stares at them all, unblinking, unwavering in her sincerity. She appears totally sane. But what she's saying can't be true. Can it? Matthew has no idea what to think any more.

'It wasn't me who threatened Christian with a knife. I would never do that. It was Eliza who hated her. That's the truth. I liked Christian. Eliza became obsessed with getting a human sacrifice – she was furious that I could see the Devil and she couldn't. She thought that if she gave him Christian, she'd get to talk to him too.'

Eliza is shaking her head primly from side to side. She couldn't look less like a devil worshipper if she tried.

Mr Alexander has no doubt. He gets up to cross-examine, irritation crackling off him.

'You cannot seriously expect that the court will believe that you spoke to the Devil?'

'I did, though.'

'Or that you did not set up the Ouija board and the tarot cards so that they would give Christian the false information that she was going to die?'

'It was true. I didn't set it up.' Every answer she makes is given with what seems to be total honesty. Her eyes are open, her head erect. She sounds proud, almost, as she asserts her case. 'It's how the cards fell. It was her fate. I can't help that the Devil was working through me.'

Matthew feels a chill pass through him. She's deadly serious. Or completely deluded. He thinks back to the psychiatrist who gave evidence at the beginning of the case, the fact that she was so adamant that there is nothing wrong with Isobel's sanity.

She must be lying, then. Because the alternative is too horrific for him to contemplate. It cannot possibly be true.

On to the cat in the shed. She asserted that the fake funeral was not intended to torment Christian. It was to ease her passage through to the afterlife. Christian was clinging too much on to living and it was killing her soul, strange as the paradox might seem. Isobel would have wanted Christian to do the same for her if the situation were reversed.

Same with the butchered pigeon. Isobel denied that this was animal cruelty. The pigeon was already injured – she was just putting it out of its misery, and for a greater good as well. She believed truly that she was helping Christian.

Eliza had no such desire. She was the one who brought malice to the table. She was the one who wanted to hurt Christian, to see how far they could push her physically. Eliza was the one obsessed with making Christian suffer.

Eliza was the one who seized the knife from Isobel and brandished it in Christian's face, chasing her and screaming threats as she did.

The words are demented. Isobel, not so. She's totally matter-of-fact, calm in her attempt to counter Mr Alexander's questions.

The only time that she becomes agitated is when he puts it to her that she's lying about the conversations with Christian's mother and father. She simply won't accept that either of them told her about their daughter's heart condition.

'No, they didn't. Neither of them did. It's not true.'

Shakes of the head around the jury. Not good to attack the bereaved parents. Isobel has not helped her case.

It's worse still when Miss Brodie stands up to cross-examine on behalf of Eliza. Isobel is immediately hostile. The open expression disappears, replaced by scowls and frowns. She will accept no suggestion whatsoever that she was doing it all on purpose to bully Christian.

'That's not true. Eliza knows it. Ask your client.'

'When you say that the planchette moved of its own volition, you're lying there as well, aren't you? You were making it move to the letters that spelt out DIE CHRISTIAN.'

'I wasn't, no. It was a spirit talking to us from the other side. Ask your client.'

Over and over again. *Ask your client. Ask your client. Eliza knows the truth.*

ELIZA WAS THE ONE WITH THE KNIFE.

At last the girl's ordeal is over. As far as Matthew can see, she hasn't won over a single heart or mind. This suspicion is confirmed when they convene in the jury room at the end of court.

'Mad or bad,' Neil says. 'That's it. Definitely dangerous to know.'

Everyone laughs. Everyone other than Matthew.

'We can't consider whether she's mad, though. At least I don't think so.' That's Jasmine. 'She's not putting it forward as a defence. She's saying it's true and asking us to believe her. The prosecution are saying she's not mad, and she's not trying to say she is.'

Matthew nods. It's a fair summary. Encapsulates the problem in one. If the jury accepts she's telling the truth, they're having to accept something they will find impossible. A legal defence of insanity is not permitted them, unless the judge tells them differently at the end.

'Which means she must be lying,' Emma says. 'That's what I think, anyway. She's lying through her back teeth. She enjoyed playing these twisted games and she wanted to see how far she could push it with Christian.'

Jasmine objects. 'Maybe she was into bullying her. But it doesn't mean that she wanted her dead, does it?'

'There was that phrase they said at the start,' Dharam says. His voice cuts through the rest of the chatter. Everyone turns to face him. 'Wicked recklessness. That's the prosecution case. The girls didn't need to intend to kill her for it to be murder. This is enough, that's the whole case. They knew that scaring her into a heart attack could kill her and they went ahead and did it anyway.'

'They?' Emma says. 'I don't see a they in this. I just see Isobel. Don't you agree?'

Murmurs round the table.

'I think we should do a poll,' she says. 'Let's get an idea of where people are right now. They did that on *Twelve Angry Men*. I watched it the other night. Everyone who thinks Isobel is guilty raise your hand.'

'They did it anonymously,' Matthew said. 'They didn't have to raise their hands.'

She turns on him. 'Why would we need to be anonymous? Surely everyone feels the same?'

Matthew catches Dharam's eye across the table. The other man shakes his head, a tiny movement, but enough. Matthew says nothing. He doesn't need the warning. Now is not the time. He needs to marshal his forces, work out exactly how to approach this.

One promise he makes himself, though, on the way out of court. Whatever it takes, he is going to make this jury cast the verdict that Matthew thinks is right. Nothing less will do.

He just needs to work out exactly what that is.

THURSDAY

54

Another terrible night's sleep. More nightmares. Isobel, Eliza, wheeling around his mind, pleading with him. Eliza wringing her hands, which are dripping in blood. Isobel stabbing a pigeon through the heart, once, twice, three times, a beatific expression on her face. The heart balloons rolling after him, chasing him wherever he goes. *It was her no it was her no it was her no it was her.* They're both guilty, neither of them is guilty, only one of them is guilty, murder, culpable homicide, innocent, not guilty, guilty guilty guilty . . .

Final witness for the defence. That's what the judge tells them when the jury gets into court. Closing speeches will be today as well, and if they're lucky (the judge's tone indicates this, rather than her words) they can get through her directions as well. The case will certainly be completed by tomorrow lunchtime at the latest, before the jury is sent out for their deliberations.

The end is in sight. Matthew feels a lightening in the air around him, as if the jury is dropping its shoulders, breathing a collective sigh of relief. They're nearly there.

But first, Isobel's father. Rupert Smyth. He doesn't look like a Rupert. Given the account that Isobel's mother gave of him, a domestic abuser, a coercive controller, Matthew is expecting someone tall and imposing to walk into the courtroom, a man used to throwing his weight around and getting what he wants. Instead, a mole-like man in thick glasses emerges blinking into the witness box, as if he hasn't seen bright lights for some time.

His voice is hesitant, the way that he gives his name apologetic, as if he's sorry to be taking up any of the court's valuable time. Matthew thinks back to the elegant self-confidence of Fiona Smyth, how well put together she was. This man couldn't be more her contrast.

Isobel stands by the advocate's lectern. Her face is as ever half-hidden by her hair, but she looks more open and warm when she looks at her father than Matthew has seen at any point in the proceedings.

'What do you want to tell the court?' she says, smiling at her father. There's a simplicity to the question that touches Matthew's heart.

He clears his throat. Coughs again. Pushes his glasses up and rubs at his eyes for a moment. Then he puts both hands down on the bar in front of him, leaning on the witness box as if for support. 'You were such a lovely little girl,' he says. He looks over at the jury. 'I don't know what you've been told about my Isobel, what her mother has said, but I would urge you to hear me out. You're not seeing the girl that I see.'

A loud tutting from the public gallery. Matthew looks over to see that Fiona, Isobel's mother, is sitting there, her face frozen in an expression of deep disapproval. It does not deter Rupert. He continues to talk to the court, telling a story of an ordinary child who behaved in an ordinary way, the usual fallings-out and ups and downs of any primary schoolgirl.

'I don't know why it was, but her mother always wanted her to be more of a problem than she was. It's as if she'd thought herself into the role of the mother of the difficult child, and nothing was going to shift that position in her head. Fiona had the most remarkable ability to turn everything to bad.'

Witch Trial

More tutting. The woman in question is now shaking her head, disapproval radiating off her.

'I never noticed anything untoward about Isobel's behaviour. Sure, she was robust and took an interest in subjects that others didn't. But all this stuff about bullying? I never believed a word of it.'

'What do you think of magic?' Isobel asks. Her mother laughs from the public gallery, quickly muffles the sound.

'We do not know what we do not know,' he says. *'There are more things in Heaven and Earth, Horatio, than are dreamt of in your philosophy.* Hamlet, as I'm sure you're aware. I do not think that it's possible entirely to rule out that there is another dimension out there, where the supernatural dwells. Some may be gifted with the ability to see this. I have always wondered whether Isobel was one of them.'

Matthew squints at him. Mole-like the man may appear to be, but he has taken on some authority as he speaks, his shoulders squared.

'I have some interests in the area myself,' Rupert continues, 'and I have often been struck by the insights provided by my daughter.'

The Devil rearing up at Matthew, the smell of rot in the air. Suddenly he's cold, that same sense of dread infusing him as it did before, on the castle esplanade. On North Berwick Law. An image creeps into his mind – this man, seemingly harmless, wielding a knife while his daughter watches along, cutting into the living flesh of a bird. He shakes his head – it's come out of nowhere. Nothing to say that the man is evil rather than harmless as he appears.

Mercifully it's the end of the evidence as far as Isobel is concerned. Though not cross-examination. Mr Alexander is the first to rise.

'Can you tell the court what your professional title is, please?'

'I'm a professor at the university,' Rupert says.
'What are you a professor in?'
'I'm a professor of parapsychology.'
Matthew has never heard of it.
'Can you tell the court what this is?'
'It's the history and psychology of magic and the paranormal, conducting research into the pseudo-psi (things which look psychic but may not be), beliefs in the paranormal and the history of accounts and studies of anomalous phenomena.'
'Is belief in witchcraft one of your areas of study?'
'Yes, it is.'
Mr Alexander looks over at the jury and spreads his hands wide. He may as well say *and there it is, the source of all the nutty thoughts*. He hasn't quite laboured his point enough, though.
'Have you often talked about your work to Isobel?'
'Yes. She has always been fascinated by it.'
A long pause while the advocate depute looks through his notes.
'You said that one of your areas of study is something you call pseudo-psi, things which look psychic but aren't?'
'Yes.'
'So presumably you had a lot of material available about the ways that unscrupulous people prey on the vulnerable with fraudulent practices intended to look like visitations of spirits and the like?'
Rupert blinks. 'I suppose so, yes.'
'No further questions.'
Miss Brodie's turn for Eliza. 'Just a couple of questions, given your area of expertise. In your experience, would it be possible to fake a tarot card reading so that it looked as if the cards were selected at random, but they were already set up for an unwitting victim to select?'

'Well, of course, yes.' He's looking a bit brighter now, happy that his knowledge is being tested. Matthew's heart sinks.

'Let's take a Ouija board – could one of the people present at the séance push the planchette in such a way that it was not conspicuous to the other participants?'

'Yes. Naturally. All of these psychic phenomena are ripe for charlatans. People are so desperate to believe in the paranormal that they will shut their eyes to any number of signs that all is not as it seems.'

Miss Brodie nods. She's hit the jackpot. Rupert may have attended court to assist his daughter, but he's damned her out of his own mouth.

55

Means. Motive. Opportunity. Mr Alexander paints a convincing picture in his closing speech.

'Forget the smoke and mirrors,' he says. 'Forget the talk about the paranormal, about witchcraft. It was simply a vehicle for the campaign of bullying which you have heard from several witnesses was carried out by Isobel and Eliza, culminating in their final act, the lunging at Christian with the knife, the attempt to pin her down from which she had to escape. This caused her to believe she was about to be attacked and precipitated the fatal heart attack. Legally speaking, this is enough on its own. It's established in Scots law that a situation like this equals murder. It doesn't even matter which girl you think was brandishing the knife – the prosecution say that both Isobel and Eliza were in this together.' He pauses as if for effect. 'It makes no difference either whether you believe the girls knew about Christian's heart condition, or not. Perpetrators must take their victims as they find them. It does not, in fact, matter whether there was a pre-existing heart condition at all. The prosecution case is that either Eliza or Isobel, acting together, were so threatening towards Christian with that knife that they scared her into a heart attack.'

Matthew feels a sense of relief at this. The issue he has with the post-mortem is still unresolved. Whichever way he looks at the photos, at the report, he's nagged anew by the sense that something's wrong with the picture. But it doesn't matter now. Even if Marianne had full-blown Munchausen's by Proxy and was lying through her teeth all through Christian's short life, it's irrelevant now.

Mr Alexander continues. 'However, it is also the prosecution case that Isobel and Eliza did know. They were made aware by two separate people that their unkindness was having a direct impact on the health of Christian and could cause serious illness. With that knowledge, the girls made a conscious decision not just to continue their campaign of psychological torture, but to intensify it, resulting in the terrifying events on the morning of May Day which caused Christian to flee and gave her the heart attack that killed her. It's as simple as that.'

There's more to it, of course, but that's the gist of it as far as Matthew is concerned. He's doing his best to concentrate but his mind is flipping this way and that.

'You may think that Isobel is not fit to plead, given her assertions throughout that every incident that took place concerning her and the victim was of supernatural origin. You may think due to this that she should be considered to have had diminished responsibility at the time of the offence. This is not the case that is being put forward on her behalf. Nor is it a finding that is supported by any psychiatric evidence either at the time or from the psychiatrist from whom you heard evidence in court. This can leave you with the conclusion only that she is lying, members of the jury, in her attempts to minimise her involvement.'

Not mad at all then. Just bad.

Or the impossible. It's true.

Matthew knows the evidence doesn't add up. But his gut tells him otherwise.

Mr Alexander turns his attentions to Eliza. 'You may take the view that Eliza was less culpable in these matters than Isobel. It was the evidence of Mr and Mrs Shaw that they told Isobel of Christian's heart condition, after all. But I would invite you to find that under the principle of art and part, Eliza is as culpable as Isobel in this campaign of bullying designed to cause harm. They were both in it together. Whichever of them wielded the knife in the last, fatal encounter.'

Eliza was as bad as Isobel, in other words. Matthew looks from one girl to the other. He knows which one looks more guilty. He knows that this is what the jury is going to think, too.

Miss Brodie's closing speech takes an even shorter amount of time. It was all Isobel's fault. Eliza had nothing to do with it. Sasha is lying. So is Isobel. Isobel was the one with the knife, not her. There's no evidence to suggest that she was made directly aware of Christian's heart condition and the case should never have been brought against her. She's more sinned against than sinning and should be fully exonerated. It's a tragedy and Eliza needs to be seen as another victim of Isobel's machinations.

Isobel stands up briefly to say that the court has heard what she had to say. She can't make anyone believe her, but witchcraft is true. The psychic world is real. She didn't make anything happen to Christian – she was simply a conduit of information that very sadly turned out to be true. She did nothing to contribute to Christian's death. The prediction was real, Christian's fate predestined regardless of any action taken by Isobel – she had just wanted to ease her friend over into the next life as had been ordained. It might be more convenient to dismiss it as nonsense and to say that she is lying, but Isobel owns the fact that she is a witch with magical powers – is proud to be a witch with magical powers. As far as the day in question is concerned, it was Eliza who had the knife. Eliza who actively hated Christian. Eliza who was wanting to kill the girl.

Not Isobel's fault.

Days of evidence have been reduced to less than two hours. Matthew can hardly believe that they've got to this point. Even though there's still half an hour to go before lunch, the judge tells them to go away and have a good meal before coming back to listen to her summing-up.

Matthew should know what he thinks. He still doesn't, though. The speeches have been compelling from both Mr Alexander and Miss Brodie. So many different people could be lying – so many different truths. He thinks about what Gill said, that the jury can come to whatever verdict they choose according to their conscience. It doesn't help. He hasn't the first idea what his conscience is telling him.

It's a sunny day. He can't bear the idea of being cooped up in the jury room so he sets off at a brisk walk, making sure to avoid Gill on the way out. No more conversation – not right now. He needs time, space. If he's quick about it, he can get to the top of Arthur's Seat, look at the spot where Sasha tried to take her life. Where the coffins were found. It might help to focus his mind.

56

It was as well he put trainers on today, the upside of his dress standards slipping as the trial goes on. When he thinks back to himself on the first day, all booted and suited, he can hardly recognise that person. Now he's in jeans and a sweatshirt, even the chinos and smart shirt abandoned.

It's not just his clothes. He looks like shit, too. His patients wouldn't recognise him. Knackered, haggard, his eyes bloodshot and strained. He might have shaved but only roughly. The rash is still troubling him; the itch of it has been building, the burning intensifying. It's spread across his cheek now as well. He runs his fingers along his cheek gently, feeling the bumps under his skin. As soon as this is all over he'll get himself to a dermatologist, sort it out once and for all.

He's fought his way past the tourists on the Royal Mile, the queues waiting for tours outside the palace. The Scottish parliament is on his right and he walks past that quickly, dodging a camera crew interviewing some man in a green tie, a lone protester with a placard that he doesn't bother to read.

On to the path now, up the hill, Salisbury Crags to his right. The sky is beginning to turn grey, a couple of drops of water on his face an indication that rain is on the way, but Matthew doesn't break his stride. There's a compulsion driving him now, a sense that he must get to the top regardless, the single most important thing that he can do. It's not like the fear that drove him up North Berwick Law – then, he was running away. Now he is driven towards the summit, by a force he can't describe, but which he certainly can't resist.

He's broken into long strides, easily overtaking groups of teenagers as they straggle up behind a keen teacher in an orange cagoule. It's still drizzling, but there's a break in the clouds above. He'll get there and back without getting soaked. If he can keep up the pace, that is. His breathing has started to get heavy, his heart pounding harder with each step. He's let his fitness slide lately, too.

Everything's slipping out of his control, he can see that now. Fitness, skin, his own cognitive skills. Matthew is used to being decisive, to knowing what course of action needs to be taken on any given occasion and enacting it. He never sits in uncertainty – he's known for it in the wards and operating theatres of the hospital. That's why he gets on so well with work. They can trust him to know what to do.

He should know what to do with this trial. It should be obvious. It's obvious to everyone else, he knows that. Eliza is innocent of everything, Isobel is guilty of the lot. It makes the most sense. Occam's razor – the simplest explanation is always the best. The evidence against Isobel is the most compelling; it makes no sense that so many witnesses would lie.

He's nearly at the top now, his steps heavier and heavier. Once he's there, he can rest, at least for a moment. He glances at the trig point at the very top before crossing over to the top of the crag on the westerly precipice. It's quieter on this side, fewer people coming and going. He'll just sit for a moment, get his breath back. Gather his thoughts.

There's shouting around him, a lively game of It with small children darting from one side of the trig point to the other. Matthew keeps his back resolutely turned. Seems to him this is a straight choice – Eliza or Isobel. One of them is lying. It's as simple as that. Their faces dance around him, angel, devil, plausible, implausible, easy, hard. It's clear what the easy path is – go along with the crowd, the majority who have already made their views clear. They like the look of Eliza, simple as that.

They're right. He knows they're right, at the core of him. But why is he resisting this so much? Why does he feel that there's something else at play?

Because she's mine

A roar in his head. Around his head. He clutches it in both hands.

You will not deny me

Now he's trying to shake off the noise, escape it, dancing from foot to foot until he's close to the edge.

Isobel is telling the truth

The roar continues, the words taking shape in front of him, patterns in the clouds forming Isobel's face, the sulky expression gone, pure love there instead. A breath of air, only the faintest whisper and the clouds have shifted shape, Eliza's face emerging, a forked tongue flickering round her lips.

Eliza is too proud. She must be punished

Globe-shaped hearts bouncing around her, distended so much they're about to burst.

Isobel is not guilty. Say it, say the words

Matthew opens his mouth to speak but the words won't come out. Fear or no fear, he still doesn't know, isn't sure. Can he say it if it isn't true? What does he actually believe?

Come closer to the edge, Matthew, closer. See what I can make you do

And now he's right up at the point on the edge of the hill where one more step will have him falling down headlong. But he still can't say it, still can't bring himself to make the commitment to the words that are teetering on the tip of his tongue.

Not guilty. Not guilty. Not guilty. Dance a little closer, Matthew, dance a little closer

He's over the edge now, one leg balancing just a little closer now, just a little closer and—

'Matthew!'

The scream brings him back to his senses. He looks down and sees the drop properly for the first time, how far he would fall. His head spins and for a moment his eyes are dark again before he brings himself back under control, stepping back carefully on to firmer ground.

'What are you doing?'

It's Gill. Of course it's Gill, always popping up where he expects her least. The grim inevitability of it.

'Why do you keep following me?' he says. Rage starts building in him at the sight of her, the face that he once thought so beautiful repulsive to him now. She's not a Hitchcock blonde; she's a harridan, a virago, constantly interfering with him and making him break his oath to the court. Everything that's happened has been her fault. He's sure of it.

'I was worried about you,' she says. But instead of words, he hears hissing instead, the forked tongue that he saw in Eliza's mouth also flicking out from Gill's. Her eyes are rimmed with red. There's a scent coming off her but it's not delicate, floral; it's rank, decay, the rot of meat left unattended too long, riddled with flies.

There are flies buzzing round her head too, great clouds of them, darting towards him, ducking away, forming themselves into giant horns that protrude on either side of her head. He runs at her, his fist raised. This has to stop, she needs to leave him alone.

Stop

A roar in his head and suddenly all is calm. The sky is clear blue now, Gill the blonde woman again, her face full of concern. A fragrance of roses on the air. He falls to his knees.

'What are you doing?' she says again and now it's in words, not hisses, or buzzing, or any of the terrible noises that were coming out of her mouth before.

'I wanted to get some fresh air,' he says, pushing himself up to his feet. He looks at her closely, waiting to see if any more demonic signs present themselves. There's nothing, though. It's safe.

For now.

'Have you decided yet what you're going to do?' she says. A faint crackling in the distance, a whiff of sulphur. Matthew shakes his head. He's saying no more to her.

They walk downhill together, but at the bottom of the Royal Mile he tells her he needs to return on his own. She doesn't argue. But as he walks away, she calls him back.

'I'm still on Isobel's side, you know,' she says. 'I know you agree with me. Don't let yourself get pulled along just because it's what everyone else thinks.'

Matthew nods. One grim movement. This is the last encouragement he needs. He turns, walks away. Resolution running right through him.

57

Matthew gets back into court just in time. No one asks him where he's been – there's a fractious air, as though the jury has been arguing in his absence. That surprises him; as far as he can see, everyone is against Isobel, but perhaps he may find more support. Maybe he's not the only one hoping she's found not guilty.

That is, if finding her not guilty is what he's going to do.

The judge begins her summing-up. He sits back, pen in hand, ready to take notes of any salient points. He wants to know about whether there's any wiggle room for discussion about Isobel's mental health. It starts off well enough, information about burdens and standards of proof, an analysis of the evidence presented at the beginning of the trial. But the longer that the judge talks, the more that Matthew's head starts to hurt. He's struggling to make out what she's saying, as well, her words increasingly drowned out by that buzzing he heard before in his ears.

Shouldn't he raise his hand, tell the court that he's not well enough to continue? He isn't ill, though. It's not that. He's overwhelmed with the sense that only he understands the truth, only he has the power to stop this from all going terribly wrong. He looks over again at the girls in the dock.

Smoke and mirrors – that was the phrase that the advocate

depute used when he talked about the role that witchcraft has allegedly played in this case. He's not wrong, either, that there's been a lot of deflection in the case, sleight of hand tricks to keep them all looking in the wrong direction. Eliza with her picture-perfect ways, her winning smiles. Isobel who doesn't play the game at all. She scowls at the court, refuses to engage, tells them a version of the truth that no one sensible could ever accept.

Matthew knows the truth, though. The Devil does exist. He's talked to Matthew, shown him his hand. Isobel wasn't tormenting Christian – she was simply telling her what was going to happen. It's irrelevant that Christian's parents had told her to lay off; death was always Christian's destiny. Isobel was not the instrument of it, only the messenger.

The instrument was Eliza, working towards her own selfish ends. Arrogantly taking it on herself to jump the gun rather than let Isobel take the lead as the Devil had ordained. Christian's fate was already sealed – the Devil had called it all. Eliza should have had faith in him, not decided to act herself. She overstepped the mark; she deserves to be punished. The jury might not yet understand it, but Matthew is going to make them believe it. By any means possible.

The judge keeps talking. The buzzing in Matthew's head has subsided and he could listen now, if he wanted to. He could make a careful note so that he could refer back to it in his deliberations. There's no need. He knows everything that he needs to know.

He's got a plan. Scanning this bunch of deadweights, losers – he's the only consultant surgeon here, a natural born leader. He can swing it, he's certain of it. He'll need to be clever about it, but Matthew is nothing if not clever. Probably the most intelligent man in the room.

He sits up, a pen in his hand, scribbles some illegible notes.

Witch Trial

Not that he's listening to the judge – he doesn't need to do that, after all, but he needs to look as if he is. This is going to take some careful management. Emma will be one to watch; she mentioned seeing him with Gill before. He can handle her, though.

At last, the summing-up comes to an end. He hasn't listened to a word of it, but he arranges his face in an attentive manner, stands up when everyone else does. The one thing he needs to know is that it's a simple majority for a finding of guilty. A finding of not guilty, too. Even not proven would be acceptable at a push. All he needs to do is to persuade seven of them to join him in the verdict. That's it.

There's no way he can't succeed.

58

Into the jury room. Not fractious any more; any sense of oppression has gone. They're nearly free. What's more, it's their time now. All this listening, this barrage of evidence, has finally come to an end. Matthew couldn't be more relieved.

Dharam takes a seat at the head of the table. 'I think we're agreed that I'm to be the foreman?'

Emma bridles, her arms crossed firmly across her pale pink cardigan. 'I don't remember that we had actually agreed that.'

'Let's put it to a vote.' Jasmine, ever sensible. 'All in favour of Dharam as foreman, please raise your hand.'

Twelve hands are raised. Only Dharam's and Emma's stay down. Struck by a sudden thought, Matthew hesitates. Not that it makes any difference – the vote is already decisive.

'Right, that's sorted.'

Emma makes a harrumphing sound. Matthew looks at her. She's clearly feeling sidelined by the way that this is all going. Despite the innate hostility that he feels towards her, perhaps she could be more useful than he initially assumed. She catches his eye and he smiles in an apologetic manner, shrugs. *Don't blame me, I tried*. For the first time in days, she smiles back.

She's got entrenched views, though. He knows that. She's been the one banging on most about what Isobel looks like. But that means she's stupid. Easily prejudiced people often are.

She'll be no match for Matthew. He's certain he can bring her round.

He checks round the rest of the table. The main players for him are Neil, Russell, Aisha, Dharam and Jasmine. Emma too. Maybe it's just that these are the people who've most impinged themselves on his consciousness, but they're the ones to whom he's spoken most. Nicola leans forward – he should add her to that number, too. They've had the odd conversation in the last week, she seems sensible.

His role as foreman now formalised, Dharam clears his throat. 'I think it's best if we go back to the original definition of murder. I'll read it out. "Murder is constituted by any wilful act causing the destruction of life, whether wickedly intended to kill, or displaying such wicked recklessness as to imply a disposition depraved enough to be regardless of consequences." Everyone with me?'

They all nod. They've had it broken down for them so many times already, but Matthew supposes one more time can't hurt.

Dharam continues. 'The judge broke it down. The question we need to answer is did the girls threaten Christian with the knife, causing the fatal heart attack? That's what it boils down to. We can find them both guilty, or we can choose to believe Eliza or Isobel. It's one against the other.'

'Did anyone mention culpable homicide?' Jasmine says. 'I'd zoned out a bit by then.'

Matthew stares at her blankly. He must have missed that bit too. An alternative charge. No matter – if it comes to it, he'll manage the situation. He's not going to let them convict Isobel of any version of killing, not if he can help it. What Gill said has given him wings.

A man sitting opposite Matthew starts talking. Matthew can't remember his name at first – he's barely spoken throughout the trial. Elliot Graham, that's it. He's explaining the alternative charge in an unpleasantly nasal, pedantic voice. 'If we don't find the knife incident proved then we could find that the bullying is an unlawful act first and then that the death has resulted—'

'Let's just concentrate on the murder aspect first,' Dharam says, cutting the man off. He must feel as hostile to the concept of an alternative charge as Matthew, though for different reasons, Matthew is sure. 'We need to see what we all think about the knife. Wouldn't you agree?'

Nods round the table.

'Who wants to start?'

Emma. Predictably enough. 'I've said from the start that I don't like the look of that Isobel. She has an unkind face. Given Christian's dad is so clear that he told her that Christian had the heart condition, I think it's cut and dried. What I'm less convinced about is Eliza's involvement.'

More nods. Time for Matthew to speak up. 'I'm not sure that we're looking at this entirely the right way,' he says. 'I know exactly what you mean about the way the girls look, but what really concerns me is whether Isobel is being stitched up. Also, I don't think she's fit to stand trial. Regardless of what the psychiatrist says.'

Noises of interest. Dharam turns to him. 'What do you mean?'

'That Eliza. I've got a gut feeling about her. You might say she's got a trustworthy face, but don't you all think she's just a bit too good to be true?'

'OK, so what about Isobel? What are you saying about her?'

Matthew takes a deep breath. The pattern on the yellow wallpaper on the wall opposite him arranges itself briefly into a face, crowned with horns. It winks at Matthew. Good – he's on the right track now. He knows he can persuade them to believe she's not well – he can act the part. The fact that he believes every word she said in court is neither here nor there. It's time for him to play devil's advocate. 'I'm saying that I think she's psychotic. She's totally unwell. I got the impression that she believed everything implicitly, all these tarot readings, the Ouija board, the animal sacrifices – the lot of it. There's no way any of that is true.' The face in the wall scowls, rearing up from the wallpaper in a way that makes Matthew's heart jump before it subsides again, laughing.

'So what?' Emma says.

'So if she believes it's true, she's got to be mad. Which means she's got diminished responsibility. Which means she's not guilty. Whether or not she wielded the knife. Which I don't believe she did, incidentally.'

The head nods, nods again, moving up and down so fast it turns into a blur. Matthew blinks. It's gone.

'That put the cat among the pigeons and no mistake,' Russell says. They're walking out of the court building having been sent home after an hour of discussion fails to provide a verdict. Matthew wonders if they also feel collectively that it might be a bit off to come back with a verdict in such a short period of time – there's less of an argument happening over what he said than he anticipated. People are more open than they seemed.

'Is it what you really think?' Neil says.

'I don't think we should discuss it without the others present,' Matthew says.

'Yes, of course. Sorry,' Neil says.

There's a little group of them standing outside court. Matthew looks around the group.

'All I will say is this, you can trust what I say. I only give my opinion if it's something I really believe. I've learnt how important that is through my work as a transplant surgeon.' *Trust me, I'm a doctor.*

A little flutter around the group, his credentials duly noted.

Matthew's work here is done. There's a faint sound of baaing in his ears. As he looks at his fellow jurors standing around him, their faces morph in the way that the tiles did in the bathroom earlier in the week. They're on all fours now, dirty fleeces, red and blue sprays of paint on their sides. Good little sheep, that's it. He puts his snout up to the moon and howls.

FRIDAY

59

No sleep. No matter. Matthew will sleep for weeks when this is over. Once he's caught up with the backlog at work, that is. Once he's put in the necessary legwork to get back on track with Rosalind and Daisy, too. But they'll be all right, he knows it. When he explains everything properly to them, they'll be fine with it. They'll have read about the case in the papers, he's sure of it – they'll be proud to think of the role that Matthew has played in such an important trial.

He dresses before the sun is even up, so hyped is he to get into court and see this case to its conclusion. As he decided yesterday, he wears a suit and tie, checking the knot in the mirror before discarding it. Too formal. He's got to strike the right note between authoritative and authoritarian, like the best parenting skills that magazine articles recommend. He mustn't look too much like the headmaster, more like the friendly deputy who's great at motivating the team.

There are pages of notes on his kitchen table – he spent hours last night strategising how to ensure he'll get the result he wants, breaking the jury down into its constituent parts, character analysis, witness comparison, the works. There are mind maps, Venn diagrams – his head is on fire with inspiration. He's got this in the palm of his hand.

Early as it is when he arrives at court, Emma is waiting

outside. He halts momentarily at the sight of her before continuing walking towards the building. He can't keep avoiding her forever – he needs to remember the realisation that he came to yesterday, that she might be amenable to persuasion.

'I hoped I'd see you here,' she says as he approaches.

'Were you waiting for me?' He's surprised by this.

'Yes. I wanted to talk to you. It's about what you said yesterday.' She looks around in a furtive manner. 'Can we go somewhere? Have a quick chat?'

'A café?'

'No. I don't want to be overheard.'

He thinks for a moment. 'Let's go to the churchyard. No one will be there at this time.'

She walks fast, easily keeping pace with his stride. They make short work of George IV Bridge and go through the gate of Greyfriars Kirk. It's still quiet, wreathed in strands of mist, the overcast sky lending a spectral air. There are only a couple of people visible, women in black gowns and striped scarfs staring intently at some grave. Matthew pays them no heed, crossing with Emma to the far end of the kirkyard, into a recessed area dedicated to a forgotten family mausoleum.

'What do you want to talk about?' Matthew says. He knows the answer, of course, but she needs to spit it out.

She looks around her carefully before answering. She's very pale, Matthew notices, dark circles under her eyes as if she hasn't slept well. He's not the only one troubled by the case.

'I had some friends round for a drink last night,' she says. 'And, well. I did something we're not supposed to do.'

'You talked about the case?' He puts his hand out to her. 'Don't worry, I'm not judging.'

She nods, her face full of shame. 'I did. Yes. Worse than that, too.'

'In what way?'

'One of my friends – her neighbour is a medium. She knows all about the spirit world. We called her and asked her to come over, and then we did a séance.'

A long pause. The mist seems to thicken around them. Matthew doesn't know what to say. In one way, he's relieved that the trial has had this effect on someone else as well. He's not the only one to have been pulled into the world of the supernatural. But he's not sure he wants to hear more.

Emma looks up at him. She moves closer and closer, taking hold of his arm with one bony hand. Its grip is surprisingly strong, digging into his forearm.

'She said the most terrible things,' Emma says. 'Her voice was all deep and croaky. She didn't sound like herself at all.'

'Did you ask her about the trial?'

Emma nods. Even more shame crosses her face. Where she was pale before, she's now bright red. 'I don't want to tell you exactly what she said. She knew … things. Things no one knows. It was so terrible. But there was something about the trial, too.'

'What was that?' He's started whispering now, matching her hissed tones.

'That you're right. I was wrong. It wasn't Isobel. She's not guilty of this.'

She lets go of his arm, stands back. Her eyes are wide open now, staring past his shoulder as if she's seen a ghost. He looks behind him but there's nothing there.

But in the air, a hint of decay. Looks like he's not the only one in sympathy with the Devil.

'You won't tell anyone?'

Matthew is striding ahead, gripped by a compulsion to get away from Emma as fast as he can. She won't let him, though.

'Matthew. Matthew! Stop!'

He comes to a halt, faces her. 'I won't tell anyone.'

'Swear. You need to swear. I mean it. I can't bear it if they need to start the trial all over again because of me.'

He sighs. 'I swear I won't tell anyone. You can trust me.'

Hollow laughter in his head. But they're locked in this together – a dance of death. He needs her not guilty verdict for Isobel. It doesn't matter how it's achieved.

'How are we going to persuade the others?' she says, standing closer to him again. He resists the urge to back away from the stale smell of her breath, the mustiness of her hair. He's in this now, up to his neck.

'I think you changing your mind will have a great effect,' he says. 'You have a great influence over the room, I can feel it.'

Some pink returns to her cheeks. A faint smile. 'Thank you. I'll do my best. I don't want to let her down.'

The revulsion in him fades. It's good to have an ally. Even if not the one he would choose. And given how much she's railed against Isobel based purely on the girl's appearance, the sudden turnaround will have an effect on the rest of the jury; he's sure of it.

60

Through security for the last time. Well, if Matthew has anything to do with it. He can see no need for jury deliberations to last longer than the morning. Now he's got Emma on-side, it's going to be a breeze.

The heady optimism carries him up the stairs and into the jury room where he's brought back down to earth with a thud.

'I've been thinking about what you said last night,' Dharam says, 'and I'm very concerned. I don't think that we can decide to impose our own verdict like that and say that we think she's got diminished responsibility. We would be completely disregarding the oath that we made.'

'I agree,' Jasmine says. 'Though to be fair, I'm concerned about it. I've been thinking about it all night. Perhaps we could put a question to the judge about it, ask them to expand on why it wasn't further explored? Also, we could ask about this business of finding a verdict according to our conscience?'

Matthew swallows down the tide of panic that threatens to submerge him. No questions to the judge; anything but that. He can't risk his machinations being exposed in this way. It would be a catastrophe.

'I have a feeling this only applies in English law,' Neil says. 'I did some googling last night.'

Everyone's heads turn to him, a current of electricity running through them.

'We're not an independent country yet,' Elliot says. 'Different legal systems, maybe, but the underlying principles are still the same.'

Annoying voice or not, Matthew could kiss him.

'This is all getting a bit out of hand,' Dharam says. He's looking very worried, his face tight. Internet research, jury members going off piste – it's no surprise. As foreman he's completely lost control. The last thing Matthew needs is for him to try and change this, though. He's got to think of something to say.

Inspiration strikes. 'How about this? Not proven. We could say not proven. Then it isn't completely that she's got away with it. But we can avoid convicting her given how unhappy we feel about her mental health.'

As one, the jurors seem to relax, sinking back in their chairs. It's clear that no one wants to be the cause of a retrial.

'Who agrees with a not proven verdict?'

Hands go up round the table. Not everyone. But Matthew looks round with a growing sense of excitement. Emma's is up from the start, Neil and Russell soon follow. More. Six, seven. A little hesitation, and Jasmine raises hers. Dharam nods, puts his up. That's nine. More than half. He's done it. He's brought them round.

They have a verdict.

'What about Eliza?' Dharam says. 'Would we say not proven for her as well?'

Matthew shakes his head. 'I think this one is a little more complicated. Or actually, less. We're not saying that Isobel didn't do what's alleged, after all. We're just saying it's not proven because we're not convinced that she was mentally competent at the time or even now. Diminished responsibility, after all. But Eliza – there's nothing wrong with her as far as anyone can tell.'

Emma nods. 'I've been thinking about it. You all know I was so in favour of Eliza, hated Isobel. I thought about it a lot last night, though, and I've changed my mind. I agree that Isobel isn't well. She's got tricky parents as well – that mother who seems to hate her, the weird father who believes in magic or whatever it is he does as well. What's Eliza's excuse? She's there blaming Isobel for everything, but what if it was all her? What if she did go at Christian?'

Jasmine shakes her head. 'I think that if we're saying it's not proven against Isobel, when there really is evidence against her, it's not very fair to say that Eliza is guilty.'

'Does fairness come into this?' Russell says. 'She's done everything she can to project the blame away from herself. Maybe Eliza is the one most to blame?'

Matthew's intentions have taken on a life of their own. He's lit the fire, and now he doesn't even need to fan the flames.

'It'll look really perverse if we find the case not proven against Isobel but yet find Eliza guilty,' Dharam says. 'I don't think we can justify that verdict. Unless we are saying that we believe Eliza is lying.'

Emma. 'Maybe she is. I've never trusted that butter-won't-melt expression of hers.'

Matthew's head is buzzing. He could laugh at Emma's volte-face, but it's too useful for him. Besides, he's out of energy now. The lack of sleep is finally catching up with him. He had one mission, to have Isobel found not guilty, and this has been achieved, best as he can. Not proven isn't exactly what was demanded, but it's close enough. He stares over at the wallpaper, waiting for the face to reveal itself again, show its approval, or whether it thinks he should do more.

Nothing. It must be all right. His work here is done. He sits back and lets the arguments continue. He's got no skin in this game.

They break for coffee. Under the supervision of a security guard, those that wish to smoke are accompanied to an inner courtyard. Matthew elects to go with them to get some fresh air.

'This is not what I thought jury deliberations would be,' Nicola says in a low voice, the smoke from her Marlboro billowing into his face.

'What did you think they'd be like?'

'Professional. This feels just like someone is making it up as they go along.'

'I suppose we are,' Matthew says. 'Maybe that's the issue with the rules against revealing what's said. How can anyone ever know what a jury's motivation is in finding a particular verdict when nothing about it can ever be revealed and there's no accountability? All sorts could happen and no one would be any the wiser.'

'I guess there's a reason why there's only a one per cent conviction rate for rape,' she says, sucking on her cigarette.

'I don't know anything about that,' Matthew says. 'But I think I'd prefer to be tried by a jury than by a judge alone.'

Nicola turns to face him, looks him up and down. For a moment he can see what she sees – a white upper-middle class man in a suit. She smiles at him, not altogether kindly. 'I suppose you would.'

Back inside. Time is ticking along and they're still arguing. Matthew continues to sit it out, worried that he might undermine the not proven that's locked in for Isobel. It's between Jasmine and Nicola now – Nicola's of the view that Eliza is definitely guilty, Jasmine that fairness trumps all and the verdict for her should be not proven too.

Elliot pipes up. 'I wouldn't mind if we can finish by lunch

Witch Trial

time,' he says. 'There's a matinée on at the Festival Theatre which I'd like to see.'

No one takes issue with this. They all seem fed up.

'Let's put it to a vote,' Dharam says. 'We can see where we've got to now. Everyone for Eliza being found guilty, please raise your hand.'

Four go up immediately, Nicola's waved the most vigorously, the others more slowly. That's it.

'And for not proven.'

Four again. Still five left to decide. Only a couple of votes needed either way. Matthew hasn't yet raised his hand.

'I really don't think it's fair that Isobel should get away with it and not Eliza,' Sarah Thompson says. She's one of the youngest in the room, has barely said a word throughout the entire proceedings. 'I say not proven for her too.'

Five votes for not proven. Only three votes needed now.

'I can't really argue with that,' Roderick says. 'I feel sorry for Christian's family, but we need to think of the living here. Not the dead. Even if they did do it, I don't think they'll ever do anything like this again. They're so young. They can learn.' His hand goes up.

Two votes more. Then it's over.

Flashes before his eyes, the face leering from the wallpaper. Eliza's smile floating in the room, a grim parody of the Cheshire cat. She's laughing, an ugly, jeering sound that cuts through him. She can't get away with this – it's obvious to him now what he needs to do. The Devil's instructions are fully clear. Not just get Isobel off, but ensure that Eliza's locked up. The punishment she deserves.

'I'm sorry, I think she's guilty. We need to think about Christian, too,' Matthew says. 'Justice for her family.' He raises his hand. Only one vote to go.

Emma looks at him. Looks away. She clears her throat. 'I'm

going to change my vote,' she says. 'I think Matthew is right. There needs to be some kind of justice. My verdict is that Eliza is guilty.'

Back in court. The public gallery is full, the atmosphere electric, tension crackling all around. Matthew catches Gill's eye, looks away. There's a throng of schoolgirls near the back of the room, all wearing witches' hats. He's surprised they haven't been kicked out. Christian's parents are in the front row, their faces grey and tight. This matters, it really matters. The reality of it starts to hit him.

'Ladies and gentlemen, who speaks for you?' the clerk asks. Dharam gets to his feet.

'Have you decided upon your verdict in this case?'

'We have.'

'What is your verdict on the charge against the first-named accused, Eliza Lawson?'

'Guilty.'

A gasp from the public gallery, sparks of nervous excitement in the air. The judge's face is inscrutable.

'Is that guilty of murder?'

'Yes.'

'And in the matter of the charge against Isobel Smyth, what is your verdict?'

'Not proven.'

The judge starts to speak, but it's drowned out by a great cry from the public gallery, a thud. A woman screams. A commotion all around her.

'He's down, my husband's down! Somebody help us.'

'Is there a doctor here? Quick, we need a doctor!'

Matthew feels hands pulling at him, pushing him. Before he knows it, he's standing in front of the patient. Eliza's father, slumped on to the ground.

'Help him. Somebody help him! Is there anyone here that knows CPR?'

Neil and Russell are shaking at Matthew's arm, shouting at him. 'Come on, you're the heart surgeon, you know what to do.'

That's when the buzzing starts. The darkness, too, black rearing up to swallow him. He holds his hands up in front of him, his useless, helpless hands.

Then he collapses to the floor.

End of Exhibit 1

Psychiatric Report

1 June 2019

Patient Name: Matthew Phillips
Date of Birth: 14.11.1970
Date of admission: 22.5.2019
Report date: 1.6.2019
Consultant Psychiatrist: Mr Stephen Lowe
Location: Ward C, Craiglockhart Psychiatric Hospital

Reason for Referral:
Matthew Phillips was referred to the psychiatric team following a major psychotic breakdown, resulting in his involuntary admission under the Mental Health Act (Care and Treatment) (Scotland) Act (section 36). The patient was brought in by emergency services following erratic behaviour, hallucinations, and a marked deterioration in functioning.

Presenting Complaint:
The patient was found wandering in the Pentland Hills in bare feet, dressed inappropriately for the weather. He was shouting incoherently and attempted to assault the member of the public who approached him. On the arrival of the emergency services, he said repeatedly that 'the devil was going to save him' and that he had 'done what the devil told him to do'. Upon arrival on the ward, he was disorganised, confused and suffering auditory hallucinations. He was paranoid, accusing medical staff of plotting to harm him, and stating that his wife wanted him dead as did his former work colleagues.

History of Present Illness:
Matthew had been displaying increased signs of stress and paranoia for approximately six months prior to the breakdown. He was increasingly abusing alcohol and his marriage was coming under strain. His wife noticed significant mood swings, decreased sleep and increased irritability. He began to isolate himself, reporting to his wife that his colleagues were 'conspiring against him to destroy his career'. In January of this year he was put on indefinite sick leave from work following a complaint of professional misconduct (he was reported by his superior Dominic North to be under the influence of alcohol in the operating theatre) and after this he moved out of the family home into a separate flat; indeed this was also in January of this year. He continued to see his wife and daughter regularly for a while but after claiming to be on the jury in a high-profile murder trial completely cut off contact with them (the truth of this assertion is still to be assessed), disposing of his mobile telephone and refusing all attempts at communication.

In the days leading up to the admission, he was seen by neighbours to be behaving in an erratic way in the common parts of the property, and loud banging and incoherent shouting were heard coming from his flat to the extent that police were called although no action was taken. On the day before the admission he encountered his downstairs neighbour at the front door and violently assaulted her, accusing her of spying on him and being in league with 'the angels of God'. Later that afternoon he was reported to have been aggressive towards a bus driver near Hillend Ski Centre but ran off before the police attended. The day of the admission he was found as stated above in a dishevelled state wandering on the hills.

Past Psychiatric History:
- No previous psychiatric admissions.
- Brief episode of depression five years ago, managed with therapy and SSRIs, which he discontinued after six months.
- No prior history of psychosis or hallucinations.

Personal History:
- Born and raised in the UK.
- Stable upbringing with no significant trauma.
- Holds a degree in medicine and works as a heart transplant surgeon.
- Married for twenty-four years, living until recently with his wife and teenaged daughter.
- Some history of alcohol use disorder.

Family Psychiatric History:
No known psychiatric illnesses in the family.

Mental State Examination:
Appearance: Matthew appeared dishevelled, with poor personal hygiene, although his hands were spotlessly clean despite the presence of dermatitis presenting in the form of an eczema rash across his hands and arms and extending to his face. He seemed agitated and restless.

Mood and affect: He reported feeling 'frustrated' and 'scared' but denied feelings of depression. He also reported being 'the cleverest person in this place' and that no one was his equal in power or knowledge. His affect was inappropriate, at times laughing when discussing serious concerns. His conversation was full of religiosities and showed a marked preoccupation with the Devil and an unknown woman called Gill Martin with whom he appears to be obsessed.

Thought Content: Matthew exhibited clear delusional content with persecutory and religious themes. He was convinced that his former colleagues were conspiring to destroy him personally and professionally, and in addition that the Devil was giving him instructions as to how to live. He described visual hallucinations, claiming to have seen the Devil appearing from clouds and wallpaper, and described auditory hallucinations that told him to direct a jury to find a certain verdict. He did not report hearing those voices during the interview.
Perception: Matthew did not seem to understand that these hallucinatory experiences described above were not real, indicating a lack of insight.

Risk Assessment:
Matthew presents a high risk of harm to others, given the nature of his paranoid delusions and command hallucinations urging violence. He also poses a risk to himself due to his poor insight and judgement, which could result in accidental self-harm. At the time of assessment, he remains highly agitated and unpredictable.

Diagnosis:
Primary Diagnosis: Acute Psychotic Disorder, likely triggered by underlying stress and untreated mental health issues.
Differential Diagnosis: Consideration of schizophrenia spectrum disorder or substance-induced psychosis (though no drug use has been reported).

Management Plan:

1. **Hospitalisation:** Continued inpatient care under Section 44 of the Mental Health Act as above.

2. **Pharmacological Treatment:**
   - Initiation of antipsychotic medication (Olanzapine 10mg daily) to manage hallucinations and delusions.
   - PRN (as needed) medication for acute agitation (Lorazepam 2mg).
3. **Psychological Intervention:** Once stabilised, referral to Cognitive Behavioural Therapy to address delusional thinking and promote insight.
4. **Monitoring:**
   - Daily assessment of mental state and response to medication.
   - Regular risk assessments, with special attention to potential harm to self or others.
   - Physical health monitoring, including sleep patterns, nutritional intake, and weight.
5. **Family Involvement:** Engage with the patient's wife for collateral information and support.
6. **Discharge Planning:** Once stable, discharge will be considered with a robust follow-up plan including outpatient psychiatric services and community support.

Prognosis:
Given Matthew's lack of prior psychotic episodes and the current severity of his condition, the prognosis is cautiously optimistic, provided he responds well to treatment. Long-term follow-up and adherence to medication will be critical in preventing relapse.

Stephen Lowe
Consultant Psychiatrist

Letter to psychiatrist from Rosalind Phillips

17 November 2019

Dear Dr Lowe,

You asked me to write to you if there is anything that concerns me particularly with regards to my husband Matthew's behaviour and demeanour. As you know, he continues to be held under section at the Craiglockhart Hospital, which status I do not wish to challenge. It is, in my opinion, very much the safest place for him at this time.

While there have been significant improvements in his mental state, I remain deeply concerned about his frame of mind. This is down to the continued tenor of his conversations in which he repeatedly expresses his concern about what he says his actions were when he was a juror on that 'witch trial' which was in the newspapers some months ago (the case of the schoolgirls at that boarding school, I'm sure that you recall it). I have still been unable to ascertain whether he really was on the jury for this as no one will give me official confirmation. While it is certainly true that he received a jury citation around the time of this trial, as this arrived at our home address and I saw it, given the nature of his breakdown and the other delusions from which he has been suffering, it is impossible for me to say with complete certainty that he was definitely involved.

Certain or not, it is clear that he has spent excessive time reading about it, not helped by the mass of articles and pieces on the internet which he has accessed since. He remains deeply preoccupied by the case, and it forms the bulk of his conversation. I hope that this obsession could be addressed in more detail by his psychiatric team.

Matthew is also persistent in his desire to contact a journalist who he says he knows by the name of Gill Martin. I have been unable to trace any person of this name, though note that it is the name adopted by a demonic character in the novel by James Hogg entitled *The Private Memoirs and Confessions of a Justified Sinner*. Again, it is impossible to say whether the person really exists or if she is another product of Matthew's deluded mind, but my sense is that it is more likely to be the latter case than the former.

What concerns me most of all about this obsession with the trial is not Matthew's interest in it per se, but rather that he is trying to make contact with outside organisations with regard to it. The hospital tells me that he has made repeated attempts to write to newspapers and solicitors' firms to give them the 'inside story' of the trial. So far it appears that they have successfully intercepted all letters, but it may be the case that something slips through the net. I would ask that a very close eye be kept on this, please.

Best wishes,
Rosalind Phillips

Letter to Matthew Phillips from solicitor

20 January 2020

Elwes Mitchell Solicitors
Charlotte Square
Edinburgh

Dear Sir,

We note your letter of 13 December 2019 asking for an urgent meeting to discuss matters arising from your participation on the jury of a trial concerning our former client Isobel Smyth. We regret to inform you that under the Contempt of Court Act we are unable to enter into any discussion whatsoever with you on this subject, and we would ask that you do not contact us on this or any other subject again.

Yours faithfully,
David Aikman

Letter to Matthew Phillips from advocate

2 February 2020

Endeavour Chambers
Royal Mile
Edinburgh

Dear Mr Phillips,

I note your letter to me dated December of 2019, asking to raise urgent discussions in relation to the trial of my client Eliza Lawson last year due to your place on the jury. I am prevented by law from entering into any discussion with you on the subject, and request that you do not contact me again.

Best wishes,
Jennifer Brodie

Advertisement run in *Private Eye* and the personals of *The Times*

27 February 2020

REMEMBER THE LOBSTER SHACK. Desperately seeking Gill Martin. Please contact Matthew Phillips at PO Box 73. Listen to your conscience. I need your help. MP

Letter to Gill Martin from Matthew Phillips

25 March 2020

Dear Gill (I know that's not your name, but I can think of you in no other way),

Thank you so much for making contact with me at last. I have been trying to find you for months. It's a matter of huge importance that we talk about the case. I need your help. I may be responsible for a grave miscarriage of justice. I don't know if you realised it, but I was extremely unwell at the time when we first met. I can't even be sure how much of the conversations that I think we had were real. I need to get some clarity on this, and it would be very helpful if we could see each other face to face and talk about what happened.

There's a poem by John Berryman, the one where Henry thinks that he has done something terrible but he finds in fact that he hasn't, no one is gone. It's a bit like OCD, where people imagine they're paedophiles or murderers when they're not. My sickness is the opposite. I have done something wrong, I know it. I just don't know exactly what. Not yet. I have a feeling that I have done something terrible, but the truth is only just emerging to me. Please let me know as soon as you can when we can meet – I am currently in hospital but visitors are permitted.

Thank you so much. I hope to see you in the near future.

Matthew

Amazon reviews of *Witch Trial*, a book self-published by the author Gill Martin in January 2023, removed by court order in July 2023

6 January 2023
From United Kingdom
Stacey Tong
*** Interesting premise quite well executed but lacking plausibility
Reviewed in the United Kingdom on 6 January 2023

I managed to read this book in one day and enjoyed it quite a lot to start with although as it went on it annoyed me more and more. The central premise that the main accused girl actually believed in witchcraft stretched all credulity. It was obvious that the narrator Matthew was going through some kind of a breakdown and I found the ending incredibly frustrating in the way that it just broke off with no explanation of what happened next. How could he just black out like that? The first half was a lot better than the second half. Some of the writing was all right which is why I have given it two and a half stars rounded up to three but a lot more could have been done with the premise. And seriously, a note to the author – learn how to end a novel properly. That was rubbish.

17 January 2023
From United Kingdom
Scott McSporran
** Knock-off of classic novel
Reviewed in the United Kingdom on 17 January 2023

Firstly I do not understand why it has to say reviewed in the United Kingdom – it should say reviewed in Scotland as that is where I am. This encapsulates why we need independence to stop our beautiful country being eradicated like this. Anyway this book is all right, nothing special, but what's so obvious is that the author is ripping off the brilliant James Hogg book *Confessions and Private Memoir of a Justified Sinner* which just shouldn't be allowed. No one has any original ideas these days.

2 February 2023
From United Kingdom
Bookish Tours
* Hated every character
Reviewed in the United Kingdom on 2 February 2023

If I could give this no stars I would. No way would I organise a tour based on any location mentioned in this book because I wouldn't want to end up near any person featured as I hated them all so much. Avoid it like the plague.

15 February 2023
From United Kingdom
Witchy Girl
***** Amazing amazing amazing
Reviewed in the United Kingdom on 15 February 2023

Oh my god this is amazing – it's only a real-life account of possibly the most insane murder trial that has ever happened. Buckle up kids because this is wild. That witch trial where the girls had a coven and scared someone to death? The Devil actually did his thing and looked out for our girl Isobel – she is our shero getting away with murder like that. The minute that b***h Eliza tried to pin the blame on her she was toast and it's great that the juror did what the Devil told him to do. I don't think this kind of story is actually allowed to be out there for legal reasons so be quick to download it before it gets banned – if the author wants to get in touch with me please do so we can look at ways to distribute it in case it does get taken down.

20 March 2023
From United Kingdom
Bill Nimmo
* Blatant contempt of court – should be banned
Reviewed in the United Kingdom on 20 March 2023

This novel purports to be a true story and is obviously based on a notorious trial that took place in Edinburgh at the beginning of 2019 when one accused was found guilty of murder and a verdict of not proven was brought in against the second accused. The story is primarily narrated by a juror who claims to have manipulated the other jurors in the case and details are revealed of the deliberations which if true, demonstrate the most blatant contempt of court I have ever seen (and I am a retired judge). To make matters worse, the way that the book is written shows little to no understanding of Scots law. I have drawn this to the attention of the authorities and trust that this will be removed from the Amazon website very soon. Prosecutions will follow, mark my words.

Newsletter from Witchy Girl to subscribers to her blog

27 February 2023

WITCHY GIRL JUST SENT A NEW MESSAGE TO SUBSCRIBERS

Crazy times, my subscribers, and I've decided to make this post public too as it covers some really important matters. I did not expect to be writing to you all again after Eliza was sentenced – as far as any of us knew, that was the end of it. HOW WRONG COULD WE BE???

So it all kicked off with that book. *Witch Trial*? Any of you read it? The one that went viral on #booktok. I came to it late, thanks to HexyBitch who posted about it on Reddit. That blew the lid off and no mistake. This man who was on the jury, turns out that he thought he was talking to the Devil all the way through. He was seeing things, convinced that he was being told what to do. So he manipulated the jury, got them to find the case not proven against Isobel (I mean that NEVER made sense, that she was let off) and convict Eliza. Then he got someone to write a book about it.

Eliza's family got hold of that (well, her mum. Her dad had a heart attack at the end of the trial, remember?). They made people pay attention. No one wanted to do anything about it, but they involved the police, solicitors, the lot. They found the man in the end – he was in some mental institution. He confessed to the lot – he's being prosecuted for contempt of court. He won't say how he got the book out there but we'll find out in the end, I'm sure.

So they took the case to the High Court, appealed it. Got Eliza's conviction overturned. But the case is going to be tried again. Both of them, Eliza and Isobel too. They've said that even though Isobel got off, it was what they call a 'tainted acquittal' (like 'Tainted Love', god I love Marc Almond . . .). So there's going to be another murder trial, some time in 2026.

Just when you thought it was all over . . .

I'm going to apply for permission to record the case, do a proper podcast on all of it. Seems like it's very important to have it done with full scrutiny, make sure that no one else is behaving badly. Those poor girls, being persecuted for their beliefs like this. I can't believe it's all starting again.

If you want to get full access to everything, please consider becoming a full subscriber to my Patreon. It's the only way that I can afford to do this – no one is paying me to report on the case, even though it's a matter of such importance. You will be supporting justice. If you can't afford to take on the subscription, please spread the word far and wide. The court needs to know that we are all watching. Every step of the way.

Psychiatric report (update)

17 September 2023

Psychiatric Report

Patient Name: Matthew Phillips
Date of Birth: 14.11.1970
Report date: 17.9.2023
Consultant Psychiatrist: Dr Stephen Lowe

This report is prepared at the request of the High Court in Edinburgh for the purposes of assessing firstly whether Matthew Phillips is fit to plead to the offence of contempt of court, and secondly whether he was suffering from any mental illness at the time of the alleged commission of the offence that might have given rise to a defence of diminished responsibility.

I was first introduced to Matthew when he was sectioned at Craiglockhart following a severe psychotic breakdown in May 2019. While some doubt attached to the veracity of his assertions at the time, it later transpired that he had in fact been on the jury in the murder trial of Eliza Lawson and Isobel Smyth. The main theme of this trial was witchcraft, and as such it had a negative effect on Matthew's frame of mind. Matthew's state of mind was already vulnerable because he had been signed off sick following tensions in his place of work due to a whistleblowing situation regarding allegations of sexual harassment and bullying against Matthew's immediate superior, the surgeon Dominic North.

It should be noted that the allegations of misuse of alcohol mentioned in my earlier report have been shown to be untrue, the only source being the aforementioned Mr North who had his own reasons for undermining Matthew's credibility.

A psychiatric report that I prepared at that time following initial discussions with Matthew is available to the court. I have no doubt that in the months surrounding the date of Matthew's admission to hospital under section 2 of the Mental Health Act, he was suffering from a severe psychotic breakdown, and in my view did not have the capacity to form criminal intention at that time, which would cover the first charge of contempt of court.

I am instructed that the second charge of contempt of court relates to the 2023 publication of a self-published novel ("Witch Trial") which contains a lightly fictionalised account of the trial and the jury's deliberations from Matthew's perspective. I understand that Matthew has pleaded guilty to this charge and accepts full culpability for his actions in causing this information to be put into the public domain contrary to any legal obligations incumbent on him as a member of a jury. I also understand that Matthew was assisted in this matter by a novelist whose name he has consistently refused to give to the court despite this person's obvious criminality in assisting him to break the law in this way, even potentially encouraging him, though I understand this is a matter currently under criminal investigation.

Matthew and I have discussed at length his mental state around the decision he made to talk to the novelist in question and give them the information that was needed for this book to be written and published. He asserts that it was the right decision and that no other route was open to him – he feels very strongly that he caused a miscarriage of justice in 2019 when he manipulated the jury and he wanted to right that wrong by getting his version of the events of the trial out into the public domain in some way. He attempted to speak to solicitors and to the advocate who represented Eliza Lawson but no one would engage with him so it seemed to him that he had no choice other than to follow this route.

While there is no doubt that the psychotic breakdown that led to Matthew's hospitalisation was severe, I am happy as his psychiatrist to say that he has made a full recovery. I am less happy to have to report this to the court as there can therefore be no doubt that he is fit to plead and has no defence in law (due to psychiatric reasons at least) to the second charge of contempt of court.

Please do not hesitate to contact me if I can be of any further assistance to the court.

Stephen Lowe
Consultant Psychiatrist

Character reference on behalf of Matthew Phillips

My name is Zaid Rahim and I write in support of my former colleague Matthew Phillips. I understand that he has pleaded guilty to contempt of court in that he has caused the secret deliberations of a jury to be revealed publicly, and I take this offence very seriously. However, I wish to provide some context for the offence, as I understand it, and also to give you a view of Matthew that may otherwise be lacking. In my opinion, he is a good man, who has been prepared to sacrifice his career in order to support me and to do the right thing. I feel no doubt that the actions that led to the commission of this offence were for a motivation that was good, if misguided, rather than malicious.

In order to explain properly, it will require me to go into detail that may on first glance appear irrelevant to the case in point, but I would ask you to bear with me.

I have been working as a surgeon within the transplant team at the Western General Hospital in Edinburgh for the last ten years. Over these years I have witnessed the lead surgeon Dominic North (recently convicted) repeatedly bully, undermine and harass those in junior positions to him, particularly women. I myself have been the target of this behaviour. I will admit that for a long time I kept my head down in the hope that his behaviour would cease, but at the end of 2018 it came to a point that I could no longer keep quiet, following a sexual assault by Mr North on one of my younger female colleagues while we were all in the operating theatre for a transplant procedure.

I raised the matter with Mr North, only to find myself the subject of a serious complaint which stemmed from an incident some months earlier when unbeknownst to me, my drinks were spiked with alcohol at a work dinner (I am teetotal). Complaints were made against me for inappropriate behaviour, and while it appeared that the matter was resolved at the time, a record was kept on file. When Mr North became aware that I was willing to initiate a complaint against him, and support my female colleague in her allegations, it was made clear to me that I would face a professional misconduct hearing as a result of the complaint that had been held on file.

There was only one witness who could both clear my name in terms of the alcohol allegations and provide a witness statement in support of the complainant against Mr North: Matthew Phillips, who witnessed both the doctoring of my drinks with alcohol, and also Mr North's behaviour. He had a choice to make: to blow the whistle on the terrible behaviour in the department, and in doing so, potentially sacrifice his career, or to say nothing, and preserve his professional situation. When Mr North became aware that Matthew was preparing to give evidence against him, he took steps to have Matthew suspended from work, alleging professional misconduct, threatening him with a referral to the General Medical Council and a Maintaining High Professional Standards investigation.

It's at this point that Matthew was signed off sick from work due to the distress that he was suffering. It is fair to say that he had not at this stage decided whether to provide the necessary evidence in my favour, and the strain of the dilemma was playing on him. At this time, he was called to be on the jury.

While I cannot explain what motivation led Matthew to behave as he did on the jury and subsequent to that, I will say that once he had recovered from the breakdown that led to his hospitalisation, he made a full statement that cleared my name and also supported the female complainant. This evidence led directly not just to Mr North's dismissal from the hospital, but ultimately to his criminal conviction for indecent assault. Matthew gave evidence at that trial.

I have been fully reinstated at work. Matthew has resigned due to his health and the impact of everything that has happened, which marks a sad and premature end to what should have been a glittering career. I am in no doubt that if Mr North had not behaved as he did, poisoning the department which he led for so many years, there would have been nothing to stop Matthew from rising to the top. He has been a victim of these circumstances as much as I.

These considerations may not seem relevant to you when weighing up the criminal actions that Matthew has committed, but I would beg you to bear in mind that as stated above, all such behaviour happened against a backdrop of great personal and professional strain, in which Matthew did eventually make the decision to do the right thing regardless of the effect that it would have on his own career.

While I cannot pretend to know the full workings of Matthew's mind at the time of the trial, I would venture a guess that his attempt to stand up for a person he perceived to be an underdog, however misguided he may have been, was done in order to serve the ends of justice. His intentions were good. I understand fully that no individual should ever behave like this, and that it undermines the integrity of the jury system in a way that's entirely unacceptable, but I feel it's important to note that it was not for selfish reasons or any hope of personal gain.

I would also like to add one additional detail in support of Matthew's character. In the novel that is the subject of this prosecution, it is put forward that he is having an extra-marital relationship with a younger colleague called Olivia. While it may not be specifically pertinent to the case, I would like to make it clear that there has never been anyone of that name working in the hospital, and that to the best of my knowledge (bearing in mind that it is a small department in which gossip is rife) Matthew has never been involved in any adulterous situation. He is a devoted family man and this part of the story was only the product of his deluded thoughts.

Yours faithfully,
Zaid Rahim
Transplant surgeon

DOCUMENT BUNDLE IN THE RETRIAL OF ELIZA LAWSON AND ISOBEL SMYTH FOR THE MURDER OF CHRISTIAN SHAW

STATEMENT OF PETER SHAW

21 January 2024

I make this statement fully of my own free will. I am aware that I am opening myself up to the possibility of prosecution. Regardless, I need to tell the court that when I gave evidence in the earlier trial of Isobel Smyth and Eliza Lawson, aspects of what I said were untrue. Specifically, when I asserted that I had explicitly informed Isobel of my daughter Christian's heart condition, I was not telling the truth. I did not tell her or Eliza Lawson anything about Christian's health, nor did I give any warning that their course of conduct might jeopardise Christian's health.

    I apologise to the court for the fact that I lied. I understand that I may well face a charge of perjury. I told the court what I wish I had done, rather than what I actually did. It has been hard to accept my daughter's death, but I understand that this is not the way to find justice.

STATEMENT OF MARIANNE SHAW

21 January 2024

I make this statement entirely of my own free will. I am aware that I am opening myself up to the possibility of prosecution. I give this statement to address why I withheld the diary of my daughter Christian Shaw as evidence in the original trial of Isobel Smyth and Eliza Lawson, despite the fact that it held information pertinent to the case.

I did not withhold it in order to pervert the course of justice, but rather because I was ashamed of some of the contents. Christian complains in numerous passages that I was controlling her life and that I was forcing an illness on her that did not exist.

She was not wrong. I consistently overplayed her diagnosis and exaggerated her symptoms. I argued with doctors when they told me that Christian was in an improved state of health, that there were no physiological issues any more. I persuaded them still to exercise an abundance of caution, to prescribe her medication that she did not, in fact, need. This was not, however, for reasons of malice. I do not have Munchausen's by Proxy. I was not inducing illness in her. The medication – beta-blockers – had no significant negative effect. I was attempting to protect her from her father's insistence that she be sent to boarding school from the age of nine, which I felt strongly was not in her best interests.

I am told that this may have affected the case against the appellants Isobel Smyth and Eliza Lawson adversely. Be that as it may, the fact remains that Christian suffered a fatal heart attack that day, precipitated by their actions. She may not have had the pre-existing heart condition as was asserted to the court in the trial. I understand that further tests are being carried out to ascertain exactly what happened, tests which were not carried out at the time because of the misleading narrative that I provided.

I apologise to the court for my actions.

EXTRACTS FROM THE DIARY OF CHRISTIAN SHAW FOUND HIDDEN IN HER BEDROOM IN THE FAMILY HOUSE IN EDINBURGH

7th November 2017

I don't know what to do. They're not talking to me and it's terrible. I can't handle it, it feels like I don't exist any more.

13th March 2018

I honestly don't know why Eliza hates me so much. Is she jealous? That's what my mum would say, that she wants something I've got. What, though? Her parents aren't divorced. They give her lots of money. She's rich – they've got a big house, Sasha told me that. It's not like Isobel likes me any better, though maybe that's the problem. Isobel used to be nice to me, before all this happened. We both liked the Cure though Eliza hates them. We both loved Practical Magic even though Eliza said it was shit. So maybe she felt left out and wanted to keep Isobel for herself? I'm not sure how Sasha fits into that, though I guess she's a bit of a hanger-on.

22nd April 2018

I cracked today. Can't believe it. I just can't go on like this any more. I think it's making me sick. Even though I know my mum was talking shit about my health all those years ago, it's not right now. Something's changed. I can feel my heart going weird, missing beats. I keep having these horrific dreams. Sometimes even when I'm awake.

Witch Trial

Eliza gave me these capsules to take last year. She said they were health supplements, that they'd help me sleep better, come to terms with everything. I wonder now if they're making me feel worse. I'm going to talk to her about it, though I know she'll be angry with me. She always wants me to do what she says.

I know I should talk to the doctor but then they'll take me out of school and I don't want to be away in case I miss something and it gets even worse. I know it sounds mad, but it feels like it's a bit more under my control if I'm here and able to see what they're doing, however bad it is. Anyway. I talked to Eliza. I tried fronting up to her, told her that she's got to make it stop. I'm going to get ill.

She just laughed.

POST-MORTEM REPORT ON
CHRISTIAN SHAW: UPDATED

I have been asked to comment on my colleague's post-mortem report on the deceased schoolgirl Christian Shaw, specifically in relation to his conclusions on her cardiac condition. The conclusions of that report were completed after false information was provided, namely an untrue narrative of myocarditis and cardiopathy provided erroneously by the mother of the deceased.

My analysis of the images of the heart does not find dilated cardiomyopathy as the original pathologist stated. In that case one would expect to find that the heart was globular or balloon-shaped due to the generalised dilation of all four chambers. That was not the case here.

I find rather that the images show valvular heart disease, namely a thickening of the heart valve in the left ventrical. The asymmetric appearance of the heart that we see displayed supports that finding.

As to what would have caused this thickening of the heart valve, additional toxicology tests have been carried out. Analysis of the remaining blood sample has shown high levels of psilocybin, the active compound to be found in the banned psychedelic, magic mushrooms. It has been established that regular doses of psilocybin, even at a low level, have the potential to cause thickening of the heart valves with the potential to cause heart disease and eventual cardiac arrest. On the balance of probabilities, I find that to be the explanation for what has happened here.

Witch Trial

I want to make one final comment, which is that my colleague should not be overly criticised for the findings that he made. Cardiomyopathy is notoriously difficult to diagnose, and the deceased's medical history always plays an important part in that diagnosis. It creates part of the narrative but also runs the risk of creating a confirmation bias, whereby the doctor sees only what they expect to see.

Closing Speech for the second accused Isobel Smyth in retrial for murder of Christian Shaw

So what is the evidence that we have heard, members of the jury? That Isobel dresses in an unconventional way. That her hair is dyed black. That she has multiple facial piercings and a belief in witchcraft that is not shared by the majority of people. Let me be clear, none of these eccentricities is anything more than that. It is not a criminal offence to be different. She is not a killer, and we have heard no single piece of evidence to suggest that she is.

There is no escaping the fact that her behaviour towards Christian was unpleasant. You may feel that bullying should be a crime, but it is not currently so. Sadly, teenage girls have behaved badly towards each other since time immemorial – I have no doubt also that this will continue until the end of time. But it is very important that you should not allow your natural desire to punish Isobel for this unacceptable behaviour to blind you to the truth of this matter, that if anyone is responsible for Christian's murder, it is Eliza.

Let us break this down. You have been given no evidence to suggest that Isobel was aware of Christian's health, but you have been shown an extract from Christian's diary which shows that Eliza gave her unspecified capsules which she was taking on a daily basis. Given the updated toxicology report, it is no stretch to conclude that these capsules contained psilocybin – magic mushrooms. Eliza has elected not to give evidence in this case, and has refused to give any explanation as to what her account of this might be – you might feel that you can draw an inference from her silence that shows she was well aware of the illegality of her action in persuading Christian to take a harmful, illegal substance.

You may also feel you can draw an inference from the arrest and conviction of Eliza's father for dealing controlled substances, namely his leading role in the company 'Shrooms' which was behind the large-scale distribution of products derived from magic mushrooms farmed on his land, containing psilocybin.

You have been given a litany of woeful behaviour on Isobel's part in terms of the sacrifices and supernatural-themed ceremonies that she carried out at Eliza's suggestion, but it is not a stretch to suggest that Isobel was also a victim of the illicit administration of hallucinogenic drugs, which would have severely affected her judgement and ability to differentiate reality from the drug-hazed fantasy in which she was living at the time. She has given evidence to the effect that she has never knowingly ingested magic mushrooms, despite the traces of psilocybin in blood samples taken from her at the time.

You have heard evidence from Isobel in which she has made a whole-hearted apology for her behaviour towards Christian. She fully accepts that she bullied her friend. She knows that so-called sacrifices are wrong, and is deeply ashamed of her mistreatment of other living creatures. She has owned up entirely to the part that she played in this, and in her own words, will never forgive herself for what happened. However, this is not guilt of murder. She never brandished a knife at Christian. She has asserted repeatedly that Eliza took it from her hand and she had no way of knowing that this would happen.

Eliza, on the other hand, has refused to give evidence. Now that, of course, is no indication of guilt. But it is notable that when given the opportunity to make a proper account of herself, she has declined that route. Isobel has told you of multiple conversations between her and Eliza in which Eliza told her how much she hated Christian, and how much she wished she were dead. Eliza could have denied this – she has not done so. No cross-examination was made of that point, so it is in my submission beyond any reasonable doubt that these conversations took place.

Introduction to podcast hosted by Edinburgh University law students

... The only surprise is that it hasn't happened sooner, but at last we've got another case to add to the canon of trials where jurors have behaved unbelievably badly. Remember that famous English case from 1995, R v Young? The one where some of the jurors did a Ouija board and tried to contact the victim? It's happened again, but this time in spades. So, the witch trial that happened a couple of years ago – not just was this a massive story at the time, but it's spawned an unbelievable amount of nonsense since. There was that novel about it – that's led to the case being reopened. The juror who spilt the beans is being prosecuted for contempt of court, they're still trying to track down the author of the book. And I've discovered today that one of the *other* jurors in the case, a woman called Emma Fraser, she's been convicted of contempt of court for carrying out a séance on the eve of the verdict. She tried to deny it but the juror who wrote the book gave evidence against her – she'd told him all about it. She tried to argue that his testimony wasn't credible because of his psychosis, but the jury believed him all the same. Looks like she's one of those religious nuts who thinks the Devil is actually real which is why she got in touch with a medium, to try and find out if it was true. The sort of woman just waiting to be fleeced by mediums, totally credulous. I mean, everyone says how great our jury system is, but when you have idiots like this on it, you have to wonder ...

Plea in mitigation (pre-sentencing) on behalf of Matthew Phillips in trial for contempt of court

My lady, as you know, I represent Matthew Phillips in this matter. You have indicated that you are considering a custodial sentence for the offence of contempt of court to which he has pleaded guilty. The sacrosanct nature of the discussions of the jury room is at the heart of our justice system; that total confidentiality is to be protected at all costs. Mr Phillips understands this. He knows exactly how serious an offence it is that he has committed, but I would urge you to consider a non-custodial option in the alternative, for the following reasons.

Firstly, he pleaded guilty at the first opportunity, thus saving the court time and money. He has not attempted to defend himself against what he accepts is an egregious breach of the law that protects the integrity of the deliberations of a jury.

Secondly, it is right to point out that during the run-up to this offence, my client was seriously mentally ill. The court has seen the psychiatric reports which detail the psychosis from which he was suffering. I understand that it's the view of the court that even though it is not the basis of a separate charge due to his mental breakdown, my client could and even should be facing consequences for the way in which he behaved while he was on the jury. He knows that he is very lucky not to be so doing.

Thirdly, my client was not acting with any malice. To support this proposition, I have a novel submission to make with regard to this, which I would ask the court at least to consider. It is said that aspects of a psychotic breakdown are influenced directly by the context in which the patient finds himself. As your ladyship will see, this has entirely been the case here. If I may remind the court, my client had been signed off sick from work in January of 2019, and was facing a momentous decision, which was whether to fly in the face of popular opinion at work and give evidence that would potentially destroy the career of his immediate superior, Dominic North, a man who was both charismatic and very popular. A man who was later convicted of indecent assault, and struck off the register as a doctor.

I would submit that this had some parallels with the facts of the trial of Isobel Smyth and Eliza Lawson, in which all sense dictated that the accused Eliza Lawson would be acquitted, as the more charismatic and popular of the two. Even down to their physical appearance, Ms Lawson was the more attractive choice in the cut-throat defence that was put forward.

But as your ladyship will recall, the matter concluded recently in a retrial in which the original verdicts, those manipulated by Mr Phillips, were upheld. Isobel Smyth was acquitted, Eliza Lawson was convicted of murder, even though the latter accused seemed on the face of it to be innocent. The retrial gave rise to numerous revelations, where additional evidence by way of the victim's diary was adduced, and where other witnesses admitted that they had lied in the first trial. Is it too much of a stretch to say that Mr Phillips's senses were attuned in some way to the truth of what happened, even if that did not correspond to the evidence that was given in the first trial?

This is further supported by the nature of the hallucinations that he reported at the time of the trial, the globe-shaped hearts that pursued him on a number of occasions. It has been established that in the first trial, the pathologist misdiagnosed the heart condition of the deceased by failing to spot that the heart of the deceased was the wrong shape for the condition he was asserting. Matthew Phillips realised this, at least at a sub-conscious level.

I appreciate that this does not align with the oath that jurors make, to find a verdict according to the evidence in front of them. But I hope it may allay any concerns that Mr Phillips was acting wilfully, or with any malice. He may have undermined the role of the jury in multiple ways, but in doing so, he ensured that justice was done.

Thirdly, Mr Phillips made concerted efforts to put right what he feared was a miscarriage of justice caused by his actions during the trial. When he realised through his recovery from psychosis how wrong his original behaviour had been, he contacted solicitors and also the defence solicitors to tell them what he had done: no one wanted to engage with him, so terrified were they that they would be implicated in a charge of contempt of court. I am not for a moment claiming that he was under any duress, but it was certainly Mr Phillips's belief that he had no other option than to cause this account to be published so that it was public. Something would then have to be done.

In this, Mr Phillips was not wrong. Despite the fact that the publication of the 'Witch Trial' book was in direct contravention of the law, it did have the desired effect. The case was reopened. It is not down to him that Eliza was convicted as before: this was down to the dishonesty of other witnesses in the initial trial. Without Mr Phillips's intervention, an innocent girl would have gone to prison, and this is a fact that I would ask the court to bear in mind.

Finally, I would ask the court to consider the liability of the person who actually facilitated the publication of this document. I understand that it is an aggravating feature of the case that Mr Phillips will not give the real name of the person known as Gill Martin who assisted him in ghost-writing his memoir or uploaded it to the internet. But I would suggest that this indicates even now the undue influence under which he was placed by Ms Martin. She has clearly taken advantage of my client's vulnerable state and once located, should face the full force of the law. I cannot imagine what possible motivation Ms Martin might have had for publishing a novel which flies so blatantly in the face of the law, and I trust that Mr Phillips is not punished for her illegal behaviour as well as his own. In my submission, he is a man more sinned against than sinning.

Isle of Muck monthly newsletter

Finally, a warm welcome to Matthew and Rosalind Phillips who have recently joined our small community, taking over the tea shop from Mrs Perry whose ginger cakes will be sorely missed. Matthew and Rosalind bring a wealth of different life experience to the island, and while not officially a doctor any more, it's going to be helpful to have someone with medical knowledge living so close by! We're glad that they've put aside all their recent difficulties and decided to make a home with us here.

Sentencing remarks in the case of HM *Advocate* v. *Harriet Tyce*, author of *Witch Trial*

Harriet Tyce, stand up. I have heard what your advocate has to say in mitigation and I disregard it entirely. There is no justification whatsoever for your actions in 2019 and beyond. You wilfully interfered with the process of justice by speaking repeatedly to a juror in the case which you were observing, you compounded this offence by responding to his letter, and as for the actions you took in encouraging him to divulge the secrets of the jury room to you and then having the effrontery to write it up and publish it online, words almost fail me.

It is an aggravating factor that in writing this so-called account, you had the temerity to portray the thoughts and feelings of witnesses in the case as if it were genuinely what they were experiencing at the time, thus causing them great distress. Reverend Thomas was particularly upset at the derogatory way in which you compared him to the appalling priest in the popular television series, *Fleabag*.

I also note that you were at some pains to assign more positive attributes to your own character, in particular the repeated comparisons between Gill Martin and Hitchcock film stars. You would do well to ask yourself in all honesty whether you do, in fact, look anything like Eva Marie Saint, in *On the Waterfront* or indeed any other film in which that actor appears.

Never, in my lengthy career as an advocate involved in criminal trials, nor in all the years that I have sat on the bench as a judge, have I seen a contempt of court as outrageous as this.

You have told the court you were in attendance merely to observe the case as research for a potential future novel, and that you found yourself pulled into the case almost against your will. You claim that you had nothing but good intentions at heart, and that you felt sorry for the accused Isobel Smyth, in part because your own teenage experiences caused you to identify strongly with her. You claim that you were seeking to subvert the prevailing narrative that you say was drawn wrongly against the accused, Isobel Smyth, even if you have accepted that by allowing your sympathy for the girl to overtake your objective judgement, you fell prey to the same confirmation bias of which you accused the rest of the court.

I disregard these attempts at mitigation entirely. Whatever your early motivation, it is apparent to me that you deliberately interfered with the juror Matthew Phillips, and exploited his vulnerabilities. Worse, you have manipulated the court to your own ends. However high-minded you claim to have been, it is unarguable that you have published a novel on this subject for financial gain, and you have also benefited in terms of sales of your other books from the publicity that has surrounded your prosecution, which eventual outcome was inevitable as you would well have known. The advocate depute referred in his speech to the well-known quotation that there is no such thing as bad publicity and I would add as a side-note that this is a deeply regrettable aspect of human nature, and one of which you have taken full advantage.

This was jury interference of the highest order and whatever your opinions of the case, you had no right to proceed in the manner in which you did. As far as I can see, you have been a more than willing participant in this egregious interference, motivated purely by self-interest. Reference is sometimes made to the sliver of ice in the novelist's heart; I can see nothing here but ice and a cold, hard desire for publicity.

The maximum sentence that I can pass here is one of two years' custody. I am asked to take into consideration the fact that your accomplice Matthew Phillips was given a non-custodial sentence. I have considered the point, and I reject it.

As someone with legal qualifications, even if only from the English bar, you should have known perfectly well that what you were doing flew in the face of every legal restriction that exists. Compounding the offence is the fact that even in your attempts to write up a trial held under Scots law, you made mistakes with procedure. I find it to be a further aggravating feature that you were so slipshod in your portrayal of what purported to be a true story.

There is no mitigation available to you. Your plea of guilty was late and I do not grant you any discount for it. You have gravely damaged the course of justice and wasted a large amount of public money on causing there to be a retrial. It's with all that in mind that I sentence you to two years in custody.

Take her down.

Acknowledgements

I am incredibly lucky to be published by Wildfire; the support they give as I continue to evolve in my writing is something I appreciate greatly. My thanks to Jack Butler for his extensive and insightful editorial notes – I will miss working with you. My thanks also to Rachel Hart – here's to the beginning of a beautiful editorial relationship! I am very grateful to everyone at Wildfire, particularly Alex Clarke and Joseph Edwards and to the wider Headline team, whose skills at publicity, sales and marketing are unsurpassed. Rosie Margesson, you are a publicist par excellence, and I look forward to your return.

None of this would be possible without my brilliant agent, Veronique Baxter, and the team at David Higham Associates. My thanks to her and to Gráinne Fox for everything they do. My thanks also to Jennifer Thomas and Nacho Martin at United Agents.

This book is dedicated to my father, a former Senator of the College of Justice and Lord Commissioner of Justiciary in Scotland. It was due to a conversation with him that I realised that it should be set in Edinburgh, both because of the extensive and terrible history of the persecution of witches in Scotland, but also because of the more prosaic consideration that there are no opening speeches in Scots law, which makes the job for a writer of surprising the reader that bit easier. I'm very grateful both for that inspiration and also for his time in looking at the text. Any mistakes I have made in my rendition of the trial are entirely down to my own ignorance, as the sentencing judge is quick to point out . . .

Thank you to my writing friends providing such support and entertainment. Sarah Pinborough – we got this! Criminal Minds and the Submission Kru distract me far more than they should and I am grateful for every excess moment I spend on screen time with them. I am lucky enough to have had amazing quotes from many authors – some of them not even my friends! – and I am deeply grateful to every one of you who takes the time to read my work.

Book sellers, bloggers, reviewers, readers – authors are nothing without you. I appreciate every single one of you. I know how many other books and films and television series and dog videos there are out there and the fact that you give me your time is very important to me. Thank you very much. A special thank you to Hester, Bex, David and all the team who might just have given this book an extra push to reach more readers . . .

Finally, thank you to my friends outside of the writing world for providing such welcome distraction. And to my family, Nat, Freddy and Eloise – I love you all. I'm glad I've finally written a book that really isn't unsuitable for you to read!

Works That Informed Witch Trial

This book took a lot of research, and I came across some fascinating resources while I was preparing to write it. I thought I would share them here; in case they're of interest to any readers.

Books

Barker, Alan – *Scared to Death*
Fagan, Jenni – *Hex*
Gans, Jeremy – *The Ouija Board Jurors*
Garner, Helen – *This House of Grief*
Gilman, Charlotte Perkins – *The Yellow Wallpaper*
Grove, Trevor – *The Juryman's Tale*
Hill, Susan – *The Woman in Black*
Hoffman, Alice – The *Practical Magic* series
Hogg, James – *The Private Memoirs and Confessions of a Justified Sinner*
Jackson, Shirley – *The Haunting of Hill House*
James, Henry – *The Turn of the Screw*
King, Stephen – *The Shining*
Knight, Sam – *The Premonitions Bureau*
Malcolm, Janet – *Iphigenie in Forest Hills: Anatomy of a Murder Trial*
Mitchell, David – *Slade House*
Nelson, Maggie – *The Red Parts*
Paver, Michelle – *Dark Matter*
Robbins, Danny – *Into the Uncanny*
Ross, Peter – *A Tomb with a View*
Russell, Craig – *The Devil's Playground*

Storr, Will – *Will Storr vs. the Supernatural*
Waterhouse, Dr Benji – *You Don't Have to Be Mad to Work Here*
Waters, Sarah – *Affinity*; *The Little Stranger*

Articles and Online Reading

Isabella Von Ghoul – '20 Years of the Craft: Why We Needed More of Rochelle' (2019), https://isabellaprice.wordpress.com/2019/02/22/20-years-of-the-craft-why-we-needed-more-of-rochelle/

Keen – 'Understanding the "Scary" Tarot Cards: The Nine of Swords', https://www.keen.com/articles/tarot/understanding-the-scary-tarot-cards-nine-of-swords

Films and Documentaries

Anatomy of a Fall (dir. Justine Triet)
Investigating Witchcraft (presented by Suranne Jones)
Saint Omer (dir. Alice Diop)
Vertigo (dir. Alfred Hitchcock)

© Charlotte Knee Photography

Harriet Tyce is the million-copy, *Sunday Times* bestselling author of four novels. She grew up in Edinburgh and studied English at Oxford University before doing a law conversion course at City University. After practising as a criminal barrister in London for nearly a decade, she subsequently completed an MA in Creative Writing – Crime Fiction at the University of East Anglia. Her first novel, *Blood Orange*, published in 2019 to huge critical acclaim and she has since written multiple *Sunday Times* bestsellers. *Witch Trial* is her fifth novel. Harriet lives in North London.